MARY ROBERTS RINEHART'S
Mystery Book

MARY ROBERTS RINEHART'S

 Mystery Book

THE CIRCULAR STAIRCASE

THE MAN IN LOWER TEN

THE CASE OF JENNIE BRICE

RINEHART & COMPANY, INC.

NEW YORK   TORONTO

Contents

THE CIRCULAR STAIRCASE   3

THE MAN IN LOWER TEN   143

THE CASE OF JENNIE BRICE   271

The
Circular
Staircase

1

THIS IS THE STORY of how a middle-aged spinster lost her mind, deserted her domestic gods in the city, took a furnished house for the summer out of town, and found herself involved in one of those mysterious crimes that keep our newspapers and detective agencies happy and prosperous. For twenty years I had been perfectly comfortable; for twenty years I had had the window boxes filled in the spring, the carpets lifted, the awnings put up, and the furniture covered with brown linen; for as many summers I had said good-bye to my friends, and, after watching their perspiring hegira, had settled down to a delicious quiet in town, where the mail comes three times a day and the water supply does not depend on a tank on the roof.

And then the madness seized me. When I look back over the months I spent at Sunnyside I wonder that I survived at all. As it is, I show the wear and tear of my harrowing experiences. I have turned very gray—Liddy reminded me of it only yesterday, by saying that a little bluing in the rinse water would make my hair silvery instead of a yellowish white. I hate to be reminded of unpleasant things and I snapped her off.

"No," I said sharply, "I'm not going to use bluing at my time of life, or starch either."

Liddy's nerves are gone, she said, since that awful summer, but she has enough left, goodness knows! And when she begins to go around with a lump in her throat all I have to do is to threaten to return to Sunnyside and she is frightened into a semblance of cheerfulness, from which you may judge that the summer there was anything but a success.

The newspaper accounts have been so garbled and incomplete—one of them mentioned me but once, and then only as the tenant at the time the thing happened—that I feel it my due to tell what I know. Jamieson, the detective, said himself he could never have done without me, although he gave me little enough credit in print.

I shall have to go back several years—thirteen, to be exact—to start my story. At that time my brother died, leaving me his two children. Halsey was eleven then, and Gertrude was seven. All the responsibilities of maternity were thrust upon me suddenly; to perfect the profession of motherhood requires precisely as many years as the child has lived, like the man who started to carry the calf and ended by walking along with the bull on his shoulders. However, I did the best I could. When Gertrude got past the hair-ribbon age, and Halsey put on long trousers—and a wonderful help that was to the darning!—I sent them away to good schools. After that, my responsibility was chiefly postal, with three months every summer in which to replen-

3

ish their wardrobes, look over their lists of acquaintances, and generally to take my foster motherhood out of its nine months' retirement in camphor.

I missed the summers with them when, somewhat later, at boarding school and college, the children spent much of their vacations with friends. Gradually I found that my name signed to a check was even more welcome than when signed to a letter, though I wrote them at stated intervals. But when Halsey had finished his electrical course and Gertrude her boarding school, and both came home to stay, things were suddenly changed. The winter Gertrude came out was nothing but a succession of sitting up late at night to bring her home from things, taking her to the dressmakers' between naps the next day, and discouraging ineligible youths with either more money than brains or more brains than money. Also, I acquired a great many things: to say lingerie for undergarments, "frocks" and "gowns" instead of dresses, and that beardless sophomores are not college boys but college men. Halsey required less personal supervision, and as they both got their mother's fortune that winter my responsibility became purely moral. Halsey bought a car, of course, and I learned how to keep my eyes off the speedometer, and, after a time, never to stop to look at the dogs one has run down. People are apt to be unpleasant about their dogs.

The additions to my education made me a properly equipped maiden aunt, and by spring I was quite tractable. So when Halsey suggested camping in the Adirondacks and Gertrude wanted Bar Harbor we compromised on a good country house with a golf course near, and within motor distance of town and telephone distance of the doctor. That was how we went to Sunnyside.

We went out to inspect the property, and it seemed to deserve its name. Its cheerful appearance gave no indication whatever of anything out of the ordinary. Only one thing seemed unusual to me: the housekeeper, who had been left in charge, had moved from the house to the gardener's lodge a few days before. As the lodge was far enough away from the house, it seemed to me that either fire or thieves could have completed their work of destruction undisturbed. The property was an extensive one: the house on the top of a hill, which sloped away in great stretches of green lawn and clipped hedges to the road; and across the valley, perhaps a couple of miles away, the Greenwood Club House. Gertrude and Halsey were infatuated.

"Why, it's everything you want," Halsey said. "View, air, good water and good roads. As for the house, it's big enough for a hospital, if it has a Queen Anne front and a Mary Anne back." Which was ridiculous: it was pure Elizabethan.

Of course we took the place. It was not my idea of comfort, being much too large and sufficiently isolated to make the servant question serious. But I give myself credit for this: whatever has happened since I have never blamed Halsey and Gertrude for taking me there. And another thing. If the series of catastrophes there did nothing else it taught me one thing, that somehow, somewhere, from perhaps a half-civilized ancestor who wore a sheepskin garment and trailed his food or his prey, I have in me the instinct of the chase. Were I a man I should be a trapper of criminals, trailing them as relentlessly as no doubt my sheepskin-clad ancestor did his wild boar. But being an unmarried woman, with the handicap of my sex, my first acquaintance with crime will probably be my last. Indeed it came near enough to being my last acquaintance with anything.

The property was owned by Paul Armstrong, the president of the Traders' Bank, who at the time we took the house was in the West with his wife and daughter and a Doctor Walker, the Armstrong family physician. Halsey knew Louise Armstrong, had been rather attentive to her the winter before, but as Halsey was always attentive to somebody I had not thought of it seriously, although she was a charming girl. I knew of Mr. Armstrong only through his connection with the bank, where the children's money was largely invested and through an ugly story about the son, Arnold Armstrong, who was reported to have forged his father's name for a considerable amount to some bank paper. However, the story had had no interest for me.

I cleared Halsey and Gertrude away to a house party, and moved out to Sunnyside the first of May. The roads were bad but the trees were in leaf, and there were still tulips in the borders around the house. The arbutus was fragrant in the woods under the dead leaves, and on the way from the station, a short mile, while the car stuck in the mud, I found a bank showered with tiny forget-me-nots. The birds—don't ask me what kind; they all look alike to me, unless they have a hallmark of some bright color—the birds were chirping in the hedges, and everything breathed of peace. Liddy, who was born and bred on a brick pavement, got a little bit down-spirited when the crickets began to chirp, or scrape their legs together, or whatever it is they do, at twilight.

The first night passed quietly enough. I have always been grateful for that one night's peace. It shows what the country might be, under favorable circumstances. Never after that night did I put my head on my pillow with any assurance how long it would be there; or on my shoulders, for that matter.

On the following morning Liddy and Mrs. Ralston, my own housekeeper, had a difference of opinion, and Mrs. Ralston left on the eleven-o'clock train. Just after luncheon Burke, the butler, was taken unexpectedly with a pain in his right side, much worse when I was within hearing distance, and by afternoon he too was started cityward. That night the cook's sister had a baby— the cook, seeing indecision in my face, made it twins on second thought— and, to be short, by noon the next day the household staff was down to Liddy and myself. And this in a house with twenty-two rooms and five baths!

Liddy wanted to go back to the city at once, but the milk boy said that Thomas Johnson, the Armstrongs' colored butler, was working as a waiter at the Greenwood Club and might come back. I have the usual scruples about coaxing people's servants away, but few of us have any conscience regarding institutions or corporations—witness the way we beat railroads and streetcar companies when we can—so I called up the club, and about eight o'clock Thomas Johnson came to see me. Poor Thomas!

Well, it ended by my engaging Thomas on the spot, at outrageous wages and with permission to sleep in the gardener's lodge, empty since the house was rented. The old man—he was white-haired and a little stooped, but with an immense idea of his personal dignity—gave me his reasons hesitatingly.

"I ain't sayin' nothin', Mis' Innes," he said, with his hand on the doorknob, "but there's been goin's-on here this las' few months as ain't natchal. 'Tain't one thing an' 'tain't another—it's jest a door squealin' here an' a winder closin' there, but when doors an' winders gets to cuttin' up capers and there's nobody nigh 'em it's time Thomas Johnson sleep somewhar's else."

Liddy, who seemed to be never more than ten feet away from me that night, and was afraid of her shadow in that great barn of a place, screamed a little, and turned a yellow-green. But I am not easily alarmed.

It was entirely in vain I represented to Thomas that we were alone, and that he would have to stay in the house that night. He was politely firm, but he would come over early the next morning and if I gave him a key he would come in time to get some sort of breakfast. I stood on the huge veranda and watched him shuffle along down the shadowy drive, with mingled feelings, irritation at his cowardice and thankfulness at getting him at all. I am not ashamed to say that I double-locked the hall door when I went in.

"You can lock up the rest of the house and go to bed, Liddy," I said severely. "You give me the creeps standing there. A woman of your age ought to have better sense." It usually braces Liddy to mention her age: she owns to forty, which is absurd. Her mother cooked for my grandfather, and Liddy must be at least as old as I. But that night she refused to brace.

"You're not going to ask me to lock up, Miss Rachel!" she quavered. "Why, there's a dozen French windows in the drawing-room and the billiard-room wing, and every one opens on a porch. And MaryAnne said that last night there was a man standing by the stable when she locked the kitchen door."

"MaryAnne was a fool," I said sternly. "If there had been a man there, she would have had him in the kitchen and been feeding him what was left from dinner inside of an hour, from force of habit. Now don't be ridiculous. Lock up the house and go to bed. I'm going to read."

But Liddy set her lips tight and stood still. "I'm not going to bed," she said. "I am going to pack up, and tomorrow I am going to leave."

"You'll do nothing of the sort," I snapped. Liddy and I often desire to part company, but never at the same time. "If you are afraid I will go with you, but for goodness' sake don't try to hide behind me."

The house was a typical summer residence on an extensive scale. Wherever possible on the first floor the architect had done away with partitions, using arches and columns instead. The effect was cool and spacious, but scarcely cozy. As Liddy and I went from one window to another, our voices echoed back at us uncomfortably. There was plenty of light—the electric plant down in the village supplied us—but there were long vistas of polished floor, and mirrors which reflected us from unexpected corners until I felt some of Liddy's foolishness communicate itself to me.

The house was very long, a rectangle in general form, with the main entrance in the center of the long side. The brick-paved entry opened into a short hall, to the right of which, separated only by a row of pillars, was a huge living room. Beyond that was the drawing room, and in the end the billiard room. Off the billiard room, in the extreme right wing, was a den or cardroom with a small hall opening on the east veranda, and from there went up a narrow circular staircase. Halsey had pointed it out with delight.

"Just look, Aunt Rachel," he had said with a flourish. "The architect that put up this joint was wise to a few things. Arnold Armstrong and his friends could sit here and play cards all night and stumble up to bed in the early morning, without having the family send in a police call."

Liddy and I got as far as the cardroom and turned on all the lights. I tried the small entry door there, which opened on the veranda, and examined the windows. Everything was secure and Liddy, a little less nervous now, had just pointed out to me the disgracefully dusty condition of the hardwood floor, when suddenly the lights went out. We waited a moment. I think Liddy was stunned with fright, or she would have screamed. And then I clutched her by the arm and pointed to one of the windows opening on the porch. The sudden change threw the window into relief, an oblong of grayish light, and showed us a figure standing close, peering in. As I looked it darted across the veranda and out of sight in the darkness.

2

LIDDY'S KNEES seemed to give way under her. Without a sound she sank down, leaving me staring at the window in petrified amazement. She began then to moan under her breath, and in my excitement I reached down and shook her.

"Stop it," I whispered. "It's only a woman, maybe a maid of the Armstrongs'. Get up and help me find the door." She groaned again. "Very well," I said, "then I'll have to leave you here. I'm going."

She moved at that, and with her holding to my sleeve we felt our way, with numerous collisions, to the billiard room and from there to the drawing room. The lights came on then, and with the long French windows unshuttered I had a creepy feeling that each one sheltered a peering face. In fact, in the light of what happened afterward, I am pretty certain we were under surveillance during the entire ghostly evening. We hurried over the rest of the locking up and got upstairs as quickly as we could. I left the lights all on, and our footsteps echoed cavernously. Liddy had a stiff neck the next morning from looking back over her shoulder, and that night she refused to go to bed.

"Let me stay in your dressing room, Miss Rachel," she begged. "If you don't I'll sit in the hall outside the door. I'm not going to be murdered with my eyes shut."

"If you're going to be murdered," I retorted, "it won't make any difference whether they are shut or open. But you may stay in the dressing room, if you will lie on the couch. When you sleep in a chair you snore."

She was too far gone to be indignant, but after a while she came to the door and looked in to where I was composing myself for sleep with Drummond's *Spiritual World*.

"That wasn't a woman, Miss Rachel," she said, with her shoes in her hand. "It was a man in a long coat."

"What woman was a man?" I discouraged her without looking up, and she went back to the couch.

It was eleven o'clock when I finally prepared for bed. In spite of my assumption of indifference I locked the door into the hall, and finding the transom did not catch I put a chair cautiously before the door—it was not necessary to rouse Liddy—and climbing up put on the ledge of the transom a small dressing mirror, so that any movement of the frame would send it crashing down. Then secure in my precautions I went to bed.

I did not go to sleep at once. Liddy disturbed me just as I was growing drowsy, by coming in and peering under the bed. She was afraid to speak, however, because of her previous snubbing, and went back, stopping in the doorway to sigh dismally.

Somewhere downstairs a clock with a chime sang away the hours, eleven-thirty, forty-five, twelve. And then the lights went out to stay. The Casanova Electric Company shuts up shop and goes home to bed at midnight. When one has a party I believe it is customary to fee the company, which will drink hot coffee and keep awake a couple of hours longer. But the lights were out for good that night. Liddy had gone to sleep, as I knew she would. She was a very unreliable person, always awake and ready to talk when she wasn't wanted and dozing off to sleep when she was. I called her once or twice, the only result being an explosive snore that threatened her very windpipe; then I got up and lighted a bedroom candle.

My bedroom and dressing room were above the big living room on the first floor. On the second floor a long corridor ran the length of the house, with rooms opening from both sides. In the wings were small corridors crossing the main one, so the plan was simplicity itself. And just as I got back into bed I heard a sound from the east wing apparently, that made me stop frozen, with one bedroom slipper half off, and listen. It was a rattling metallic sound, and it reverberated along the empty halls like the crash of doom. It was for all the world as if something heavy, perhaps a piece of steel, had rolled clattering and jangling down the hardwood stairs leading to the cardroom.

In the silence that followed Liddy stirred and snored again. I was exasperated. First she kept me awake by silly alarms, then when she was needed she slept like Joe Jefferson, or Rip Van Winkle; they are always the same to me. I went in and shook her, and I give her credit for being wide awake the minute I spoke.

"Get up," I said, "if you don't want to be murdered in your bed."

"Where? How?" she yelled vociferously, and jumped up.

"There's somebody in the house," I said. "Get up. We'll have to get to the telephone."

"Not out in the hall!" she gasped. "Oh, Miss Rachel, not out in the hall!" She was trying to hold me back, but I am a large woman and Liddy is small. We got to the door somehow and Liddy held a brass andiron, which it was all she could do to lift, let alone brain anybody with. I listened and, hearing nothing, opened the door a little and peered into the hall. It was a black void, full of terrible suggestion, and my candle only emphasized the gloom. Liddy squealed and drew me back again, and as the door slammed the mirror I had placed on the transom came down and hit her on the head. That completed our demoralization. It was some time before I could persuade her she had not been attacked from behind by a burglar, and when she found the mirror smashed on the floor she wasn't much better.

"There's going to be a death!" she wailed. "Oh, Miss Rachel, there's going to be a death!"

"There will be," I said grimly, "if you don't keep quiet, Liddy Allen."

And so we sat there until morning, wondering if the candle would last until dawn, and arranging what trains we could take back to town. If we had only stuck to that decision and gone back before it was too late!

The sun came finally, and from my window I watched the trees along the drive take shadowy form, gradually lose their ghostlike appearance, become gray and then green. The Greenwood Club showed itself a dab of white against the hill across the valley, and an early robin or two hopped around in the dew. Not until the milk boy and the sun came, about the same time, did I dare to open the door into the hall and look around. Everything was as we had left it. Trunks were heaped here and there, ready for the trunk room, and through an end window of stained glass came a streak of red and yellow daylight that was eminently cheerful. The milk boy was pounding somewhere below, and the day had begun.

Thomas Johnson came ambling up the drive about half past six and we could hear him clattering around on the lower floor, opening shutters. I had to take Liddy to her room upstairs, however, she was quite sure she would find something uncanny there, and in fact when she did not, having now the courage of daylight, she was actually disappointed.

Well, we did not go back to town that day.

The discovery of a small picture fallen from the wall of the drawing room was quite sufficient to satisfy Liddy that the alarm had been a false one, but I was anything but convinced. Allowing for my nerves and the fact that small noises magnify themselves at night, there was still no possibility that the picture had made the series of sounds I heard. To prove it however I dropped it again. It fell with a single muffled crash of its wooden frame, and incidentally ruined itself beyond repair. I justified myself by reflecting that if the Armstrongs chose to leave pictures in unsafe positions, and to rent a house with a family ghost, the destruction of property was their responsibility, not mine.

I warned Liddy not to mention what had happened to anybody, and telephoned to town for servants. Then after a breakfast which did more credit to Thomas's heart than his head I went on a short tour of investigation. The sounds had come from the east wing, and not without some qualms I began there. At first I found nothing. Since then I have developed my powers of observation, but at that time I was a novice. The small cardroom seemed undisturbed. I looked for footprints, which is I believe the conventional thing to do, although my experience has been that as clues both footprints and thumbmarks are more useful in fiction than in fact. But the stairs in that wing offered something.

At the top of the flight had been placed a tall wicker hamper, packed with linen which had come from town. It stood at the edge of the top step, almost barring passage, and on the step below it was a long fresh scratch. For three steps the scratch was repeated, gradually diminishing, as if some object had fallen, striking each one as it dropped. Then for four steps nothing. On the fifth step below was a round dent in the hard wood. That was all, and it seemed little enough, except that I was positive the marks had not been there the day before.

It bore out my theory of the sound, which had been for all the world like the bumping of a metallic object down a flight of steps. The four steps had been skipped. I reasoned that an iron bar for instance would do something of the sort, strike two or three steps end down, then turn over, jumping a few steps and landing with a thud.

Iron bars, however, do not fall downstairs in the middle of the night alone. Coupled with the figure on the veranda, the agency by which it climbed might be assumed. But—and here was the thing which puzzled me most—the doors were all fastened that morning, the windows unmolested, and the particular door from the cardroom to the outside veranda had a combination lock of which I held the key, and which had not been tampered with.

I fixed on an attempt at burglary as the most natural explanation, an attempt frustrated by the falling of the object, whatever it was, which had roused me. Two things however I could not understand: how the intruder had escaped with everything locked, and why he had left the small silver which, in the absence of a butler, had remained downstairs overnight.

Under pretext of learning more about the place that morning Thomas Johnson led me through the house and the cellars, without result. Everything was in good order and repair. Money had been spent lavishly on construction and plumbing, the house was full of conveniences, and I had no reason to repent my bargain save the fact that in the nature of things night must come again. And other nights must follow—and we were a long way from a police station.

In the afternoon a taxi came up from Casanova with a fresh relay of servants. The driver took them with a flourish to the servants' entrance, and then drove around to the front of the house, where I was awaiting him.

"Two dollars," he said in reply to my question. "I don't charge full rates, because, bringin' 'em up all summer as I do it pays to make a special price. When they got off the train, I sez to myself: 'There's another bunch for Sunnyside, cook, parlormaid and all.' Yes'm, six summers and a new lot never less than once a month. They won't stand for the country and the lonesomeness, I reckon."

But with the presence of the "bunch" of servants my courage revived, and late in the afternoon came a message from Gertrude that she and Halsey would arrive that night at about eleven o'clock, coming in the car from Richfield. Things were looking up, and when Beulah, my cat and a most intelligent animal, found some early catnip on a bank near the house and rolled in it in a feline ecstasy, I decided that getting back to nature was the thing to do.

While I was dressing for dinner Liddy rapped at the door. She was hardly herself yet, but privately I think she was worrying about the broken mirror and its augury more than anything else. When she came in she was holding something in her hand, and she laid it on the dressing table carefully.

"I found it in the linen hamper," she said. "It must be Mr. Halsey's, but it seems queer how it got there."

It was the half of a link cuff button of unique design, and I looked at it carefully.

"Where was it? In the bottom of the hamper?" I asked.

"On the very top," she replied. "It's a mercy it didn't fall out on the way."

When Liddy had gone I examined the fragment attentively. I had never seen it before, and I was certain it was not Halsey's. It was of Italian workmanship and consisted of a mother-of-pearl foundation encrusted with tiny seed pearls, strung on horsehair to hold them. In the center was a small ruby. The trinket was odd enough but not intrinsically of great value. Its interest for me lay in this: Liddy had found it lying in the top of the hamper which had blocked the east wing stairs.

That afternoon the Armstrongs' housekeeper, a youngish good-looking woman, applied for Mrs. Ralston's place and I was glad enough to take her. She looked as though she might be equal to a dozen of Liddy, with her snapping black eyes and heavy jaw. Her name was Anne Watson, and I dined that evening for the first time in three days.

3

I HAD DINNER served in the breakfast room. Somehow the huge dining room depressed me and Thomas, cheerful enough all day, had allowed his spirits to go down with the sun. He had a habit of watching the corners of the room, left shadowy by the candles on the table, and altogether it was not a festive meal.

Dinner over I went into the living room. I had three hours before the children could possibly arrive, and I got out my knitting. I had brought along two dozen pairs of slipper soles in assorted sizes—I always send knitted slippers to the Old Ladies' Home at Christmas—and now I sorted over the wools with a grim determination not to think about the night before. But my mind was not on my work. At the end of a half hour I found I had put a row of blue scallops on Sally Klinefelter's lavender slippers, and I put them away.

I got out the cuff link and went with it to the pantry. Thomas was wiping silver and the air was heavy with tobacco smoke. I sniffed and looked around, but there was no pipe to be seen.

"Thomas," I said, "you have been smoking."

"No, ma'am." He was injured innocence itself. "It's on my coat, ma'am. Over at the club the gentlemen—"

But Thomas did not finish. The pantry was suddenly filled with the odor of singeing cloth. Thomas gave a clutch at his coat, whirled to the sink, filled a tumbler with water and poured it into his right pocket with the celerity of practice.

"Thomas," I said, when he was sheepishly mopping the floor, "smoking is a filthy and injurious habit. If you must smoke you must, but don't stick a lighted pipe in your pocket again. Your skin's your own. You can blister it if you like. But this house is not mine, and I don't want a conflagration. Did you ever see this cuff link before?"

No, he never had, he said, but he looked at it oddly.

"I picked it up in the hall," I added indifferently. The old man's eyes were shrewd under his bushy eyebrows.

"There's strange goin's-on here, Mis' Innes," he said, shaking his head. "Somethin's goin' to happen sure. You ain't took notice that the big clock in the hall is stopped, I reckon?"

"Nonsense," I said. "Clocks have to stop, don't they, if they're not wound?"

"It's wound up all right, and it stopped at three o'clock last night," he answered solemnly. "More'n that, that there clock ain't stopped for fifteen years, not since Mr. Armstrong's first wife died. And that ain't all—no, ma'am. Last three nights I slep' in this place, after the electrics went out I had a token. My oil lamp was full of oil, but it kep' goin' out, do what I would. Minute I shet my eyes out that lamp'd go. There ain't no surer token of death.

The Bible sez, Let yer light shine! When a hand you can't see puts yer light out, it means death, sure."

The old man's voice was full of conviction. In spite of myself I had a chilly sensation in the small of my back, and I left him mumbling over his dishes. Later on I heard a crash from the pantry and Liddy reported that my cat Beulah, who is coal black, had darted in front of Thomas just as he picked up a tray of dishes; that the bad omen had been too much for him, and he had dropped the tray.

The roar of the motor as the car climbed the hill was the most welcome sound I had heard for a long time, and with Gertrude and Halsey actually before me, my troubles seemed over for good. Gertrude stood smiling in the hall, with her hat quite over one ear, and her hair in every direction over her shoulders. Gertrude is a very pretty girl no matter how her hair is, and I was not surprised when Halsey presented a good-looking young man, who bowed at me and looked at Trude—that is the ridiculous nickname Gertrude brought from school.

"I've brought a guest, Aunt Ray," Halsey said. "I want you to adopt him into your affections and your Saturday-to-Monday list. Let me present John Bailey, only you must call him Jack. In twelve hours he'll be calling you 'aunt': I know him."

We shook hands and I got a chance to look at Mr. Bailey. He was a tall fellow, perhaps thirty, and he wore a small mustache. I remember wondering why. He seemed to have a good mouth and when he smiled his teeth were above the average. One never knows why certain men cling to a messy upper lip that must get into things, any more than one understands some women building up their hair on wire atrocities. Otherwise, he was very good to look at, stalwart and tanned, with the direct gaze that I like. I am particular about Mr. Bailey, because he was a prominent figure in what happened later.

Gertrude was tired from the trip and went up to bed very soon. I made up my mind to tell them nothing until the next day, and then to make as little of our excitement as possible. After all, what had I to tell? An inquisitive face peering in at a window, a crash in the night, a scratch or two on the stairs and half a cuff button! As for Thomas and his forebodings, it was always my belief that a Negro is at least one part superstition.

It was Saturday night. The two men carried their highballs to the billiard room, and I could hear them talking as I went upstairs. It seemed that Halsey had stopped at the Greenwood Club for gasoline and found Bailey there with the Sunday golf crowd. Mr. Bailey had not been hard to persuade— probably Gertrude knew why—and they carried him off triumphantly. I roused Liddy to get them something to eat—Thomas was beyond reach in the lodge—and paid no attention to her evident terror of the kitchen regions. Then I went to bed. The men were still in the billiard room when I finally dozed off and the last thing I remember was the howl of a dog in front of the house. It wailed a crescendo of woe that trailed off hopefully, only to break out afresh from a new point of the compass.

At three o'clock in the morning I was roused by a revolver shot. The sound seemed to come from just outside my door. For a moment I could not move. Then I heard Gertrude stirring in her room and the next moment she had thrown open the connecting door.

"Aunt Ray! Aunt Ray!" she called hysterically. "Someone must have been killed! What on earth—"

"Thieves," I said shortly. "Thank goodness, there are some men in the house tonight." I was getting into my slippers and a bathrobe, and Gertrude with shaking hands was lighting a lamp. Then we opened the door into the hall where crowded on the upper landing of the stairs the maids, white-faced and trembling, were peering down. I was greeted by a series of low screams and questions, and I tried to quiet them. Gertrude had dropped on a chair and sat there limp and shivering.

I went at once across the hall to Halsey's room and knocked, then I pushed the door open. It was empty. The bed had not been occupied!

"He must be in Mr. Bailey's room," I said excitedly, and followed by Liddy we went there. Like Halsey's, it had not been occupied. Gertrude was on her feet now, but she leaned against the door for support.

"They have both been killed!" she gasped. She caught me by the arm and dragged me toward the stairs. "They may only be hurt. We've got to find them," she said, her eyes dilated with excitement.

I don't remember how we got down the stairs. I do remember expecting every moment to be killed. The cook was at the telephone upstairs calling the Greenwood Club, and Liddy was behind me afraid to come and not daring to stay behind. We found the living room and the drawing room undisturbed. Somehow I felt that whatever we found would be in the cardroom or on the staircase, and nothing but the fear that Halsey was in danger drove me on; with every step my knees seemed to give way under me. Gertrude was ahead and in the cardroom she stopped, holding her candle high. Then she pointed silently into the hall beyond. Huddled there on the floor, face down and with his arms extended, was a man.

Gertrude ran forward with a gasping sob. "Jack," she cried, "oh, Jack!"

Liddy had run, screaming, and the two of us were there alone. It was Gertrude who turned him over until we could see his white face, and then she drew a deep breath and dropped limply to her knees. It was the body of a man, in a dinner coat and white waistcoat, stained now with blood. The body of a man I had never seen before.

4

Gertrude gazed at the face in a kind of fascination. Then she put out her hands blindly and I thought she was going to faint.

"He's killed him!" she muttered almost inarticulately, and at that and because my nerves were going I gave her a good shake.

"What do you mean?" I said frantically. There was a depth of grief and conviction in her tone that was worse than anything she could have said. The shake braced her, anyhow, and she seemed to pull herself together. But not another word would she say. She stood gazing down at that gruesome figure on the floor while Liddy, ashamed of her flight and afraid to come back alone, drove before her three terrified women servants into the drawing room, which was as near as any of them would venture.

Once in the drawing room, Gertrude collapsed and went from one fainting spell into another. I had all I could do to keep Liddy from drowning her with cold water, while the maids huddled in a corner, as much use as so many sheep. In a short time, although it seemed hours, a car came rushing up, and Anne Watson, who had waited to dress, opened the door. Three men from the Greenwood Club in all kinds of improvised costumes hurried in. I recognized a Mr. Jarvis, but the others were strangers.

"What's wrong?" the Jarvis man asked. We made a strange picture, no doubt. "Nobody hurt, is there?" He was looking at Gertrude.

"Worse than that, Mr. Jarvis," I said. "I think it is murder."

At the word there was a commotion. The cook began to cry, and Mrs. Watson knocked over a chair. The men were visibly impressed.

"Not any member of the family?" Mr. Jarvis asked, when he had got his breath.

"No," I said. "Nobody I know." And motioning Liddy to look after Gertrude I led the way with a lamp to the cardroom door. One of the men gave an exclamation, and they all hurried across the room. Mr. Jarvis took the lamp from me—I remember that—and then, feeling myself getting dizzy and lightheaded I closed my eyes. When I opened them their brief examination was over, and Mr. Jarvis was trying to put me in a chair.

"You must get upstairs," he said firmly, "you and Miss Gertrude too. This has been a terrible shock. In his own home, of all things!"

I stared at him without comprehension. "Who is it?" I asked with difficulty. There was a band drawn tight around my throat.

"It's Arnold Armstrong," he said, looking at me oddly, "and he has been murdered, here in his father's house."

After a minute I gathered myself together and Mr. Jarvis helped me into the living room. Liddy had got Gertrude upstairs, and the two strange men from the club stayed with the body. The reaction from the shock and strain was tremendous: I was collapsed—and then Mr. Jarvis asked me a question that brought back my wandering faculties.

"Where's Halsey?" he asked.

"Halsey!" Suddenly Gertrude's stricken face rose before me, and the empty rooms upstairs. Where was Halsey?

"He was here, wasn't he?" Mr. Jarvis persisted. "He stopped at the club on his way over."

"I don't know where he is," I said feebly.

One of the men from the club came in, asked for the telephone, and I could hear him excitedly talking, saying something about coroners and the police. Mr. Jarvis leaned over to me.

"Why don't you trust me, Miss Innes?" he said. "If I can do anything I will. But tell me the whole thing."

I did finally from the beginning, and when I told of Jack Bailey's being in the house that night he gave a long whistle.

"I wish they were both here," he said when I finished. "Whatever took them away, it would look better if they were here. Especially—"

"Especially what?"

"Especially since Jack Bailey and Arnold Armstrong were notoriously bad friends. It was Bailey who got Arnold into trouble last spring. Something about the bank. And then, too—"

"Go on," I said. "If there is anything more, I ought to know."

"There's nothing more," he said evasively. "There's just one thing we may bank on, Miss Innes. Any court in the country will acquit a man who kills an intruder in his house, at night. If Halsey—"

"You can't think Halsey did it!" I mumbled. There was a queer feeling of physical nausea coming over me.

"No, no, not at all," he said, with forced cheerfulness. "Come, Miss Innes, you're a ghost of yourself. I'm going to help you upstairs and call your maid. This has been too much for you."

Liddy helped me back to bed, and under the impression that I was in danger of freezing to death put a hot-water bottle over my heart and another at my feet. Then she left me. It was early dawn now, and from voices under my window I surmised that Mr. Jarvis and his companions were searching the grounds. As for me, I lay in bed with every faculty awake. Where had Halsey gone? How had he gone, and when? Before the murder, certainly, but who would believe that? If either he or Jack Bailey had heard an intruder in the house and shot him—as they might have been justified in doing—why had they run away? The whole thing was unheard of, outrageous, and perfectly damnable.

About six o'clock Gertrude came in. She was fully dressed, and I sat up nervously.

"Poor Rachel," she said. "What a shocking night you have had!" She came over and sat down on the bed, and I saw that she looked practically exhausted.

"Is there anything new?" I asked anxiously.

"Nothing. The car's gone, but Warner"—Warner was our chauffeur—"Warner is at the lodge and knows nothing about it."

"Well," I said, "if I ever get my hands on Halsey Innes I shan't let go until I have told him a few things. When we get this cleared up I am going back to the city to be quiet. One more night like the last two will end me. Don't talk to me about the peace of the country."

Whereupon I told Gertrude of the noises the night before, and the figure on the veranda in the east wing. As an afterthought I brought out the pearl cuff link.

"I have no doubt now," I said, "that it was Arnold Armstrong the night before last too. He had a key, probably. But why he should steal into his father's house I can't imagine. He could have come with my permission easily enough. Anyhow whoever it was that night left this little souvenir."

Gertrude took one look at the cuff link and went as white as the pearls in it. She clutched at the foot of the bed, and stood staring. As for me I was quite as astonished as she was.

"Where did you find it?" she asked finally, with a desperate effort at calm. And while I told her she stood gazing out the window with a look I could not fathom on her face. It was a relief when Mrs. Watson tapped at the door and brought me some tea and toast. The cook was in bed and completely demoralized, she reported; and Liddy, brave with the daylight, was looking for footprints around the house. The police and the coroner, having to come from a distance, had not yet arrived. And Mrs. Watson herself was a wreck; she was blue-white around the lips, and she had one hand tied up. She said she had fallen downstairs in her excitement. It was natural of course that the thing would shock her, having been the Armstrongs' housekeeper for several years and knowing Mr. Arnold well.

Gertrude had slipped out during my talk with Mrs. Watson, and I dressed and went downstairs. The billiard and card rooms were locked until the police got there, and the men from the club had gone back for more conventional clothing.

I could hear Thomas in the pantry, alternately wailing for Mr. Arnold, as he called him, and citing the tokens that had precursed the murder. The house seemed to choke me and slipping a shawl around me I went out on the drive. At the corner by the east wing I met Liddy. Her skirts were draggled with dew to her knees, and her hair was still in crimps.

"Go right in and change your clothes," I said sharply. "You're a sight, and at your age!"

She had a golf stick in her hand, and she said she had found it on the lawn. There was nothing unusual about it, but it occurred to me that a golf stick with a metal end might have been the object that had scratched the stairs near the cardroom. I took it from her and sent her up for dry garments. Her daylight courage and self-importance and her shuddering delight in the mystery irritated me beyond words. After I left her I made a circuit of the building. Nothing seemed to be disturbed. The house looked as calm and peaceful in the morning sun as it had the day I had been coerced into taking it. There was nothing to show that inside had been mystery and violence and sudden death.

In one of the tulip beds back of the house an early crow was pecking viciously at something that glittered in the light. I picked my way gingerly over through the dew and stooped. Almost buried in the soft ground was a revolver. I scraped the earth off it with the tip of my shoe and picking it up slipped it into my pocket. Not until I had got into my bedroom and double-locked the door did I venture to take it out and examine it. One look was all I needed. It was Halsey's own gun. I had unpacked it the day before and put it on his shaving stand, and there could be no mistake. His name was on a small silver plate on the handle.

I seemed to see a network closing around my boy, innocent as I knew he was. The revolver—I am afraid of them, but anxiety gave me courage to ex-amine it—the revolver had still two bullets in it. I could only breathe a prayer of thankfulness that I had found it before any sharp-eyed detective had come around.

I decided to keep what clues I had—the cuff link, the golf stick and the revolver—in a secure place until I could see some reason for displaying them. The cuff link had been dropped into a little filigree box on my toilet table. I opened the box and felt around for it, but to my horror the box was empty. The cuff link had disappeared!

5

AT EIGHT O'CLOCK that morning the Casanova hack brought up three men. They introduced themselves as the coroner of the county and two de-tectives from the city. The coroner led the way at once to the locked wing, and with the aid of one of the detectives examined the rooms and the body. The other detective, after a short scrutiny of the dead man, busied himself with the outside of the house. It was only after they had got a fair idea of things as they were that they sent for me.

I received them in the living room, and I had made up my mind exactly what to tell. I had taken the house for the summer, I said, while the Arm-strongs were in California. In spite of a rumor among the servants about strange noises—I cited Thomas—nothing had occurred the first two nights. On the third night I believed that someone had been in the house. I had heard a crashing sound, but being alone with one maid had not investigated. The house had been locked in the morning and apparently undisturbed.

Then as clearly as I could I related how, the night before, a shot had roused us; that my niece and I had investigated and found a body, that I did not know who the murdered man was until Mr. Jarvis from the club informed me, and that I knew of no reason why Mr. Arnold Armstrong should steal into his father's house at night. I should have been glad to allow him entree there at any time.

"Have you reason to believe, Miss Innes," the coroner asked, "that any member of your household, imagining Mr. Armstrong was a burglar, shot him in self-defense?"

"I have no reason for thinking so," I said quietly.

"Your theory is that Mr. Armstrong was followed here by some enemy, and shot as he entered the house?"

"I don't think I have a theory," I said. "The thing that has puzzled me is why Mr. Armstrong should enter his father's house two nights in succession, stealing in like a thief, when he needed only to ask entrance to be admitted."

The coroner was a very silent man. He listened to what I had to say, but he seemed anxious to make the next train back to town. He set the inquest for the following Saturday, gave Jamieson, the younger of the two detectives and the more intelligent looking, a few instructions, and after gravely shaking hands with me and regretting the unfortunate affair took his departure, accompanied by the other detective.

I was just beginning to breathe freely when Jamieson, who had been standing by the window, came over to me.

"The family consists of yourself alone, Miss Innes?"

"My niece is here," I said.

"There is no one but yourself and your niece?"

"My nephew." I had to moisten my lips.

"Oh, a nephew. I should like to see him, if he is here."

"He is not here just now," I said as quietly as I could. "I expect him at any time."

"He was here yesterday evening?"

"No—yes."

"Didn't he have a guest with him? Another man?"

"He brought a friend with him to stay over Sunday, a Mr. Bailey."

"Mr. John Bailey, the cashier of the Traders' Bank, I believe." And I knew that someone at the Greenwood Club had been talking. "When did they leave?"

"Very early. I don't know at just what time."

Jamieson turned suddenly and looked at me.

"Please try to be more explicit," he said. "You say your nephew and Mr. Bailey were in the house last night, and yet you and your niece with some women servants found the body. Where was your nephew?"

I was entirely desperate by that time.

"I don't know," I said. "But be sure of this: Halsey knows nothing of this thing, and no amount of circumstantial evidence can make an innocent man guilty."

"Sit down," he said, pushing forward a chair. "There are some things I have to tell you, and in return please tell me all you know. Believe me, things always come out. In the first place, Mr. Armstrong was shot from above. The bullet was fired at close range, entered below the shoulder and came out, after passing through the heart, well down the back. In other words, I believe the murderer stood on the stairs and fired down. In the second place, I found on the edge of the billiard table a charred cigar which had burned itself partly out, and a cigarette which had consumed itself to the cork tip. Neither one had been more than lighted, then put down and forgotten. Have you any idea what it was that made your nephew and Mr. Bailey leave their cigars and their game, take out the car without calling the chauffeur, and all this certainly before three o'clock in the morning?"

"I don't know," I said; "but depend on it, Mr. Jamieson, Halsey will be back himself to explain everything."

"I sincerely hope so," he said. "Miss Innes, has it occurred to you that Mr. Bailey might know something of this?"

Gertrude had come downstairs and as he spoke she came in. I saw her stop suddenly, as if she had been struck.

"He does not," she said in a tone that was not her own. "Mr. Bailey and my brother know nothing of this. The murder was committed at three. They left the house at a quarter before three."

"How do you know that?" Jamieson asked oddly. "Do you know at what time they left?"

"I do," Gertrude answered firmly. "At a quarter before three my brother and Mr. Bailey left the house, by the main entrance. I was there when they went."

"Gertrude," I said excitedly, "you're dreaming! Why, at a quarter to three—"

"Listen," she said. "At half past two the downstairs telephone rang. I hadn't gone to sleep and I heard it. Then I heard Halsey answer it, and in a few minutes he came upstairs and knocked at my door. I—we talked for a minute, then I put on my dressing gown and slippers, and went downstairs with him. Mr. Bailey was in the billiard room. We all talked together for perhaps ten minutes. Then it was decided that they had to leave to attend to something—"

"Can't you be more explicit?" Jamieson asked. "What did they have to attend to?"

"I am only telling you what happened, not why it happened," she said evenly. "Halsey went for the car and instead of bringing it to the house and rousing people he went by the lower road from the stable. Mr. Bailey was to meet him at the foot of the lawn. Mr. Bailey left—"

"Which way?" Jamieson asked sharply.

"By the main entrance. He left at a quarter to three. I know exactly."

"The clock in the hall is stopped, Miss Innes," said Jamieson. Nothing seemed to escape him.

"He looked at his watch," she replied, and I could see Mr. Jamieson's eyes snap as if he had made a discovery. As for myself, during the whole recital I had been plunged into the deepest amazement.

"Will you pardon me for a personal question?" The detective was a young-ish man, and I thought he was somewhat embarrassed. "What are your relations with Mr. Bailey?"

Gertrude hesitated. Then she came over and put her hand lovingly in mine.

"I am engaged to marry him," she said simply.

I had grown so accustomed to surprises that I could only gasp again. As for Gertrude, the hand that lay in mine was icy cold.

"And after that," Jamieson went on, "you went directly to bed?"

Gertrude hesitated.

"No," she said finally. "I'm not nervous, and after I had put out the light I remembered something I had left in the billiard room. I felt my way back there through the darkness."

"Will you tell me what it was you had forgotten?"

"I can't tell you," she said slowly. "But I didn't leave the billiard room at once—I waited awhile."

"Why?" The detective's tone was imperative. "This is very important, Miss Innes."

"I was crying," Gertrude said in a low tone. "When the French clock in the drawing room struck three I got up, and then I heard a step on the east porch, just outside the cardroom. Someone with a key was working with the latch. I thought of course of Halsey. When we took the house he called that his entrance, and he had carried a key for it ever since. The door opened and I was about to ask what he had forgotten when there was a flash and a report. Some heavy body dropped, and I guess I was scared out of my wits. Anyhow I ran through the drawing room and got upstairs. I scarcely remember how."

"You didn't see the dead man?"

"No."

She dropped into a chair, and I thought Jamieson must have finished. But he was not through.

"You certainly clear your brother and Mr. Bailey admirably," he said. "The testimony is important, especially in view of the fact that your brother and Mr. Armstrong had quarreled rather seriously some time ago."

"Nonsense," I broke in. "Things are bad enough, Mr. Jamieson, without inventing bad feeling where it doesn't exist. Gertrude, I don't think Halsey even knew young Armstrong, did he?"

But Jamieson was sure of his ground.

"The quarrel," he persisted, "was about Mr. Armstrong's conduct to you, Miss Gertrude. He had been annoying you, paying you unwelcome attentions. That's the fact, isn't it?"

And I had never seen the man!

When she nodded a "yes" I saw the tremendous possibilities involved. If this detective could prove that Gertrude feared and disliked the murdered man and that young Armstrong had been annoying her for some reason, all that added to Gertrude's confession of her presence in the billiard room at the time of the crime looked strange, to say the least. The prominence of his family assured a strenuous effort to find the murderer, and if we had nothing worse to look forward to we were sure of a disgusting publicity.

Jamieson shut his notebook with a snap, and thanked us.

"I have an idea," he said, with a grim sort of smile, "that at any rate the ghost is laid here. Whatever the rappings have been—and the colored man says they began when the family went west three months ago—they're likely to stop now."

Which shows how much he knew about it. The ghost was not laid; with the murder of Arnold Armstrong he or it only seemed to take on fresh vigor.

Jamieson left then and when Gertrude had gone upstairs, as she did at once, I sat and thought over what I had just heard. Her engagement, which had come as a surprise to me, paled now beside the significance of her story. If Halsey and Jack Bailey had left before the crime, why was Halsey's revolver in the tulip. bed? What was the mysterious cause of their sudden flight? What had Gertrude left in the billiard room that she had gone back for? What was the significance of the cuff link? And where was it?

I was not left long in peace. For hours that morning police officers prowled the place, photographs were taken, and men were everywhere. In due time however the body was removed, and we had at least an interval of quiet. Gertrude was shut in her room, and Liddy should have been shut in a lunatic asylum.

But before the body was taken away I was asked to look at it. Whatever lines of dissipation had been in young Armstrong's face had been wiped away by death. But he had been handsome. And young. I felt a stab of pity for him.

6

WHEN JAMIESON LEFT he had enjoined absolute secrecy on everybody in the household. The Greenwood Club promised the same thing, and as there are no Sunday afternoon papers the murder was not publicly known until Monday. The police however notified the Armstrong family lawyer, and early in the afternoon he came out.

Mr. Harton was a small, thin man, and he looked as if he did not relish his business that day.

"This is very unfortunate, Miss Innes," he said, after we had shaken hands. "Most unfortunate and mysterious. With the father and mother in the West, I find everything devolves on me, and as you can understand it is an unpleasant duty."

"No doubt," I said absently. "Mr. Harton, I am going to ask you some questions, and I hope you will answer them. I feel that I am entitled to some knowledge, because my family and I myself are in a most ambiguous position."

I don't know whether he understood me or not. He took off his glasses and wiped them.

"I shall be very happy," he said with old-fashioned courtesy. "I know very little, of course."

"Thank you. Mr. Harton, did Mr. Arnold Armstrong know that Sunnyside had been rented?"

"I think—yes, he did. In fact, I myself told him about it."

"And he knew who the tenants were?"

"Yes."

"He had not been living with the family for some years, I believe?"

"No. Unfortunately there had been trouble between Arnold and his father. For the past two years he had lived in town."

"Then it would be unlikely that he came here last night to get possession of anything belonging to him?"

"I should think it hardly possible," he admitted. "To be perfectly frank, Miss Innes, I can't think of any reason whatever for his coming here as he did. He had been staying at the clubhouse across the valley for the last week, Jarvis tells me, but that only explains how he came here, not why."

He gave me a shrewd look through his spectacles. "I know him only slightly," he said, "but I understand he—well, he lived his own life. If he came back it was a case of the Prodigal Son, Miss Innes. That's all I can say."

He was greatly upset. I could see that. But he did not elaborate except to mutter something about the sins of the fathers being visited on the children, which left me pondering.

He asked to see the scene of the crime, and as we started Mrs. Watson appeared at the cardroom door. Evidently he knew her, for he spoke to her.

"I'm sorry about this, Mrs. Watson," he said, "Who would have expected such a thing?"

But she only shook her head and passed us without speaking. She went on, and Mr. Harton viewed the spot where the body had been found without comment. Someone—perhaps Mrs. Watson herself—had washed the blood from the carpet in the hall. I stepped over the place and going to the door at the foot of the circular staircase opened it and glanced out.

If I could only have seen Halsey coming at his usual harebrained pace up the drive, if I could have heard the throb of the motor, I would have felt that my troubles were over. But there was nothing to be seen. The countryside lay sunny and quiet in its peaceful Sunday afternoon calm, and far down the drive Jamieson was walking slowly, stooping now and then as if to examine the road. When I turned back Mr. Harton was furtively wiping his spectacles.

"I have known him since he was a boy," he said. "Whatever he was he didn't deserve this."

Before he left he told me something of the Armstrong family. Paul Armstrong, the father, had been married twice. Arnold was a son by the first marriage. The second Mrs. Armstrong had been a widow with a child, a little girl. This child, now perhaps twenty, was Louise Armstrong, having taken her stepfather's name, and was at present in California with the family.

"They will probably return at once," he concluded, "and part of my errand here today is to see if you will relinquish your lease here in their favor."

"We would better wait and see if they care to come," I said. "It seems unlikely, and my town house is being remodeled." At that he let the matter drop, but it came up unpleasantly enough later.

At six o'clock the house had more or less settled down, and at seven-thirty, after an early dinner, Mr. Harton went. Gertrude had not come down, and there was no news of Halsey. Jamieson had taken a lodging in the village, and I had not seen him since midafternoon. It was about nine o'clock, I think, when the bell rang and he was ushered into the living room.

"Sit down," I said grimly. "Have you found anything that will incriminate me, Mr. Jamieson?"

He had the grace to look uncomfortable. "No," he said. "If you had killed Mr. Armstrong, I imagine you would have left no clues. You are a very intelligent woman, Miss Innes."

After that we got along better. I was knitting, while he was fishing in his pocket. After a minute he brought out two scraps of paper. "I have been to the clubhouse," he said, "and among Mr. Armstrong's effects I found these. One is curious. The other is puzzling."

The first was a sheet of club note paper on which was written over and over the name "Halsey B. Innes." It was Halsey's flowing signature to a dot, but it lacked Halsey's ease. The ones toward the bottom of the sheet were much better than the top ones. Jamieson smiled at my face.

"His old tricks," he said. "That one is merely curious. This one, as I said before, is puzzling."

The second scrap, folded and refolded into a compass so tiny that the writing had been partly obliterated, was part of a letter. The lower half of a sheet, not typed, but written in a cramped hand.

". . . . . by altering the plans for . . . . rooms may be possible. The best way, in my opinion, would be to . . . . the plan for . . . . in one of the . . . . rooms . . . . chimney."

That was all.

"Well?" I said, looking up. "There is nothing in that, is there? A man ought to be able to change the plan of his house without becoming an object of suspicion."

"There is little in the paper itself," he admitted. "But why should Arnold Armstrong carry that around unless it meant something? He never built a house, you may be sure of that. If it is this house it may mean anything, from a secret room—"

"To an extra bathroom," I said scornfully. "Haven't you a thumbprint too?"

"I have," he said, with a smile, "and the print of a foot in a tulip bed, and a number of other things. The oddest part is, Miss Innes, that the thumb-mark is probably yours and the footprint certainly."

His audacity was the only thing that saved me. His amused smile put me on my mettle, and I ripped out a perfectly good scallop before I answered.

"Why did I step into the tulip bed?" I asked, with interest.

"You picked up something," he said good-humoredly, "which you are going to tell me about later."

"Am I indeed?" I was politely curious. "With this remarkable insight of yours, I wish you would tell me where I shall find my four-thousand-dollar car."

"I was just coming to that," he said. "You will find it about thirty miles away at Andrews Station in a garage where it is being repaired."

I laid down my knitting then and looked at him. "And Halsey?" I managed to say.

"We are going to exchange information," he said. "I am going to tell you that, when you tell me what you picked up in the tulip bed."

We looked steadily at each other. It was not an unfriendly stare; we were only measuring weapons. Then he smiled a little and got up.

"With your permission," he said, "I am going to examine the cardroom and the staircase again. You might think over my offer in the meantime."

He went on through the drawing room, and I listened to his footsteps growing gradually fainter. I dropped my pretense at knitting and leaning back I thought over the last forty-eight hours. Here was I, Rachel Innes, a spinster, a granddaughter of old John Innes of Revolutionary days, a D.A.R., a Colonial Dame, mixed up with a vulgar and revolting crime and even attempting to hoodwink the law! Certainly I had left the straight and narrow way.

I was roused by hearing Mr. Jamieson coming rapidly back through the drawing room. He stopped at the door.

"Miss Innes," he said quickly, "will you come with me and light the hall over here? I have locked somebody in the small room at the head of the card-room stairs."

I jumped up at once.

"You mean the murderer?" I gasped.

"Possibly," he said quietly, as we hurried together up the stairs. "Someone was hiding on the staircase when I went back. I spoke, but instead of an answer whoever it was turned and ran up. I followed but as I turned the corner at the top a figure darted through this door and closed it. The key was on my side and I turned it. It's a closet, I think." We were in the upper hall now. "If you will show me the electric switch, Miss Innes, you would better wait in your own room."

Trembling as I was, I was determined to see that door opened. I hardly knew what I feared, but so many terrible and inexplicable things had happened that suspense was worse than certainty.

"I'm perfectly cool," I said, "and I intend to stay right here."

The lights flashed up along that end of the corridor, throwing the doors into relief. At the intersection of the small hallway with the larger the circular staircase wound its way up, as if it had been an afterthought of the architect. And just around the corner in the small hallway was the door Jamieson had indicated. I was still unfamiliar with the house and I did not remember the door. My heart was thumping wildly in my ears, but I nodded to him to go ahead. I was perhaps eight or ten feet away when he turned the key. I think he had a gun in his hand.

"Come out," he said quietly. There was no response. "Come out," he repeated. "I've got you." Then suddenly, he stepped aside and threw the door open.

From where I stood I could not see beyond the door, but I saw Jamieson's face change and heard him mutter something. Then he bolted down the stairs, three at a time. When my knees had stopped shaking, I moved forward, slowly, nervously, until I had a partial view of what was beyond the door. It seemed at first to be a closet, empty. After that I went close and examined it, to stop with a shudder. Where the floor should have been was black void and darkness, from which came the indescribable damp smell of the cellars.

Jamieson had locked somebody in the clothes chute. As I leaned over I fancied I heard a groan. Or was it the wind?

7

I WAS PANIC-STRICKEN. As I ran along the corridor I was confident that the mysterious intruder and probable murderer had been found, and that he lay dead or dying at the foot of the chute. I got down the staircase somehow, and through the kitchen to the basement stairs. Jamieson had been before me and the door stood open. Liddy was standing in the middle of the kitchen, holding a frying pan by the handle as a weapon.

"Don't go down there," she yelled when she saw me moving toward the basement stairs. "Don't you do it, Miss Rachel. That Jamieson's down there now. There's only trouble comes of hunting ghosts. They lead you into bottomless pits and things like that. Please, Miss Rachel, don't—" as I tried to get past her.

She was interrupted by Jamieson's reappearance. He ran up the stairs two at a time, and his face was flushed and furious.

"The whole place is locked," he said angrily. "Where's the laundry key kept?"

"It's kept in the door," Liddy snapped. "That whole end of the cellar is kept locked, so nobody can get at the clothes. And then the key's left in the door, so that unless a thief was as blind as some detectives he could walk right in."

"Liddy," I said sharply, "come down with us and turn on all the lights."

She offered her resignation as usual on the spot, but I took her by the arm and she came along finally. She switched on all the lights and pointed to a door just ahead.

"That's the door," she said sulkily. "The key's in it."

The key was not in it, however. Mr. Jamieson shook it, but it was a heavy door and well locked. Then he stooped and began punching around the key-hole with the end of a lead pencil, and when he stood up his face was exultant.

"It's locked on the inside," he said in a low tone. "There is somebody in there."

"Lord have mercy!" gasped Liddy, and turned to run.

"Liddy," I called, "go through the house at once and see who is missing, or if anyone is. We'll have to clear this thing at once. Mr. Jamieson, if you will watch here I will go to the lodge and find Warner, the chauffeur. Thomas would be no use. Together you may be able to force the door."

"A good idea," he assented. "But there are windows, of course, and there is nothing to prevent whoever was in there from getting out that way."

"Then lock the door at the top of the basement stairs," I suggested, "and patrol the house from the outside."

We agreed to this, and I had a feeling that the mystery of Sunnyside was about to be solved. I ran down the steps and along the drive. Just at the corner I ran full tilt into somebody who seemed to be as much alarmed as I was. It was not until I had recoiled a step or two that I recognized Gertrude, and she me.

"Good gracious, Rachel," she exclaimed, "what is the matter?"

"There's somebody locked in the laundry," I panted. "That is unless—You didn't see anyone crossing the lawn or skulking around the house, did you?"

"I think we have mystery on the brain," Gertrude said wearily. "No, I haven't seen anyone except old Thomas, who looked for all the world as if he had been caught stealing the spoons. What on earth have you locked in the laundry?"

"I can't wait to explain," I replied. "I must get Warner from the lodge. If you came out for air you'd better change your shoes." That was when I noticed Gertrude was limping. Not much, but sufficiently to make her progress very slow and seemingly painful.

"You've hurt yourself," I said sharply.

"I turned my ankle," she explained. "I thought perhaps I might see Halsey coming home. He ought to be back. I don't understand."

I hurried on down the drive. The lodge was some distance from the house, in a grove of trees where the drive met the country road. There were two white stone pillars to mark the entrance, but the iron gates, once closed and tended by the lodgekeeper, now stood permanently open. Times had changed, and the lodge at Sunnyside was merely a sort of supplementary servants' quarters. It was as convenient in its appointments as the big house and infinitely easier to care for.

As I went down the drive my thoughts were busy. Who could it be that

Jamieson had trapped in the cellar? Would we find a body or someone badly injured? Scarcely either. Whoever had fallen had been able to lock the laundry door on the inside. But if the fugitive had come from outside the house, how did he get in? If it was some member of the household, who could it have been? That was when a feeling of horror almost overwhelmed me. Gertrude! Gertrude and her injured ankle. Gertrude limping slowly up the drive when I had thought she was in bed!

I tried to put the thought away, but it would not go. If Gertrude had been on the circular staircase that night why had she run from Jamieson? The idea, puzzling as it was, seemed borne out by this circumstance. Whoever had taken refuge at the head of the stairs could scarcely have been familiar with the house, or with the location of the chute. The mystery seemed to deepen constantly. What possible connection could there be between Halsey and Gertrude, and the murder of Arnold Armstrong? And yet every way I turned I seemed to find something that pointed to such a connection.

At the foot of the drive the road described a long sloping horseshoe-shaped curve around the lodge. There were lights there, streaming cheerfully out onto the trees, and from an upper room came wavering shadows, as if someone with a lamp was moving around. I had come almost silently in my evening slippers, and I had my second collision of the evening on the road just above the house. I ran full tilt into a man in a long coat who was standing in the shadow beside the drive, with his back to me and watching the lighted windows.

"What the hell!" he ejaculated furiously, and turned around. When he saw me, however, he did not wait for any retort on my part. He faded away—this is not slang; he did—he absolutely disappeared in the dusk without my getting more than a glimpse of his face. I had a vague impression of unfamiliar features and of a sort of cap with a visor. Then he was gone.

I went to the lodge and rapped. It required two or three poundings to bring Thomas to the door, and he opened it only an inch or so.

"Where is Warner?" I asked.

"I think he's in bed, ma'am."

"Get him up," I said, "and for goodness' sake open the door, Thomas. I'll wait for Warner."

"It's kind o' close in here, ma'am," he said, obeying gingerly, and disclosing a cool and comfortable-looking interior. "Perhaps you'd keer to set on the porch an' rest yo'self."

It was so evident that Thomas did not want me inside that I went in.

"Tell Warner he is needed in a hurry," I repeated, and turned into the little sitting room. I could hear Thomas going up the stairs, could hear him rouse Warner, and the steps of the chauffeur as he hurriedly dressed. But my attention was busy with the room below.

On the center table, open, was a pigskin traveling bag. It was filled with gold-topped bottles, and it breathed opulence, luxury, femininity from every inch of surface. How did it get there? I was still asking myself the question when Warner came running down the stairs and into the room. He was completely but somewhat incongruously dressed, and his open, boyish face looked abashed. He was a country boy, absolutely frank and reliable, and of fair education and intelligence. One of the small army of American youths who turn a natural aptitude for mechanics into the special field of the automobile, and earn good salaries in a congenial occupation.

"What is it, Miss Innes?" he asked anxiously.

"There is someone locked in the laundry," I replied. "Mr. Jamieson wants you to help him break the lock. Warner, whose bag is this?"

He was in the doorway by this time and he pretended not to hear.

"Warner," I called, "come back here. Whose bag is this?"

He stopped then, but he did not turn around.

"It's—I think it belongs to Thomas," he said, and hurried up the drive.

To Thomas! An English fitted bag with mirrors and cosmetic jars of which Thomas could not even have guessed the use! However, I put the bag in the back of my mind, which was fast becoming stored with absurd and apparently irreconcilable facts, and followed Warner to the house.

Liddy had come back to the kitchen. The door to the basement stairs was double-barred, and had a table pushed against it. And beside her on the table was most of the kitchen paraphernalia.

"Did you see if there was anyone missing in the house?" I asked, ignoring the array of saucepans, rolling pins, and the poker from the range.

"Rosie is missing," Liddy said with unction. She had objected to Rosie, the parlor maid, from the start. "Mrs. Watson went into her room and found she had gone without her hat. People that trust themselves a dozen miles from the city, in strange houses, with servants they don't know, needn't be surprised if they wake up some morning and find their throats cut."

After which carefully veiled sarcasm Liddy relapsed into gloom. Warner came in then with a handful of small tools, and Jamieson went with him to the basement. Oddly enough I was not alarmed. With all my heart I wished for Halsey, but I was not frightened. At the door he was to force, Warner put down his tools and looked at it. Then he turned the handle. Without the slightest difficulty the door opened, revealing the blackness of the drying room beyond!

Jamieson gave an exclamation of disgust. "Damnation!" he said. "Confound such careless work! I might have known."

It was true enough. We got the lights on finally and looked all through the three rooms that constituted this wing of the basement. Everything was quiet and empty. An explanation of how the fugitive had escaped injury was found in a heaped-up basket of clothes under the chute. The basket had been overturned but that was all. Jamieson examined the windows. One was unlocked and offered an easy escape. The window or the door to the yard outside? Which way had the fugitive escaped? The door seemed most probable, and I hoped it had been so. I could not have borne just then to think that it was my poor Gertrude we had been hounding through the darkness. And yet I had met Gertrude not far from that very door.

I went upstairs at last, tired and depressed. Mrs. Watson and Liddy were making tea in the kitchen. In certain walks of life the teapot is the refuge in times of stress, trouble or sickness. They give tea to the dying and they put it in the baby's nursing bottle. Also Mrs. Watson was fixing a tray to be sent in to me, and when I asked her about Rosie she confirmed her absence.

"She's not here," she said; "but I wouldn't think much of that, Miss Innes. Rosie is a pretty young girl, and perhaps she has a friend in the neighborhood. It will be a good thing if she has. The maids stay much better when they have something like that to hold them here."

Gertrude had gone back to her room, and while I was drinking my cup of hot tea Jamieson came in.

"Suppose we take up the conversation where we left off an hour and a half ago," he suggested. "But before we go on, I want to say this. The person who escaped from the laundry was a woman with a foot of moderate size and well arched. She wore nothing but a stocking on her right foot, and, in spite of the unlocked door she escaped by the window. Which seems rather curious."

Again I thought of Gertrude's sprained ankle. At least I was sure she was wearing slippers on both feet. Nevertheless I was uneasy. She *had* been limping.

8

"MISS INNES," Jamieson began, "what is your opinion of the figure you saw on the east veranda the night you and your maid were in the house alone?"

"It was a woman," I said positively.

"And yet your maid affirms with equal positiveness that it was a man."

"Nonsense," I broke in. "Liddy had her eyes shut. She always shuts them when she's frightened."

"You never thought then that the intruder who came later that night might be a woman? The woman in fact whom you saw on the veranda?"

"I had reasons for thinking it was a man," I said, remembering the pearl cuff link.

"Now we're getting down to business," he said, smiling. "What were your reasons for thinking that?"

I hesitated, and his smile faded.

"Listen," he said. "If you have any reason for believing that your midnight guest was Mr. Armstrong, other than his visit here the next night, you ought to tell me. We can take nothing for granted. If for instance the intruder who dropped the bar and scratched the staircase—yes, of course I know about that

—if this visitor was a woman, why should not the same woman have come back the following night, met Mr. Armstrong on the circular staircase, and either in alarm or for some other reason shot him?"

"It was a man," I reiterated stubbornly. And then, because I could think of no other reason for my statement, I told him about the broken pearl cuff link. He was more than interested.

"Will you give me the link," he said, when I finished, "or, at least, let me see it? It may be most important."

"Won't the description do?"

"Not so well as the original." He eyed me suspiciously.

"Well, I'm very sorry," I said, as calmly as I could. "The thing is lost. It must have fallen out of a box on my dressing table. Anyhow I can't find it."

Whatever he thought of my explanation, and I knew he doubted it, he made no sign. He asked me to describe the link accurately and I did so, while he glanced at a list he took from his pocket.

"One set monogram cuff links," he read, "one set plain dinner links with small pearl, one set cuff links, antique with woman's head set with diamonds and emeralds. There is no mention of such a link as you describe, and yet if your theory is right Mr. Armstrong must have worn back that night to the club one complete cuff link, and a half perhaps of the other."

The idea was new to me. If it had not been the murdered man who had entered the house that night, who had it been?

"There are a number of unusual things connected with this case," the detective went on. "Miss Gertrude Innes testified that she heard someone fumbling with the lock last night, that the door opened, and that almost immediately the shot was fired. Now, Miss Innes, here is the strange part of that. Arnold Armstrong had no key with him. There was no key in the lock or on the floor. In other words, the evidence points absolutely to the fact that Mr. Armstrong was admitted to the house from within."

"It's impossible," I broke in. "Mr. Jamieson, do you know what your words imply? Do you know that you are practically accusing Gertrude Innes of admitting that man?"

"Not quite that," he said, with his friendly smile. "In fact, Miss Innes, I am quite certain she didn't do anything of the sort. But as long as I learn only bits of the truth from both you and her what can I do? I know you picked up something in the flower bed, but you refuse to tell me what it was. I know Miss Gertrude went back to the billiard room to get something, yet she refuses to say what. You suspect what happened to the cuff link after you found it, but you won't tell me. So far, all I am sure of is this: I do not believe Arnold Armstrong was the midnight visitor who so alarmed you by dropping—shall we say?—a golf stick. And I believe that when he did come he was admitted by someone in the house. Who was that person? Liddy?"

I stirred my tea angrily.

"I have always heard," I said, "that undertakers' assistants are jovial young men. A man's sense of humor seems to be in inverse proportion to the gravity of his profession."

"A man's sense of humor is often a barbarous and a cruel thing," he admitted. "It is to the feminine as the hug of a bear is to the scratch of something with claws. I don't know which is worse." He glanced up abruptly. "Is that you, Thomas? Come in."

Thomas stood in the doorway. He looked alarmed and apprehensive, and I remembered the pigskin traveling bag in the lodge. Thomas came just inside the door and stood with his arms hanging and his eyes under their shaggy gray brows fixed on Jamieson.

"Thomas," said the detective, not unkindly, "I sent for you to tell us what you told Sam Bohannon at the club, the day before Mr. Arnold was found here dead. Let me see. You came here Friday night to see Miss Innes, didn't you? And came to work here Saturday morning?"

For some unexplained reason Thomas looked relieved.

"Yas, suh," he said. "You see it were like this: When Mistah Armstrong and the fam'ly went away Mis' Watson an' me we was lef' in charge till the place was rented. Mis' Watson, she've bin here a good while an' she warn't skeery. So she slep' in the house. I'd bin havin' tokens—I tol' Mis' Innes some of 'em—an' I slep' in the lodge. Then one day Mis' Watson she came to me an' she sez, 'Thomas, you'll hev to sleep up in the big house. I'm too nervous to do it any more.' But I jes' reckon to myself that ef it's too skeery fer her it's too skeery for me. We had it then sho' nuff, and it ended up with Mis' Watson stayin' in the lodge nights an' me lookin' fer work at de club."

"Did Mrs. Watson say that anything had happened to alarm her?"

"No, suh. She was jes' natchally skeered. Well, that was all, far's I know, until the night I come over to see Mis' Innes. I come across the valley, along the path from the clubhouse, and I goes home that way. Down in the creek bottom I almost run into a man. He wuz standin' with his back to me, an' he was workin' with one of these yere electric light things that fit in yer pocket. He was havin' trouble. One minute it'd flash out an' the nex' it'd be gone. I hed a view of 'is dress shirt an' tie as I passed. I didn't see his face. But I know it warn't Mr. Arnold. It was a taller man than Mr. Arnold. Beside that Mr. Arnold was playin' cards when I got back to the clubhouse, same's he'd been doin' all day."

"And the next morning you came back along the same path," pursued Jamieson relentlessly.

"The nex' mornin' I come back along the path, an' down where I dun see the man night befoh I picked up this here." The old man held out a tiny object, and Jamieson took it. Then he held it on his extended palm for me to see. It was the other half of the pearl cuff link.

But Jamieson was not quite through questioning him.

"And so you showed it to Sam, at the club, and asked him if he knew anyone who owned such a link, and Sam said—what did Sam say?"

"Wal, Sam, he 'lowed he'd seen such a pair of cuff buttons in a shirt be-longin' to Mr. Bailey. Mr. Jack Bailey, suh."

"I'll keep this link, Thomas, for a while," the detective said. "That's all I wanted to know. Good night."

As Thomas shuffled out Jamieson watched me sharply.

"You see, Miss Innes," he said, "Mr. Bailey insists on mixing himself with this thing. If Mr. Bailey came here that Friday night expecting to meet Ar-nold Armstrong, and missed him—If, as I say, he had done this, might he not, seeing him enter the following night, have struck him down as he had in-tended before?"

"But the motive?" I gasped. "Why on earth would he do it?"

"There could be motive proved, I think. Arnold Armstrong and John Bailey have been on bad terms since Bailey, as cashier of the Traders' Bank, brought Arnold almost into the clutches of the law. Then don't forget that both men have been paying attention to your niece. Bailey's flight looks bad, too."

"And you think Halsey helped him to escape?"

"What do you think? Suppose I reconstruct that evening as I see it. Bailey and Armstrong had quarreled at the club. I learned this today. After that your nephew brought Bailey over here. And it looks as though Armstrong, prompted by jealous, insane fury followed them both, coming across by the path. He entered the billiard-room wing, perhaps rapping and being admitted by your nephew. And just inside he was shot by someone on the circular staircase. The shot fired, your nephew and Bailey left the house at once, going toward the garage and the car. They drove off by the lower road, which pre-vented their being heard, and when you got downstairs everything was quiet."

"That's not what Gertrude says," I objected.

He lit a cigarette before he spoke.

"Miss Gertrude only brought forward her explanation the following morn-ing. Quite frankly I don't believe it, Miss Innes. It's the story of a loving and frightened woman."

"And this thing tonight? The clothes chute."

"It may upset my whole view of the case," he admitted. "I have no idea of jumping to any conclusion yet. We may, for instance, come back to the figure on the porch. If it was a woman you saw that night through the window we might start with other premises. Or your nephew's explanation when we find him may turn us in a new direction. It's possible he shot Arnold Armstrong as a burglar and then escaped, shocked at what he had done. In any case how-ever I feel confident that the body was here when he left. Mr. Armstrong left the club, ostensibly for a moonlight saunter, about half after eleven o'clock. It was three when the shot was fired."

I leaned back bewildered. It seemed to me that the evening had been full of significant happenings, had I only had the brains to understand them. Had Gertrude been the fugitive in the clothes chute? In that case who was the man on the drive near the lodge? And whose gold-mounted dressing bag had I seen in the lodge sitting room?

It was late when Jamieson finally got up to go. I went with him to the door, and together we stood looking out over the valley. Below lay the small village of Casanova with its Old World houses, its blossoming trees and its peace. Above on the hill across the valley were the lights of the Greenwood Club. It was even possible to see the curving row of parallel lights which marked the carriage road. Rumors about the club came back to me. Founded by a group of wealthy men from the city, a good bit more took place there than the golf which was its ostensible purpose. There was, I knew, a good bit of drinking and gambling, and once a year ago there had been a suicide under those very lights.

Jamieson left soon, taking a short cut to the village, and I still stood there. It must have been after eleven, and the monotonous tick of the big clock on the stairs behind me was the only sound. Then I was conscious that someone was running up the drive. In a minute a woman darted into the area of light made by the open door, and caught me by the arm. It was Rosie, a Rosie in a state of collapse from terror and, not the least important, clutching one of my Coalport plates and a silver spoon.

She stood staring into the darkness behind, still holding the plate. I got her into the house and took the plate from her. Then I stood and looked down at her where she crouched tremblingly against the doorway.

"Well," I asked, "didn't your young man enjoy his meal?"

She couldn't speak. She looked at the spoon she still held as if she was unconscious of it. Then she stared at me.

"I appreciate your desire to have everything nice for him," I went on, "but the next time you might take the Limoges china. It's more easily duplicated and less expensive."

"I haven't a young man. Not here." She had got her breath now, and dropped into a chair. "I've been chased by somebody, Miss Innes."

"Did he chase you out of the house and back again?" I asked dryly.

She began to cry, not silently but noisily, hysterically. I stopped her by giving her a good shake.

"What in the world is the matter with you?" I snapped. "Has the day of good common sense gone by?—Sit up and tell me the whole thing."

Rosie sat up then and sniffled.

"I was coming up the drive—" she began.

"You'd better start with when you went down the drive, with my dishes and my silver," I interrupted. But seeing more signs of hysteria I gave in. "Very well, you were coming up the drive—"

"I had a basket of—of silver and dishes on my arm, and I was carrying the plate, because I was afraid I'd break it. Part way up the road a man stepped out of the bushes and held his arm like this, spread out, so I couldn't get past. He said 'Not so fast, young lady; I want you to let me see what's in that basket.'"

She got up in her excitement and took hold of my arm.

"It was like this, Miss Innes," she said, "and say you was the man. When he said that, I screamed and ducked under his arm like this. He caught at the basket and I dropped it. I ran as fast as I could, and he came after me as far as the trees. Then he stopped. Oh, Miss Innes, I know it was the murderer. I'm sure of it."

"Don't be foolish," I said. "Whoever killed Mr. Armstrong would put as much space between himself and this house as he could."

But she was hysterical again. I saw it was no use asking her about the basket and its contents, or why she had been out. She was shaking all over, and I doubt if she even heard what I said.

"Get on up to your bed," I told her. "And remember this. If I hear of your telling this cock-and-bull story to the other maids I'll deduct from your wages for every broken dish I find in the drive."

I listened to her as she went upstairs, running past the shadowy places and slamming her door. Then I sat down and looked at the Coalport plate and the silver spoon. I had brought from town my own china and silver, and from all appearances I would have little enough to take back. But though I might jeer at Rosie as much as I wished, the fact remained that someone had been on the drive that night who had no business there. Although neither had Rosie, for that matter.

I could fancy Liddy's face when she missed the extra pieces of china. She had opposed Rosie from the start, and if Liddy once finds a prophecy fulfilled, especially an unpleasant one, she never allows me to forget it. It seemed to me that it was absurd to leave that china dotted along the road for her to find the next morning; so with a sudden resolution I opened the door again and stepped out into the darkness. As the door closed behind me I half regretted my impulse. Then I shut my teeth and went on.

I have never been a nervous woman, as I have said before. Moreover, a minute or two in the darkness enabled me to see things fairly well. Beulah gave me rather a start by rubbing unexpectedly against my feet. Then we two side by side went down the drive.

There were no fragments of china, but where the trees began I picked up a silver spoon. So far Rosie's story was borne out. But I began to wonder if it was not indiscreet, to say the least, this midnight prowling in a neighborhood with such a deservedly bad reputation. Then I saw something gleaming which proved to be the handle of a cup, and a step or two farther on I found a V-shaped bit of a plate. But the most surprising thing of all was to find the basket sitting comfortably beside the road with the rest of the broken crockery piled neatly within, and a handful of small silver, spoons, forks, and the like on top. I could only stand and stare. Evidently Rosie's story was true. But where had she carried her basket? And why had the thief, if he was a thief, picked up the broken china out of the road and left it along with his booty?

It was with my nearest approach to a nervous collapse that I heard the familiar throbbing of a motor, and as it came closer I recognized the outline of my car.

Halsey had come back.

Strange enough it must have seemed to Halsey too, to come across me in the middle of the night, with the long skirt of my gray silk dress over my shoulders to keep off the dew, while holding a red and green basket under one arm and a black cat under the other. What with relief and joy I began to cry right there, and very nearly wiped my eyes on Beulah in the excitement.

9

"GOOD GOD, RAY!" Halsey said from the gloom behind the lamps. "What in the world are you doing here?"

"Taking a walk," I said, trying to be composed. I don't think the answer struck either of us as being ridiculous at the time. "Where have you been? I've been slowly losing my mind."

"Get in and let me take you up to the house." He was in the road, and had Beulah and the basket out of my arms in a moment. I could see the car plainly now and Warner was at the wheel, Warner in an ulster and a pair of slippers over Heaven knows what. Jack Bailey was not there. I got in, and we went slowly and cautiously up to the house.

We did not talk. What we had to say was too important to commence there, and besides it took all kinds of coaxing to get the car up the last grade. It was apparently almost out of gas. Only when we had closed the front door and stood facing each other in the hall did Halsey say anything. Then he slipped his strong young arm around my shoulders and turned me so I faced the light.

"Poor Rachel!" he said gently. And I nearly wept again. "Look here, I have to see Gertrude. I have a lot to say to her."

Then Gertrude herself came down the stairs. She had not been to bed evidently, for she still wore the white negligee she had worn earlier in the evening, and she limped somewhat. During her slow progress down the stairs I had time to notice one thing. Jamieson had said the woman who escaped from the cellar had worn no shoe on her right foot. Gertrude's right ankle was the one she had sprained.

The meeting between brother and sister was tense but without tears. Halsey kissed her, and there were signs of strain and anxiety in both young faces.

"Is everything all right?" she asked.

"Right as can be," Halsey said with forced cheerfulness.

I lighted the living room and we went in there. Only a half hour before I had sat with Jamieson in that very room, listening while he overtly accused both Gertrude and Halsey of at least a knowledge of the death of Arnold Armstrong. Now Halsey was here to speak for himself. I should learn everything that had puzzled me.

"I saw it in the paper tonight for the first time," he was saying. "It knocked me silly. When I think of this houseful of women, and a thing like that occurring! What happened? Who did it?"

Gertrude's face was still set and white. "We don't know, Halsey," she said. "You and Jack left almost at the time it happened. The police think that you, that all of us, know something about it. The detective thinks so too."

"The hell he does!" Halsey's eyes were fairly starting from his head. "Sorry, Aunt Ray, but the fellow's a lunatic."

"It's up to you to explain a lot of things," I said dryly. "Where you went that night, or rather morning, and why you went as you did. This has been a terrible time for all of us."

He stood staring at me, and I could see indecision and something like alarm in his face.

"I can't tell you where I went, Aunt Ray," he said, after a moment. "As to why, you'll learn that soon enough. But Gertrude knows that Jack and I left the house before this thing happened."

"Mr. Jamieson doesn't believe me," Gertrude said drearily. "Halsey, if the worst comes, if they should arrest you, you must talk. You'll have to."

"I'm not talking to anyone, not yet," he said, with a new sternness in his voice. "Aunt Ray, it was necessary for Jack and me to leave that night. I cannot tell you why. It was essential. That's all. As to where we went, if I have to depend on that as an alibi I still won't talk. The whole thing is absurd, a trumped-up charge that cannot possibly be serious."

"Has Jack Bailey gone back to the city," I demanded, "or to the club? You can tell that much, can't you?"

"Neither," he said defiantly. "At the present moment I don't know where he is."

"Halsey," I asked gravely, leaning forward, "have you the slightest suspicion who killed Arnold Armstrong? The police think he was admitted by someone in this house, and that he was shot down from above by someone on the circular staircase."

"Well, I didn't do it, nor did Jack," he maintained. But I fancied I caught a sudden glance at Gertrude, a flash of something that looked like a warning.

After that, as quietly and calmly as I could, I went over the whole story from the night Liddy and I had been alone to the finding of the body, including the curious experience of Rosie and her pursuer that same evening. The basket still stood on the table, a mute witness to this last mystifying occurrence.

"There's something else," I said hesitatingly, at the last. "Halsey, I've never told this even to Gertrude, but the morning after the crime I found, outside in the garden, a revolver. It was yours, Halsey."

For an appreciable moment he stared at me. Then he turned to Gertrude, looking bewildered.

"My gun, Trude!" he exclaimed. "Jack took it with him, didn't he?"

To my amazement she did not answer. Instead she got up and taking a cigarette from a box proceeded to light it. I was near enough to see that her hands were shaking.

"If he did, you'd better not say so," I said tartly. "Jamieson will be sure Jack came back and shot him. He thinks one of you did now."

"He didn't come back," Halsey said stiffly. "Gertrude, when you brought down a revolver that night for Jack to take with him, what one did you bring? Mine?"

Gertrude had recovered by that time.

"No," she said. "Yours was loaded, and I knew the state Jack was in. I gave him one I have had for a year or two. It wasn't loaded."

Halsey threw up both hands.

"If that isn't like a girl!" he said. "Why didn't you do what I asked you to? You send Bailey off with an empty gun and throw mine in a tulip bed, of all places on earth! Mine was a thirty-eight caliber. The inquest will show of course that the bullet that killed Armstrong was a thirty-eight and that it came from my gun. Where the hell does that leave me?"

"You forget," I broke in, "that I have the revolver, and that no one knows about it."

But Gertrude flushed with anger.

"I cannot stand it any more," she said. "I didn't throw your revolver into the tulip bed. I think you did it yourself!"

They glared at each other across the big library table, with young eyes all at once hard and suspicious. Then Gertrude held out both hands to him.

"We can't quarrel," she said brokenly. "Just now, with so much at stake. It's shameful. I know you are as innocent as I am. Make me believe it, Halsey."

He soothed her as best he could, and the breach seemed to be healed. But long after I went to bed he sat downstairs in the living room alone, and I knew he was going over the case as he had learned it. Some things were clear to him that were dark to me. He knew, and Gertrude knew too, why Jack Bailey and he had gone away that night as they had. He knew where they had been, and why Jack had not returned with him. It seemed to me that without fuller confidence from both the children—they are always children to me—I should never be able to learn anything.

As I was finally getting ready for bed, Halsey came upstairs and knocked at my door. When I had got into a negligee—I used to say wrapper before Gertrude came back from school—I let him in. He stood in the doorway a moment, and then to my amazement he went into agonies of silent mirth. I sat down on the side of the bed and waited in severe silence for him to stop, but he only seemed to grow worse. When he had recovered he took me by the elbow and pulled me in front of the mirror.

"'How to be beautiful,'" he quoted. "'Advice to maids and matrons,' by the Lady Who Knows." And then I saw myself. I had neglected to remove my wrinkle eradicators and I presume my appearance was odd. I believe that it is a woman's duty to care for her looks, but it is much like telling a necessary

lie. One ought not to be found out. By the time I had jerked the things off
Halsey was serious again, and I listened to his story.

"Look, old girl," he began, extinguishing his cigarette on the back of my
ivory hairbrush, "I would give a hell of a lot to tell you the whole thing. But I
can't, for a day or so anyhow. Only one thing I might have told you a long
time ago. If you had known it, you wouldn't have suspected me for a moment
of—of having anything to do with killing Armstrong. God only knows what
I might do to a fellow like that if there was enough provocation, and if I had a
gun in my hand—under ordinary circumstances. But I care a great deal about
Louise Armstrong, Rachel. I hope to marry her someday. Is it likely I would
kill her brother?"

"Her stepbrother," I corrected. "No, of course it isn't likely, or possible.
Why didn't you tell me, Halsey?"

"Well, there were two reasons," he said slowly. "One was that you had a
girl already picked out for me—"

"Nonsense," I broke in, and felt myself growing red. "I merely showed her
to you. She was a nice girl, Halsey."

But he ignored that.

"And the second reason," he pursued, "was that the Armstrongs would have
none of me."

I sat bolt upright at that and gasped.

"The Armstrongs!" I repeated. "With old Peter Armstrong driving a stage
across the mountains while your grandfather was governor during the War
between the States!"

"Well, the war governor's dead and out of the matrimonial market," Halsey
interrupted. "And the present Innes admits himself he isn't good enough for
Louise. But of course—"

"Exactly," I said despairingly, "and naturally you're taken at your own
valuation. The Inneses are not always so self-depreciatory."

"Not always, no," he said, looking at me with his boyish smile. "Fortunately
Louise doesn't agree with her family. She's willing to take me, war governor
or no, provided her mother consents. She isn't overly fond of her stepfather
but she adores her mother. And now, can't you see where this thing puts me?
Down and out with all of them."

"But the whole thing is outrageous," I argued. "And besides, Gertrude's
sworn statement that you left before Arnold Armstrong came would clear you
at once."

Halsey got up and began to pace the room, and his air of cheerfulness
dropped like a mask.

"She can't swear it," he said finally. "Gertrude's story was true as far as it
went, but she didn't tell everything. Armstrong came here at two-thirty that
night, came into the billiard room and stayed about five minutes. We were
all here. He came to bring something."

"Halsey," I cried, "you must tell me the whole truth. Every time I see a way for you to escape you block it yourself with this wall of mystery. What did he bring?"

"A telegram for Bailey," he said. "It came by special messenger from town. Bailey had started for here, and the messenger had gone back to the city. The steward gave it to Arnold, who had been drinking all day and couldn't sleep, and was coming for a stroll in this direction anyhow."

"And he brought it and then left?"

"Yes."

"What was in the telegram?"

"I can tell you as soon as certain things are made public. It is only a matter of days now," he added gloomily.

"And Gertrude's story of a telephone message?"

"Poor Trude!" he said. "She's a loyal kid. Aunt Ray, there was no such message. I expect your detective already knows that and discredits all Gertrude told him."

"And when she went back, it was to get the telegram? Did you leave it there?"

"We may have. We were pretty well excited. Or she may have thought we had. When you get to thinking about it, Aunt Ray, it looks bad for all three of us, doesn't it? And yet I'll swear none of us even inadvertently killed that poor devil."

I looked at the closed door into Gertrude's dressing room, and lowered my voice.

"The same horrible thought keeps troubling me," I said, lowering my voice. "Halsey, Gertrude probably had your revolver. She must have examined it anyhow that night. After you and Jack had gone, what if that ruffian came back, and she—"

I couldn't finish. Halsey stood looking at me with shut lips.

"She might have heard him fumbling at the door—he had no key, the police say—and thinking it was you or Jack she admitted him. When she saw her mistake she ran up the stairs a step or two and because she was afraid of him she fired at him."

"Don't even think it," he said sharply. "It's nonsense."

"What about your gun? It was almost buried in that flower bed. What about her ankle? How did she sprain it?"

"What about her ankle? Any girl can do a thing like that. Look at the heels they wear."

But I had to tell him, if only to have him say I was crazy.

"I think she fell down the clothes chute," I half whispered. And to my dismay he looked as if I had signed a death warrant.

10

THE MORNING AFTER Halsey's return was Tuesday. Arnold Armstrong had been found dead at the foot of the circular staircase at three o'clock on Sunday morning. There was to be a funeral service that day, the inquest having been deferred to the end of the week. But the interment of the body was to wait until the Armstrongs arrived from California. No one, I think, was very sorry that Arnold Armstrong was dead, but the manner of his death aroused some sympathy and an enormous amount of curiosity. Mrs. Ogden Fitzhugh, a cousin, took charge of the arrangements and everything, I believe, was as quiet as possible. I gave Thomas Johnson and Mrs. Watson permission to go into town to pay their last respects to the dead man, but for some reason they did not care to go.

Halsey spent part of the day with the detective, Jamieson, but he said nothing of what happened. He looked grave and anxious, and he had a long conversation with Gertrude late in the afternoon.

Tuesday evening found us quiet, with the quiet that precedes an explosion. Gertrude and Halsey were both gloomy and distracted, and as Liddy had already discovered that some of the china was broken—it is impossible to have any secrets from an old servant—I was not in a pleasant humor myself. When Warner brought up the afternoon mail and the evening papers at seven I was curious to know what the papers said of the murder. We had turned away at least a dozen reporters. But I read over the headline that ran halfway across the top of the *Gazette* twice before I comprehended it. Halsey had opened the *Chronicle* and was staring at it fixedly.

"The Traders' Bank closes its doors" was what I read. I put down the paper and looked across the table.

"Did you know about this?" I asked Halsey.

"I expected it. But not so soon," he replied.

"And you?" to Gertrude.

"Jack told us something," Gertrude said, her voice flat. "It looks bad for him now, Halsey, doesn't it?"

"Jack!" I said scornfully. "Your Jack's flight is easy enough to explain now. And you helped him, both of you, to get away! You get that from your mother. It isn't an Innes trait. Do you know that every dollar you have, both of you, is in that bank?"

Gertrude tried to speak, but Halsey stopped her.

"That isn't all, Gertrude," he said quietly; "Jack's under arrest."

"Under arrest!" She leaped to her feet and tore the paper out of his hand. She glanced at the heading, then she crumpled the newspaper into a ball and flung it to the floor. While Halsey, looking stricken and white, was trying to smooth it out and read it, she dropped her head on the table and sobbed stormily.

I have the clipping somewhere, but just now I can remember only the essentials.

On the afternoon before, while the Traders' Bank was in the rush of closing hour, between two and three, Mr. Jacob Trautman, president of the Pearl Brewing Company, came into the bank to pay off a loan. As security for the loan he had deposited some three hundred International Steamship Company 5's, in total value three hundred thousand dollars. Mr. Trautman went to the loan clerk and, after certain formalities had been gone through, the loan clerk went to the vault. Mr. Trautman, who was a large and genial Jewish gentleman, waited for a time, whistling under his breath. The loan clerk did not come back, and after an interval Mr. Trautman saw him emerge from the vault and go to the assistant cashier. The two went hurriedly to the vault. A lapse of another ten minutes, and the assistant cashier came out and approached Mr. Trautman. He was noticeably white and trembling. Mr. Trautman was told that through an oversight the bonds had been misplaced, and was asked to return the following morning, when everything would be made all right.

Mr. Trautman, however, was a shrewd businessman, and he did not like the appearance of things. He left the bank apparently satisfied, and within thirty minutes he had called up three different members of the Traders' Board of Directors. At three-thirty there was a hastily convened board meeting, with some stormy scenes, and late in the afternoon a national bank examiner was in possession of the books. The bank had not opened for business on Tuesday. The article went on:

At twelve-thirty o'clock the Saturday before, as soon as the business of the day was closed, Mr. John Bailey, the cashier of the defunct bank, had taken his hat and departed. During the afternoon he had called up Mr. Aronson, a member of the board, saying he was ill and might not be at the bank for a day or two. As Bailey was highly thought of, Mr. Aronson merely expressed regret. From that time until Monday night, when Mr. Bailey had surrendered to the police, little was known of his movements. Sometime after one o'clock on Saturday he had entered the Western Union office at Cherry and White streets and had sent two telegrams. He was at the Greenwood Country Club on Saturday night, and appeared unlike himself. Nothing was said as to where he had been in the interval. It was reported that he would be released under heavy bond sometime that day, Tuesday.

The article closed by saying that, while the officers of the bank refused to talk until the examiner had finished his work, it was known that securities aggregating a million and a quarter were missing. Then there was a diatribe on the possibility of such an occurrence; on the folly of a one-man bank, and of a Board of Directors that met only to lunch together and to listen to a brief report from the cashier, and on the poor policy of a government that arranges a three- or four-day examination twice a year.

The mystery, it insinuated, had not been cleared by the arrest of the cashier. Before now minor officials had been used to cloak the misdeeds of men higher up. Inseparable as the words "speculation" and "peculation" have grown to be, John Bailey was not known to be in the stock market. His only words after his surrender had been "Send for Mr. Armstrong at once." The telegraph message which had finally reached the president of the Traders' Bank, in an interior town in California, had been responded to by a telegram from Doctor Walker, the young physician who was traveling with the Armstrong family, saying that Paul Armstrong was very ill and unable to travel.

That was how things stood that Tuesday before dinner. The Traders' Bank had suspended payment, and John Bailey was under arrest, charged with wrecking it. Paul Armstrong lay very ill in California, and his only son had been murdered two days before. I sat dazed and bewildered. The children's money was gone. That was bad enough, though I had plenty if they would let me share it. But Gertrude's grief was beyond any power of mine to comfort. The man she was in love with stood accused of a colossal embezzlement and even worse. For in the instant that I sat there I seemed to see the coils closing around John Bailey as the murderer of Arnold Armstrong.

Gertrude lifted her head at last and stared across the table at Halsey. "Why did he do it?" she said bleakly. "Couldn't you stop him, Halsey? It was suicidal to go back."

Halsey was looking steadily through the windows of the breakfast room, but it was evident he saw nothing.

"It was the only thing he could do, Trude," he said at last. "Aunt Ray, when I found Jack at the Greenwood Club last Saturday night he was frantic. I can't talk until Jack tells me I may, but he is absolutely innocent of all this. I thought, Trude and I thought, we were helping him. But it was the wrong way. He came back. Isn't that the act of an innocent man?"

"Then why did he leave at all?" I asked, unconvinced. "What innocent man would run away from here at three o'clock in the morning? Doesn't it look as though he thought it was impossible to escape?"

Gertrude rose angrily. "You are not even just!" she flamed. "You don't know anything about it, and you think he is guilty."

"I know we have all lost a great deal of money," I said. "I shall believe Mr. Bailey innocent the moment he is shown to be. You profess to know the truth, but you won't tell me! What am I to think?"

Halsey leaned over and patted my hand.

"You must take us on faith," he said. "Jack Bailey hasn't a penny that doesn't belong to him. The truth will come out in a day or so."

"I'll believe that when it's proved," I said grimly. "In the meantime, I take no one on faith. The Inneses never do."

Gertrude, who had been standing aloof at a window, turned suddenly. "But when the bonds are offered for sale, Halsey, won't the thief be detected at once?"

Halsey turned with a superior smile.

"It wouldn't be done that way," he said. "They would be taken out of the vault by someone who had access to it, and used as collateral for a loan in other banks. It would be possible to realize eighty per cent of their face value."

"In cash?"

"In cash."

"But the man who did it, he would be known?"

"Yes. I tell you both, as sure as I stand here, I believe that Paul Armstrong looted his own bank. I believe he has a million at least as the result, and that he will never come back. I'm worse than a pauper now. I can't ask Louise to share nothing a year with me, and when I think of this disgrace for her I'm crazy."

The most ordinary events of life seemed pregnant with possibilities that evening, and when Halsey was called to the telephone I ceased all pretense at eating. When he came back from the telephone his face showed that something had occurred. He waited, however, until Thomas left the dining room. Then he told us.

"Paul Armstrong is dead," he announced gravely. "He died this morning in California. Whatever he did, he is beyond the law now."

Gertrude turned pale.

"And the only man who could have cleared Jack can never do it!" she said despairingly.

"Also," I replied coldly, "Mr. Armstrong is forever beyond the power of defending himself. When your Jack comes to me with some two hundred thousand dollars in his hands, which is about what you've lost, I'll believe him innocent."

Halsey threw his cigarette away and turned on me.

"There you go!" he exclaimed. "If he were the thief he could return the money, of course. If he's innocent he probably hasn't a tenth of that amount in the world. In his hands! That's like a woman."

Gertrude, who had been pale and despairing during the early part of the conversation, had flushed an indignant red. She got up and drew herself to her slender height, looking down at me with the scorn of the young and positive.

"You are the only mother I ever had," she said tensely. "I had given you all I would have given my mother had she lived, my love and trust. And now when I need you most you fail me. I tell you, John Bailey is a good man, an honest man. If you say he's not, you—you—"

"Gertrude," Halsey broke in sharply. She dropped beside the table and burying her face in her arms broke into a storm of tears.

"I love him so much," she sobbed, in a surrender that was totally unlike her. "I never thought it would be like this. I can't bear it. I can't."

Halsey and I stood helpless before the storm. I would have tried to comfort her, but she had put me away, and there was something aloof in her grief, something new and strange. When at last her sorrow had subsided to the dry shaking sobs of a tired child, without raising her head she put out one groping hand.

"Aunt Ray!" she whispered. In a moment I was on my knees beside her, her arm around my neck and her cheek against my hair.

"Where am I in all this?" Halsey said suddenly, and tried to put his arms around us both. It was a welcome distraction, and Gertrude was soon herself again. The little storm had cleared the air. Nevertheless, my opinion remained unchanged. There was much to be cleared up before I would consent to any renewal of my acquaintance with John Bailey. And Halsey and Gertrude knew it, knowing me.

11

IT WAS ABOUT half past eight when we left the dining room, and still engrossed with one subject, the failure of the bank and its attendant evils, Halsey and I went out into the grounds for a stroll. Gertrude followed us shortly. "The light was thickening," to appropriate Shakespeare's description of twilight, and once again the tree toads and the crickets were making night throb with their tiny life.

It was almost oppressively lonely in spite of its beauty, and I felt a sickening pang of homesickness for my city at night, for the clatter of horses' feet on cemented paving, for the lights, the voices, the sound of children playing. The country after dark oppresses me. The stars, quite eclipsed in the city by the electric lights, here become insistent, assertive. Whether I want to or not I find myself looking for the few I know by name and feeling ridiculously new and small by contrast, always an unpleasant sensation.

After Gertrude joined us we avoided any further mention of the murder. To Halsey as to me there was ever present, I am sure, the thought of our conversation of the night before. As we strolled back and forth along the drive Jamieson unexpectedly emerged from the shadow of the trees.

"Good evening," he said, managing to include Gertrude in his bow. Gertrude had never been even ordinarily courteous to him, and she nodded coldly. Halsey was more cordial, although we were all constrained enough. He and Gertrude went on together, leaving the detective to walk with me. As soon as they were out of earshot he turned to me.

"Do you know, Miss Innes," he said, "the deeper I go into this thing the more strange it seems to me. I am very sorry for Miss Gertrude. It looks as if Bailey, whom she has tried so hard to save, is guilty as hell. After her plucky fight for him it seems hard."

I looked through the dusk to where Gertrude's light dinner dress gleamed among the trees. She *had* made a plucky fight, poor child. Whatever she might have been driven to do, I could find nothing but a deep sympathy for her. If she had only come to me with the whole truth then!

"Miss Innes," Jamieson was saying, "in the last three days, have you seen any suspicious figures around the grounds? Any woman, for instance."

"No," I replied. "I have a houseful of maids who will bear watching, one and all. But there has been no strange woman near the house or Liddy would have seen her, you may be sure. She has a telescopic eye."

Jamieson looked thoughtful.

"It may not amount to anything," he said slowly. "It is difficult to get any perspective on things around here, because everyone down in the village is sure he saw the murderer, either before or since the crime. And half of them will stretch a point or two as to facts to be obliging. But the man who drives the taxi down there tells a story that may possibly prove to be important."

"I've heard it, I think. Was it the one the parlormaid brought up yesterday, about a ghost wringing its hands on the roof? Or perhaps it's the one the milk boy saw, a tramp washing a dirty shirt, presumably bloody, in the creek below the bridge?"

I could see the gleam of his teeth as he smiled.

"Neither," he said. "But Matthew Geist, which is our friend's name, claims that on Saturday night at nine-thirty a lady in black, with a heavy black veil over her face, as though she was in mourning—"

"I knew it would be a veiled lady," I broke in.

"A veiled lady," he persisted, "who was apparently young and beautiful, engaged his taxi and asked to be driven to Sunnyside. Near the gate however she made him stop, in spite of his remonstrances, saying she preferred to walk to the house. She paid him and he left her there. Now, Miss Innes, you had no such visitor, I believe?"

"None," I said decidedly.

"Geist thought it might be another member of the family, or even a new maid, as you had got a supply that day. But he said her getting out near the gate puzzled him. Anyhow, we have now one veiled lady who, with the ghostly intruder of Friday night, makes two assets I hardly know what to do with."

"It is mystifying," I admitted, "although I can think of one possible explanation. The path from the Greenwood Club to the village enters the road near the lodge gate. A woman who wished to reach the Country Club without being seen might choose such a method. There are plenty of women there."

I think this gave him something to ponder, for in a short time he said good night and left. But I myself was far from satisfied. I was determined on one thing. If my suspicions, for I had suspicions, were true, I would make my own investigations and Jamieson should learn only what was good for him to know.

We went back to the house and Gertrude, who was more like herself since her talk with Halsey, sat down at the mahogany desk in the living room to write a letter. Halsey prowled up and down the entire east wing, and after a little I joined him in the billiard room and together we went over the details of the discovery of the body.

The cardroom was quite dark. Where we sat in the billiard room only one of the side brackets was lighted and we spoke in subdued tones, as the hour and the subject seemed to demand. When I spoke of the figure Liddy and I had seen on the porch through the cardroom window Friday night Halsey sauntered into the darkened room, and together we stood there, much as Liddy and I had done that other night.

The window was the same grayish rectangle in the blackness as before. A few feet away in the hall was the spot where the body of Arnold Armstrong had been found. I was a bit nervous, and I put my hand on Halsey's sleeve. Suddenly from the top of the staircase above us came the sound of a cautious footstep. At first I was not sure, but Halsey's attitude told me he had heard and was listening. The step, slow, measured, infinitely cautious, was nearer now. Halsey tried to loosen my fingers, but I was in a paralysis of fright.

The swish of a body against the curving rail as if for guidance was plain enough, and now whoever it was had reached the foot of the staircase and had caught a glimpse of our rigid silhouettes against the billiard room doorway. Halsey threw me off then and strode forward.

"Who's there?" he called, and took a half dozen rapid strides toward the foot of the staircase. Then I heard him mutter something, there was the crash of a falling body and the slam of the outer door. I screamed, I think. Then I remember turning on the lights and finding Halsey, white with fury, trying to untangle himself from something warm and fleecy. He had cut his forehead on the lowest step of the stairs, and he was a ghastly sight. He flung the white object at me and jerking open the outer door raced outside into the darkness.

Gertrude had come on hearing the noise, and now we stood, staring at each other over—of all things on earth—a white silk and wool blanket, exquisitely fine! It was the most unghostly thing in the world, with its lavender border and its faint scent. Gertrude was the first to speak.

"What happened? Who had it?" she asked.

"Halsey tried to stop someone on the stairs and fell. Gertrude, that blanket isn't mine. I have never seen it before."

She held it up and looked at it. After that she went to the door to the veranda and threw it open. Perhaps a hundred feet from the house were two figures who moved slowly toward us as we looked. When they came within range of the light I recognized Halsey, and with him Mrs. Watson, the housekeeper.

12

THE MOST COMMONPLACE incident takes on a new appearance if the attendant circumstances are unusual. There was no reason on earth why Mrs. Watson should not have carried a blanket down the east wing staircase, if she so desired. But to take a blanket down at eleven o'clock at night, with every precaution as to noise, and when discovered to fling it at Halsey and bolt—Halsey's word, and a good one—into the grounds, this made the incident more than significant.

They moved slowly across the lawn and up the steps. Halsey was talking quietly, and Mrs. Watson was looking down and listening. She was a woman of a certain amount of dignity, most efficient, so far as I could tell, although Liddy would have found fault if she had dared. But just now Mrs. Watson's face was an enigma. She was defiant, I think, under her mask of submission, and she still showed the effect of nervous shock.

"Mrs. Watson," I said severely, "will you be so good as to explain this rather unusual occurrence?"

"I don't think it so unusual, Miss Innes." Her voice was deep and very clear, but just now it was somewhat shaky. "I was taking a blanket down to Thomas, who isn't well, and I used this staircase as being nearer the path to the lodge. When Mr. Innes called and then rushed at me I was alarmed and flung the blanket at him."

Halsey was examining the cut on his forehead in a small mirror on the wall. It was not much of an injury, but it had bled freely and his appearance was rather terrifying.

"Thomas ill?" he said, over his shoulder. "Why, I thought I saw Thomas out there as you made that cyclonic break out the door and across the porch."

I could see that under pretense of examining his injury he was watching her through the mirror.

"Is this one of the servants' blankets, Mrs. Watson?" I asked, holding up its luxurious folds to the light.

"Everything else is locked away," she replied. Which was true enough, no doubt. I had rented the house without bed furnishings.

"If Thomas is ill," Halsey said, "some member of the family ought to go down to see him. You needn't bother, Mrs. Watson. I will take the blanket."

She drew herself up quickly as if in protest, but she found nothing to say. She stood smoothing the folds of her dead-black dress, her face as white as chalk above it. Then she seemed to make up her mind.

"Very well, Mr. Innes," she said. "Perhaps you'd better go. I have done all I could."

She turned and went up to the circular staircase, moving slowly and with a certain dignity. Below, the three of us stared at one another across the intervening white blanket.

"Upon my word," Halsey broke out, "this place is a walking nightmare. I have the feeling that we three outsiders, who have paid our money for the privilege of staying in this spook factory, are living on the very top of things. We're on the lid, so to speak. Now and then we get a sight of the things inside, but we are not a part of them."

"Do you suppose," Gertrude asked doubtfully, "that she really meant that blanket for Thomas?"

"Thomas was standing beside that magnolia tree," Halsey replied, "when I ran after Mrs. Watson. It's down to this, Aunt Ray. Rosie's basket and Mrs. Watson's blanket can mean only one thing: there is somebody hiding or being hidden in the lodge. It wouldn't surprise me if we hold the key to the whole situation now. Anyhow, I'm going to the lodge to investigate."

Gertrude wanted to go too, but she looked so shaken that I insisted she should not. I sent for Liddy to help her to bed, and then Halsey and I started for the lodge. The grass was heavy with dew, and manlike Halsey chose the shortest way across the lawn. Halfway there, however, he stopped.

"We'd better go by the drive," he said. "This isn't a lawn; it's a field. Where's the gardener these days?"

"There isn't any," I said meekly. "We have been thankful enough so far to have our meals prepared and served and the beds made. The gardener who belongs here is working at the club."

"Remind me tomorrow to send out a man from town," he said. "I know the very fellow."

I record this scrap of conversation, just as I have tried to put down anything and everything that had a bearing on what followed, because the gardener Halsey sent the next day played an important part in the events of the next few weeks. Events which culminated as you know by stirring the country profoundly. At that time, however, I was busy trying to keep my feet dry, and paid little or no attention.

Along the drive I showed Halsey where I had found Rosie's basket with the bits of broken china piled inside. He was rather skeptical. Or at least he so pretended.

"Warner probably," he said when I had finished. "Began it as a joke on Rosie and ended by picking up the broken china out of the road, knowing it would play hob with the tires of the car." Which shows how near one can come to the truth and yet miss it altogether.

At the lodge everything was quiet. There was a light in the sitting room downstairs, and a faint gleam as if from a shaded lamp in one of the upper rooms. Halsey stopped and examined the place with calculating eyes.

"I don't know, Aunt Ray," he said dubiously; "this is hardly a woman's affair. If there's a scrap of any kind, you scram in a hurry." Which was Halsey's solicitous care for me put into vernacular.

"I shall stay right here," I said, and crossing the small veranda, now shaded and fragrant with honeysuckle, I hammered the knocker on the door.

Thomas opened the door himself, Thomas, fully dressed and in his customary health. I had the blanket over my arm.

"I brought the blanket, Thomas," I said; "I am sorry you are so ill."

The old man stood staring at me and then at the blanket. His confusion under other circumstances would have been ludicrous.

"What! Not sick?" Halsey said from the step. "Thomas, I'm afraid you've been malingering."

Thomas seemed to have been debating something with himself. Now he stepped out on the porch and closed the door gently behind him.

"I reckon you bettah come in, Mis' Innes," he said, speaking cautiously. "It's got so I dunno what to do, and it's boun' to come out some time er ruther."

He threw the door open then and I stepped inside, Halsey close behind. In the sitting room the old Negro turned with quiet dignity to Halsey.

"You bettah sit down, suh," he said. "It's a place for a woman, suh."

Things were not turning out the way Halsey expected. He sat down near the center table with his hands thrust in his pockets, and watched me as I followed Thomas up the narrow stairs. At the top a woman was standing, and a second glance showed me it was Rosie. She shrank back a little, but I said nothing. And then Thomas motioned to a partly open door, and I went in.

The lodge boasted three bedrooms upstairs, all comfortably furnished. In this one, the largest and airiest, a night lamp was burning, and by its light I could make out a plain white metal bed. A girl was asleep there, or in a half stupor, for she muttered something now and then. Rosie had taken her courage in her hands and on coming in had turned up the light. It was only then that I knew. Fever-flushed, ill as she was, I recognized Louise Armstrong.

I stood gazing down at her in a stupor of amazement. Louise here, hiding at the lodge, ill and alone! Rosie came up to the bed, smoothed the white counterpane, and turned down the light.

"I am afraid she's worse tonight," she ventured at last. I put my hand on the sick girl's forehead. It was burning with fever, and I turned to where Thomas lingered in the hallway.

"Will you tell me what you mean, Thomas Johnson, by not telling me this before?" I demanded indignantly.

Thomas quailed.

"Mis' Louise wouldn' let me," he said earnestly. "I wanted to. She ought to 'a' had a doctor the night she came, but she wouldn' hear to it. Is she—is she very bad, Mis' Innes?"

"Bad enough," I said coldly. "Send Mr. Innes up."

Halsey came up the stairs slowly, looking rather interested and inclined to be amused. For a moment he could not see anything distinctly in the darkened room. He stopped, glanced at Rosie and at me, and then his eyes fell on the restless head on the pillow. I think he felt who it was before he really saw her, for he crossed the room in a couple of strides and bent over the bed.

"Louise!" he said softly. But she did not reply, and her eyes showed no recognition. Halsey was young, and illness was new to him. He straightened himself slowly, still watching her, and caught my arm.

"She's dying, Aunt Ray!" he said huskily. "Dying! Why, she doesn't know me!"

"Fudge!" I snapped, being apt to grow irritable when my sympathies are aroused. "She's doing nothing of the sort. And don't pinch my arm. If you want something to do, go and choke Thomas."

But at that moment Louise roused from her stupor to cough, and at the end of the paroxysm, as Rosie laid her back exhausted, she knew us. That was all Halsey wanted. To him consciousness was recovery. He dropped on his knees beside the bed, and tried to tell her she was all right, and that we would bring her around in a hurry, and how beautiful she looked—only to break down utterly and have to stop. And at that I came to my senses, and put him out.

"This instant!" I ordered, as he hesitated. "And send Rosie here."

He did not go far. He sat on the top step of the stairs, only leaving to telephone for a doctor and getting in everybody's way in his eagerness to fetch and carry. I got him away finally, by sending him to fix up the car as a sort of ambulance, in case the doctor would allow the sick girl to be moved. He sent Gertrude down to the lodge loaded with all manner of impossible things, including an armful of Turkish towels and a box of mustard plasters; and as the two girls had known each other somewhat before, Louise brightened perceptibly when she saw her.

When the doctor from Englewood—the Casanova doctor, Doctor Walker, being away—had started for Sunnyside, and I had got Thomas to stop trying to explain what he did not understand himself, I had a long talk with the old man, and this is what I learned.

On the Saturday evening before, about ten o'clock, he had been reading in the sitting room downstairs when someone rapped at the door. The old man was alone and at first he was uncertain about opening the door. He did so finally, and was amazed at being confronted by Louise Armstrong. Thomas was an old family servant, having been with the present Mrs. Armstrong since she was a child, and he was overwhelmed at seeing Louise.

He saw that she was excited and tired, and he drew her into the sitting room and made her sit down. After a while he went to the house and brought Mrs. Watson, and they talked until late. The old man said Louise was in trouble, and seemed frightened. Mrs. Watson made some tea and Louise drank it, but she made them both promise to keep her presence a secret. She had not known that Sunnyside was rented, and whatever her trouble was this complicated things. She seemed puzzled. Her stepfather and her mother were still in California. That was all she would say about them. Why she had run away no one could imagine. Arnold Armstrong was at the Greenwood Club and at last Thomas, not knowing what else to do, went over there along the path. It was almost midnight. Part way over he met Armstrong himself and brought him to the lodge. Mrs. Watson had gone to the house for some bed linen, it having been arranged that under the circumstances Louise would be better at the lodge until morning. Arnold Armstrong and Louise had a long conference, during which he was heard to storm and become very violent. When he left it was after two. He had gone up to the house—Thomas did not know why—and at three o'clock he was shot at the foot of the circular stair-case.

The following morning Louise had been ill. She had asked for Arnold, and was told he had left town. Thomas had not the moral courage to tell her of the crime. She refused a doctor, and shrank morbidly from having her pres-ence known. Mrs. Watson and Thomas had had their hands full, and at last Rosie had been enlisted to help them. She carried necessary provisions to the lodge, and helped to keep the secret.

Thomas told me quite frankly that he had been anxious to keep Louise's presence hidden for the reason that they had all seen Arnold Armstrong that night, and he himself for one was known to have had no very friendly feeling for the dead man. As to the reason for Louise's flight from California, or why she had not gone to the Fitzhughs' or to some of her people in town, he had no more information than I had. With the death of her stepfather and the prospect of the immediate return of the family, things had become more and more impossible. I gathered that Thomas was as relieved as I at the turn events had taken. No, she did not know of either of the deaths in the family.

Taken all around, I had only substituted one mystery for another. If I knew now why Rosie had taken the basket of dishes, I did not know who had spoken to her and followed her along the drive. If I knew that Louise was in the lodge, I did not know why she was there. If I knew that Arnold Armstrong had spent some time there the night before he was murdered, I was still no nearer the solution of the crime.

Who was the midnight intruder who had so alarmed Liddy and myself? Who had fallen down the clothes chute? Was Jack Bailey a rascal or a victim of circumstance? Time was to answer all these things, but not too soon. Not soon enough.

13

THE DOCTOR from Englewood came very soon, and I went up with him to see the sick girl. Halsey had gone to supervise the fitting of the car with blankets and pillows, and Gertrude was opening and airing Louise's own rooms at the house. Her private sitting room, bedroom and dressing room were as they had been when we came. They occupied the end of the east wing, near the circular staircase, and we had not even opened them.

The girl herself was too ill to notice what was being done. When with the help of the doctor, who was a fatherly man with a family of girls at home, we got her to the house and up the stairs into bed, she dropped into a feverish sleep, which lasted until morning. Doctor Stewart—that was the Englewood doctor—stayed almost all night, giving the medicine himself and watching her closely. Afterwards he told me that she had had a narrow escape from pneumonia, and that the cerebral symptoms had been rather alarming. I said I was glad it wasn't an "itis" of some kind, anyhow, and he smiled solemnly.

He left after breakfast, saying that he thought the worst of the danger was over, and that she must be kept very quiet.

"The shock of two deaths I suppose has done this," he remarked, picking up his case. "It has been most deplorable. She is certainly suffering from shock."

I set him right at once.

"She doesn't know of either one, doctor," I said. "So don't mention them to her."

He looked as surprised as a medical man ever does.

"I don't know the family," he said, preparing to get into his car. "Young Walker down in Casanova has been attending them. I understand he is going to marry this girl."

"You have been misinformed," I said stiffly. "Miss Armstrong is going to marry my nephew."

He smiled as he turned on the ignition.

"Young ladies are changeable these days," he said. "We thought the wedding was to occur soon. Well, I'll stop in this afternoon to see how she's getting along. Just keep her warm and quiet."

He drove away then, and I stood looking after him. He was a doctor of the old school, of the class of family practitioner that is fast dying out. A loyal and honorable gentleman who was at once physician and confidential adviser to his patients. When I was a girl we called in the doctor either when we had the measles or when mother's sister died in the far West. He cut out redundant tonsils and brought the babies with the same air of inspiring self-confidence. Nowadays it requires a different specialist for each of these occurrences. When babies cried, old Doctor Wainwright gave them peppermint and dropped warm sweet oil in their ears, with sublime faith that if it was not colic it was earache. When, at the end of a year, Father met him on the street and asked for a bill, he used to go home, estimate what his services were worth for that period, divide it in half—I don't think he kept any books —and send Father a statement in a cramped hand on a sheet of ruled white paper. He was an honored guest at all the weddings, christenings, and funerals —yes, funerals—for everyone knew he had done his best, and there was no gainsaying in the ways of Providence.

Ah well, Doctor Wainwright is gone, and I am an elderly woman with an increasing tendency to live in the past. The contrast between my old doctor at home and the Casanova doctor, Frank Walker, always rouses me to wrath and digression.

Some time about noon of that day, Wednesday, Mrs. Ogden Fitzhugh telephoned me. I had the barest acquaintance with her, and that only because she managed to be put on the governing board of the Old Ladies' Home, where she ruins their digestions by sending them ice cream and cake on every holiday. Beyond that and her reputation at bridge, which was insufferably bad—she was the worst player at the bridge club—I knew little of her. It was she who had taken charge of Arnold Armstrong's funeral, however, and I went at once to the telephone.

"Yes," I said, "this is Miss Innes."

"Miss Innes," she said volubly, "I have just received a very strange telegram from my cousin, Mrs. Armstrong. Her husband died yesterday in California and—Wait, I will read you the message."

I knew what was coming, and I made up my mind at once. If Louise Armstrong had a good and sufficient reason for leaving her people and coming home, a reason moreover which kept her from going at once to Mrs. Ogden Fitzhugh and that brought her to the lodge at Sunnyside instead, it was not my intention to betray her. Louise herself must notify her people. I do not justify myself now, but I was in a peculiar position toward the Armstrong family. I was connected most unpleasantly with a cold-blooded crime, and my niece and nephew were practically beggared, either directly or indirectly, through the head of the family.

Mrs. Fitzhugh had found the message.

" 'Paul died yesterday. Heart disease,' " she read. " 'Wire at once if Louise is with you.' You see, Miss Innes, Louise must have started east and Fanny is alarmed about her."

"Yes," I said.

"Louise is not here," Mrs. Fitzhugh went on, "and none of her friends—the few who are still in town—has seen her. I called you because Sunnyside was not rented when she went away, and Louise might have gone there."

"I am sorry, Mrs. Fitzhugh, but I can't help you," I said, and was immediately filled with compunction. Suppose Louise grew worse? Who was I to play Providence in this case? The anxious mother certainly had a right to know that her daughter was in good hands. So I broke in on Mrs. Fitzhugh's voluble excuses for disturbing me.

"Mrs. Fitzhugh," I said. "I was going to let you think I knew nothing about Louise Armstrong, but I have changed my mind. Louise is here, with me." There was a clatter of ejaculations at the other end of the wire. "She is very ill and not able to be moved. Moreover, she is unable to see anyone. I wish you would wire her mother that she is with me, and tell her not to worry. No, I do not know why she came east."

"But, my dear Miss Innes—" Mrs. Fitzhugh began. I cut in ruthlessly.

"I will send for you as soon as she can see you," I said. "No, she is not in a critical state now, but the doctor says she must have absolute quiet."

When I had hung up the receiver I sat down to think. So Louise had fled from her people in California, and had come east alone. It was not a new idea, but why had she done it? It occurred to me that Doctor Walker might be concerned in it, might possibly have bothered her with unwelcome attentions. But it seemed to me that Louise was hardly a girl to take refuge in flight under such circumstances. She had always been high-spirited, with the build and outspokenness of the outdoor girl. It would have been much more in keeping with Louise's character as I knew it to resent vigorously any unwelcome attentions from anyone. It was the suitor whom I should have expected to see in headlong flight, not the girl in the case.

The puzzle was no clearer at the end of a half hour. I picked up the morning papers which were still full of the looting of the Traders' Bank, the interest at fever height again because of Paul Armstrong's death. The bank examiners were still working on the books and said nothing for publication. John Bailey had been released on bail. The body of Paul Armstrong would arrive Sunday and would be buried from the Armstrong town house. There were rumors that the dead man's estate had been a comparatively small one. But the last paragraph was the important one.

Walter P. Broadhurst of the Marine Bank had produced a large number of American Traction bonds, which had been placed as security with the Marine Bank for a loan of one hundred and sixty thousand dollars, made to Paul Armstrong just before his California trip. The bonds were a part of the missing bonds from the Traders' Bank. While this involved the late president of the wrecked bank, to my mind it by no means cleared its cashier.

The gardener mentioned by Halsey came out about two o'clock in the afternoon, and walked up from the station. I was favorably impressed by him. His references were good—he had been employed by the Brays until they went to Europe, and he looked young and vigorous. He asked for one assistant, and I was glad enough to get off so easily. He was a pleasant-faced young fellow, although rather shabbily dressed. He had black hair and blue eyes, and his name was Alexander Graham. I have been particular about Alex, because as I said before he played an important part later.

That afternoon I had a new insight into the character of the dead banker. I had my first conversation with Louise. She sent for me, and against my better judgment I went. There were so many things she could not be told, in her weakened condition, that I dreaded the interview. It was much easier than I expected, however, because she asked no questions.

Gertrude had gone to bed, having been up almost all night, and Halsey was absent on one of those mysterious absences of his that grew more and more frequent as time went on, until it culminated in the event of the night of June the tenth. Liddy was in attendance in the sickroom. There being little or nothing to do, she seemed to spend her time smoothing the wrinkles from the counterpane. Louise lay under a field of virgin white, folded back at an angle of geometrical exactness and necessitating a readjustment every time the sick girl turned.

Liddy heard my approach and came out to meet me. She seemed to be in a perpetual state of goose flesh, and she had got in the habit of looking past me when she talked, as if she saw things. It had the effect of making me look over my shoulder to see what she was staring at, and was intensely irritating.

"She's awake," Liddy said, looking uneasily down the circular staircase, which was beside me. "She was talkin' in her sleep something awful. About dead men and coffins."

"Liddy," I said sternly, "did you breathe a word about everything not being right here?"

Liddy's gaze had wandered to the door of the clothes chute, now bolted securely.

"Not a word," she said, "beyond asking her a question or two, which there was no harm in. She says there never was a ghost known here."

I glared at her, speechless, and closing the door into Louise's dressing room, to Liddy's great disappointment, I went on to the bedroom beyond.

Whatever Paul Armstrong had been, he had been lavish with his step-daughter. Gertrude's rooms at home were always beautiful, but the three rooms in the east wing at Sunnyside, set apart for the daughter of the house, were much more expensive. From the walls to the rugs on the floor, from the furniture to the appointments of the bath with its pool sunk into the floor instead of the customary unlovely tub, everything was luxurious. In the bedroom Louise was watching for me. It was easy to see that she was much improved. The flush was going, and the peculiar gasping breathing and coughing of the night before were now a comfortable and easy respiration.

She held out her hand and I took it between both of mine.

"What can I say to you, Miss Innes?" she said slowly. "To have come like this—"

I thought she was going to break down, but she did not.

"You're not to think of anything but of getting well," I said, patting her hand. "When you're better I am going to scold you for not coming here at once. This is your home, my dear, and of all people in the world Halsey's old aunt ought to make you welcome."

She smiled a little, sadly, I thought.

"I ought not to see Halsey," she said. "Miss Innes, there are a great many things you will never understand, I'm afraid. I am an impostor on your sympathy, because I stay here and let you lavish care on me, and all the time I know you are going to despise me."

"Nonsense!" I said briskly. "Why, what would Halsey do to me if I even ventured such a thing? He is in such a state that if I dared to be anything but rapturous over you he would throw me out a window. He would be quite capable of it."

She seemed scarcely to hear me. She had eloquent brown eyes—the Inneses are fair, and are prone to a grayish-green optic that is better for use than appearance—and they seemed now to be clouded with trouble.

"Poor Halsey!" she said softly. "Miss Innes, I can't marry him, and I am afraid to tell him. I am a coward—a coward!"

I sat beside the bed and stared at her. She was too ill to argue with, and besides sick people take queer fancies.

"We'll talk about that when you are stronger," I said gently.

"But there are some things I must tell you," she insisted. "You must wonder how I came here, and why I stayed hidden at the lodge. Dear old Thomas has been almost crazy, Miss Innes. I didn't know that Sunnyside was rented. I knew my mother wanted to rent it, without telling my stepfather, but the news must have reached her after I left. When I started east I had only one idea, to be alone, to bury myself here. Then I must have taken a cold on the train."

"You came east in clothing suitable for California," I said, "and like all girls nowadays I don't suppose you wear much." But she was not listening.

"Miss Innes," she said, "has my stepbrother Arnold gone away?"

"What do you mean?" I asked, startled. But Louise was literal.

"He didn't come back to the lodge that night," she said, "and it was frightfully important that I should see him again."

"I believe he has gone away," I replied uncertainly. "Isn't it something we could attend to instead?"

But she shook her head. "I must do it myself," she said dully. "My mother must have rented Sunnyside without telling my stepfather, and—Miss Innes, did you ever hear of anyone being wretchedly poor in the midst of luxury? Did you ever long and long for money, money to use without question, money that no one would take you to task about? My mother and I have been surrounded for years with every indulgence, everything that would make a display. But we have never had any money, Miss Innes. That must have been why Mother rented this house. My stepfather pays our bills but that's all. It's the most maddening, humiliating existence in the world. I could take honest poverty better."

"Never mind," I said. "When you and Halsey are married you can be as honest as you like, and you will certainly be poor."

She looked puzzled at that. I had no time to explain, however, for Halsey came to the door at that moment and I could hear him coaxing Liddy.

"Shall I bring him in?" I asked Louise, uncertain what to do. The girl seemed to shrink back among her pillows at the sound of his voice. I was vaguely irritated with her. There are few young fellows like Halsey, straightforward, honest, and willing to sacrifice everything for the one woman. I knew one once, more than thirty years ago, who was like that. He died a long time ago, and sometimes I take out his picture with its cane and its queer silk hat and look at it. But of late years it has grown too painful. He is always young and I am an old woman. I would not bring him back if I could.

Perhaps it was some such memory that made me call out sharply.

"Come in, Halsey." And then I took my sewing and went into the dressing room beyond to play propriety. I did not try to hear what they said, but every word came through the open door with curious distinctness. Halsey had evidently gone over to the bed, and I suppose he kissed her. There was silence for a moment, as if words were superfluous things.

"I have been almost wild, darling"—Halsey's voice. "Why didn't you trust me and send for me before?"

"It was because I couldn't trust myself," she said in a low tone. "I'm too weak to struggle today. I've wanted you so dreadfully."

There was something I did not hear, then Halsey again.

"We could go away," he was saying. "What does it matter about anyone in the world but just the two of us? To be always together like this, hand in hand. Louise darling, don't tell me it isn't going to be. I won't believe you."

"You don't know; you don't know," she repeated dully. "Halsey, I care. You know that. But not enough to marry you the way things are."

"That is not true, Louise," he said sternly. "You can't look at me with your honest eyes and say that."

"I can't marry you," she repeated miserably. "It's bad enough, isn't it? Don't make it worse. Someday before long, you'll be glad."

"Then it's because you have never really cared for me." There were depths of hurt pride in his voice. "You saw how much I loved you, and you let me think you cared. That isn't like you, Louise. There is something you haven't told me. Is it because there is someone else?"

"Yes," almost inaudibly.

"Louise! Hell, I don't believe it."

"It's true," she said. "Halsey, you mustn't try to see me again. As soon as I can I am going away from here, where you are all so much kinder than I deserve. And whatever you hear about me try to think as well of me as you can. I'm going to marry another man. Just try not to hate me, won't you?"

I could hear him cross the room to the window. Then after a pause he went back to her. I could hardly sit still. I wanted to go in and give her a good spanking, weak as she was. The dratted little fool!

"Then it's all over," he was saying with a long breath. "Everything goes into the discard. All the things we planned and hoped shot to bits. Well, I'm no crybaby, and I'll give up the minute you say you're in love with the other fellow."

"I haven't said that. But nevertheless I'm going to marry him."

I could hear Halsey's low triumphant laugh.

"To hell with him," he said. "Sweetheart, as long as you care for me I am not afraid. And you do care. I know it."

The wind slammed the door between the two rooms just then, and I could hear nothing more although I moved my chair quite close. After a discreet interval I went into the other room, and found Louise alone. She was staring at the cherub painted on the ceiling over the bed, and because she looked exhausted I did not disturb her.

14

WE HAD DISCOVERED Louise at the lodge Tuesday night. It was Wednesday I had my interview with her. Thursday and Friday were uneventful, save as they marked improvement in our patient. Gertrude spent almost all the time with her, and the two had grown to be great friends. But certain things hung over me constantly: the coroner's inquest on the death of Arnold Armstrong, to be held Saturday, and the arrival of Mrs. Armstrong and young Doctor Walker, bringing the body of the dead president of the Traders' Bank. We had not told Louise of either death.

Then, too, I was anxious about the children. With their mother's inheritance swept away in the wreck of the bank, and with their love affairs in a disastrous condition, things could scarcely be worse. Added to that the cook and Liddy had a flare-up over the proper way to make beef tea for Louise, and of course the cook left.

Mrs. Watson had been glad enough, I think, to turn Louise over to our care, and Thomas went upstairs night and morning to greet his young mistress from the doorway. Poor Thomas! He had the faculty—found still in some old Negroes—of making his employer's interest his. It was always "we" with Thomas. I miss him sorely, pipe-smoking, obsequious, not overreliable but kindly old man!

On Thursday Mr. Harton, the Armstrongs' attorney, called up from town. He had been advised, he said, that Mrs. Armstrong was coming east with her husband's body and would arrive Monday. He came with some hesitation, he went on, to the fact that he had been further instructed to ask me to relinquish my lease on Sunnyside, as it was Mrs. Armstrong's desire to come directly there.

I was aghast.

"Leave?" I said. "Surely you are mistaken, Mr. Harton. And come here! I should think, after what happened here only a few days ago, she would never wish to come back!"

"Nevertheless," he replied, "she is most anxious to come. This is what she says: 'Use every possible means to have Sunnyside vacated. Must go there at once.'"

"Mr. Harton," I said testily, "I am not going to do anything of the kind. We have suffered enough at the hands of this family. I rented the house at an exorbitant figure and I have moved out here for the summer. My city home is dismantled and in the hands of decorators. I have been here one week, during which I have not had a single night of uninterrupted sleep, and I intend to stay until I have recuperated. Moreover, if Mr. Armstrong died insolvent, as I believe was the case, his widow ought to be glad to be rid of so expensive a piece of property."

The lawyer cleared his throat.

"I am very sorry you have made this decision," he said. "Miss Innes, Mrs. Fitzhugh tells me Louise Armstrong is with you."

"She is."

"Has she been informed of this—double bereavement?"

"Not yet," I said. "She has been very ill. Perhaps tonight she can be told."

"It is very sad. Very sad," he said. "I have a telegram for her, Mrs. Innes. Shall I send it out?"

"Better open it and read it to me," I suggested. "If it's important that will save time."

There was a pause while Mr. Harton opened the telegram. Then he read it slowly, judicially.

" 'Watch for Nina Carrington. Home Monday. Signed F.L.W.' "

"Humph!" I grunted. " 'Watch for Nina Carrington. Home Monday.' Very well, Mr. Harton, I will tell her, whoever Nina is. But she is not in condition to watch for anyone."

"Well, Miss Innes, if you decide to—er—relinquish the lease, let me know," the lawyer said.

"I will not relinquish it," I replied, and I imagined his irritation from the way he hung up the receiver.

I wrote the telegram down word for word, afraid to trust my memory, and decided to ask Doctor Stewart how soon Louise might be told the truth. The closing of the Traders' Bank I considered unnecessary for her to know, but the death of her stepfather and stepbrother must be broken to her soon or she might hear it in some unexpected and shocking manner.

Doctor Stewart came about four o'clock, bringing his leather bag into the house with a great deal of care, and opening it at the foot of the stairs to show me a dozen big yellow eggs nesting among the bottles.

"Real eggs," he said proudly. "None of your anemic store eggs but the real thing, some of them still warm. Feel them! Eggnog for Louise."

He was beaming with satisfaction, and before he left he insisted on going back to the pantry and making an eggnog with his own hands. Somehow all the time he was doing it I had a vision of Doctor Willoughby, my nerve specialist in the city, trying to make an eggnog. I wondered if he ever prescribed anything so plebeian and so delicious. And while Doctor Stewart whisked the eggs he talked.

"I said to Mrs. Stewart," he confided, a little red in the face from the exertion, "after I went home the other day, that you would think me an old gossip for saying what I did about Walker and Louise."

"Nothing of the sort," I protested.

"The fact is," he went on, evidently justifying himself, "I got that piece of information just as we get a lot of things, through the kitchen end of the house. Young Walker's chauffeur—Walker's more fashionable than I am, and he goes around the country in a big car—well, his chauffeur comes to see our maid, and he told her the whole thing. I thought it was probable, because Walker spent a lot of time up here last summer when the family was here. And besides Riggs, that's Walker's man, had a very pat little story about the doctor's building a house on this property at the foot of the hill. The sugar, please."

The eggnog was finished. Drop by drop the liquor had cooked the egg and now with a final whisk, a last toss in the shaker, it was ready, a symphony in gold and white. The doctor sniffed it.

"Real eggs, real milk, and a touch of real Kentucky bourbon," he said.

He insisted on carrying it up himself, but at the foot of the stairs he paused.

"Riggs said the plans were drawn for the house," he said, harking back to the former subject. "Drawn by Houston, the architect in town. So I naturally believed him."

When the doctor came down I was ready with a question.

"Doctor," I asked, "is there anyone in the neighborhood named Carrington? Nina Carrington?"

"Carrington?" He wrinkled his forehead. "Carrington? No, I don't remember any such family. There used to be Covingtons down the creek."

"The name was Carrington," I said, and the subject lapsed.

Gertrude and Halsey went for a long walk that afternoon, and Louise slept. Time hung heavy on my hands, and I did as I had fallen into a habit of doing lately—I sat down and thought things over. One result of my meditations was that I got up abruptly and went to the telephone. I had taken the most intense dislike to this Doctor Walker, whom I had never seen and who was being talked of in the countryside as the fiancé of Louise Armstrong.

I knew Sam Houston well. There had been a time, when Sam was a good deal younger than he is now and before he married Anne Endicott, when I knew him even better. So now I felt no hesitation in calling him over the telephone. But when his office boy had given way to his confidential clerk, and that functionary had condescended to connect his employer's desk telephone, I was somewhat at a loss as to how to begin.

"Why, how are you, Rachel?" Sam said sonorously. "Going to build that house at Rock View?" It was a twenty-year-old joke of his.

"Sometime, perhaps," I said. "Just now I want to ask you a question about something that is none of my business."

"I see you haven't changed an iota in a quarter of a century." This was intended to be another jest. "Ask ahead. Everything but my domestic affairs is at your service."

"Try to be serious," I said. "And tell me this: has your firm made any plans for a house recently, for a Doctor Walker at Casanova?"

"Yes, we have. Why?"

"Where was it to be built? I have a reason for asking."

"It was to be on the Armstrong place. Mr. Armstrong himself consulted me, and the inference was—in fact, I'm quite certain—the house was to be occupied by Mr. Armstrong's daughter, who was engaged to marry Walker."

When Sam had inquired for the different members of my family and had finally rung off I was certain of one thing. Louise Armstrong was in love with Halsey, and the man she was going to marry was Doctor Walker. Moreover, this decision was not new. Marriage had been contemplated for some time. There must certainly be some explanation, but what was it?

That day I repeated to Louise the telegram Mr. Harton had opened. She seemed to understand, but an unhappier face I have never seen. She looked like a criminal whose reprieve is over, with the day of execution approaching.

15

THE NEXT DAY, Friday, Gertrude broke the news of her stepfather's death to Louise. She did it as gently as she could, telling her first that he was very ill and finally that he was dead. Louise received the news in the most unexpected manner, and when Gertrude came out to tell me how she had stood it I think she was almost shocked.

"She just lay and stared at me, Aunt Ray," she said. "Do you know, I believe she's glad! And she's too honest to pretend anything else. What sort of man was Paul Armstrong anyhow?"

"He was a bully as well as a rascal, Gertrude," I said. "But I am convinced of one thing, Louise will send for Halsey now, and they will make it all up."

For Louise had steadily refused to see Halsey all that day, and the boy was frantic.

We had a quiet hour, Halsey and I, that evening, and I told him several things: about the request that we give up the lease to Sunnyside, about the telegram to Louise, about the rumors of an approaching marriage between the girl and Doctor Walker, and last of all about my own interview with her the day before.

He sat back in a big chair, with his face in the shadow, and my heart fairly ached for him. He was so big and so boyish. When I had finished he drew a long breath.

"Whatever Louise does," he said, "nothing will convince me that she doesn't care for me. And up to two months ago, when she and her mother went west, I was the happiest fellow on earth. Then something made a difference. She wrote me that her people were opposed to the marriage, that her feeling for me was what it had always been, but that something had happened which had changed her ideas as to the future. I was not to write until she wrote me, and whatever occurred I was to think the best I could of her. It sounded like a puzzle. When I saw her yesterday, it was the same thing, only perhaps worse."

"Halsey," I asked, "have you any idea of the nature of the interview between Louise and Arnold the night he was murdered?"

"It was stormy. Thomas says once or twice he almost broke into the room, he was so scared for Louise."

"Another thing," I said. "Have you ever heard Louise mention a woman named Carrington, Nina Carrington?"

"Never," he said positively.

Try as we would, our thoughts always came back to that fatal Saturday night, and the murder. Every conversational path led to it, and we all felt that Jamieson was tightening the threads of evidence around John Bailey. The detective's absence was hardly reassuring. He must have had something to work on in town, or he would have returned.

The papers reported that the cashier of the Traders' Bank was ill in his apartment at the Knickerbocker, a situation not surprising, everything considered. The guilt of the defunct president was no longer in doubt. The missing bonds had been advertised and some of them discovered. In every instance they had been used as collateral for large loans, and the belief was current that not less than a million and a half dollars had been realized. Practically everyone connected with the bank had been placed under arrest and then released on heavy bond.

Was Armstrong alone in his guilt, or was the cashier his accomplice? Where was the money? The estate of the dead man was comparatively small, a city house on a fashionable street, Sunnyside, which was largely mortgaged, an insurance policy of fifty thousand dollars, and some personal property—this was all. The rest lost in speculation probably, the papers said. There was one thing that looked uncomfortable for Jack Bailey. He and Paul Armstrong together had promoted a railroad company in New Mexico, and it was rumored that together they had sunk large sums of money there.

The business alliance between the two men added to the belief that Bailey knew something of the looting. His unexplained absence from the bank on Monday lent color to the suspicion against him. The strange thing seemed to be his surrendering himself as he had. To me it seemed the shrewd calculation of a clever crook. I was not actively antagonistic to Gertrude's lover, but I meant to be convinced, one way or the other. I took no one on faith.

That night the Sunnyside ghost began to walk again. Liddy had been sleeping in Louise's dressing room on a couch, and the approach of dusk was a signal for her to barricade the entire suite. Situated as it was beyond the circular staircase nothing but an extremity of excitement would have made her pass it after dark. I confess myself that the place seemed to me to have a sinister appearance; but we kept that wing well lighted, and until the lights went out at midnight it was really cheerful, if one did not know its history.

On Friday night then I had gone to bed, resolved to go at once to sleep. Thoughts that insisted on obtruding themselves I pushed resolutely to the back of my mind, and I systematically relaxed every muscle. I fell asleep soon, and was dreaming that Doctor Walker was building his new house immediately in front of my windows. I could hear the thump-thump of the hammers, and finally I awakened to a knowledge that somebody was pounding on my door.

I was up at once and with the sound of my footstep on the floor the low knocking ceased, to be followed immediately by sibilant whispering through the keyhole.

"Miss Rachel! Miss Rachel!" somebody was saying, over and over.

"Is that you, Liddy?" I asked, my hand on the knob.

"For the love of mercy let me in!" she said in a low tone.

She must have been leaning against the door, for when I opened it she fell in. She was greenish-white, and had a red-and-black barred flannel petticoat over her shoulders.

"Listen," she said, standing in the middle of the floor and holding on to me. "Oh, Miss Rachel, it's the ghost of that dead man hammering to get in!"

Sure enough, there was a dull thud—thud—thud from some place near. It was muffled. One felt rather than heard it, and it was impossible to locate. One moment it seemed to come, three taps and a pause, from the floor under us. The next, thud—thud—thud, it came apparently from the wall.

"It's not a ghost," I said decidedly. "If it was a ghost it wouldn't rap: it would come through the keyhole." Liddy looked at the keyhole. "But it sounds very much as though someone is trying to break into the house."

Liddy was shivering violently. I told her to get me my slippers and she brought me a pair of kid gloves, so I found my things myself and prepared to call Halsey. As before, the night alarm had found the electric lights gone. The hall save for its night lamp was in darkness as I went across to Halsey's room, and it was a relief to find him there, very sound asleep and with his door unlocked.

"Wake up, Halsey," I said, shaking him.

He stirred a little. Liddy was half in and half out the door, afraid as usual to be left alone and not quite daring to enter. Her scruples seemed to fade all at once, however. She gave a suppressed yell, bolted into the room, and stood tightly clutching the footboard of the bed. Halsey was gradually waking.

"I've seen it," Liddy wailed. "A woman in white down the hall!"

I paid no attention.

"Halsey," I persevered, "someone is breaking into the house! For heaven's sake, get up."

"It isn't our house," he said sleepily. And then he roused to the exigency of the occasion. "All right, Ray," he said, still yawning. "If you'll let me get into something—"

It was all I could do to get Liddy out of the room. The demands of the occasion had no influence on her. She had seen the ghost, she persisted, and she wasn't going into the hall. But I got her over to my room at last, more dead than alive, and made her lie down on the bed.

The tappings which seemed to have ceased for a while had commenced again but they were fainter. Halsey came over in a few minutes, and stood listening and trying to locate the sound.

"Persistent devil, isn't he?" he said. "Where's my gun, Aunt Rachel?"

As will have been noticed, both Gertrude and Halsey seldom call me "aunt" at all—I am Ray or Rachel, but in real emergency I become Aunt Rachel. This was such a time. And I got the revolver in a hurry. While I was locating it he saw Liddy and realized that Louise was alone.

"You let me attend to this fellow, whoever it is, Aunt Rachel, and go to Louise, will you? She may be awake and having a fit."

So in spite of her protests I left Liddy alone and went back to the east wing. Perhaps I went a little faster than usual past the yawning blackness of the circular staircase, and I could hear Halsey creaking cautiously down the main staircase. The rapping, or pounding, had ceased, and the silence was almost painful. Then suddenly from apparently under my very feet there rose a woman's scream, a cry of terror that broke off as suddenly as it came. I stood frozen and still. Every drop of blood in my body seemed to leave the surface and gather around my heart. In the dead silence that followed, it throbbed as if it would burst. More dead than alive I stumbled into Louise's bedroom.

She was not there.

16

I STOOD LOOKING at the empty bed. The coverings had been thrown back, and Louise's silk dressing gown was gone from the foot, where it had been lying. The night lamp burned dimly, revealing the emptiness of the place. I picked it up, but my hand shook so that I put it down again, and got somehow to the door.

There were voices in the hall and Gertrude came running toward me.

"What is it?" she cried. "What was that noise? Where is Louise?"

"She is not in her room," I said stupidly. "I think she must have been the one who screamed."

Liddy had joined us now, carrying a light. We stood huddled together at the head of the circular staircase, looking down into its shadows. There was nothing to be seen, and it was absolutely quiet down there. Then we heard Halsey running up the main staircase. He came quickly down the hall to where we were standing.

"There's no sign of anyone trying to get in," he said. "I thought I heard someone shriek. Who was it?"

Our stricken faces told him the truth.

"Someone did scream down there," I said. "And Louise is not in her room."

With a jerk Halsey took the light from Liddy and ran down the circular staircase. I followed him, more slowly. My legs seemed to be paralyzed, for I could scarcely walk. At the foot of the stairs Halsey gave an exclamation and put down the light.

"Aunt Rachel!" he called sharply.

At the foot of the staircase, huddled in a heap with her head on the lower step, was Louise Armstrong. She lay limp and white, her dressing gown dragging loose from one sleeve of her pajamas, and her heavy dark hair spread above her as if she had slipped down.

She was not dead. Halsey put her down on the floor and began to rub her cold hands, while Gertrude and Liddy ran for stimulants. As for me, I sat there at the foot of that ghostly staircase—sat, because my knees wouldn't hold me—and wondered where it would all end. Louise was still unconscious but she was breathing better, and I suggested that we get her back to bed before she came to. There was something grisly and horrible to me, seeing her there in almost the same attitude and in the same place where we had found her brother's body. And to add to the similarity, just then the hall clock, far off, struck faintly three o'clock.

It was four before Louise was able to talk, and the first rays of dawn were coming through her windows, which faced the east, before she could tell us coherently what had occurred. I give it as she told it. She lay propped up in bed, and Halsey sat beside her and held her hand while she talked.

"I was not sleeping well," she began, "partly, I think, because I had slept during the afternoon. Liddy brought me some hot milk at ten o'clock and I slept until twelve. Then I wakened and I got to thinking about things and worrying, so I could not go to sleep.

"I was wondering why I had not heard from Arnold since I saw him that night at the lodge. I was afraid he was ill, because he was to have done something for me, and he had not come back. It must have been three when I heard someone rapping down below. I sat up and listened to be quite sure, and the rapping kept up. It was cautious, and I was about to call Liddy. Then suddenly I thought I knew what it was. The east entrance and the circular staircase were always used by Arnold when he was out late, and sometimes when he forgot his key he would rap and I would go down and let him in.

"I thought he had come back to see me—I didn't think about the time, for his hours were always erratic. But I was afraid I was too weak to get down the stairs. The knocking kept up, and just as I was about to call Liddy she ran through the room and out into the hall. I got up then, feeling weak and dizzy, and put on my dressing gown. If it was Arnold, I knew I had to see him.

"It was very dark everywhere, but of course I knew my way. I felt along for the stair rail and went down as quickly as I could. The knocking had stopped, and I was afraid I was too late. I got to the foot of the staircase and over to the door onto the east veranda. I had never thought of anything but that it was Arnold, until I got to the door. It was unlocked and opened about an inch, and everything was black. It was perfectly dark outside, and I felt queer and shaky. Then I thought perhaps Arnold had used his key. He did strange things sometimes when he had been drinking, so I turned around. Just as I reached the foot of the staircase I thought I heard someone coming. My nerves were going anyhow there in the dark, and I could scarcely stand. I got up as far as the third or fourth step. Then I felt that someone was coming toward me on the staircase. The next instant a hand met mine on the stair rail, and someone brushed past me. That was when I screamed. Then I must have fainted."

That was Louise's story. There could be no doubt of its truth, and the thing that made it inexpressibly awful to me was that the poor girl had crept down to answer the summons of a brother who would never need her kindly offices again. Twice now without apparent reason someone had entered the house by means of the east entrance, had apparently gone his way unhindered through the house, and gone out again as he had entered. Had this unknown visitor been there a third time, the night Arnold Armstrong was murdered? Or a fourth, the time Jamieson had locked someone in the clothes chute?

Sleep was impossible, I think, for any of us. We dispersed finally to bathe and dress, leaving Louise little the worse for her experience. But I determined that before the day was over she must know the true state of affairs. Another decision I made, and I put it into execution immediately after breakfast. I had one of the unused bedrooms in the east wing, back along the small corridor, prepared for occupancy; and from that time on Alex, the gardener, slept there. One man in that barn of a house was an absurdity, with things happening all the time, and I must say that Alex was as unobjectionable as anyone could possibly have been.

The next morning Halsey and I made an exhaustive examination of the circular staircase, the small entry at its foot, and the cardroom opening from it. There was no evidence of anything unusual the night before, and had we not ourselves heard the rapping noises I should have felt that Louise's imagination had run away with her. The outer door was closed and locked, and the staircase curved above us, for all the world like any other staircase of the sort.

Halsey, who had never taken seriously my account of the night Liddy and I were there alone, was grave enough now. He examined the paneling of the wainscoting above and below the stairs, looking for a secret door, and suddenly there flashed into my mind the recollection of a scrap of paper that Jamieson had found among Arnold Armstrong's effects. As nearly as possible I repeated its contents to him while Halsey took them down in a notebook.

"I wish you had told me that before," he said, as he put the memorandum carefully away. However, we found nothing at all in the house, and I expected little from any examination of the porch and grounds. But as we opened the outer door something fell into the entry with a clatter. It was a cue from the billiard room.

Halsey picked it up with an exclamation.

"That's careless enough," he said. "Some of the servants must have been amusing themselves."

I was far from convinced. Not one of the servants would go into that wing at night unless driven by dire necessity. And a billiard cue! As a weapon of either offense or defense it was an absurdity, unless one accepted Liddy's hypothesis of a ghost. Even then, as Halsey pointed out, a billiard-playing ghost would be a very modern evolution of an ancient institution.

That afternoon Gertrude, Halsey and I attended the coroner's inquest in town. Doctor Stewart had been summoned also, it transpiring that in that early Sunday morning, when Gertrude and I had gone to our rooms, he had been called to view the body. We went, the four of us, in the car, preferring the execrable roads to the matinee train with half of Casanova staring at us. And on the way we decided to say nothing about Louise and her interview with her stepbrother the night he died. The girl was in trouble enough as it was.

17

IN GIVING THE GIST of what happened at the inquest, I have only one excuse, to recall to the reader the events of the night of Arnold Armstrong's murder. Many things had occurred which were not brought out at the inquest and some things were told there which were new to me. Altogether it was a gloomy affair, and the six men in the corner who constituted the coroner's jury were evidently the merest puppets in the hands of that all-powerful gentleman, the coroner.

Gertrude and I sat well back, for there were a number of people we knew: Barbara Fitzhugh, in extravagant mourning—she always went into black on the slightest provocation, because it was becoming—and Mr. Jarvis, the man who had come over from the Greenwood Club the night of the murder. Mr. Harton was there, too, looking impatient as the inquest dragged, but alive to every particle of evidence. From a corner Jamieson was watching the proceedings intently.

Doctor Stewart was called first. His evidence was told briefly, and amounted to this: on the Sunday morning previous, at a quarter before five, he had been called to the telephone. The message was from a Mr. Jarvis, who asked him to come at once to Sunnyside, as there had been an accident there and Mr. Arnold Armstrong had been shot. He had dressed hastily, gathered up some instruments, and driven to Sunnyside.

He was met by Mr. Jarvis, who took him at once to the east wing. There, just as he had fallen, was the body of Arnold Armstrong. There was no need of the instruments. The man was dead. In answer to the coroner's question he said the body had not been moved, save to turn it over. It lay at the foot of the circular staircase. Yes, he believed death had been instantaneous. The body was still somewhat warm and rigor mortis had not set in. It occurred late in cases of sudden death. No, he believed the probability of suicide might be eliminated; the wounds could have been self-inflicted, but with difficulty, and no weapon had been found.

The doctor's examination was over, but he hesitated and cleared his throat.

"Mr. Coroner," he said, "at the risk of taking up valuable time, I would like to speak of an incident that may or may not throw some light on this matter."

The audience was alert at once.

"Kindly proceed, doctor," the coroner said.

"My home is in Englewood, two miles from Casanova," the doctor began. "In the absence of Doctor Walker a number of Casanova people have been consulting me. A month ago—five weeks, to be exact—a woman whom I had never seen came to my office. She was in deep mourning and kept her veil down, and she brought for examination a child, a boy of six. The little fellow was ill. It looked like typhoid, and the mother was frantic. She wanted a permit to admit the youngster to the Children's Hospital in town here, where I am a member of the staff, and I gave her one. The incident would have escaped me, but for a curious thing. Two days before Mr. Armstrong was shot I was sent for to go to the Country Club. Someone had been struck with a golf ball that had gone wild. It was late when I left—I was on foot, and about a mile from the club on the Claysburg road I met two people. They were disputing violently, and I had no difficulty in recognizing Mr. Armstrong. The woman, beyond doubt, was the one who had consulted me about the child."

At this hint of scandal Mrs. Ogden Fitzhugh sat up very straight. Jamieson was looking slightly skeptical, and the coroner made a note.

"The Children's Hospital, you say, doctor?" he asked.

"Yes. But the child, who entered as Lucien Wallace, was taken away by his mother two weeks ago. I have tried to trace them and failed."

All at once I remembered the telegram sent to Louise by someone signed F.L.W., presumably Doctor Walker. Could this veiled woman be the Nina Carrington of the message? But it was only idle speculation. I had no way of finding out, and the inquest was proceeding.

The report of the coroner's physician came next. The post-mortem examination showed that the bullet had entered the chest in the fourth left intercostal space and had taken an oblique course downward and backward, piercing both heart and lungs. The left lung was collapsed, and the exit point of the ball had been found in the muscles of the back to the left of the spinal column. It was improbable that such a wound had been self-inflicted, and its oblique downward course pointed to the fact that the shot had been fired from above. In other words, as the murdered man had been found dead at the foot of a staircase, it was probable that the shot had been fired by someone higher up on the stairs. There were no marks of powder. The bullet, a thirty-eight caliber, had been found in the dead man's clothing and was shown to the jury.

Mr. Jarvis was called next, but his testimony amounted to little. He had been summoned by telephone to Sunnyside, had come over at once with the steward and Mr. Winthrop, at present out of town. They had been admitted by the housekeeper, and had found the body lying at the foot of the staircase. He had made a search for a weapon, but there was none around. The outer entry door in the east wing had been unfastened and was open about an inch.

I had been growing more and more nervous. When the coroner called Mr. John Bailey, the room was filled with suppressed excitement. Jamieson went forward and spoke a few words to the coroner, who nodded. Then Halsey was called.

"Mr. Innes," the coroner said, "will you tell under what circumstances you saw Mr. Arnold Armstrong the night he died?"

"I saw him first at the Country Club," Halsey said quietly. He was rather pale, but very composed. "I stopped there with my automobile for gasoline. Mr. Armstrong had been playing cards. When I saw him there, he was coming out of the cardroom, talking to John Bailey."

"The nature of the discussion—was it amicable?"

Halsey hesitated.

"They were having a dispute," he said. "I asked Mr. Bailey to leave the club with me and come to Sunnyside over Sunday."

"Isn't it a fact, Mr. Innes, that you took Mr. Bailey away from the clubhouse because you were afraid there would be blows?"

"The situation was unpleasant," Halsey said evasively.

"At that time had you any suspicion that the Traders' Bank had been wrecked?"

"No."

"What occurred next?"

"Mr. Bailey and I talked in the billiard room until two-thirty."

"And Mr. Arnold Armstrong came there, while you were talking?"

"Yes. He came just before half past two. He rapped at the east door, and I admitted him."

The silence in the room was intense. Jamieson's eyes never left Halsey's face.

"Will you tell us the nature of his errand?"

"He brought a telegram which had come to the club for Mr. Bailey."

"He was sober?"

"Perfectly, at that time. Not earlier."

"Was not his apparent friendliness a change from his former attitude?"

"Yes. I didn't understand it."

"How long did he stay?"

"About five minutes. Then he left, by the east entrance."

"What occurred then?"

"We talked for a few minutes, discussing a plan Mr. Bailey had in mind. Then I went to the stables where I kept my car, and got it out."

"Leaving Mr. Bailey alone in the billiard room?"

Halsey hesitated.

"My sister was there."

Mrs. Ogden Fitzhugh had the audacity to turn and stare at Gertrude.

"And then?"

"I took the car along the lower road, not to disturb the household. Mr. Bailey came down across the lawn, through the hedge, and got into the car on the road."

"Then you know nothing of Mr. Armstrong's movements after he left the house?"

"Nothing. I read of his death Monday evening for the first time."

"Mr. Bailey did not see him on his way across the lawn?"

"I think not. If he had seen him he would have spoken of it."

"Thank you. That is all. Miss Gertrude Innes."

Gertrude's replies were fully as concise as Halsey's. Mrs. Fitzhugh subjected her to a sharp inspection, commencing with her hat and ending with her shoes. I flatter myself she found nothing wrong with either her clothes or her manner, but poor Gertrude's testimony was the reverse of comforting.

She had been summoned, she said, by her brother after Mr. Armstrong had gone. She had waited in the billiard room with Mr. Bailey until the automobile was ready. Then she had locked the door at the foot of the staircase, and taking a lamp had accompanied Mr. Bailey to the main entrance of the house, and had watched him cross the lawn. Instead of going at once to her room she had gone back to the billiard room for something which had been left there. The cardroom and billiard room were in darkness.

She had groped around, found the article she was looking for, and was on the point of returning to her room when she had heard someone fumbling at the east outer door. She had thought it was probably her brother, and had been about to go to the door when she heard it open. Almost immediately there was a shot, and she had run panic-stricken through the drawing room and had roused the house.

"You heard no other sound?" the coroner asked. "There was no one with Mr. Armstrong when he entered?"

"It was perfectly dark. There were no voices and I heard nothing. There was just the opening of the door, the shot, and the sound of somebody falling."

"Then, while you went through the drawing room and upstairs to alarm the household, the criminal, whoever it was, could have escaped by the east door?"

"Yes."

"Thank you. That will do."

I flatter myself that the coroner got little enough out of me. I saw Jamieson smiling to himself, and the coroner gave me up after a time. I admitted I had found the body, said I had not known who it was until Mr. Jarvis told me, and ended by looking up at Barbara Fitzhugh and saying that in renting the house I had not expected to be involved in any family scandal. At which she turned purple.

The verdict was that Arnold Armstrong had met his death at the hands of a person or persons unknown, and we all prepared to leave. Barbara Fitzhugh flounced out without waiting to speak to me, but Mr. Harton came, as I knew he would.

"You have decided to give up the house, I hope, Miss Innes," he said. "Mrs. Armstrong has wired me again."

"I am not going to give it up," I maintained, "until I understand some things that are puzzling me. The day the murderer is discovered I will leave."

"Then, judging by what I have heard, you will be back in the city very soon," he said. And I knew that he suspected the discredited cashier of the Traders' Bank.

Jamieson came up to me as I was about to leave the coroner's office.

"How is your patient?" he asked, with his odd little smile.

"I have no patient," I replied, startled.

"I will put it in a different way, then. How is Miss Armstrong?"

"She—she is doing very well," I stammered.

"Good," cheerfully. "And our ghost? Is it laid?"

"Mr. Jamieson," I said suddenly, "I wish you would do one thing. I wish you would come to Sunnyside and spend a few days there. The ghost is not laid. I want you to spend one night at least watching the circular staircase. The murder of Arnold Armstrong was a beginning, not an end, I'm sure of that."

He looked serious.

"Perhaps I can do it," he said. "I have been doing something else, but —well, I'll come out tonight."

We were very silent during the trip back to Sunnyside. I watched Gertrude closely and somewhat sadly. To me there was one glaring flaw in her story, and it seemed to stand out for everyone to see. Arnold Armstrong had had no key, and yet she said she had locked the east door. He must have been admitted from within the house: over and over I repeated it to myself.

That night, as gently as I could, I told Louise the story of her stepbrother's death. She sat in her big pillow-filled chair and heard me through without interruption. It was clear that she was shocked beyond words, but if I had hoped to learn anything from her expression, I had failed. She was as much in the dark as we were.

18

MY ASKING the detective out to Sunnyside raised an unexpected storm of protest from Gertrude and Halsey. I was not prepared for it, and I scarcely knew how to account for it. To me Jamieson was far less formidable under my eyes where I knew what he was doing than he was off in the city, twisting circumstances and motives to suit himself, and learning what he wished to know about events at Sunnyside in some occult way. I was glad enough to have him there, when excitements began to come thick and fast.

A new element was about to enter into affairs. Monday, or Tuesday at the latest, would find Doctor Walker back in his green-and-white house in the village, and Louise's attitude to him in the immediate future would signify Halsey's happiness or wretchedness, as it might turn out. Then too the return of her mother would mean of course that she would have to leave us, and I had become greatly attached to her.

From the day Jamieson came to Sunnyside there was a subtle change in Gertrude's manner to me. It was elusive, difficult to analyze, but it was there. She was no longer frank with me, although I think her affection never wavered. At the time I laid the change to the fact that I had forbidden all communication with John Bailey, and had refused to acknowledge any engagement between the two. Gertrude spent much of her time wandering through the grounds, or taking long cross-country walks. Halsey played golf at the Country Club day after day, and after Louise left, as she did the following week, Jamieson and I were much together. He played a fair game of cribbage, but he cheated at solitaire.

The night the detective arrived, Saturday, I had a talk with him. I told him of the experience Louise Armstrong had had the night before, on the circular staircase, and about the man who had so frightened Rosie on the drive. I saw he thought the information was important, and to my suggestion that we put an additional lock on the east wing door he opposed a strong negative.

"I think it probable," he said, "that our visitor will be back again, and the thing to do is to leave things exactly as they are, to avoid arousing suspicion. Then I can watch for at least a part of each night and probably Mr. Innes will help us out. I would say as little to Thomas as possible. The old man knows more than he's willing to admit."

I suggested that Alex, the gardener, would probably be willing to help, and Jamieson undertook to make the arrangement. For one night, however, he preferred to watch alone. Apparently nothing occurred. The detective sat in absolute darkness on the lower step of the stairs, dozing, he said afterwards, now and then. Nothing could pass him in either direction, and the door in the morning remained as securely fastened as it had been the night before. And yet one of the most inexplicable occurrences of the whole affair took place that very night.

Liddy came to my room on Sunday morning with a face as long as the moral law. She laid out my things as usual, but I missed her customary garrulousness. I was not regaled with the new cook's extravagance as to eggs, and she even forbore to mention "that Jamieson," on whose arrival she had looked with silent disfavor.

"What's the matter, Liddy?" I asked at last. "Didn't you sleep last night?"

"No, ma'am," she said stiffly.

"Did you have two cups of coffee with your dinner?" I inquired.

"No, ma'am," indignantly.

I sat up and almost upset my hot water. I always take a cup of hot water with a pinch of salt before I get up. It tones the stomach.

"Liddy Allen," I said, "stop combing that switch and tell me what is wrong with you."

Liddy heaved a sigh.

"Girl and woman," she said, "I've been with you twenty-five years, Miss Rachel, through good temper and bad—" The idea! and what I have taken from her in the way of sulks!—"but I guess I can't stand it any longer. My trunk's packed."

"Who packed it?" I asked, expecting from her tone to be told she had wakened to find it done by some ghostly hand.

"I did; Miss Rachel, you won't believe me when I tell you this house is haunted. Who was it fell down the clothes chute? Who was it scared Miss Louise almost into her grave?"

"I'm doing my best to find out," I said. "What in the world are you driving at?"

She drew a long breath. "There is a hole in the trunk-room wall, dug out since last night. It's big enough to put your head in, and the plaster's all over the place."

"Nonsense!" I said. "Plaster is always falling."

But Liddy merely looked superior.

"Just ask Alex," she said. "When he put the new cook's trunk there last night the wall was as smooth as this. This morning it's dug out, and there's plaster on the cook's trunk. Miss Rachel, you can get a dozen detectives and put one on every stair in the house, and you'll never catch anything. There's some things you can't handcuff."

Liddy was right. As soon as I could I went up to the trunk room, which was directly over my bedroom. The plan of the upper story of the house was like that of the second floor, generally speaking. But one end—over the east wing —had been left only roughly finished, the intention having been to convert it into a ballroom; and various storerooms, including a large airy linen room, opened from a long corridor like that on the second floor. And in the trunk room, as Liddy had said, was a fresh break in the plaster.

Not only in the plaster, but through the lathing the aperture extended. I reached into the opening, and three feet away, perhaps, I could touch the bricks of the partition wall. For some reason the architect in building the house had left a space there that struck me, even in the surprise of the discovery, as a considerable waste of room.

"You're sure the hole wasn't here yesterday?" I asked Liddy, whose expression was a mixture of satisfaction and alarm. In answer she pointed to the new cook's trunk—that necessary adjunct of the migratory domestic. The top was covered with fine white plaster, as was the floor. But there were no large pieces of mortar lying around, no bits of lathing. When I mentioned this to Liddy she merely raised her eyebrows. Being quite confident that the gap was of unholy origin, she did not concern herself with such trifles as a bit of mortar and lath. No doubt they were even then heaped neatly on a gravestone in the Casanova churchyard!

I brought Jamieson up to see the hole in the wall, directly after breakfast. His expression was very odd when he looked at it, and the first thing he did was to try to discover what object, if any, such a hole could have. He got a piece of candle, and by enlarging the aperture a little was able to examine what lay beyond. The result was nil. The trunk room, although heated by steam heat like the rest of the house, boasted of a fireplace and mantel as well. The opening had been made between the flue and the outer wall of the house. On inspection there was revealed, however, only the brick of the chimney on one side and the outer wall of the house on the other; in depth the space extended only to the flooring. The breach had been made about four feet from the floor, and inside were all the missing bits of plaster. It had been a methodical ghost.

It was very much of a disappointment. I had expected a secret room, at the very least, and I think even Jamieson had fancied he might at last have a clue to the mystery. There was evidently nothing more to be discovered. Liddy reported that everything was screne among the servants, and that none of them had been disturbed by the noise. The maddening thing, however, was that the nightly visitor had evidently more than one way of gaining access to the house, and we made arrangements to redouble our vigilance as to windows and doors that night.

Halsey was inclined to pooh-pooh the whole affair. He said a break in the plaster might have occurred months ago and gone unnoticed, and that the dust had probably been stirred up the day before. After all we had to let it go at that, but we put in an uncomfortable Sunday. Gertrude went to church, and Halsey took a long walk in the morning. Louise was able to sit up, and she allowed Halsey and Liddy to assist her downstairs late in the afternoon. The east veranda was shady, green with vines and plants, cheerful with cushions and lounging chairs. We put Louise in a steamer chair and she sat there passively enough, her hands clasped in her lap.

We were very silent. Halsey sat on the rail with a pipe, openly watching Louise as she looked broodingly across the valley to the hills. There was something baffling in the girl's eyes, and gradually Halsey's boyish features lost their glow at seeing her about again, and settled into grim lines. He was like his father just then.

We sat until late afternoon, Halsey growing more and more moody. Shortly before six he got up and went into the house, and in a few minutes he came out and called me to the telephone. It was Anna Whitcomb, in town, and she kept me for twenty minutes, telling me the children had had the measles, and how Madame Sweeny had botched her new gown. Only she used an *i* instead of an *o*.

When I finished Liddy was behind me, her mouth a thin line.

"I wish you would try to look cheerful, Liddy," I groaned. "Your face would sour milk." But Liddy seldom replied to my gibes. She folded her lips a little tighter.

"He called her up," she said oracularly. "He called her up, and asked her to keep you at the telephone, so he could talk to Miss Louise. A thankless child is sharper than a serpent's tooth."

"Nonsense!" I said brusquely. "I might have known enough to leave them. It's a long time since you and I were in love, Liddy, and I suppose we forget."

Liddy sniffed.

"No man ever made a fool of me," she replied virtuously.

"Well, something did," I retorted.

19

"MR. JAMIESON," I said, when we found ourselves alone after dinner that night, "the inquest yesterday seemed to me the merest recapitulation of things that were already known. It developed nothing new beyond Doctor Stewart's story, and that was volunteered."

"An inquest is only a necessary formality, Miss Innes," he replied. "Unless a crime is committed in the open, the inquest does nothing beyond getting evidence from witnesses while events are still in their minds. The police step in later. You and I both know how many important things never transpired. For instance, the dead man had no key, and yet Miss Gertrude testified to a fumbling at the lock and then the opening of the door. The piece of evidence you mention, Doctor Stewart's story, is one of those things we have to take cautiously. The doctor has a patient who wears black and does not raise her veil. So it is the typical mysterious lady! Then the good doctor comes across Arnold Armstrong, who was a graceless scamp—de mortuis, what's the rest of it?—and he is quarreling with a lady in black. Behold, says the doctor, they are one and the same."

"Why was Mr. Bailey not present at the inquest?"

The detective's expression was peculiar.

"Because his physician testified that he is ill, and unable to leave his bed."

"Ill!" I exclaimed. "Neither Halsey nor Gertrude has told me it was serious."

"There are more things than that, Miss Innes, that are puzzling. Bailey gives the impression that he knew nothing of the crash at the bank until he read it in the paper Monday night, and that he went back and surrendered himself immediately. I do not believe it. Jonas, the watchman at the Traders' Bank, tells a different story. He says that on the Thursday night before, about eight-thirty, Bailey went back to the bank. Jonas admitted him, and he says the cashier was in a state almost of collapse. Bailey worked until midnight, then he closed the vault and went away. The occurrence was so unusual that the watchman pondered over it all the rest of the night.

"Then what did Bailey do when he went back to the Knickerbocker Apartments that night? He packed a suitcase ready for instant departure. But he held off too long, waiting for something. My personal opinion is that he waited to see Miss Gertrude before getting out of the country. Then, when he had shot down Arnold Armstrong that night, he had to choose between two evils. He did the thing that would immediately turn public opinion in his favor, and surrendered himself as an innocent man. The strongest thing against him is his preparation for flight, and his deciding to come back after the murder of Arnold Armstrong. He was shrewd enough to disarm suspicion as to the graver charge."

The evening dragged along slowly. Mrs. Watson came to my bedroom before I went to bed and asked if I had any iodine. She showed me a badly swollen hand, with reddish streaks running up toward the elbow; she said it was the hand she had hurt the night of the murder a week before, and that she had not slept well since. It looked to me as if it might be serious, and I told her to let Doctor Stewart see it.

The next morning she went up to town on the eleven-o'clock train and was admitted to the Emergency Hospital, suffering from blood poisoning. I fully meant to go up and see her there, but other things later drove her entirely from my mind. I telephoned to the hospital that day, however, and ordered a private room for her and whatever comforts she might be allowed.

Mrs. Armstrong arrived Monday evening with her husband's body, and the services were set for the next day. The house on Chestnut Street in town had been opened, and Tuesday morning Louise left us to go home. She sent for me before she went, and I saw she had been crying.

"How can I thank you, Miss Innes?" she said. "You have taken me on faith, and you haven't asked me any questions. Sometime perhaps I can tell you. And when that time comes you will all despise me, Halsey too."

I tried to tell her how glad I was to have had her, but there was something else she wanted to say. She said it finally, when she had bade a constrained good-bye to Halsey and the car was waiting at the door.

"Miss Innes," she said in a low tone, "if they—if there is any attempt made to have you give up the house, do it if you possibly can. I'm afraid to have you stay."

I didn't like it. It was a definite warning, but if she knew what it was all about she should have told me. I wondered if Halsey had not made a mistake, after all. But I could do nothing. Gertrude went into town with her that day and saw her safely home. She reported a decided coolness in the greeting between Louise and her mother, and that Doctor Walker was there, apparently in charge of the arrangements for the funeral. Halsey disappeared shortly after Louise left and came home about nine that night, muddy and tired. As for Thomas, he went around dejected and sad, and I saw the detective watching him closely at dinner. Even now I wonder. What did Thomas know? What did he suspect?

At ten o'clock the household had settled down for the night. Liddy, who was taking Mrs. Watson's place, had finished examining the tea towels and the corners of the shelves in the refrigerator and had gone to bed. Alex, the gardener, had gone heavily up the circular staircase to his room, and Jamieson was examining the locks of the windows. Halsey dropped into a chair in the living room and stared moodily ahead. Once he roused.

"What sort of looking chap is Walker, Gertrude?" he asked.

"Rather tall, very dark. and smooth-shaven. Not bad-looking," Gertrude said, putting down the book she had been pretending to read. Halsey kicked a coffee table viciously.

"Lovely place this village must be in the winter," he said irrelevantly. "A girl would be buried alive here."

It was then someone rapped at the knocker on the heavy front door. Halsey got up leisurely and opened it, admitting Warner. He was out of breath from running, and he looked half abashed.

"I am sorry to disturb you," he said, "but I didn't know what else to do. It's about Thomas."

"What about Thomas?" I asked. Jamieson had come into the hall and we all stared at Warner.

"He's acting queer," Warner explained. "He's sitting down there on the edge of the porch, and he says he has seen a ghost. The old man looks bad, too. He can scarcely speak."

"He's as full of superstition as an egg is of meat," I said. "Halsey, bring some whisky and we will all go down."

He got a bottle from the side board in the dining room. Gertrude threw a shawl around my shoulders, and we all started down over the hill. I had made so many nocturnal excursions around the place that I knew my way perfectly. But Thomas was not on the veranda nor was he inside the house. The men exchanged significant glances, and Warner got a lantern.

"He can't have gone far," he said. "He was trembling so that he couldn't stand when I left."

Jamieson and Halsey together made the rounds of the lodge, occasionally calling the old man by name. But there was no response. No Thomas came, bowing and showing his white teeth through the darkness. I began to be vaguely uneasy for the first time. Gertrude, who was never nervous in the dark, outside, went alone down the drive to the gate and stood there looking along the yellowish line of the road, while I waited on the tiny veranda.

Warner was puzzled. He came around to the edge of the steps and stood looking at them as if they ought to know and explain.

"He might have stumbled into the house," he said, "but he couldn't have climbed the stairs. Anyhow, he's not inside or outside that I can see." The other members of the party had come back now, and no one had found any trace of the old man. His pipe, still warm, rested on the edge of the rail, and inside on the table his old gray hat showed that its owner had not gone far.

He was not far, after all. From the table my eyes traveled around the room, and stopped at the door of a closet. I hardly know what impulse moved me, but I went in and turned the knob. It burst open with the impetus of a weight behind it, and something fell partly forward in a heap on the floor. It was Thomas, Thomas without a mark of injury on him. And dead.

20

WARNER WAS on his knees in a moment, fumbling at the old man's collar to loosen it. But Halsey caught his hand.

"Let him alone," he said. "You can't help him. He's dead."

We stood there, each avoiding the other's eyes. We spoke low and reverently in the presence of death, and we tacitly avoided any mention of the suspicion that was in every mind. When Jamieson had finished his cursory examination he got up and dusted the knees of his trousers.

"There is no wound," he said, and I know I for one drew a long breath of relief. "From what Warner says and from his hiding in the closet, I should say he was scared to death. Fright and a weak heart, together."

"But what could have done it?" Gertrude asked. "He was all right this evening at dinner. Warner, what did he say when you found him on the porch?"

Warner looked shaken. His honest, boyish face was colorless.

"Just what I told you, Miss Innes. He'd been reading the paper downstairs. I had put up the car, and feeling sleepy I came down to the lodge to go to bed. As I went upstairs Thomas put down the paper and taking his pipe went out on the porch. Then I heard an exclamation from him."

"What did he say?" demanded Jamieson.

"I couldn't hear, but his voice was strange. It sounded startled. I waited for him to call out again, but he didn't, so I went downstairs. He was sitting on the porch step, looking straight ahead, as if he saw something among the trees across the road. And he kept mumbling about having seen a ghost. He looked queer and I tried to get him inside, but he wouldn't move. Then I thought I'd better go up to the house."

"Didn't he say anything else you could understand?" I asked.

"He said something about the grave giving up its dead."

Jamieson was going through the old man's pockets and Gertrude was composing his arms folding them across his white shirt bosom, always so spotless. Jamieson looked up at me.

"What was that you said to me, Miss Innes, about the murder at the house being a beginning and not an end? By Jove, I believe you were right!"

In the course of his investigations the detective had come to the inner pocket of the dead butler's black coat. Here he found some things that interested him. One was a small flat key with a red cord tied to it, and the other was a bit of white paper, on which was written something in Thomas's cramped hand. Jamieson read it: then he gave it to me. It was an address in fresh ink—

LUCIEN WALLACE, 14 Elm Street, Richfield.

As the card went around, I think both the detective and I watched for any possible effect it might have, but beyond perplexity there seemed to be none.

"Richfield!" Gertrude exclaimed. "Why, Elm Street is the main street; don't you remember, Halsey?"

"Lucien Wallace," Halsey said. "That is the child Stewart spoke of at the inquest."

Warner, with his mechanic's instinct, had reached for the key. What he said was not a surprise.

"Yale lock," he said. "Probably a key to the east entry."

There was no reason why Thomas, an old and trusted servant, should not have had a key to that particular door, although the servants' entry was in the west wing. But I had not known of this key, and it opened up a new field of conjecture. Just now, however, there were many things to be attended to, and leaving Warner with the body we all went back to the house. Jamieson walked with me, while Halsey and Gertrude followed.

"I suppose I shall have to notify the Armstrongs," I said. "They will know if Thomas had any people and how to reach them. Of course I expect to defray the expenses of the funeral, but his relatives must be found. What do you think frightened him, Mr. Jamieson?"

"It's hard to say," he replied slowly, "but I think we may be certain it *was* fright, and that he was hiding from something. I am sorry in more than one way. I have always believed that Thomas knew or suspected something that he wouldn't tell. Do you know how much money there was in that worn-out wallet of his? Nearly a hundred dollars! Almost two months' wages, yet those darkies seldom have a penny. Well, what Thomas knew will probably be buried with him."

Halsey suggested that the grounds be searched, but Jamieson vetoed the suggestion.

"You would find nothing," he said. "Anybody clever enough to get into Sunnyside and tear a hole in the wall while I watched downstairs is not to be found by going around the shrubbery with a lantern."

With the death of Thomas I felt that a climax had come in affairs at Sunnyside. The night that followed was quiet enough. Halsey watched at the foot of the staircase, and a complicated system of bolts on the other doors seemed to be effectual.

Once in the night I wakened and thought I heard the tapping again. But all was quiet, and I had reached the stage where I refused to be disturbed for minor occurrences.

The Armstrongs were notified of Thomas's death, and I had my first interview with Doctor Walker as a result. He came up early the next morning, just as we finished breakfast, in a professional-looking black car. I found him striding up and down the living room, and in spite of my preconceived dislike I had to admit that the man was presentable. A big fellow he was, tall and dark, as Gertrude had said, smooth-shaven and erect, with prominent features and a square jaw. He was painfully spruce in his appearance, and his manner was almost obtrusively apologetic.

"I must make a double excuse for this early visit, Miss Innes," he said as he sat down. The chair was lower than he expected, and his dignity required collecting before he went on. "My professional duties are urgent and long neglected, and"—a fall to the everyday manner—"something must be done about the butler's body."

"Yes," I said, sitting on the edge of my chair. "I merely wished the address of Thomas's people. You might have telephoned if you were busy."

He smiled.

"I wanted to see you about something else," he said. "As for Thomas, it is Mrs. Armstrong's wish that you allow her to attend to the expense. About his relatives, I have already notified his brother in the village. It was heart disease, I think. Thomas always had a bad heart."

"Heart disease and fright," I said, still on the edge of my chair. But the doctor had no intention of leaving.

"I understand you have a ghost up here, and that you have the house filled with detectives to exorcise it," he said, smiling faintly.

For some reason I felt I was being pumped, as Halsey says. "You have been misinformed," I replied.

"What, no ghost, no detectives!" he said, still with his smile. "What a disappointment to the village!"

I resented his attempt at playfulness. It had been anything but a joke to us.

"Doctor Walker," I said tartly, "I fail to see any humor in the situation. Since I came here one man has been shot and another one has died from shock. There have been intruders in the house and strange noises. If that is funny, there is something wrong with my sense of humor."

"You miss the point," he said, still good-naturedly. "The thing that is funny to me is that you insist on remaining here, under the circumstances. I should think nothing would keep you."

"You are mistaken. Everything that occurs only confirms my resolution to stay until the mystery is cleared."

"I have a message for you, Miss Innes," he said, rising at last. "Mrs. Armstrong asked me to thank you for your kindness to Louise, whose trip east, coming at the time it did, put her to great inconvenience. Also—and this is a delicate matter—she asked me to appeal to your natural sympathy for her at this time, and to ask you if you would not reconsider your decision about the house. Sunnyside is her home. She loves it dearly, and just now she wants to come here for quiet and peace."

"She must have had a change of heart," I said, ungraciously enough. "Louise told me her mother despised the place. Besides this is no place for quiet and peace just now. Anyhow, doctor, while I don't care to force an issue, I shall certainly remain here, for a time at least."

"For how long?" he asked.

"My lease is for six months. I shall stay until some explanation is found for certain things. My own family is involved now, and I shall do everything to clear the mystery of Arnold Armstrong's murder."

The doctor stood looking down, slapping his gloves thoughtfully against the palm of a well-looked-after hand.

"You say there have been intruders in the house?" he asked. "You are sure of that, Miss Innes?"

"Certain."

"In what part?"

"In the east wing."

"Can you tell me when these intrusions occurred, and what the purpose seemed to be? Was it robbery?"

"No," I said decidedly. "As to time, once on Friday night a week ago, again the following night, when Arnold Armstrong was murdered, and again last Friday night."

The doctor looked serious. He seemed to be debating some question in his mind, and to reach a decision.

"Miss Innes," he said, "I am in a peculiar position: I understand your attitude, of course; but do you think you are wise? Ever since you have come here there have been hostile demonstrations against you and your family. I'm not a croaker, but wouldn't it be safer to go back to town? To leave before anything occurs that will cause you lifelong regret."

"I am willing to take the responsibility," I said coldly. "Warnings don't scare me."

I think he gave me up then as a poor proposition. He asked to be shown where Arnold Armstrong's body had been found, and I took him there. He scrutinized the whole place carefully, examining the stairs and the lock. When he had taken a formal farewell I was confident of one thing. Doctor Walker would do anything he could to get me away from Sunnyside.

21

IT WAS MONDAY EVENING when we found the body of poor old Thomas. Monday night had been uneventful; things were quiet at the house and the peculiar circumstances of the old man's death had been carefully kept from the servants. Rosie took charge of the dining room and pantry, in the absence of a butler, and except for the warning of the Casanova doctor everything breathed of peace.

Affairs at the Traders' Bank were progressing slowly. The failure had hit small stockholders very hard, the minister of the little Methodist chapel in Casanova among them. He had received as a legacy from an uncle a few shares of stock in the Traders' Bank, and now his joy was turned to bitterness. He had to sacrifice everything he had in the world, and his feeling against Paul Armstrong, dead as he was, must have been bitter in the extreme. He was asked to officiate at the simple services when the dead banker's body was interred in Casanova churchyard, but the good man providentially took cold and a substitute was called in.

A few days after the services he called to see me, a kindly-faced little man in a shabby suit and an ancient tie. I think he was uncertain as to my connection with the Armstrong family, and dubious whether I considered Mr. Armstrong's taking away a matter for condolence or congratulation. He was not long in doubt.

I liked the little man. He had known Thomas well, and had promised to officiate at the services in the rickety African Zion Church. He told me more of himself than he knew, and before he left I astonished him—and myself, I admit—by promising a new carpet for his church. He was much affected, and I gathered that he had yearned over his ragged chapel as a mother over a half-clothed child.

"You are laying up treasure, Miss Innes," he said brokenly, "where neither moth nor rust corrupt, nor thieves break through and steal."

"It is certainly a safer place than Sunnyside," I admitted. And the thought of the carpet permitted him to smile. He stood just inside the doorway, looking from the luxury of the house to the beauty of the view.

"The rich ought to be good," he said wistfully. "They have so much that is beautiful, and beauty is ennobling. And yet while I ought to say nothing in view of this lovely spot, to him these trees and lawns were not the work of God. They were property, at so much an acre. He loved money, Miss Innes. He offered up everything to his golden calf. Not power, not ambition, was his fetish. It was money." Then he dropped his pulpit manner and turned to me with his engaging smile.

"In spite of all this luxury," he said, "the country people here have a saying that Mr. Paul Armstrong could sit on a dollar and see all around it. Unlike the summer people, he gave neither to the poor nor to the church. He loved money for its own sake."

"And there are no pockets in shrouds!" I said cynically.

I sent him home in the car, with a bunch of hothouse roses for his wife, and he was quite overwhelmed. As for me, I had a generous glow that was cheap at the price of a church carpet. I had received less gratification and less gratitude when I presented the new silver communion set to St. Barnabas.

I had a great many things to think about in those days. I made out a list of questions and possible answers, but I seemed only to be working around in a circle. I always ended where I began. The list was something like this:

Who had entered the house the night before the murder?

Thomas claimed it was Mr. Bailey, whom he had seen on the footpath, and who owned the pearl cuff link.

Why did Arnold Armstrong come back after he had left the house the night he was killed?

No answer. Was it on the mission Louise had mentioned?

Who admitted him?

Gertrude said she had locked the east entry. There was no key on the dead man or in the door. He must have been admitted from within, by someone who belonged there, or who had already arrived in the house.

Who had been locked in the clothes chute?

Someone unfamiliar with the house, obviously. Only two people were missing from the household, Rosie and Gertrude. Rosie had been at the lodge with Louise. Therefore—but was it Gertrude? Might it not have been the mysterious intruder again?

Who had accosted Rosie on the drive?

Again perhaps the nightly visitor. It seemed more likely someone who suspected a secret at the lodge. Was Louise under surveillance?

Who had passed Louise on the circular staircase?

Could it have been Thomas? The key to the east entry made this a possibility. But why was he there, if it was indeed he?

Who had made the hole in the trunk-room wall?

It was not merely vandalism. It had been done quietly and with deliberate purpose. If I had only known how to read the purpose of that gaping aperture, what I might have been saved in anxiety and mental strain!

Why had Louise left her people and come home to hide at the lodge?

There was no answer as yet to this, or to the next questions.

Why did both she and Doctor Walker warn us away from the house?

Who was Lucien Wallace?

What did Thomas see in the shadows the night he died?

What was the meaning of the subtle change in Gertrude?

Was Jack Bailey an accomplice or a victim in the looting of the Traders' Bank?

What all-powerful reason made Louise determine to marry Doctor Walker?

The examiners were still working on the books of the Traders' Bank, and it was probable that several weeks would elapse before everything was cleared up. The firm of expert accountants who had examined the books some two months before testified that every bond, every piece of valuable paper, was there at that time. It had been shortly after their examination that the president, who had been in bad health, had gone to California. Jack Bailey was still ill at the Knickerbocker, and in this as in other ways Gertrude's conduct puzzled me. She seemed indifferent, refused to discuss matters pertaining to the bank, and never to my knowledge either wrote to him or went to see him. Gradually I came to the conclusion that Gertrude, with the rest of the world, believed her lover guilty and although I believed it myself, for that matter, I was irritated by her indifference. Girls in my day did not meekly accept the public's verdict as to the man they loved.

But presently something occurred that made me think that under Gertrude's surface calm there was a seething flood of suppressed excitement.

Tuesday morning the detective made a careful search of the grounds, but he found nothing. In the afternoon he disappeared, and it was late that night when he came home. He said he would have to go back to the city the following day, and arranged with Halsey and Alex to guard the house.

Liddy came to me on Wednesday morning with her black silk apron held up like a bag, and her eyes big with virtuous wrath. It was the day of Thomas's funeral in the village, and Alex and I were in the conservatory cutting flowers for the old man's casket. Liddy is never so happy as when she is making herself wretched, and now her mouth drooped while her eyes were triumphant.

"I always said there were plenty of things going on here right under our noses that we couldn't see," she said, holding out her apron.

"I don't see with my nose," I remarked. "What have you got there?"

Liddy pushed aside a half dozen geranium pots, and in the space thus cleared she dumped the contents of her apron, a handful of tiny bits of paper. Alex had stepped back but I saw him watching her curiously.

"Wait a moment, Liddy," I said, "you have been going through the library paper basket again!"

Liddy was arranging her bits of paper with the skill of long practice and paid no attention.

"Did it ever occur to you," I went on, putting my hand over the scraps, "that when people tear up their correspondence it is for the express purpose of keeping it from being read?"

"If they wasn't ashamed of it they wouldn't take so much trouble, Miss Rachel," Liddy said oracularly. "More than that, with things happening every day, I consider it my duty. If you don't read and act on this, I shall give it to that Jamieson, and I'll venture he'll not go back to the city today."

That decided me. If the scraps had anything to do with the mystery, ordinary conventions had no value. So Liddy arranged the scraps, like working out a puzzle picture, and she did it with much the same eagerness. When it was finished she stepped aside while I read it.

"Wednesday night, nine o'clock. Bridge," I read aloud. Then, aware of Alex's stare, I turned on Liddy.

"Someone is to play bridge tonight at nine o'clock," I said. "Is that your business, or mine?"

Liddy was aggrieved. She was about to reply when I scooped up the pieces and left the conservatory.

"Now then," I said, when we got outside, "will you tell me why you choose to take Alex into your confidence? He's no fool. Do you suppose he thinks anyone in this house is going to play bridge tonight at nine o'clock, by appointment? I suppose you have shown it in the kitchen, and instead of my being able to slip down to the bridge tonight quietly and see who is there, the whole household will be going in a procession."

"Nobody knows it," Liddy said humbly. "I found it in the basket in Miss Gertrude's dressing room. Look at the back of the sheet." I turned over some of the scraps, and, sure enough, it was a blank deposit slip from the Traders' Bank. So Gertrude was going to meet Jack Bailey that night by the bridge! And I had thought he was ill! It hardly seemed like the action of an innocent man, this avoidance of daylight and of his fiancée's people. I decided to make certain by going to the bridge that night.

After luncheon Jamieson suggested that I go with him to Richfield, and I consented.

"I am inclined to place more faith in Doctor Stewart's story," he said, "since I found that scrap in old Thomas's pocket. It bears out the statement that the woman with the child and the woman who quarreled with young Armstrong are the same. It looks as if Thomas had stumbled onto some affair that was more or less discreditable to the dead man, and out of loyalty to the family had kept it to himself. Then, you see, your story about the woman at the cardroom window begins to mean something. It is the nearest approach to anything tangible that we have had yet."

Warner took us to Richfield in the car. It was about twenty-five miles by railroad, but by taking a series of atrociously rough short cuts we got there very quickly. It was a pretty little town on the river, and back on the hill I could see the Mortons' big country house, where Halsey and Gertrude had been staying until the night of the murder.

Elm Street was almost the only street and number fourteen was easily found. It was a small white house, dilapidated without having gained anything picturesque, with a bay window and a porch only a foot or so above the bit of lawn. There was a baby carriage in the path, and from a swing at the side came the sound of conflict. Three small children were disputing vociferously, and a faded young woman with a kindly face was trying to hush the clamor. When she saw us she untied her gingham apron and came around to the porch.

"Good afternoon," I said. Jamieson lifted his hat, without speaking. "I came to inquire about a child named Lucien Wallace."

"I'm glad you've come," she said. "In spite of the other children I think the little fellow is lonely. We thought perhaps his mother would be here today."

Jamieson stepped forward.

"You are Mrs. Tate?" I wondered how the detective knew.

"Yes, sir."

"Mrs. Tate, we want to make some inquiries. Perhaps in the house—"

"Come right in," she said hospitably. And soon we were in the little shabby parlor, exactly like a thousand of its type. Mrs. Tate sat uneasy, her hands folded in her lap.

"How long has Lucien been here?" Mr. Jamieson asked.

"Since a week ago last Friday. His mother paid one week's board in advance; the other has not been paid."

"Was he ill when he came?"

"No, sir, not what you'd call sick. He was getting better of typhoid, she said, and he's picking up fine."

"Will you tell me his mother's name and address?"

"That's the trouble," the young woman said, frowning. "She gave her name as Mrs. Wallace, and she said she had no address. She was looking for a boardinghouse in town. She said she worked in a department store and couldn't take care of the child properly, and he needed fresh air and milk. I had three children of my own, and one more didn't make much difference in the work. But I wish she would pay this week's board."

"Did she say what store it was?"

"No, sir, but all the boy's clothes came from King's. They're far too good for the country."

There was a chorus of shouts and shrill yells from the front door, followed by the loud stamping of children's feet and a throaty "whoa, whoa!" Into the room came a tandem team of two chubby youngsters, a boy and a girl, harnessed with a clothesline and driven by a laughing boy of about seven in tan overalls. The small driver caught my attention at once. He was a beautiful child, and although he showed traces of recent severe illness his skin had now the clear transparency of health.

"Whoa, Flinders," he shouted. "You're goin' to smash the wagon."

Jamieson coaxed him over by holding out a lead pencil, striped blue and yellow.

"Now then," he said, when the boy had taken the lead pencil and was testing its usefulness on the detective's cuff, "I'll bet you don't know what your name is!"

"I do," said the boy. "Lucien Wallace."

"Great! And what's your mother's name?"

"Mother, of course. What's your mother's name?" And he pointed to me! I am going to stop wearing black. It doubles a woman's age.

"And where did you live before you came here?" Jamieson was polite enough not to smile.

"Grossmutter," he said. And I saw Jamieson's eyebrows go up.

"German," he commented. "Well, young man, you don't seem to know much about yourself."

"I've tried it all week," Mrs. Tate broke in. "The boy knows a word or two of German, but he doesn't know where he lived or anything about himself."

Jamieson wrote something on a card and gave it to her.

"Mrs. Tate," he said, "I want you to do something. Here is some money for the telephone call. The instant the boy's mother appears here call up that number and ask for the person whose name is there. You can run across to the drugstore on an errand and do it quietly. Just say, 'The lady has come.'"

"'The lady has come,'" repeated Mrs. Tate. "Very well, sir, and I hope it will be soon. The milk bill alone is almost double what it was."

"How much is the child's board?" I asked.

"Seven dollars a week, including his washing."

"Very well," I said. "Now, Mrs. Tate, I'm going to pay last week's board and a week in advance. If the mother comes, she is to know nothing of this visit. Absolutely not a word. And in return for your silence you may use this extra money for something for your own children."

Her tired, faded face lighted up and I saw her glance at the little Tates' small feet. Shoes, I divined, the feet of the genteel poor being almost as expensive as their stomachs.

As we went back Jamieson made only one remark. I think he was laboring under the weight of a great disappointment.

"Is King's a children's outfitting place?" he asked.

"Not especially. It's a general department store."

He was silent after that, but he went to the telephone as soon as we got home and called up King and Company, in the city. After a time he got the general manager, and they talked for some time. When Mr. Jamieson hung up the receiver he turned to me.

"The plot thickens," he said with his ready smile. "There are four women named Wallace at King's, none of them married, and none over twenty. I think I shall go up to the city tonight. I want to go to the Children's Hospital. But before I go, Miss Innes, I wish you would be more frank with me than you have been yet. I want you to show me the revolver you picked up in the tulip bed."

So he had known all along!

"It was a revolver, Mr. Jamieson," I admitted, cornered at last, "but I can't show it to you. It is not in my possession."

22

AT DINNER THAT NIGHT Jamieson suggested sending a man out in his place for a couple of days, but Halsey was certain there would be nothing more, and felt that he and Alex could manage the situation. The detective went back to town early in the evening and by nine o'clock Halsey, who had been playing golf, as a man does anything to take his mind away from trouble, was sleeping soundly on the big davenport in the living room.

I sat and knitted, pretending not to notice when Gertrude got up and wandered out into the starlight. As soon as I was satisfied that she had gone, however, I went out cautiously. I had no intention of eavesdropping, but I wanted to be certain that it was Jack Bailey she was meeting. Too many things had occurred in which Gertrude was or appeared to be involved to allow anything to be left in question.

I went slowly across the lawn, skirted the hedge to a break not far from the lodge, and found myself on the open road. Perhaps a hundred feet to the left the path led across the valley to the Country Club, and only a little way off was the footbridge over Casanova Creek. But just as I was about to turn down the path I heard steps coming toward me, and I shrank into the bushes. It was Gertrude, going back quickly toward the house.

I was surprised. I waited until she had had time to get almost to the house before I started. And then I stepped back again into the shadows. The reason why Gertrude had not kept her tryst was evident. Leaning on the parapet of the bridge in the moonlight and smoking a pipe was Alex, the gardener. I could have throttled Liddy for her carelessness in reading the torn note where he could hear. And I could cheerfully have choked Alex to death for his interference.

But there was no help for it. I turned and followed Gertrude slowly back to the house.

The frequent invasions of the house had effectually prevented any relaxation after dusk. We had redoubled our vigilance as to bolts and window locks, but as Jamieson had suggested we allowed the door at the east entry to remain as before, locked by the Yale lock only. To provide only one possible entrance for the invader, and to keep a constant guard in the dark at the foot of the circular staircase, seemed to be the only method.

In the absence of the detective Alex and Halsey arranged to change off, Halsey to be on duty from ten to two and Alex from two until six. Each man was armed, and as an additional precaution the one off duty slept in a room near the head of the circular staircase and kept his door open, to be ready for emergency.

These arrangements were carefully kept from the servants, who were only commencing to sleep at night and who retired one and all with barred doors and lamps that burned until morning.

The house was quiet again Wednesday night. It was almost a week since Louise had encountered someone on the stairs, and it was four days since the discovery of the hole in the trunk-room wall. Arnold Armstrong and his father rested side by side in the Casanova churchyard, and at the Zion African Church on the hill a new mound marked the last resting place of poor Thomas.

Louise was with her mother in town, and beyond a polite note of thanks to me we had heard nothing from her. Doctor Walker had taken up his practice again, and we saw him now and then flying along the road, always at top speed. The murder of Arnold Armstrong was still unsolved, and I remained firm in the position I had taken—to stay at Sunnyside until the thing was at least partly cleared up.

Yet for all its quiet it was on Wednesday night that perhaps the boldest attempt was made to enter the house. On Thursday afternoon the laundress sent word she would like to speak to me, and I saw her in my private sitting room, a small room beyond the dressing room.

MaryAnne was embarrassed. She had rolled down her sleeves and tied a white apron around her waist, and she stood making folds in it with fingers that were red and shiny from soapsuds.

"Well, Mary," I said encouragingly, "what's the matter? Don't dare to tell me the soap is out."

"No, ma'am, Miss Innes." She had a nervous habit of looking first at my one eye and then at the other, her own optics shifting ceaselessly, right eye, left eye, right eye, until I found myself doing the same thing. "No, ma'am. I was askin' did you want the ladder left up the clothes chute?"

"The what?" I screeched, and was sorry the next minute. Seeing her suspicions were verified, MaryAnne had gone white, and stood with her eyes shifting more wildly than ever.

"There's a ladder up the clothes chute, Miss Innes," she said. "It's up that tight I can't move it, and I didn't like to ask for help until I spoke to you."

It was useless to dissemble; MaryAnne knew now as well as I did that the ladder had no business to be there. I did the best I could, however. I put her on the defensive at once.

"Then you didn't lock the laundry last night?"

"I locked it tight, and put the key in the kitchen on its nail."

"Very well, then you forgot a window."

MaryAnne hesitated.

"Yes'm," she said at last. "I thought I locked them all, but there was one open this morning."

I went out of the room and down the hall, followed by MaryAnne. The door into the clothes chute was securely bolted, and when I opened it I saw the evidence of the woman's story. A pruning ladder had been brought from where it had lain against the stable and now stood upright in the clothes shaft, its end resting against the wall between the first and second floors.

I turned to MaryAnne.

"This is due to your carelessness," I said. "If we had all been murdered in our beds it would have been your fault." She shivered. "Now, not a word of this through the house, and send Alex to me."

The effect on Alex was to make him apoplectic with rage, and with it all I fancied there was an element of satisfaction. As I look back so many things are plain to me that I wonder I could not see at the time. It is all known now, and yet the whole thing was so remarkable that perhaps my stupidity was excusable.

Alex leaned down the chute and examined the ladder carefully.

"It's caught," he said with a grim smile. "The fools, to have left a warning like that! The only trouble is, Miss Innes, they won't be apt to come back for a while."

"I shouldn't regard that in the light of a calamity," I replied dryly.

Until late that evening Halsey and Alex worked at the chute. They got down the ladder at last and put a new bolt on the door. As for myself, I sat and wondered if I had a deadly enemy, intent on my destruction.

I was growing more and more alarmed. Liddy had given up all pretense at bravery and slept regularly in my dressing room on the couch, with a prayer book and a game knife from the kitchen under her pillow, thus preparing for both the natural and the supernatural. And that was the way things stood that Thursday night, when I myself took a hand in the struggle.

23

ABOUT NINE O'CLOCK that night Liddy came into the living room and reported that one of the housemaids declared she had seen two men slip around the corner of the stable. Gertrude had been sitting staring in front of her, jumping at every sound. Now she turned on Liddy pettishly.

"Good heavens, Liddy," she said, "you're a bundle of nerves. What if Eliza did see some men around the stable? It may have been Warner and Alex."

"Warner is in the kitchen, miss," Liddy said, with dignity. "And if you had come through what I have you would be a bundle of nerves, too. Miss Rachel, I'd be thankful if you'd give me my month's wages tomorrow. I'll be going to my sister's."

"Very well," I said, to her evident amazement. "I will make out the check. Warner can take you down to the noon train."

Liddy's face was really funny.

"You'll have a nice time at your sister's," I went on. "Five children, hasn't she?"

"That's it," Liddy said, suddenly bursting into tears. "Send me away after all these years, and your new bathrobe only half done, and nobody knowin' how to fix the water for your bath."

"It's time I learned to prepare my own bath." I was knitting complacently. But Gertrude got up and put her arms around Liddy's shaking shoulders.

"You are two big babies," she said soothingly. "Neither one of you could get along for an hour without the other. So stop quarreling and be good. Liddy, go right up and lay out Aunty's night things. She is going to bed early."

After Liddy had gone I began to think about the men at the stable, and I grew more and more anxious. Halsey was aimlessly knocking the billiard balls around in the billiard room, and I called to him.

"Halsey," I said when he sauntered in, "is there a policeman in Casanova?"

"Constable," he said laconically. "Veteran of the war, one arm. In office to conciliate the Legion crowd. Why?"

"Because I'm uneasy tonight." And I told him what Liddy had said. "Is there anyone you can think of who could be relied on to watch the outside of the house tonight?"

"We might get Sam Bohannon from the club," he said thoughtfully. "It wouldn't be a bad scheme. He's a smart darky, and with his mouth shut and his shirt front covered you couldn't see him a yard off in the dark."

Halsey conferred with Alex, and the result in an hour was Sam. His instructions were simple. There had been numerous attempts to break into the house. It was the intention, not to drive intruders away, but to capture them. If Sam saw anything suspicious outside he was to tap at the east entry, where Alex and Halsey were to alternate in keeping watch through the night.

It was with a comfortable feeling of security that I went to bed that night. The door between Gertrude's rooms and mine had been opened, and, with the doors into the hall bolted, we were safe enough. Although Liddy persisted in her belief that doors would prove no obstacles to our disturbers.

As before, Halsey watched the east entry from ten until two. He had an eye to comfort and he kept vigil in a heavy oak chair, very large and deep. We went upstairs rather early, and through the open door Gertrude and I kept up a running fire of conversation. Liddy was brushing my hair and Gertrude was doing her own, with a long free sweep of her strong young arms.

"Did you know Mrs. Armstrong and Louise are in the village?" she called.

"No," I replied, startled. "How did you hear it?"

"I met the oldest Stewart girl today, the doctor's daughter, and she told me they hadn't gone back to town after the funeral. They went directly to that little yellow house next to Doctor Walker's and are apparently settled there. They took the house furnished for the summer."

"Why, it's a bandbox," I said. "I can't imagine Fanny Armstrong in such a place."

"It's true, just the same. Ella Stewart says Mrs. Armstrong has aged terribly and looks as if she is hardly able to walk."

I lay and thought over some of these things until midnight. The electric lights went out then, blinking once or twice in warning before they died entirely and we were embarked on the darkness of another night.

Apparently only a few minutes had elapsed, during which my eyes were becoming accustomed to the darkness, when I noticed that the windows were reflecting a faint pinkish light. Liddy noticed it at the same time and I heard her jump up. At that moment Sam's deep voice boomed from somewhere just below.

"Fire!" he yelled. "The stable's on fire!"

I could see him on the drive, and a moment later Halsey joined him. Alex was awake and running down the stairs, and in five minutes from the time the fire was discovered three of the maids were sitting on their trunks in the drive, although excepting a few sparks there was no fire nearer than a hundred yards.

Gertrude seldom loses her presence of mind, and she had gone to the telephone. But by the time the Casanova volunteer fire department came toiling up the hill the stable was a furnace, with the car safe but blistered in the road. Some gasoline cans exploded just as the volunteer department got to work, which shook their nerves as well as the burning building.

The stable, being on a hill, was a torch to attract the population from every direction. Rumor had it that Sunnyside was burning, and it was amazing how many people threw something over their night clothes and rushed to the excitement. I take it Casanova has few fires and Sunnyside was furnishing the people, in one way and another, the greatest excitements they had had for years.

The stable was off the west wing, and I hardly know how I came to think of the circular staircase and the unguarded door at its foot. Liddy was putting my clothes into sheets preparatory to tossing them out the window when I found her, and I could hardly persuade her to stop.

"I want you to come with me, Liddy," I said. "Bring a candle and a couple of blankets."

She lagged behind considerably when she saw me making for the east wing, and at the top of the staircase she balked.

"I am not going down," she said firmly.

"There is no one guarding the door there," I explained. "Who knows? This may be a scheme to draw everybody away from this end of the house and let someone in here."

The instant I had said it I was convinced I had hit on the explanation, and that perhaps it was already too late. It seemed to me as I listened that I heard stealthy footsteps on the east porch, but there was so much shouting outside that it was impossible to tell. Liddy was on the point of retreat.

"Very well," I said. "Then I shall go down alone. Run back to Mr. Halsey's room and get his revolver. But don't shoot down the stairs if you hear a noise. Remember I'll be down there. And hurry."

I put the candle on the floor at the top of the staircase and took off my bedroom slippers. Then I crept down the stairs, going very slowly and listening with all my ears. I was keyed to such a pitch that I felt no fear. Like the condemned who sleep and eat the night before execution, I was no longer able to suffer apprehension. I was past that. Just at the foot of the stairs I stubbed my toe against Halsey's big chair, and had to stand on one foot in a soundless agony until the pain subsided to a dull ache. And then I knew I was right. Someone had put a key into the lock, and was turning it. For some reason it refused to work, and the key was withdrawn. There was a muttering of voices outside, and I had only a second. Another trial and the door would open. The candle above made a faint gleam down the well-like staircase, and at that moment with only a second to spare I thought of a plan.

The heavy oak chair almost filled the space between the newel post and the door. With a crash I turned it on its side and wedged it against the door, its legs against the stairs. I could hear a faint scream from Liddy at the crash, and then she came down the stairs on a run, with the revolver held straight out in front of her.

"Thank God," she said, in a shaking voice. "I thought it was you."

I pointed to the door, and she understood.

"Call Mr. Halsey or Alex, out the windows at the other end of the house," I whispered. "Run. Tell them not to wait for anything."

She went up the stairs at that, two at a time. Evidently she collided with the candle, for it went out and I was left in darkness.

I was really astonishingly cool. I remember stepping over the chair and gluing my ear to the door, and I shall never forget feeling it give an inch or two there in the darkness, under a steady pressure from without. But the chair held, although I could hear an ominous cracking of one of the legs. Then without the slightest warning the cardroom window broke with a crash. I had my finger on the trigger of the revolver, and as I jumped it went off, right through the door. Someone outside swore roundly, and for the first time I could hear what was said.

"I'm getting the hell out of here," someone was saying.

"Did it get you?"

"Only a scratch."

Evidently they had abandoned the door and were moving toward the broken window. There was some argument I could not hear. Then as I looked into the cardroom a small man put his leg over the sill and stepped cautiously inside. I fired again, and something that was glass or china crashed to the ground. But I had not hit him. In the darkness he was moving steadily toward me, and I thought he had a gun in his hand.

It was time for retreat and I knew it. I don't recall running up the circular staircase. I must have, however, for I found Gertrude standing there looking ready to faint. Certainly I cut a peculiar figure, in my bare feet and dressing gown, with a gun in my hand. But I had no time to talk. There was the sound of footsteps in the lower hall, and someone came running up the stairs in the dark.

I had gone berserk, I think. I leaned over the stair rail and fired again. And Halsey below yelled at me.

"What are you doing up there?" he yelped. "You missed me by an inch."

"They're in the house," I managed to say. "In the cardroom."

After that I disgraced myself by fainting for the first time in my life. When I came around Liddy was rubbing my temples with hair tonic and the search was in full blast.

The men were gone. The stable burned to the ground that night, while the crowd shrieked at every falling rafter and the volunteer fire department sprayed it with a garden hose. And in the house Alex and Halsey searched every corner of the lower floor, finding no one.

The truth of my story was shown by the broken window and the overturned chair. That the man I had seen had got upstairs was almost impossible. He had not used the main staircase, there was no way to the upper floor in the east wing, and Liddy had been at the window in the west wing where the servants' stair went up. But we did not go to bed at all. Sam Bohannon and Warner helped in the search, and not a closet escaped scrutiny. Even the cellars were given a thorough overhauling without result. The door in the east entry had a hole through it where my bullet had gone, and there were a few drops of blood there. The hole slanted downward and the bullet was embedded in the porch.

"Somebody will walk lame," Halsey said, when he had marked the course of the bullet. "It's too low to have hit anything but a leg or foot."

From that time on I watched every person I met for a limp, and to this day the man who halts in his walk is an object of suspicion to me. But Casanova had no lame men. The nearest approach to it was an old fellow who tended the safety gates at the railroad, and he, I learned on inquiry, had an artificial leg. Our man had gone, and the large and expensive stable at Sunnyside was a heap of smoking rafters and charred boards. Warner swore the fire was incendiary, and in view of the attempt to enter the house there seemed to be no doubt of it.

24

I F H A L S E Y had only taken me fully into his confidence throughout the whole affair, it would have been much simpler. If he had been altogether frank about Jack Bailey, and if the day after the fire he had told me what he suspected, there would have been no further harrowing period for all of us. But young people refuse to profit by the experience of their elders, and sometimes the elders are the ones to suffer.

I was much used up the day after the fire, and Gertrude insisted on my going out for some fresh air. The car was temporarily out of commission, and she finally got a trap from the Casanova liveryman. But just as we turned from the drive into the road we passed a woman. She had put down a small valise and stood inspecting the house and grounds minutely. I should hardly have noticed her had it not been for the fact that she had been horribly disfigured by what looked like burns.

"Ugh!" Gertrude said, when we had passed. "What a face! I shall dream of it tonight. Get up, Flinders."

"Flinders?" I asked. "Is that the horse's name?"

"It is." She flicked the horse's stubby mane with the whip. It was a long time since she had driven a horse and she was enjoying it. "He didn't look like a livery horse, and the liveryman said he had bought him from the Armstrongs when they purchased a couple of cars and did away with their stable. Nice Flinders, good old boy!"

Flinders was certainly not a common name for a horse, and yet the youngster at Richfield had named his prancing, curly-haired little horse Flinders. It set me thinking.

At my request Halsey had already sent word of the fire to the agent from whom we had secured the house. Also, he had called Jamieson by telephone, and somewhat guardedly had told him of the previous night's events. Jamieson had promised to come out that night, and to bring another man with him. I did not consider it necessary to notify Mrs. Armstrong, in the village. She certainly knew of the fire, and in view of my refusal to give up the house an interview would probably have been unpleasant enough. But as we passed Doctor Walker's white-and-green house I thought of something.

"Stop here, Gertrude," I said. "I am going to get out."

"To see Louise?" she asked.

"No, I want to ask this young Walker something."

She was curious, I knew, but I did not wait to explain. I went up the walk to the house, where a brass sign at the side announced the office, and went in. The reception room was empty, but from the consulting room beyond came the sound of two voices, not very amicable.

"It's an outrageous figure," someone was storming. Then the doctor's quiet tone, evidently not arguing, merely stating something. But I had no time to listen to some person probably disputing his bill, so I coughed. The voices ceased at once. A door closed somewhere, and the doctor entered from the hall of the house. He looked sufficiently surprised at seeing me.

"Good afternoon, doctor," I said formally. "I shall not keep you from your patient. I wish merely to ask you a question."

"Won't you sit down?"

"It won't be necessary. Doctor, has anyone come to you, either early this morning or today, to have you treat a bullet wound?"

"Nothing so startling has happened to me," he said, smiling. "A bullet wound! Things must be lively at Sunnyside."

"I didn't say it was at Sunnyside. But as it happens it was. If any such case comes to you will it be too much trouble for you to let me know?"

"I shall be only too happy," he said. "I understand you have had a fire up there too. A fire and a shooting in one night is rather lively for a quiet place like that."

"It's as quiet as a boiler room," I replied, as I turned to go.

"And you are still going to stay?"

"Until I am burned out," I responded. Then on my way down the steps I turned around suddenly.

"Doctor," I asked at a venture, "have you ever heard of a child named Lucien Wallace?"

Clever as he was his face changed and stiffened. He was on his guard again in a moment.

"Lucien Wallace?" he repeated. "No, I think not. There are plenty of Wallaces around, but I don't know any Lucien."

I was as certain as possible that he did. People do not lie readily to me, and this man lied beyond a doubt. But there was nothing to be gained now. His defenses were up and I left, half irritated and wholly baffled.

Our reception was entirely different at Doctor Stewart's. Taken into the bosom of the family at once, Flinders tied outside and nibbling the grass at the roadside, Gertrude and I drank some homemade elderberry wine and told briefly of the fire. Of the more serious part of the night's experience, of course, we said nothing. But when at last we had left the family on the porch and the doctor was untying our steed I asked him the same question I had put to Doctor Walker.

"Shot!" he said. "Bless my soul, no. Why, what have you been doing up at the big house, Miss Innes?"

"Someone tried to enter the house during the fire, and was shot and slightly injured," I said hastily. "Please don't mention it. We want to make as little of it as possible."

There was one other possibility, and we tried that. At Casanova station I saw the stationmaster, and asked him if any trains left Casanova between one o'clock and daylight. There was none until six A.M. The next question, however, required more diplomacy.

"Did you notice on the six-o'clock train any person, any man, who limped a little?" I asked. "Please try to remember: we are trying to trace a man who was seen loitering around Sunnyside last night before the fire."

He was all attention in a moment.

"I was up there myself at the fire," he said volubly. "I'm a member of the volunteer company. First big fire we've had since the summerhouse burned over to the club golf links. My wife was sayin' the other day, 'Dave, you

might as well 'a' saved the money you spent on that there helmet and shirt.'
And here last night they came in handy. Blew that siren so hard I hadn't
time scarcely to get 'em on."

"And did you see a man who limped?" Gertrude put in as he stopped
for breath.

"Not at the train, ma'am," he said. "No such person got on here today.
But I'll tell you where I did see a man that limped. I didn't wait till the fire
company left. There's a fast freight goes through at four forty-five and I
had to get down to the station. I seen there wasn't much more to do anyhow
at the fire—we'd got the flames under control—" Gertrude looked at me and
smiled—"so I started down the hill. There was folks here and there goin'
home, and along by the path to the Country Club I seen two men. One was
a short fellow. He was sitting on a big rock, his back to me, and he had
something white in his hand, as if he was tying up his foot. After I'd gone on
a piece I looked back, and he was hobbling on and—excuse me, miss—he was
swearing something sickening."

"Did they go toward the club?" Gertrude asked suddenly, leaning forward.

"No, miss. I think they came into the village. I didn't get a look at their
faces, but I know every chick and child in the place and everybody knows
me. When they didn't shout at me—in my uniform, you know—I took it they
were strangers."

So all we had for our afternoon's work was this: someone had been shot
by the bullet that went through the door, he had not left the village by
train, and he had not called in a physician. Also, Doctor Walker knew who
Lucien Wallace was, and his very denial made me confident that in that one
direction at least we were on the right track.

The thought that the detective would be there that night was the most
cheering thing of all, and I think even Gertrude was glad of it. Driving home
that afternoon I saw her in the clear sunlight for the first time in several
days, and I was startled to see how thin she looked. She was colorless too,
and all her bright animation was gone.

"Gertrude," I said, "I have been a very selfish old woman. You are going
to leave this miserable house tonight. Annie Morton is going to Scotland
next week, and you are going with her."

To my surprise she flushed painfully.

"I don't want to go, Aunt Ray," she said. "Don't make me leave now."

"You're losing your health and your good looks," I said decidedly. "You
should have a change."

"I shan't stir a foot." She was equally decided. Then, more lightly: "You
and Liddy need me to arbitrate between you every day in the week."

Perhaps I was growing suspicious of everyone, but it seemed to me that
Gertrude's gaiety was forced and artificial. I watched her covertly during
the rest of the drive, and I did not like the two spots of crimson in her pale
cheeks. But I said nothing more about sending her to Scotland. I knew she
would not go.

25

THAT DAY was destined to be an eventful one, for when I entered the house and found Eliza the cook ensconced in the upper hall on a chair, with MaryAnne doing her best to stifle her with household ammonia and Liddy rubbing her wrists—whatever good that is supposed to do—I knew that the ghost had been walking again, this time in daylight.

Eliza was in a frenzy of fear. She clutched at my sleeves when I went close to her and refused to let go until she had told her story. Coming just after the fire, the household was demoralized, and it was no surprise to me to find Alex and the undergardener struggling down the stairs with a heavy trunk between them.

"I didn't want to do it, Miss Innes," Alex said. "But she was so excited I was afraid she would do as she said, drag it down herself and scratch the staircase."

I was trying to get my hat off and to keep the women quiet at the same time. "Now, Eliza, when you have washed your face and stopped bawling," I said, "come into my sitting room and tell me what has happened."

Liddy put away my things without speaking. The very set of her shoulders expressed disapproval.

"Well," I said, when the silence became uncomfortable, "things seem to be warming up."

Silence from Liddy, and a long sigh.

"If Eliza goes, I don't know where to look for another cook." More silence.

"Rosie is probably a good cook." Sniff.

"Liddy," I said at last, "don't dare to deny that you are having the time of your life. You positively gloat in this excitement. You never looked better. It's my opinion all this running around and getting jolted out of a rut has stirred up that torpid liver of yours."

"It's not myself I'm thinking about," she said, goaded into speech. "Maybe my liver was torpid and maybe it wasn't. But I know this. I've got some feelings left, and to see you standing at the foot of that staircase shootin' through the door—I'll never be the same woman again."

"Well, I'm glad of that. Anything for a change," I said coldly. And in came Eliza, flanked by Rosie and MaryAnne.

Her story, broken with sobs and corrections from the other two, was this: At two o'clock (two-fifteen, Rosie insisted) she had gone upstairs to get a picture from her room to show MaryAnne. (A picture of a lady, MaryAnne interposed.) She went up the servants' staircase and along the corridor to her room, which lay between the trunk room and the unfinished ballroom. She heard a sound as she went down the corridor, like someone moving furniture, but she was not nervous. She thought it might be men examining the house after the fire the night before, but she looked in the trunk room and saw nobody.

She went into her room quietly. The noise had ceased, and everything was quiet. Then she sat down on the side of her bed, and, feeling faint—she was subject to spells—("I told you that when I came, didn't I, Rosie?" "Yes'm, indeed she did!")—she put her head down on her pillow and—

"Took a nap. All right!" I said. "Go on."

"When I came to, Miss Innes, sure as I'm sittin' here I thought I'd die. Somethin' hit me on the face and I set up, sudden-like. And then I seen the plaster drop, droppin' from a little hole in the wall. And the first thing I knew an iron bar that long" (fully two yards by her measure) "shot through that hole and tumbled on the bed. If I'd been still sleeping" ("Fainting," corrected Rosie) "I'd 'a' been hit on the head and killed!"

"I wisht you'd heard her scream," put in MaryAnne. "And her face as white as a pillow slip when she tumbled down the stairs."

"No doubt there is some natural explanation for it, Eliza," I said. "You may have dreamed it, for one thing. But if it is true, the metal rod and the hole in the wall will show it."

Eliza looked a little bit sheepish.

"The hole's there all right, Miss Innes," she said. "But the bar was gone when MaryAnne and Rosie went up to pack my trunk."

"That wasn't all." Liddy's voice came funereally from a corner. "Eliza said that from the hole in the wall a burning eye looked down at her!"

"The wall must be at least six inches thick," I said with asperity. "Unless the person who drilled the hole carried an eye on the ends of a stick Eliza couldn't possibly have seen it."

But the fact remained, and a visit to Eliza's room proved it. I might jeer all I wished. Someone had drilled a hole in the unfinished wall of the ballroom passing between the bricks of the partition, and meeting the unresisting plaster of Eliza's room had sent the rod flying onto her bed. I had gone upstairs alone, and I confess the thing puzzled me. In two or three places in the wall small apertures had been made, none of them of any depth. But not the least mysterious thing was the disappearance of the iron implement that had been used.

I remembered a story I read once about an impish dwarf that lived in the spaces between the double walls of an ancient castle. I wondered vaguely if my original idea of a secret entrance to a hidden chamber could be right after all, and if we were housing some erratic guest who played pranks on us in the dark, and destroyed the walls so that he might listen, hidden safely away, to our amazed investigations.

MaryAnne and Eliza left that afternoon, but Rosie decided to stay. It was about five o'clock when the taxi came from the station to get them, and, to my amazement it had an occupant. Matthew Geist, the driver, asked for me and explained his errand with pride.

"I've brought you a cook, Miss Innes," he said. "When the message came to come up for two girls and their trunks I supposed there was something doing, and as this here woman had been looking for work in the village I thought I'd bring her along."

Already I had acquired the true suburbanite ability to take servants on faith. I no longer demanded written and unimpeachable references. I, Rachel Innes, have learned not to mind if the cook sits down comfortably in my sitting room when she is taking the orders for the day, and to be grateful if the silver is not cleaned with scouring soap. So that day I merely told Liddy to send the new applicant in. When she came, however, I could hardly restrain a gasp of surprise. It was the woman with the scarred face.

She stood somewhat awkwardly just inside the door, but she had an air of self-confidence that was inspiring. Yes, she could cook. She was not a fancy cook, but she could make good soups and desserts if there was anyone to take charge of the salads. And so in the end I took her. As Halsey said when we told him, it didn't matter much about the cook's face if only it was clean.

I have spoken of Halsey's restlessness. On that day it seemed to be more than ever a resistless impulse that kept him out until after luncheon. I think he hoped constantly that he might meet Louise driving over the hills in her small coupé. Possibly he did meet her occasionally, but from his continued gloom I felt sure the situation between them was unchanged.

Part of the afternoon I believe he read. Gertrude and I were out, as I have said, and at dinner we both noticed that something had occurred to distract him. He was disagreeable, which is unlike him, nervous and looking at his watch every five minutes, and he ate almost nothing. He asked twice during the meal on what train Jamieson and the other detective were coming, and had long periods of abstraction during which he dug his fork into my damask cloth and did not hear when he was spoken to. He refused dessert and left the table early, excusing himself on the ground that he wanted to see Alex.

Alex, however, was not to be found. It was after eight when Halsey ordered the car, and started down the hill at a pace which even for him was unusually reckless. Shortly after, Alex reported that he was ready to go over the house, preparatory to closing it for the night. Sam Bohannon came at a quarter before nine, and began his patrol of the grounds, and with the arrival of the two detectives to look forward to I was not especially apprehensive.

At half past nine I heard the sound of a car driven furiously up the drive. It came to a stop in front of the house, and immediately after there were hurried steps on the veranda. Our nerves were not what they should have been, and Gertrude, always apprehensive lately, was at the door almost instantly. A moment later Louise had burst into the room and stood there bareheaded and breathing hard.

"Where is Halsey?" she demanded. Above her plain black frock her eyes looked big and somber, and the rapid drive had brought no color to her face. I got up and drew forward a chair.

"He hasn't come back," I said quietly. "Sit down, child. You're not strong enough for this kind of thing."

I don't think she even heard me.

"He hasn't come back?" she asked, looking from me to Gertrude. "Do you know where he went? Where can I find him?"

"For heaven's sake, Louise," Gertrude burst out, "tell us what is wrong. Halsey's not here. He's gone to the station for Mr. Jamieson. What has happened?"

"To the station, Gertrude? You are sure?"

"Yes," I said. "Listen. There's the whistle of the train now."

She relaxed a little at our matter-of-fact tone, and allowed herself to drop into a chair.

"Perhaps I was wrong," she said heavily. "He will be here in a few moments, if everything is all right."

We sat there, the three of us, without attempt at conversation. Both Gertrude and I recognized the futility of asking Louise any questions. Quite obviously she did not intend to talk. I know all our ears were strained for the first throb of the motor as it turned into the drive and commenced the climb to the house. But ten minutes passed, fifteen, twenty. I saw Louise's hands grow rigid as they clutched the arms of her chair. I watched Gertrude's bright color slowly ebbing away, and around my own heart I seemed to feel the grasp of a giant hand.

Twenty-five minutes, and then a sound. But it was not the chug of the motor, it was the unmistakable rattle of the Casanova taxi. Gertrude drew aside the curtain and peered into the darkness.

"It's the taxi, I am sure," she said, evidently relieved. "Something has gone wrong with the car, and no wonder, the way Halsey went down the hill."

It seemed a long time before the creaking vehicle came to a stop at the door. Louise rose and stood watching, her hand at her throat. And then Gertrude opened the door, admitting Jamieson and a stocky, middle-aged man. Halsey was not with them. When the door had closed and Louise realized that Halsey had not come her expression changed. From tense watchfulness to relief, and now again to absolute despair, her face was an open page.

"Halsey?" I asked unceremoniously, ignoring the stranger. "Didn't he meet you?"

"No." Jamieson looked slightly surprised. "I rather expected the car, but we got up all right."

"You didn't see him at all?" Louise demanded breathlessly.

Jamieson knew her at once, although he had not seen her before. She had kept to her rooms until the morning she left.

"No, Miss Armstrong," he said. "I saw nothing of him. What's wrong?"

"Then we have to find him," she asserted. "Every instant is precious. Mr.

Jamieson, I have reason for believing that he is in danger, but I don't know what it is. Only he must be found."

The stocky man had said nothing. Now he went quickly toward the door. "I'll catch the taxi if I can and hold it," he said. "Is the gentleman down in the town?"

"Mr. Jamieson," Louise said impulsively, "I can use the taxi. Take my coupé—it's outside and it's fast—and drive like mad. Try to find Halsey's car. It ought to be easy to trace. Only don't lose a moment."

The new detective had gone and a moment later Jamieson drove rapidly down the drive. Louise stood looking after them. When she turned around she faced a Gertrude who stood indignant, almost tragic, in the hall.

"You know what danger Halsey is in, Louise," she said accusingly. "I believe you know this whole horrible thing, this mystery we're struggling with. If anything happens to Halsey I'll never forgive you."

Louise only raised her hands despairingly and dropped them again.

"I care as much as you do. Maybe more," she said despairingly. "I tried to warn him, but he wouldn't listen."

"Now listen, both of you," I said, as briskly as I could. "We are making a lot of trouble out of something perhaps very small. Halsey was probably late. He's always late. Any moment we may hear the car coming up the road."

But it did not come. After a half hour of suspense Louise went out quietly and did not come back. I hardly knew she was gone until I heard the station taxi moving off. And at eleven o'clock the telephone rang. It was Jamieson.

"I have found your car, Miss Innes," he said. "It has collided with a freight car on the siding above the station. No, Mr. Innes was not there, but we shall probably find him. Better send Warner for the car."

But they did not find him. At four o'clock the next morning we were still waiting for news, while Alex watched the house and Sam the grounds. At daylight I dropped into exhausted sleep. Halsey had not come back, and there was no word from the two detectives.

26

NOTHING THAT HAD GONE before had been as bad as this. The murder and Thomas's sudden death we had been able to view in a detached sort of way. But with Halsey's disappearance everything was altered. Our little circle, intact until now, was broken. We were no longer onlookers who saw a battle passing around them. We were the center of action. Of course, there was no time then to voice such an idea. My mind seemed able to hold only one thought, that Halsey had been wickedly dealt with and that every minute lost might be fatal.

Jamieson came back about eight o'clock the next morning. He was covered with mud, and his hat was gone. Altogether we were a sad-looking trio which gathered around a breakfast no one could eat. Over a cup of black coffee the detective told us that he had learned of Halsey's movements the night before. Up to a certain point the car had made it easy enough to follow him. And I gathered that Burns, the other detective, had followed a similar car for miles at dawn, only to find it was carrying a family with several children.

"He left here about ten minutes after eight," Jamieson said. "He went alone, and at eight-twenty he stopped at Doctor Walker's. I went to the doctor's about midnight, but he had been called out on a case and had not come back by four o'clock. From the doctor's it seems Mr. Innes walked across the lawn to the cottage Mrs. Armstrong and her daughter have taken. Mrs. Armstrong had gone to bed, and he said perhaps a dozen words to Miss Louise. She will not say what they were, but the girl evidently suspects what has occurred. That is, she suspects foul play but she doesn't know of what sort. Then apparently he started directly for the station. He was going very fast; the flagman at the Carol Street crossing says he saw the car pass and recognized it. Along somewhere in the dark stretch between Carol Street and the depot the car evidently swerved suddenly—perhaps someone in the road—and went full into the side of a freight train. We found it there, badly smashed."

"And Halsey?" My lips were stiff.

"No sign of him, Miss Innes. Not even any indication that he had been hurt. In a way it's curious. If he was in the car when it hit—"

Gertrude shuddered.

"We examined every inch of track. The freight had gone, but there was no sign of trouble."

"But surely he can't be gone!" I cried. "Aren't there traces in the mud? Anything?"

"There is no mud, only dust. There hasn't been any rain lately. And the footpath there is of cinders. Miss Innes, I am inclined to think that he has met some sort of trouble. I don't think he's been murdered." I shrank from the word. "Burns is back in the country, on a clue we got from the night clerk at the drugstore. There will be two more men here by noon, and word has gone out over the teletype. If he's around we'll find him."

"What about the creek?" Gertrude asked with stiff lips. "If he was knocked unconscious, they might have—"

She did not finish, but Jamieson knew what she meant.

"The creek is shallow now. If it were swollen with rain it would be different. There's hardly any water in it. Now, Miss Innes," he said, turning to me, "I must ask you some questions. Had Mr. Innes any possible reason for going away like this without warning?"

"None whatever, so far as I know."

"He went away once before," he persisted. "And you were as sure then."

"He did not leave the car jammed into the side of a freight car before."

"No, but he left it for repairs in a garage a long distance from here. Do you know if he had any personal enemies? Anyone who might wish him out of the way?"

"Not that I know of, unless—no, I cannot think of any."

"Was he in the habit of carrying money?"

"He never carried it far. No, he never had more than enough for current expenses."

He got up and began to pace the room. It was an unwonted concession to the occasion.

"Then I think we get at it by elimination. The chances are against flight. If he was hurt, we find no sign of it. It looks almost like a kidnaping. This young Doctor Walker, have you any idea why Mr. Innes should have gone there last night?"

"I can't understand it," Gertrude said thoughtfully. "I don't think he knew Doctor Walker at all. Anyhow their relations could hardly have been even friendly, under the circumstances."

Jamieson pricked up his ears, and little by little he drew from us the unfortunate story of Halsey's love affair, and the fact that Louise was going to marry the doctor.

He listened attentively.

"There are some interesting developments here," he said thoughtfully. "The woman who claims to be the mother of Lucien Wallace has not come back. Your nephew has apparently been spirited away. There is an organized attempt being made to enter this house. In fact it has been entered. Witness the incident with the cook yesterday. And I have a new piece of information." He looked carefully away from Gertrude. "Mr. John Bailey is not at his Knickerbocker apartments, and I don't know where he is. It's a Chinese puzzle. Nothing fits together, unless Mr. Bailey and your nephew have again—"

And once again Gertrude surprised me. "They are not in any plot," she said hotly. "I know where Mr. Bailey is. My brother is not with him."

The detective turned and looked at her keenly.

"Miss Gertrude," he said, "if you and Louise Armstrong would only tell me everything you know and surmise about this business, I should be able to do a great many things. I believe I could find your brother, and I might be able to—well, to do some other things." But Gertrude's face did not change.

"Nothing I know could help you to find Halsey," she said stubbornly. "I know as little of his disappearance as you do, and I can only say this: I don't trust Doctor Walker. I think he hated Halsey, and he would get rid of him if he could."

"Perhaps you are right. In fact, I had some such theory myself. But Doctor Walker went out late last night to a serious case in Summitville, and he's still there. Burns traced him. We have made guarded inquiry at the Greenwood Club, and through the village. There is absolutely nothing to go on but this. On the embankment above the railroad, at the point where we found the car, is a small house. An old woman and a daughter who is very lame live there. They say that they distinctly heard the shock when the car hit the freight, and they went to the bottom of their garden and looked over. The car was there. They could see the lights, and they thought someone had been injured. It was very dark, but they could make out two figures, standing together. The women were curious, and leaving the fence they went back and by a roundabout path down to the road. When they got there the car was still standing, the headlights broken and the front of it badly crushed, but there was no one to be seen."

He went away soon after, and to Gertrude and me was left the woman's part, to watch and wait. By luncheon nothing had been found, and I was about frantic. I went upstairs to Halsey's room finally, from sheer inability to sit across from Gertrude any longer and meet her terror-filled eyes.

Liddy was in my dressing room, suspiciously red-eyed, and trying to put a right sleeve in a left armhole of a new blouse for me. I was too much shaken to scold.

"What name did that woman in the kitchen give?" she demanded, viciously ripping out the offending sleeve.

"Bliss. Mattie Bliss," I replied.

"Bliss. M.B. Well, that's not what she has on her suitcase. It is marked N.F.C."

The new cook and her initials troubled me not at all. I put on my hat and sent for what the Casanova garage called a limousine. Having once made up my mind to a course of action I am not one to turn back. Warner drove me. He was plainly disgusted, and he drove the wreck as he would my own car, with the result that I was on the verge of catastrophe all the time I was out.

But Warner also had something on his mind, and after we had turned into the road he voiced it.

"Miss Innes," he said over his shoulder, "I overheard a part of a talk yesterday that I didn't understand. It wasn't my business to understand it, for that matter. But I've been thinking all day that I'd better tell you. Yesterday afternoon while you and Miss Gertrude were out, I had got the car in some sort of shape again after the fire, and I went to the library to call Mr. Innes to see it. I went into the living room, where Miss Liddy said he was, and halfway cross to the library I heard him talking to someone. He seemed to be walking up and down and he was in a rage, I can tell you."

"What did he say?"

"The first thing I heard was—excuse me, Miss Innes, but it's what he said. 'The damned rascal,' he said, 'I'll see him in'—well, in hell was what he said, 'in hell first.' Then somebody else spoke up. It was a woman. She said, 'I warned them, but they thought I would be afraid.'"

"A woman? Did you wait to see who it was?"

"I wasn't spying, Miss Innes," Warner said with dignity. "But the next thing caught my attention. She said, 'I knew there was something wrong from the start. A man isn't well one day and dead the next without some reason.' I thought she was speaking of Thomas."

"And you don't know who it was!" I protested. "Warner, you had the key to everything in your hands and didn't use it."

However, there was nothing to be done. I resolved to make an inquiry when I got home, and in the meantime my present errand absorbed me. This was nothing less than to see Louise Armstrong and to attempt to drag from her what she knew, or suspected, of Halsey's disappearance. But here, as in every direction I turned, I was baffled.

A neat maid answered the bell, but she stood squarely in the doorway and it was impossible to preserve one's dignity and pass her.

"Miss Armstrong is very sick and unable to see anyone," she said. I did not believe her. She was a poor liar.

"And Mrs. Armstrong, is she also ill?"

"She's with Miss Louise and can't be disturbed."

"Tell her it's Miss Innes, and that it is a matter of the greatest importance."

"It wouldn't be any good, Miss Innes. My orders are positive."

At that moment a heavy step sounded on the stairs. Past the maid's white-trapped shoulder I could see a familiar thatch of gray hair, and in a moment I was face to face with Doctor Stewart. He was very grave, and his customary geniality was tinged with restraint.

"You are the very woman I want to see," he said promptly. "Send away your car and let me drive you home. What's this about your nephew?"

"He has disappeared, doctor. Not only that, but there is every evidence that he has been either abducted or—" I could not finish. The doctor helped me into his shabby car in silence. Until we had gone a little distance he did not speak. Then he turned and looked at me.

"Now tell me about it," he said.

He heard me through without speaking, but his air of gravity did not change.

"So you think Louise knows something?" he said when I had finished. "I don't. In fact, I'm sure of it. The best evidence of it is this: she asked me if he had been heard from, or if anything had been learned. She won't allow Walker in the room, and she made me promise to see you and tell you not to give up the search for him. Find him, and find him soon. He's alive. That's the message."

"Well," I said, "if she knows all that she knows more. She's a very cruel and ungrateful girl."

"She is a very sick girl," he said gravely. "Neither you nor I can judge her until we know everything. But both she and her mother are ghosts of their former selves. Under all this, these two sudden deaths, this bank robbery, the invasions at Sunnyside and Halsey's disappearance, there is some mystery that, mark my words, will come out someday. And when it does, we shall find Louise a victim. Her mother too, perhaps."

I had not noticed where we were going, but now I saw we were beside the railroad and from a knot of men standing near the track I divined that it was here the car had been found. But the siding was empty. Except for a few bits of splintered wood on the ground there was no sign of the accident.

"Where is the freight car that was rammed?" the doctor asked a bystander.

"It was taken away at daylight, when the train was moved."

There was nothing to be gained. He pointed out the house on the embankment where the old lady and her daughter had heard the crash and seen two figures beside the car. Then we drove slowly home. I had the doctor put me down at the gate and I walked to the house, past the lodge where we had found Louise and, later, poor Thomas; up the drive where I had seen a man watching the lodge and where, later, Rosie had been frightened; past the east entrance, where so short a time before the most obstinate effort had been made to enter the house, and where, that night two weeks ago, Liddy and I had seen the strange woman. Not far from the west wing lay the blackened ruins of the stables. I felt like a ruin myself as I paused on the broad veranda before I entered the house.

Two more detectives had arrived in my absence, and it was a relief to turn over to them the responsibility of the house and grounds. Jamieson, they said, had arranged for more to assist in the search for Halsey, and the country was being scoured in all directions.

The household staff was again depleted that afternoon. Liddy was waiting to tell me that the new cook had gone, bag and baggage, without waiting to be paid. No one had admitted the visitor Warner had heard in the library, unless possibly the missing cook with the scarred face. Again I was working in a circle.

27

THE NEXT FOUR DAYS, from Saturday to the following Tuesday, we lived or existed in a state of the most dreadful suspense. We ate only when Liddy brought in a tray, and then very little. The papers of course had got hold of the story, and we were besieged by newspapermen. From all over the country false clues came pouring in and raised hopes that crumbled again to nothing. Every morgue within a hundred miles, every hospital, had been visited without result.

Jamieson personally took charge of the organized search and every evening, no matter where he happened to be, he called us by long-distance telephone. It was the same formula. "Nothing today. A new clue to work on. Better luck tomorrow." And heartsick we would put down the receiver and sit back again to our vigil.

The inaction was deadly. Liddy cried all day and, because she knew I objected to tears, sniffed audibly around the corner.

"For heaven's sake, smile!" I snapped at her. And her ghastly attempt at a grin, with her swollen nose and red eyes, made me hysterical. I laughed and cried together and pretty soon, like the two old fools we were, we were sitting together weeping into the same handkerchief.

Things were happening of course all the time, but they made little or no impression. The Emergency Hospital called up Doctor Stewart and reported that Mrs. Watson was in a critical condition. I understood also that legal steps were being taken to terminate my lease at Sunnyside. Louise was out of danger but very ill, and a trained nurse guarded her like a gorgon. There was a rumor in the village, brought up by Liddy from the butcher's, that a wedding had already taken place between Louise and Doctor Walker, and this roused me for the first time to action.

On Tuesday then I sent for the car from the garage in the village and prepared to go out. As I waited at the porte-cochère I saw the undergardener, an inoffensive grayish-haired man, trimming borders near the house. The day detective was watching him, sitting on what had been the carriage block. When he saw me he got up.

"Miss Innes," he said, taking off his hat, "do you know where Alex the gardener is?"

"Why, no. Isn't he here?" I asked.

"He's been gone since yesterday afternoon. Have you employed him long?"

"Only a couple of weeks."

"Is he efficient? A capable man?"

"I hardly know," I said vaguely. "The place looks all right, and I know very little about such things. I know much more about boxes of roses than bushes of them."

"This man," pointing to the assistant, "says Alex isn't a gardener. That he doesn't know anything about plants."

"That's very strange," I said, thinking hard. "He came to me from the Brays, who are in Europe."

"Exactly." The detective smiled. "Every man who cuts grass isn't a gardener, Miss Innes, and just now it is our policy to believe every person around here a rascal until he proves to be the other thing."

Warner came up with the car then, and the conversation stopped. As he helped me in, however, the detective said something further.

"Not a word or sign to Alex, if he comes back," he said cautiously.

I went first to Doctor Walker's. I was tired of beating about the bush, and I felt that the key to Halsey's disappearance was here at Casanova, in spite of Jamieson's theories.

The doctor was in. He came at once to the door of his consulting room, and there was no mask of cordiality in his manner.

"Please come in," he said curtly.

"I shall stay here, I think, doctor." I did not like his face or his manner.

There was a subtle change in both. He had thrown off the air of friendliness, and I thought too that he looked anxious and haggard.

"Doctor Walker," I said, "I have come to you to ask some questions. I hope you will answer them. As you know, my nephew has not yet been found."

"So I understand," he said stiffly.

"I believe if you would you could help us, and that leads to one of my questions. Will you tell me what was the nature of the conversation you held with him the night he was attacked and carried off?"

"Attacked! Carried off!" he said, with pretended surprise. "Really, Miss Innes, don't you think you exaggerate? I understand this is not the first time Mr. Innes has—disappeared."

"You're quibbling, doctor. This is a matter of life and death. Will you answer my question?"

"Certainly. He said his nerves were bad, and I gave him a prescription for them. I am violating professional ethics when I tell you even as much as that."

I could not tell him he lied. I think I looked it. But I hazarded a random shot.

"I thought perhaps," I said, watching him narrowly, "that it might be about Nina Carrington."

For a moment I thought he was going to strike me. He grew livid, and a small crooked blood vessel in his temple swelled and throbbed. Then he forced a short laugh.

"Who is Nina Carrington?" he asked.

"I am about to discover that," I replied, and he was quiet at once. It was not difficult to realize that he feared Nina Carrington a good deal more than he did the devil. As a result our leave-taking was brief. In fact we merely stared at each other over the waiting-room table, with its litter of year-old magazines. Then I turned and went out.

"To Richfield," I told Warner, and on the way I thought and thought hard.

"Nina Carrignton, Nina Carrington," the roar and rush of the wheels seemed to sing the words. "Nina Carrington, N.C." and then I knew, knew as surely as if I had seen the whole thing. There had been an N.C. on the suitcase belonging to the woman with the scarred face. How simple it all seemed. Mattie Bliss had been Nina Carrington. It was she Warner had heard in the library. It was something she had told Halsey that had taken him frantically to Doctor Walker's office, and from there perhaps to his death. If we could find the woman we might find what had become of Halsey.

We were almost at Richfield now, so I kept on. My mind was not on my errand there now. It was back with Halsey on that memorable night. What was it he had said to Louise that had sent her up to Sunnyside, half wild with fear of him? I made up my mind, as the car drew up before the Tate cottage, that I would see Louise if I had to break into the house with a gun.

Almost exactly the same scene as before greeted my eyes at the cottage:

Mrs. Tate, the baby carriage in the path, the children at the swing, all were the same.

She came forward to meet me, and I noticed that some of the anxious lines had gone out of her face. She looked young, almost pretty.

"I am glad you've come back," she said. "I think I will have to be honest and give you back your money."

"Why?" I asked. "Has the mother come?"

"No, but someone came and paid the boy's board for a month. She talked to him for a long time, but when I asked him afterward he didn't know her name."

"A young woman?"

"Not very young. About forty, I suppose. She was small and fair-haired, just a little bit gray, and very sad. She was in deep mourning, and I think when she came she expected to go at once. But the child, Lucien, interested her. She talked to him for a long time, and she looked much happier when she left."

"You are sure this was not the real mother?"

"Oh mercy, no! Why, she didn't know which of the three was Lucien. I thought perhaps she was a friend of yours, but of course I didn't ask."

"She was not scarred in the face?" I asked at a venture.

"No, indeed. A skin like a baby's. But perhaps you'll know the initials. She gave Lucien a handkerchief and forgot it. It was very fine, black-bordered, and it had three hand-worked letters in the corner—F.B.A."

"No," I said with truth enough, "she is not a friend of mine." F.B.A. was Fanny Armstrong, without a chance of doubt!

With another warning to Mrs. Tate as to silence we started back to Sunnyside. So Fanny Armstrong knew of Lucien Wallace, and was sufficiently interested to visit him and pay for his support. Who was the child's mother and where was she? Who was Nina Carrington? Did either of them know where Halsey was, or what had happened to him?

On the way home we passed the little cemetery where Thomas had been laid to rest. I wondered if Thomas could have helped us to find Halsey, had he lived. Farther along was the more imposing burial ground, where Arnold Armstrong and his father lay in the shadow of a tall granite shaft. Of the three, I think Thomas was the only one sincerely mourned.

28

THE BITTERNESS toward the dead president of the Traders' Bank seemed to grow with time. Never popular, his memory was execrated by people who had lost nothing, but who were filled with disgust by constantly hearing new stories of the man's grasping avarice. The Traders' had been a favorite bank for small tradespeople, and in its savings department it had solicited even the smallest deposits. People who had thought to be self-supporting to the last found themselves confronting the poorhouse, their few hundred dollar savings wiped away. All bank failures have this element, however, and the directors were trying to promise twenty per cent on deposits.

But like everything else those days the bank failure was almost forgotten by Gertrude and myself. We did not mention Jack Bailey. I had found nothing to change my impression of his guilt, and Gertrude knew how I felt. As for the murder of the bank president's son, I was of two minds. One day I thought Gertrude knew or at least suspected that Jack had done it; the next I feared that it had been Gertrude herself, that night alone on the circular staircase. And then the mother of Lucien Wallace would obtrude herself, and an almost equally good case might be made against her. There were times of course when I was disposed to throw all those suspicions aside and fix definitely on the unknown, whoever that might be.

I had my greatest disappointment when it came to tracing Nina Carrington. The woman had gone without leaving a trace. Scarred as she was it should have been easy to follow her, but she was not be found. A description to one of the detectives on my arrival home had started the ball rolling. But by night she had not been found. I told Gertrude then about the telegram to Louise when she had been ill before, about my visit to Doctor Walker, and my suspicions that Mattie Bliss and Nina Carrington were the same. She thought, as I did, that there was little doubt of it.

I said nothing to her, however, of the detective's suspicions about Alex. Little things that I had not noticed at the time now came back to me. I had an uncomfortable feeling that perhaps Alex was a spy, and that by taking him into the house I had played into the enemy's hand. But at eight o'clock that night Alex himself appeared, and with him a strange and repulsive individual. They made a queer pair, for Alex was almost as disreputable as the tramp, and he had a badly swollen eye.

Gertrude had been sitting listlessly waiting for the evening message from Jamieson, but when the singular pair came in as they did, without ceremony, she jumped up and stood staring. Winters, the detective who watched the house at night, followed them and kept his eyes sharply on Alex's prisoner. For that was the situation as it developed.

He was a tall lanky individual, ragged and dirty, and just now he looked both terrified and embarrassed. Alex was too much engrossed to be either, and to this day I don't think I ever asked him why he went off without permission the day before.

"Miss Innes," Alex began abruptly, "this man can tell us something very important about the disappearance of Mr. Innes. I found him trying to sell this watch."

He took a watch from his pocket and put it on the table. It was Halsey's watch. I had given it to him on his twenty-first birthday, and I was dumb with apprehension.

"He says he had a pair of cuff links also, but he sold them—"

"Fer a dollar'n half," put in the disreputable individual hoarsely, with an eye on the detective.

"He's not dead?" I implored. The tramp cleared his throat.

"No'm," he said huskily. "He was used up pretty bad, but he weren't dead. He was comin' to hisself when I—" He stopped and looked at the detective. "I didn't steal it, Mr. Winters," he whined. "I found it in the road, honest to God I did."

Mr. Winters paid no attention to him. He was watching Alex.

"I'd better tell what he told me," Alex broke in. "It will be quicker. When Mr. Jamieson calls up we can start him right. Mr. Winters, I found this man trying to sell that watch on Fifth Street. He offered it to me for three dollars."

"How did you know the watch?" Winters snapped at him.

"I'd seen it before. As a matter of fact I used it at night when I was watching at the foot of the staircase." The detective was satisfied. "When he offered the watch to me I knew it, and I pretended I was going to buy it. We went into an alley and I got the watch." The tramp shivered. It was plain how Alex had secured the watch. "Then I got the story from this fellow. He claims to have seen the whole affair. He says he was in an empty freight car, in the car the automobile struck."

The tramp broke in here and told his story, with frequent interpretations by Alex and Mr. Winters. He used a strange argot, in which familiar words took unfamiliar meanings, but it was gradually made clear to us.

On the night in question the tramp had been "pounding his ear," as he put it, in an empty boxcar along the siding at Casanova. The train was going west, and due to leave at dawn. The tramp and the "brakey" were friendly, and things were going well. About ten o'clock, perhaps earlier, a terrific crash against the side of the car roused him. He tried to open the door but could not move it. He got out on the other side, and as he did so he heard someone groan.

The habits of a lifetime made him cautious. He slipped onto the bumper of a car and peered through. An automobile had struck the car, and was badly smashed. The taillight was burning, but the headlights were out. Two men were stooping over someone who lay on the ground. Then the taller of the two started on a dogtrot along the train looking for an empty. He found one four cars away and ran back again. The two lifted the unconscious man into the empty boxcar, and getting in themselves stayed for three or four minutes. When they came out, after closing the sliding door, they cut up over the railroad embankment toward the town. One, the short one, seemed to limp.

The tramp was wary. He waited for ten minutes or so. Some women came down a path to the road and inspected the automobile. When they had gone, he crawled into the car in question and closed the door again. Then he lighted a match. The figure of a man, unconscious, gagged, and with his hands tied, lay at the far end. The tramp lost no time. He went through his pockets, found a little money and the cuff links, and took them. Then he loosened the gag—it had been cruelly tight—and went his way, again closing the door of the boxcar. Outside on the road he found the watch. He got on the fast freight east some time after and rode into the city. He had sold the cuff links, but on offering the watch to Alex he had been "copped."

The story with its cold recital of brutality was done. I hardly knew if I was more anxious or less. That it was Halsey there could be no doubt. How badly he was hurt, how far he had been carried, were the questions that demanded immediate answer. But it was the first real information we had had. At least my boy had not been murdered outright. But instead of vague terrors there was now the real fear that he might be lying in some strange hospital receiving the casual attention commonly given to charity cases. Even this, had we known it, would have been paradise to the terrible truth. I wake yet and feel myself cold and trembling with the horror of Halsey's situation for three days after his disappearance.

Winters and Alex disposed of the tramp with a warning. It was evident he had told us all he knew. We had occasion, within a day or two, to be doubly thankful that we had given him his freedom. When Jamieson telephoned that night we had news for him, but he told me what I had not realized before, that it would not be possible to find Halsey at once even with this clue. The cars by this time, three days, might be scattered over the Union. But he said to keep on hoping, that it was the best news we had had. And in the meantime, consumed with anxiety as we were, things were happening at the house in rapid succession.

We had one peaceful day, then Liddy took sick in the night. I went in when I heard her groaning and found her with a hot-water bottle to her face and her right cheek swollen until it was glassy.

"Toothache?" I asked, not too gently. "You deserve it. A woman of your age, who would rather go around with an exposed nerve in her head than have the tooth pulled! It would be over in a moment."

"So would hanging," Liddy protested, from behind the hot-water bottle. I was hunting around for cotton and laudanum.

"You have a tooth just like it yourself, Miss Rachel," she whimpered. "And I'm sure Doctor Boyle's been trying to take it out for years."

There was no laudanum and Liddy made a terrible fuss when I proposed carbolic acid, just because I had put too much on the cotton once and burned her mouth. I'm sure it never did her any permanent harm. Indeed, the doctor said afterward that living on a liquid diet had been a splendid rest for her stomach. But she would have none of the acid and she kept me awake groaning, so at last I got up and went to Gertrude's door. To my surprise, it was locked.

I went around by the hall and into her bedroom that way. The bed was turned down, and her dressing gown and pajamas lay ready in the little room next, but Gertrude was not there. She had not undressed.

I don't know what terrible thoughts came to me in the minute I stood there. Through the door I could hear Liddy grumbling, with a squeal now and then when the pain stabbed harder. Then automatically I got the medicine and went back to her.

It was fully a half hour before Liddy's groans subsided. At intervals I went to the door into the hall and looked out, but I saw and heard nothing suspicious. Finally when Liddy had dropped into a doze I even ventured as far as the head of the circular staircase, but there floated up to me only the even breathing of Winters, the night detective, sleeping just inside the entry. And then far off I heard the rapping noise that had lured Louise down the staircase that other night, two weeks before. It was over my head, and very faint, three or four short muffled taps, a pause and then again, stealthily repeated.

The sound of Winters's breathing was comforting. With the thought that there was help within call something kept me from waking him. I did not move for a moment. Ridiculous things Liddy had said about a ghost—I am not at all superstitious, except perhaps in the middle of the night with everything dark—things like that came back to me. Almost beside me was the clothes chute. I could feel it, but I could see nothing. As I stood listening intently I heard a sound near me. It was vague, indefinite. Then it ceased. There was an uneasy movement and a grunt from the foot of the circular staircase, and silence again. I stood perfectly still, hardly daring to breathe.

Then I knew I had been right. Someone was stealthily passing the head of the staircase and coming toward me in the dark. I leaped against the wall for support, for my knees were giving away. The steps were close now, and suddenly I thought of Gertrude. Of course it was Gertrude. I put out one hand in front of me but I touched nothing. My voice almost refused me, but I managed to gasp out, "Gertrude!"

"Good God!" a man's voice exclaimed just beside me. And then I collapsed. I felt myself going, felt someone catch me, and a horrible blackness, then nothing.

When I came to it was dawn. I was lying on the bed in Louise's room, with a cherub on the ceiling staring down at me, and there was a blanket from my own bed thrown over me. I felt weak and dizzy, but I managed to get up and totter to the door. At the foot of the circular staircase Winters was still asleep. Hardly able to stand I crept back to my room. The door into Gertrude's room was no longer locked. She was sleeping like a tired child. And in my dressing room Liddy hugged a cold hot-water bottle and mumbled in her sleep.

"There's some things you can't hold with handcuffs," she was muttering thickly.

29

FOR THE FIRST TIME in twenty years I kept my bed that day. Liddy was alarmed to the point of hysteria and sent for Doctor Stewart just after breakfast. Gertrude spent the morning with me, reading something, I forget what. I was too busy with my thoughts to listen. I had said nothing to the two detectives. If Jamieson had been there, I would have told him everything, but I could not go to these strange men and tell them my niece had been missing in the middle of the night, that she had not gone to bed at all, or that while I was searching for her through the house I had met a stranger who when I fainted had carried me into a room and left me there, to get better or not as it might happen.

The whole situation was incredible. Had the issues been less vital it would have been absurd. Here we were, guarded day and night by private detectives with an extra man to watch the grounds, and yet we might as well have lived in a Japanese paper house for all the protection we had.

And there was something else. The man I had met in the darkness had been even more startled than I, and about his voice when he muttered his muffled exclamation there was something vaguely familiar. All that morning while Gertrude read aloud and Liddy watched for the doctor, I was puzzling over that voice, without result.

And there were other things too. I wondered what Gertrude's absence from her room had to do with it all, or if it had any connection. I tried to think that she had heard the rapping noises before I did and gone to investigate, but I'm afraid I was a moral coward that day. I could not ask her.

Perhaps the diversion was good for me. It took my mind from Halsey, and the story we had heard the night before. But the day was a long vigil, with every ring of the telephone full of possibilities. Doctor Walker came up, sometime just after luncheon, and asked for me.

"Go down and see him," I instructed Gertrude. "Tell him I'm out. For mercy's sake don't say I'm sick. Find out what he wants, and from this time on instruct the servants that he is not to be admitted. I loathe the man."

Gertrude came back very soon, her face rather flushed.

"He came to ask us again to get out," she said, picking up her book with a jerk. "He says Louise wants to come here, now that she is recovering."

"And what did you say?"

"I said we were very sorry we couldn't leave, but we would be delighted to have Louise come up here with us. He looked daggers at me. And he wanted to know if we would recommend Eliza as a cook. He has brought a patient, a man, out from town, and is increasing his establishment. That's the way he put it."

"I wish him joy of Eliza," I said tartly. "Did he ask for Halsey?"

"Yes. I told him we were on the track, and that it was only a question of time. He said he was glad, although he didn't appear to be, but he said not to be too sanguine."

"Do you know what I believe?" I asked. "I believe, as firmly as I believe anything, that Doctor Walker knows something about Halsey, and that he could put his finger on him if he wanted to."

There were several things that day that bewildered me. About three o'clock Jamieson telephoned from the Casanova station and Warner went down to meet him. I got up and dressed hastily, and the detective was shown up to my sitting room.

"No news?" I asked, as he entered. He tried to look encouraging, without success. I noticed that he looked tired and dusty, and although he was ordinarily impeccable in his appearance it was clear he was at least two days from a razor.

"It won't be long now, Miss Innes," he said. "I have come out here on a peculiar errand, but I'll tell you about it later. First, I want to ask some questions. Did anyone come out here yesterday to repair the telephone and examine the wires on the roof?"

"Yes," I said promptly; "but it was not the telephone. He said the wiring might have caused the fire at the stable. I went up with him myself, but he only looked around. He didn't do anything."

"Good for you!" he applauded. "Don't allow anyone in the house that you don't trust, and don't trust anybody. Not everybody is an electrician who wears rubber gloves."

He refused to explain further, but he got a slip of paper out of his pocket-book and opened it carefully.

"Listen," he said. "You heard this before and scoffed. In the light of recent developments I want you to read it again. You are a clever woman, Miss Innes. Just as surely as I sit here there's something in this house that is wanted very badly by a number of people. The lines are closing up, Miss Innes."

The paper was the one he had found among Arnold Armstrong's effects, and I read it again:

". . . . . by altering the plans for . . . . rooms may be possible. The best way in my opinion would be to . . . . . . the plan for . . . . in one of the . . . . rooms . . . . chimney."

"I think I understand," I said slowly. "Someone is searching for a secret room, and he is trying in every possible way to get into the house. He's been in the house, for that matter. The hole in the wall upstairs—"

"Why do you say 'he'?" he inquired with interest.

"I've seen one of them."

But he made no comment on that. He got up, shaking down his trouser legs as he did so, and confronted me with a grave face.

"Miss Innes," he said, "I don't think there's any doubt that at least some of the money from the Traders' Bank is concealed in this house. I believe young Walker knows it, that he came back from California to get it, and when he failed to put Mrs. Armstrong and Louise back here he has consistently tried to break in. He's succeeded twice."

"Three times," I corrected him, and told him about my experience the night before. "But it wasn't Walker last night. He has someone working with him. It wasn't he who caught me when I fainted. I'd know his voice anywhere."

He lit a cigarette and paced the floor before he spoke again.

"There's something else that puzzles me," he said, stopping before me. "Who and what is the woman Nina Carrington? If she came here as Mattie Bliss, what did she tell Halsey that sent him racing to Doctor Walker's and then to see Miss Armstrong? If we could find that woman we might have the whole thing."

"Mr. Jamieson, did you ever think that Paul Armstrong might not have died a natural death?"

He gave me a curious glance.

"We're checking on that with the Coast now," he said. But there was no time for more. Gertrude came in, announcing a man below to see him.

"I want you present at this interview, Miss Innes," he said. "May Riggs come up? He has left Doctor Walker and he has something he wants to tell us."

Riggs came into the room diffidently, but Jamieson put him at his ease. He kept a careful eye on me, however, and slid into a chair by the door when he was asked to sit down.

"Now, Riggs," began Jamieson briskly, "you are to say what you have to say before this lady. She is Miss Innes and is certainly interested."

"You promised you'd keep it quiet, Mr. Jamieson." Riggs plainly did not trust me. There was nothing friendly in the glance he turned on me.

"Yes, yes. You will be protected. But first of all, did you bring what you promised?"

Riggs produced a roll of papers from under his coat and handed them over. Jamieson examined them with lively satisfaction and passed them to me. "The blueprints of Sunnyside," he said. "What did I tell you? Now, Riggs, we're ready."

"I'd never have come to you, Mr. Jamieson," he began, "if it hadn't been for Miss Armstrong. When Mr. Innes was spirited away like, and Miss Louise got sick because of it, I thought things had gone far enough. I'd done some things for the doctor before that wouldn't bear looking into, but I turned a bit squeamish."

"Did you help with my nephew's kidnaping?" I asked, leaning forward.

"No, ma'am. I didn't ever know of it until the next day, when it came out in the Casanova *Weekly Ledger*. But I know who did it all right. I'd better start at the beginning.

"When Doctor Walker went away to California with the Armstrong family there was talk in the town that when he came back he would be married to Miss Armstrong, and we all expected it. First thing I knew I got a letter from him, in the West. He seemed to be excited, and he said Miss Armstrong had taken a sudden notion to go home. He sent me some money, and I was to watch for her to see if she went to Sunnyside, and wherever she was not to lose sight of her until he got back here. I traced her to the lodge, and I guess I scared you on the drive one night, Miss Innes."

"You scared Rosie worse," I observed dryly.

Riggs grinned sheepishly.

"I only wanted to make sure Miss Louise was there. Rosie started to run, and I tried to stop her and tell her some sort of story to account for my being there. But she wouldn't wait."

"And the broken china in the basket?"

"Well, broken china's death to rubber tires," he said. "I hadn't any complaint against you people here, and your car was a good one."

So Rosie's highwayman was explained.

"Well, I telegraphed the doctor where Miss Louise was and I kept an eye on her. Just a day or so before they came home with the body I got another letter, telling me to watch for a woman whose face had bad scars from a burn. Her name was Carrington, and the doctor made things pretty strong. If I found any such woman loafing around I was not to lose sight of her for a minute until he got back.

"Well, I would have had my hands full, but the other woman didn't show up for a good while, and when she did the doctor was home."

"Riggs," I asked abruptly, "did you get into this house a day or two after I took it, at night?"

"I did not, Miss Innes. I've never been in this house before. Well, the Carrington woman didn't show up until the night Mr. Halsey disappeared. Then she came to the office late and the doctor was out. She waited around, walking the floor and acting pretty excited. When the doctor didn't come back she was in an awful way. She wanted me to hunt him, and when he didn't appear she called him names and said he couldn't fool her. There was murder being done, and she would see him swing for it.

"She struck me as being an ugly customer, and when she left about eleven o'clock and went across to the Armstrong house in the village I wasn't far behind her. She walked all around the house first, looking up at the windows. Then she rang the bell, and the minute the door was opened she was through it and into the hall."

"How long did she stay?"

"That's the queer part of it," Riggs said, looking puzzled. "She didn't come out that night at all. I went to bed at daylight and that was the last I heard of her until the next day, when I saw her on a truck at the station, covered with a sheet. She'd been struck by the express and you'd hardly have known her. She was dead, of course. The station agent said she was crossing the track to take the up-train to town when the express struck her."

I was profoundly shocked. The death itself was horrible enough. But also we had apparently reached another dead end. Even Jamieson looked stunned.

"So that's that," I said. "We're back where we started."

Riggs, however, spoke up eagerly.

"It's not as bad as that," he said. "The Carrington woman came from the town in California where Mr. Armstrong died, and she knew something. I lived with Doctor Walker seven years, and I know him well. There are few things he is afraid of, but he was afraid of her. I think he killed Mr. Armstrong out there himself. That's what I think. What else he did I don't know, but he fired me and pretty nearly strangled me for telling Mr. Jamieson here about Mr. Innes's having been in his office the night he disappeared, and about my hearing them quarreling."

Jamieson turned to me.

"What was it Warner heard the Carrington woman say to your nephew in the library, Miss Innes?" he inquired.

"She said 'I knew there was something wrong from the start. A man isn't well one day and dead the next without some reason.'"

So the Carrington woman had known or suspected something, and now she was dead. Like the two Armstrong men, and my poor Thomas. And Halsey was still God only knew where.

30

IT WAS ON WEDNESDAY that Riggs told us the story of his connection with some of the situations which had been previously unexplained. Halsey had been gone since the Friday night before, and with the passage of each day I felt that his chances were lessening. I knew well enough that he might be carried thousands of miles in the boxcar, locked in perhaps without water or food. I had read of cases where bodies had been found locked in cars on isolated sidings in the West, and my spirits went down with every hour.

His recovery was destined to be almost as sudden as his disappearance, and was due directly to the tramp Alex had brought to Sunnyside. It seems the man was grateful for his release, and when he learned something of Halsey's whereabouts from another member of his fraternity he was prompt in letting us know.

On Wednesday evening Jamieson, who had been down at the Armstrong house trying to see Louise and failing, was met near the gate at Sunnyside by an individual as repulsive and unkempt as the one Alex had captured. The man knew the detective, and he gave him a piece of dirty paper, on which were scrawled the words—"Innes at City Hospital, Johnsville." The tramp who brought the paper pretended to know nothing except that the paper had been passed along from a "friend" in Johnsville, who seemed to know the information would be valuable to us.

Again the long-distance telephone came into requisition. Jamieson called the hospital, while we crowded around him. And when there was no longer any doubt that it was Halsey, and that he would probably recover, we all laughed and cried together. I am sure I kissed Liddy, and I have had terrible moments since when I seem to remember kissing Jamieson too, in the excitement.

Anyhow by eleven o'clock that night Gertrude was on her way to Johnsville, three hundred and eighty miles away, and accompanied by Rosie. The domestic force was now down to MaryAnne and Liddy, with the undergardener's wife coming every day to help out. Fortunately Warner and the detectives were keeping bachelor hall in the lodge. Out of deference to Liddy they washed their dishes once a day, and they concocted queer messes according to their several abilities. They had one triumph which they ate regularly for breakfast, and which formed a sort of odorous aura about them the rest of the day. It was bacon and onions, fried together. They were almost pathetically grateful, however, I noticed, for an occasional broiled tenderloin steak.

It was not until Gertrude and Rosie had gone and Sunnyside had settled down for the night, with Winters at the foot of the staircase, that Jamieson broached a subject he had evidently planned before he came.

"Miss Innes," he said, stopping me as I was about to go to my room upstairs, "how are your nerves tonight?"

"I have none," I said, almost gaily. "With Halsey found, my troubles have gone."

"I mean," he persisted, "do you feel as though you could go through with something rather unusual?"

"The most unusual thing I can think of would be a peaceful night. But if anything is going to happen don't dare to let me miss it."

"Something is going to happen," he said. "And you're the only woman I can think of that I can take along." He looked at his watch. "Don't ask me any questions, Miss Innes. Put on heavy shoes and some old dark clothes, and make up your mind not to be surprised at anything."

Liddy was sleeping the sleep of the just when I went upstairs, and I hunted out my things cautiously. The detective was waiting in the hall, and I was astonished to see Doctor Stewart with him. They were talking confidentially together, but when I came down they stopped. There were a few preparations to be made, the locks to be gone over, Winters to be instructed as to renewed vigilance, and then after extinguishing the hall light we crept in the darkness through the front door and into the night.

I asked no questions. I felt that they were doing me honor in making me one of the party, and I would show them I could be as silent as they. We went across the fields, passing through the woods that reached almost to the ruins of the stable, going over stiles now and then, and sometimes climbing over fences. Only once somebody spoke, and then it was an emphatic bit of profanity from Doctor Stewart when he ran into a barbed-wire fence.

We were joined at the end of five minutes by another man, who fell into step with the doctor silently. He carried something over his shoulder which I could not make out. In this way we walked for perhaps twenty minutes. I had lost all sense of direction: I merely stumbled along in silence, allowing Jamieson to guide me this way or that as the path demanded. I hardly know what I expected. Once when through a miscalculation I jumped a little short over a ditch and landed above my shoe tops in the water and ooze I remember wondering if this was really I, and if I had ever tasted life until that summer. I walked along with the water sloshing in my shoes, and I was actually cheerful. I remember whispering to Jamieson that I had never seen the stars so lovely, and that it was a mistake, when the Lord had made the night so beautiful, to sleep through it!

The doctor was not happy, however. He kept muttering about doing unlawful things and what would happen to him when the thing came out. If it ever did. And I remember Jamieson replying that what might happen to Doctor Stewart was nothing to what the department would do to him unless he could prove his case.

We were all puffing somewhat when we finally came to a halt. I confess that just then even Sunnyside seemed a cheerful spot. We had paused at the edge of a level cleared place, bordered all around with primly trimmed evergreen trees. Between them I caught a glimpse of starlight shining down on rows of white headstones, and an occasional more imposing monument or towering shaft. In spite of myself I drew my breath in sharply. We were on the edge of the Casanova churchyard.

I saw now both the man who had joined the party and the implements he carried. It was Alex, armed with two long-handled spades. After the first shock of surprise, I flatter myself if I was not cool I was at least quiet. We went in single file between the rows of headstones, and although when I found myself last I had an instinctive desire to keep looking back over my shoulder, I found when the first uneasiness is past that a cemetery at night is much the same as any other country place, filled with vague shadows and unexpected noises. Once, indeed—but Mr. Jamieson said it was an owl and I tried to believe him.

In the shadow of the Armstrong granite shaft we stopped. I think the doctor wanted to send me back.

"It's no place for a woman," I heard him protesting angrily. But Jamieson said something about witnesses, and the doctor came over and felt my pulse.

"Anyhow, I don't believe you're any worse off here than you would be in that nightmare of a house," he said finally, and put his coat on the steps of the shaft for me to sit on.

There is an air of finality about a grave. One watches the earth thrown in, with the feeling that this is the end. Whatever has gone before, whatever is to come in eternity, that particular temple of the soul has been given back to the elements from which it came. So there is a sense of desecration, of a reversal of the everlasting fitness of things, in resurrecting a body from its mother earth. Nevertheless, I sat quietly by and watched Alex and Jamieson steaming over their work, without a single qualm except the fear of detection.

The doctor kept a keen lookout, but no one appeared. Once in a while he came over to me, and gave me a reassuring pat on the shoulder.

"I never expected to come to this," he said once. "There's one thing sure, I'll not be suspected of complicity. A doctor is generally supposed to be handier at burying folks than at digging them up."

Then the uncanny moment came when Alex and Jamieson tossed the spades on the grass, and I confess I hid my face. There was a longish period of strain I know, while the heavy coffin was being raised, and I felt my composure going. For fear I would shriek I tried to think of something else, of what time Gertrude would reach Halsey, or of anything but the grisly reality that lay just beyond me on the grass.

Then I heard a low exclamation from the detective and I felt the pressure of the doctor's fingers on my arm.

"Now, Miss Innes," he said gently. "If you will come over—"

I held on to him frantically, and somehow I got there and looked down. The lid of the casket had been raised and a silver plate on it proved we had made no mistake. But the face that showed in the light of the lantern was a face I had never seen before. The man who lay before us was not Paul Armstrong.

31

WHAT WITH the excitement of the discovery, the walk home under the stars in wet shoes and draggled skirts, and getting upstairs and undressed without rousing Liddy, I was completely used up. What to do with my shoes was the greatest puzzle of all, there being no place in the house safe from Liddy, until I decided to slip upstairs the next morning and drop them into the hole the "ghost" had made in the trunk-room wall.

I went to bed after I reached this decision, but only to a light sleep in which I lived over again the events of the night. Again I saw the group around the silent figure on the grass, and again as had happened at the grave I heard Alex's voice, tense and triumphant: "Now we've got them," he said. Only, in my nervous condition he seemed to say it over and over, until I finally took a sleeping tablet to shut out his voice.

I wakened early in spite of my fatigue, and lay there thinking. Who was Alex? I no longer believed he was a gardener. Who was the man whose body we had resurrected? And where was Paul Armstrong? Probably living safe in some extraditionless country on the fortune he had stolen. Did Louise and her mother know of the shameful and wicked deception? What had Thomas known, and Mrs. Watson? And who was Nina Carrington?

This last question, it seemed to me, was answered. In some way the woman had learned of the substitution, and had tried to use her knowledge for blackmail. Nina Carrington's own story had died with her, but however it happened it was clear that she had carried her knowledge to Halsey the afternoon Gertrude and I were looking for clues to the man I had shot on the east veranda.

Halsey had probably been half crazed by what he heard, since it was evident Louise was marrying Doctor Walker to keep the shameful secret for her mother's sake. Always reckless, he had gone at once to Doctor Walker and denounced him. There had been a scene, and he left on his way to the station to meet and notify Jamieson of what he had learned. The doctor was active mentally and physically. Accompanied perhaps by Riggs, who had shown himself not overscrupulous until he quarreled with his employer, he had gone to the railroad embankment. But what had happened after that I did not know. It seemed likely that he had knocked Halsey unconscious so that the car hit the freight. Or with Halsey out cold he had himself directed the car and jumped before it struck.

I still think my reconstruction good, if not entirely correct.

There was a telegram that morning from Gertrude.

"Halsey conscious and improving. No fracture. Home as soon as possible.   GERTRUDE."

With Halsey found and getting better, and with at last something to work on, I began that day, Thursday, with fresh courage. As Jamieson had said, the lines were closing up. That I was to be caught and almost finished in the closing was happily unknown to us all.

It was late when I got up. I lay in my bed, looking around the four walls of the room and trying to imagine behind what one of them a secret chamber might lie. Certainly in daylight Sunnyside deserved its name. Never was a house more cheery and open, less sinister in general appearance. There was not a corner apparently that was not clear and above board, and yet I believed firmly that somewhere behind its handsomely papered walls there lay a hidden space, with all the possibilities it would involve.

I did not believe that a reputable architect would supply such a hiding spot and then keep quiet about it, in view of the enormous publicity the press had given us. And that morning I called the only contractor in Casanova. He had done no work in the house himself, he said. But something had been done a year or so before. The workmen had come by truck from the city. That was all he knew, but it was enough.

I made a mental note to have the house measured during the day to discover any discrepancy between the outer and inner walls, and I tried to recall again the exact wording of the paper Jamieson had found.

The slip had said "chimney." It was the only clue, and a house as large as

Sunnyside was full of them. There was an open fireplace in my dressing room, but none in the bedroom, and as I lay there looking around I thought of something that made me sit up suddenly. The trunk room just over my head had an open fireplace and a brick chimney, and yet there was nothing of the kind in my room. I got out of bed and examined the opposite wall closely. There was apparently no flue, and I knew there was none in the hall just beneath. The house was heated by steam, as I have said before. In the living room was a huge open fireplace, but it was on the other side.

Why did the trunk room have both a radiator and an open fireplace? Architects were not usually erratic. It was not fifteen minutes before I was upstairs, armed with a tape measure in lieu of a foot rule, eager to justify Jamieson's opinion of my intelligence, and firmly resolved not to tell him of my suspicion until I had more than theory to go on. The hole in the trunk-room wall still yawned there, between the chimney and the outer wall. I examined it again, with no new result. The space between the brick wall and the plaster and lath one, however, now had a new significance. The hole showed only one side of the chimney, and I determined to investigate what lay in the space on the other side of the mantel.

I worked feverishly. Liddy had gone to the village to market, it being her firm belief that the store people sent short measure unless she watched the scales, and that since the failure of the Traders' Bank we must watch the corners, and I knew that what I wanted to do must be done before she came back. I had no tools, but after rummaging around I found a pair of garden scissors and a hatchet, and thus armed I set to work. The plaster came out easily, but the lathing was more obstinate. It gave under my blows, only to spring back into place again, and the necessity for caution made it doubly hard.

I had a blister on my palm when at last the hatchet went through and fell with what sounded like the report of a gun to my overstrained nerves. I sat on a trunk, waiting to hear Liddy fly up the stairs, with the household behind her like the tail of a comet. But nothing happened, and with a growing feeling of uneasiness I set to work enlarging the opening.

The result was absolutely nil. When I could hold a lighted candle in the opening I saw precisely what I had seen on the other side of the chimney, a space between the true wall and the false one, possibly seven feet long and about three feet wide. It was in no sense of the word a secret chamber, and it was evident it had not been disturbed since the house was built. It was a supreme disappointment.

It had been Jamieson's idea that the hidden room, if there was one, would be found somewhere near the circular staircase. In fact I knew that he had once investigated the entire length of the clothes chute, hanging to a rope, with this in view. I was reluctantly about to concede that he had been right when my eyes fell on the mantel and fireplace. The latter had evidently never been used. It was closed with a metal fire front, and only when the front refused to move, and investigation showed that it was not intended to be moved, did my spirits revive.

I hurried into the next room. Yes, sure enough there was a similar mantel and fireplace there, similarly closed. In both rooms the chimney flue extended well out from the wall. I measured with the tape line, my hands trembling so that I could scarcely hold it. They extended two feet and a half into each room, which, with the three feet of space between the two partitions, made eight feet to be accounted for. Eight feet in one direction and almost seven in the other—what a chimney it was!

But I had only located the hidden room. I was not in it, and no amount of pressing on the carving of the wooden mantels, no search of the floors for loose boards, none of the customary methods availed at all. That there was a means of entrance, and probably a simple one, I could be certain. But what? What would I find if I did get in? Was the detective right, and were the bonds and money from the Traders' Bank there? Or was our whole theory wrong? Would not Paul Armstrong have taken his booty with him when he went West? Even if he had not, if Doctor Walker was in the secret he would have known how to enter the chimney room. Then who had dug the other hole in the false partition?

I determined to keep my discovery to myself until I could make another attempt to get into the room, and was able to face Jamieson that morning with what I hope was my usual calm. He himself, however, showed a certain eagerness and suppressed excitement.

I gathered that the body had been restored to its grave and that he like myself was still playing a waiting game. Which was a mistake on my part at least.

32

LIDDY DISCOVERED the fresh break in the trunk room while we were at luncheon, and ran shrieking down the stairs. She maintained that as she entered unseen hands had been digging at the plaster, that they had stopped when she went in, and that she had felt a gust of cold damp air. In support of her story she carried in my wet and muddy shoes, which I had unluckily forgotten to hide, and held them out to the detective and myself.

"What did I tell you?" she said dramatically. "Look at 'em. They're yours, Miss Rachel, and covered with mud and soaked to the tops. I tell you, you can scoff all you like! Something's been wearing your shoes. As sure as you sit there, there's the smell of the graveyard on them. How do we know they weren't tramping through the Casanova graveyard last night, and sitting on the graves!"

Jamieson almost choked to death. "I wouldn't be at all surprised if they were doing that very thing, Liddy," he said, when he got his breath. "They certainly look like it."

I think he already had a plan on which he was working, and which was meant to be a coup. But things went so fast there was no time to carry it into effect. The first thing that occurred was a message from the Emergency Hospital that Mrs. Watson was dying and had asked for me. I did not care much about going. There may be a sort of melancholy pleasure to be had out of a funeral, with its pomp and ritual, but I shrank from a deathbed. However, Liddy got out the black things I keep for such dismal occasions, and I went. I left Jamieson and another detective going over every inch of the circular staircase, pounding, probing and measuring. I was inwardly elated to think of the surprise I was going to give them that night, and as it turned out I did surprise them, almost into collapse.

I drove from the train to the Emergency Hospital, and was at once taken to a ward. There, in a gray-walled room in a high iron bed lay Mrs. Watson. She was very weak, and she only opened her eyes and looked at me when I sat down beside her. I was conscience-stricken. We had been so engrossed that I had left this poor creature to die without even a word of sympathy.

The nurse gave her a stimulant, and in a little while she was able to talk. But so broken and half coherent was her story that I shall tell it in my own way. In an hour from the time I entered the hospital I had heard a sad and pitiful narrative, and had seen a woman slip into the unconsciousness that is only a step from death.

Briefly, the housekeeper's story was this:

She was almost forty years old, and had been the sister-mother of a large family of children. One by one they had died, and been buried beside their parents in a little town in the Middle West. There was only one sister left, the baby, Lucy. On her the older girl had lavished all the love of an impulsive and emotional nature. When Anne, the elder, was thirty-two and Lucy was nineteen, a young man had come to the town. He was going east after spending the summer at a celebrated ranch in Wyoming, one of those places where wealthy men send worthless and dissipated sons for a season of temperance, fresh air and riding. The sisters of course knew nothing of this, and the young man's ardor carried them away. In a word, seven years before Lucy Haswell had married a young man whose name was given as Aubrey Wallace.

Anne Haswell had married a carpenter in her native town, and was a widow. For three months everything went fairly well. Aubrey took his bride to Chicago, where they lived at a hotel. Perhaps the very unsophistication that had charmed him in Valley Mill jarred on him in the city. He had been far from a model husband, even for the three months, and when he disappeared Anne was almost thankful. It was different with the young wife, however. She drooped and fretted, and on the birth of her baby boy she had died. Anne took the child, and named him Lucien.

Anne had had no children of her own, and on Lucien she had lavished all her aborted maternal instinct. On one thing she was determined, however.

That was that Aubrey Wallace should educate his boy. It was a part of her devotion to the child that she should be ambitious for him. He must have every opportunity. And so she came east. She drifted around, doing plain sewing and keeping a home somewhere always for the boy. Finally, she realized that her only training had been domestic, and she put the boy in an Episcopalian home and secured the position of housekeeper to the Armstrongs. There she found Lucien's father, this time under his own name. It was Arnold Armstrong.

I gathered that there was no particular enmity at that time in Anne's mind. She told him of the boy, and threatened exposure if he did not provide for him. And for a time at least he did so. Then he realized that Lucien was the ruling passion in this lonely woman's life. He found out where the child was hidden, and threatened to take him away. Anne was frantic. The positions became reversed. Where Arnold had given money for Lucien's support, as time went on he forced money from Anne Watson instead until she was always penniless. The lower Arnold sank in the scale, the heavier his demands became. With the rupture between him and his family things were worse, and Anne took the child from the home and hid him in a farmhouse near Casanova, on the Claysburg road. There she went sometimes to see the boy, and there he had taken fever. The people were Germans, and he called the farmer's wife Grossmutter. He had grown into a beautiful boy, and he was all Anne had to live for.

The Armstrongs left for California, and Arnold's persecutions began anew. He was furious over the child's disappearance and she was afraid he would do her some hurt. She left the big house and went down to the lodge. When I had rented Sunnyside, however, she had thought the persecutions would stop. She had applied for the position of housekeeper, and secured it.

That had been on Saturday, and that night Louise arrived unexpectedly from the West. Thomas sent for Mrs. Watson and then went for Arnold Armstrong at the Greenwood Club. Anne had been fond of Louise. Apparently she reminded her of Lucy. She did not know what the trouble was, but Louise had been in a state of terrible excitement. Mrs. Watson tried to hide from Arnold when he appeared, but he did not stay long. He had quarreled with Louise and left the lodge in an ugly mood.

Watching from a window she saw him go up to Sunnyside and apparently be admitted there. But he stayed only a few minutes and then departed.

In the meantime she and Thomas had got Louise quiet, and a little before three she herself started up to the house. Thomas had a key to the east entry, and he gave it to her.

On the way across the lawn she was confronted by Arnold, who for some reason was determined to get into the house again. He had a golf stick in his hand, which he had picked up somewhere, and on her refusal to admit him he had struck her with it. One hand had been badly cut, and it was that, poisoning having set in, which caused her present condition. She broke away in a frenzy of rage and fear, and got into the house while Gertrude and Jack Bailey were at the front door. She went upstairs, hardly knowing what she was doing. Gertrude's door was open, and Halsey's revolver lay there on the bed. She picked it up and ran part way down the circular staircase, where she could hear Arnold fumbling at the lock outside. She slipped down quietly and opened the door, and he was inside before she had got back to the stairs. It was quite dark, but she could see his white shirt bosom. From the fourth step she fired. As he fell, she heard Gertrude in the billiard room scream, and she was fairly trapped. When the alarm was raised she had had no time to get upstairs. She hid outside in the grounds until everyone was down on the lower floor. Then she slipped upstairs and threw the revolver out of an upper window, going down again in time to admit the men from the Greenwood Club.

If Thomas had suspected her, he had never told. When she found the hand Arnold had injured was growing worse she gave the address of Lucien at Richfield to the old man, and almost a hundred dollars. The money was for Lucien's board until she recovered. Now she had sent for me to ask me if I would try to interest the Armstrongs in the child. When she found herself growing worse she had written to Mrs. Armstrong, telling her nothing but that Arnold's legitimate child was at Richfield, and imploring her to recognize him. She was dying, she said, the boy was an Armstrong, and entitled to his father's share of the estate. The papers were in her trunk at Sunnyside, with letters from the dead man which would prove what she said. She was going. She would not be judged by earthly laws, and somewhere else perhaps Lucy would plead for her. It was she who had crept down the circular staircase the night Jamieson had heard someone there. When he followed her, she had fled madly through the first door she came to. She had fallen down the clothes chute, and been saved by the basket of sheets underneath. I could have cried with relief. It had not been Gertrude, after all!

That was the story. Sad and tragic though it was, the very telling of it seemed to relieve the dying woman. She did not know that Thomas was dead, and I did not tell her. I promised to look after little Lucien, and sat with her until the intervals of consciousness grew shorter and finally ceased altogether. She died that night.

33

As I DROVE RAPIDLY back to the house from Casanova station in the taxi I saw the detective Burns loitering across the street from the Walker place. So Jamieson was already putting the screws on, lightly now but ready to give them a twist or two, I felt certain, very soon.

The house was quiet. Two steps of the circular staircase had been pried off without result, and beyond a second message from Gertrude, that Halsey insisted on coming home and they would arrive that night, there was nothing new. Jamieson, having failed to locate the secret room, had gone to the village. I learned afterward that he called at Doctor Walker's, under pretense of an attack of acute indigestion, and before he left had inquired about the evening trains to the city. He said he had wasted a lot of time on the case, and a good bit of the mystery was in my imagination! The doctor was under the impression that the house was guarded day and night. Well, give a place a reputation like that, and you don't need a guard at all—thus Jamieson. And sure enough, late in the afternoon the two detectives, accompanied by Jamieson himself, walked down the main street of Casanova and took a city-bound train.

That they got off at the next station and walked back again to Sunnyside at dusk was not known at the time. Personally I knew nothing of either move. I had other things to absorb me at that time.

Liddy brought me some tea while I rested after my trip, and on the tray was a small book from the Casanova library. It was called *The Unseen World* and had a cheerful cover on which a half dozen sheeted figures linked hands around a headstone.

At this point in my story, Halsey always says: "Trust a woman to add two and two together, and make six." To which I retort that if two and two plus x makes six, then to discover the unknown quantity is the simplest thing in the world. That a houseful of detectives missed it entirely was because they were busy trying to prove that two and two make four.

The depression due to my visit to the hospital left me at the prospect of seeing Halsey again that night. It was about five o'clock when Liddy left me for a nap before dinner, having put me into a gray-silk dressing gown and a pair of slippers. I listened to her retreating footsteps, and as soon as she was safely belowstairs I went up to the trunk room. The place had not been disturbed, and I proceeded once again to try to discover the entrance to the hidden room. The openings on either side, as I have said, showed nothing but perhaps three feet of brick wall. There was no sign of an entrance—no levers, no hinges, to give a hint. Either the mantel or the roof, I decided, and after a half hour at the mantel, productive of absolutely no result, I decided to try the roof.

I am not fond of a height. The few occasions on which I have climbed a stepladder have always left me dizzy and weak in the knees. The top of the Washington Monument is as impossible to me as the elevation of the presidential chair. And yet I climbed out onto the Sunnyside roof without a second's hesitation. Like a dog on a scent, like my bearskin progenitor with his spear and his wild boar, to me now there was the lust of the chase, the frenzy of pursuit, the dust of battle. I got quite a little of the latter on me as I climbed from the unfinished ballroom out through a window to the roof of the east wing of the building, which was only two stories in height.

Once out there, access to the top of the main building was rendered easy— at least it looked easy—by a small vertical iron ladder, fastened to the wall outside of the ballroom and perhaps twelve feet high. The twelve feet looked

short from below, but they were difficult to climb. I gathered my gown around
me and succeeded finally in making the top of the ladder. Once there, however, I was completely out of breath. I sat down, my feet on the top rung,
and put my hairpins in more securely, while the wind belled my dressing
gown out like a sail. I had torn a great strip of the silk loose, and now I ruthlessly finished the destruction of the thing by jerking the strip free and tying
it around my head.

From far below the smallest sounds came up with peculiar distinctness.
I could hear the paper boy whistling down the drive, and I heard something
else. I heard the thud of a stone, and a spit followed by a long and startled
meiou from Beulah. I forgot my fear of a height, and advanced boldly almost
to the edge of the roof.

It was half past six by that time, and growing dusk.

"You boy, down there!" I called.

The paper boy turned and looked around. Then seeing nobody he raised
his eyes. It was a moment before he located me. When he did he stood for
one moment as if paralyzed, then he gave a horrible yell and dropping his
papers bolted across the lawn to the road without stopping to look around.
Once he fell, and his impetus was so great that he turned an involuntary
somersault. He was up and off again without any perceptible pause, and he
leaped the hedge—which I am sure under ordinary stress would have been
quite a feat for any man.

With Johnny Sweeny a cloud of dust down the road and the dinner hour
approaching I hurried on with my investigations. Luckily the roof was flat,
and I was able to go over every inch of it. But the result was disappointing; no
trap door revealed itself, no window, nothing but a couple of pipes two inches
across and standing perhaps eighteen inches high and three feet apart, with
a cap to prevent rain from entering and raised to permit the passage of air.
I picked up a pebble from the roof and dropped it down, listening with my
ear at one of the pipes. I could hear it strike on something with a sharp,
metallic sound, but it was impossible for me to tell how far it had gone.

I gave up finally and went down the ladder again, getting in through the
ballroom window without being observed. I went back at once to the trunk
room, and sitting down on a box I gave my mind as consistently as I could to
the problem before me. If the pipes in the roof were ventilators to the secret
room, and there was no trap door above, the entrance was probably in one of
the two rooms between which it lay. Unless indeed the room had been built
with the house, and the opening then closed with a brick and mortar wall.

The mantel fascinated me. Made of wood and carved, the more I looked
the more I wondered that I had not noticed before the absurdity of such a
mantel in such a place. It was covered with scrolls and panels, and finally
by the merest accident I pushed one of the panels to the side. It moved easily,
revealing a small brass knob.

It is not necessary to detail the fluctuations of hope and despair, and not
a little fear of what lay beyond, with which I twisted and turned the knob.

It moved, but nothing seemed to happen, and then I discovered the trouble. I pushed the knob vigorously to one side, and the whole mantel swung loose from the wall almost a foot, revealing a cavernous space beyond.

I took a long breath, closed the door from the trunk room into the hall— thank Heaven, I did not lock it—and pulling the mantel-door wide open I stepped into the chimney room. I had time to get a hazy view of a small portable safe, a common wooden table and a chair, then the mantel door swung to and clicked behind me. I stood quite still for a moment in the darkness, unable to comprehend what had happened. Then I turned and beat furiously at the door with my fists. It was closed and locked again, and my fingers in the darkness slid over a smooth wooden surface without a sign of a knob.

I was furiously angry, at myself, at the mantel-door, at everything. I was not afraid of suffocating. Before the thought had come to me I had already seen a gleam of light from the two small ventilating pipes in the roof. But they supplied air and nothing else. The room itself was shrouded in blackness.

I sat down in the stiff-backed chair and tried to remember how many days one could live without food and water. When that grew monotonous and rather painful I got up and, according to the time-honored rule of people shut in unknown and ink-black prisons, I felt my way around. It was small enough, goodness knows. I felt nothing but a splintery surface of wood, and in endeavoring to get back to the chair something struck me full in the face and fell with the noise of a thousand explosions to the ground. When I had gathered up my nerves again I found it had been the bulb of a swinging electric light, and that had it not been for the accident I might have starved to death in an illuminated sepulcher.

I must have dozed off. I am sure I did not faint. I was never more composed in my life. I remember planning, if I was not discovered, who would have my things. I knew Liddy would want my heliotrope foulard, and she's a fright in lavender. Once or twice I heard mice in the partitions, and so I sat on the table with my feet on the chair. I imagined I could hear the search going on through the house, and once someone came into the trunk room. I could distinctly hear footsteps.

"In the chimney! In the chimney!" I called with all my might, and was rewarded by a piercing shriek from Liddy and the slam of the trunk-room door.

I felt easier after that, although the room was oppressively hot and enervating. I had no doubt the search for me would now come in the right direction, and after a little I got down to the chair and dropped into a doze.

How long I slept I do not know. It must have been several hours, for I had been tired from a busy day, and I wakened stiff from my awkward position. I could not remember where I was for a few minutes, and my head felt heavy and congested. Gradually I roused to my surroundings, and to the fact that in spite of the ventilators the air was bad and growing worse. I was breathing long, gasping respirations, and my face was damp and clammy. I must have been there a long time, and the searchers were probably hunting outside the house, dredging the creek or beating the woodland. I knew that another hour or two would find me unconscious, and with my inability to cry out would go my only chance of rescue. It was the combination of bad air and heat probably, for some inadequate ventilation was coming through the pipes. I tried to retain my consciousness by walking the length of the room and back, over and over, but I had not the strength to keep it up, so I sat down on the chair again, my back against the wall.

The house was very still. Once my straining ears seemed to catch a footfall beneath me, possibly in my own room. I groped for the chair from the table, and pounded with it frantically on the floor. But nothing happened. I realized bitterly that if the sound was heard at all no doubt it was classed with the other rappings which had so alarmed us recently.

It was impossible to judge the flight of time. I measured five minutes by counting my pulse, allowing seventy-two beats to the minute. But it took eternities, and toward the last I found it hard to count. My head was confused.

And then I heard sounds from below me, in the house. There was a peculiar throbbing, vibrating noise which I felt rather than heard, much like the pulsing beat of fire engines in the city. For one awful moment I thought the house was on fire, and every drop of blood in my body gathered around my heart. Then I knew. It was the engine of the car, and Halsey had come back. Hope sprang up afresh. Halsey's clear head and Gertrude's intuition might do what Liddy's hysteria and three detectives had failed to discover.

After a time I thought I had been right. There was certainly something going on down below. Doors were slamming, people were hurrying through the halls, and certain high notes of excited voices penetrated to me shrilly. I hoped they were coming closer, but after a time the sounds died away below and I was left once more to the silence and heat, to the weight of the darkness, to the oppression of walls that seemed to close in on me and stifle me.

The first warning I had was a stealthy fumbling at the lock of the mantel-door. With my mouth open to scream I stopped. Perhaps the situation had rendered me acute, perhaps it was instinctive. Whatever it was I sat without moving, while someone outside in absolute stillness ran his fingers over the carving of the mantel and found the panel.

Now the sounds below redoubled. From the clatter and jarring I knew that several people were running up the stairs, and as the sounds approached I could even hear what they said.

"Watch the staircases!" Jamieson was shouting. "Damnation, there's no light here!" And then a second later: "All together now. One—two—three—"

The door into the trunk room had evidently been locked from the inside. At the second that it gave, opening against the wall with a crash and evidently tumbling somebody into the room, the stealthy fingers beyond the mantel-door gave the knob the proper impetus, and the door swung open and closed again. Only—and Liddy always screams and puts her fingers in her ears at this point—only now I was not alone in the chimney room. There was someone else in the darkness, someone who breathed hard and was so close I could have touched him with my hand.

I was in a paralysis of terror. Outside there were excited voices and incredulous oaths. The trunks were being jerked around in a frantic search, the windows were thrown open, only to show a sheer drop of forty feet. And the man in the room with me leaned against the mantel-door and listened. His pursuers were plainly baffled, and I heard him draw a long breath and turn to grope his way through the blackness. Then he touched my hand, cold, clammy, death-like.

A hand in an empty room! He drew in his breath, the sharp intaking of horror that fills lungs suddenly collapsed. Beyond jerking his hand away instantly he made no movement. I think absolute terror had him by the throat, for he stepped back without turning, retreating foot by foot from the Dread in the corner, and I do not think he breathed.

Then with the relief of space between us I screamed, ear-splittingly, madly, and they heard me outside.

"In the chimney!" I shrieked. "Behind the mantel! The mantel!"

With an oath the figure hurled itself across the room at me, and I screamed again. In his blind fury he had missed me, and I heard him strike the wall. That one time I escaped him, and now I was across the room and had got the chair. He stood for a second, listening, then he made another rush and I struck out with my weapon. I think it stunned him, for I had a second's respite when I could hear him breathing, and someone shouted outside:

"We can't get in. How does it open?"

But the man in the room had changed his tactics. I knew he was creeping on me, inch by inch, and I could not tell from where. And then he caught me. He held his hand over my mouth, and I bit him. I was helpless, strangling, and someone was trying to break in the mantel from the wall at the side. It began to yield somewhere, for a thin wedge of yellowish light was reflected on the opposite wall. When he saw that my assailant dropped me with a curse. Then the opposite wall swung open noiselessly, closed again without a sound, and I was alone. The intruder was gone.

"In the next room!" I called wildly. "The next room!" But the sound of blows on the mantel drowned my voice. By the time I had made them understand a couple of minutes had elapsed. The pursuit was taken up then by all except Alex, who was determined to liberate me. When I stepped out into the trunk room, a free woman again, I could hear the chase far below.

I must say, for all Alex's anxiety to set me free, he paid little enough attention to my plight. He jumped through the opening into the secret room, and picked up the portable safe.

"I am going to put this in Mr. Halsey's room, Miss Innes," he said, "and I'll send one of the detectives to guard it."

I hardly heard him. I wanted to laugh and cry in the same breath, to crawl into bed and have a cup of tea and scold Liddy and do any of the thousand natural things that I had never expected to do again. And the air! The touch of the cool night air on my face!

As Alex and I reached the second floor Jamieson met us. He was grave and quiet, and he nodded comprehendingly when he saw the safe.

"Will you come with me for a moment Miss Innes?" he asked soberly, and on my assenting he led the way to the east wing. There were lights moving around below, and some of the maids were standing gaping down. They screamed when they saw me, and drew back to let me pass. There was a sort of hush over the scene. Alex behind me muttered something I could not hear, and brushed past me without ceremony. Then I realized that a man was lying doubled up at the foot of the staircase, and that Alex was stooping over him.

As I came slowly down, Winters stepped back and Alex straightened himself, looking at me across the body with impenetrable eyes. In his hand he held a shaggy gray wig, and before me on the floor lay the man whose headstone stood in Casanova churchyard—Paul Armstrong.

Winters told the story in a dozen words. In his headlong flight down the circular staircase with Winters just behind, Armstrong had pitched forward violently, struck his head against the door to the east veranda, and broken his neck. He had died as Winters reached him.

As the detective finished I saw Halsey, pale and shaken, in the cardroom doorway, and for the first time that night I lost my self-control. I put my arms around my boy, and for a moment he had to support me. But a second later over Halsey's shoulder I saw something that turned my emotion into other channels. For behind him in the shadowy cardroom were Gertrude and Alex, the gardener, and—there is no use mincing matters—he was kissing her!

I was unable to speak. Twice I opened my mouth, then I turned Halsey around and pointed. They were quite unconscious of us. Her head was on his shoulder, his face against her hair. As it happened, it was Jamieson who broke up the tableau.

He stepped over to Alex and touched him on the arm.

"And now," he said quietly, "how long are you and I to play our little comedy, Mr. Bailey?"

34

OF DOCTOR WALKER'S sensational escape that night to South America, of the recovery of over a million dollars in cash and securities in the safe from the chimney room, the papers have kept the public well informed. Of my share in discovering the secret chamber they have been singularly silent. The inner history has never been told. Lieutenant Jamieson got all kinds of credit, and some of it he deserved. But if Jack Bailey as Alex had not traced Halsey and insisted on the disinterring of Paul Armstrong's casket, if he had not suspected the truth from the start, where would the detective have been?

When Halsey learned the truth he insisted on going the next morning, weak as he was, to Louise; and by night she was at Sunnyside under Gertrude's particular care, while her mother had gone to Barbara Fitzhugh's.

What Halsey said to Mrs. Armstrong I never knew, but that he was considerate and chivalrous I feel confident. It was Halsey's way always with women.

He and Louise had no conversation together until that night. Gertrude and Alex—I mean Jack—had gone for a walk, although it was nine o'clock and anybody but a pair of young geese would have known the night air was chilly, and that it is next to impossible to get rid of a summer cold.

At half after nine, growing weary of my own company, I went downstairs to find the young people. At the door of the living room I paused. Gertrude and Jack had returned and were there, sitting together on a divan, with only one lamp lighted. They did not see or hear me, and I beat a hasty retreat to the library. But here again I was driven back. Louise was sitting in a deep chair, looking the happiest I had ever seen her, with Halsey on the arm of the chair holding both her hands.

It was no place for an elderly spinster. I retired to my upstairs sitting room and got out Sally Klinefelter's lavender slippers. Ah, well, the foster motherhood would soon have to be put away in camphor again.

The next day, by degrees, I got the whole story.

Paul Armstrong had a besetting evil, the love of money. Common enough, but he loved money not for what it would buy but for its own sake. An examination of the books showed no irregularities in the past year since John had been cashier, but before that, in the time of Anderson, the old cashier who had died, much strange juggling had been done with the records. The railroad in New Mexico had apparently drained the banker's private fortune, and he determined to retrieve it by one stroke. This was nothing less than the looting of the bank's securities, turning them into money and making his escape.

But the law has long arms. Paul Armstrong had evidently studied the situation carefully. Just as they say that the only good Indian is a dead Indian, so the only safe defaulter is a dead defaulter. He decided to die, to all appearances, and thus when the hue and cry subsided be able to enjoy his money almost anywhere he wished.

The first necessity was an accomplice. The connivance of Doctor Walker was suggested by his love for Louise. The man was unscrupulous, and with the girl as a bait Paul Armstrong soon had him fast. The plan was apparently the acme of simplicity; a small town in the West, an attack of heart disease, a body from a medical college dissecting room shipped in a trunk to Doctor Walker by a colleague in San Francisco, and palmed off for the supposed dead banker. What was simpler?

The woman, Nina Carrington, was the cog that slipped. What she only suspected, what she really knew, we never learned. Early in life she had evidently been badly burned in a fire, and so scarred that marriage was improbable. When and how her suspicions were aroused in California we never learned, but it was obviously her hope that by blackmailing Doctor Walker she could secure funds or indefinite support. In any case she made his situation desperate. To pay the woman to keep quiet would be confession. He denied the whole thing, and she went to Halsey.

It was this that had taken Halsey to the doctor the night he disappeared. He accused the doctor of the deception and threatened him with police action at once. I believe too that he saw Louise that night and demanded to know her part in the plot. However that may be, during the interval he was in the Armstrong house either Walker or Paul Armstrong—still lame where I had shot him—had concealed himself in the back of his car. Near the railroad track he had been struck over the head and after he had been removed the car was driven head on into the freight train.

In whatever manner it was done, for three days Halsey lay in the boxcar tied hand and foot, suffering tortures of thirst, delirious at times, and discovered by a tramp at Johnsville only in time to save his life.

As to Paul Armstrong, at the last moment his plans had been frustrated. Sunnyside, with its hoard in the chimney room, had been rented without his knowledge! Attempts to dislodge me having failed, he was driven to breaking into his own house. The ladder in the chute, the burning of the stable and the entrance through the cardroom window, all were in the course of a desperate attempt to get into the chimney room.

Louise and her mother had from the first been the great stumbling blocks. The plan had been to send Louise away until it was too late for her to interfere, but she came back to the hotel where they were living in California just at the wrong time. There was a terrible scene. The girl was told that something of the kind was necessary; that the bank was about to close and her stepfather would either avoid arrest and disgrace in this way or kill himself. Fanny Armstrong was a weakling, but Louise was more difficult to manage. She had no love for her stepfather, but her devotion to her mother was entire and self-sacrificing. Forced into acquiescence by her mother's appeals and overwhelmed by the situation, the girl finally consented and escaped.

From somewhere in Colorado she sent an anonymous telegram to Jack Bailey at the Traders' Bank. Trapped as she was, she did not want to see an innocent man arrested. The telegram, received on Thursday, had sent the cashier to the bank that night in a frenzy.

Louise arrived at Sunnyside and found the house rented. Not knowing what to do she sent for Arnold at the Greenwood Club, and told him a little, not all. She told him that there was something wrong, that the bank was about to close, and that his father was responsible. Of the conspiracy she said nothing. To her surprise Arnold already knew, through Bailey that night, that things were not right. Moreover, he suspected what Louise did not, that the money was hidden at Sunnyside. He had a scrap of paper that indicated a concealed room somewhere.

His cupidity was aroused at once. Eager to get Halsey and Jack Bailey out

of the house, he went up to the east entry, and in the billiard room gave
Bailey what he had refused earlier in the evening, the address of Paul Armstrong in California and a telegram which had been forwarded to the club
for Bailey from Doctor Walker. It was in response to one Bailey had sent, and
it said that Paul Armstrong was very ill.

Bailey was almost desperate. He decided to go West and see Armstrong,
and to force him to admit the facts. But the catastrophe at the bank occurred
sooner than he had expected. On the moment of starting West, at Andrews
station where Jamieson had located the car, he read that the bank had closed
and going back to town surrendered himself.

Bailey had known Paul Armstrong intimately. He did not believe the
money was gone. It was hardly possible in the interval since the securities
had been taken. Where was it? From some chance remark let fall some
months earlier by Arnold Armstrong when he had been drinking, he felt sure
there was a hidden room at Sunnyside, and tried to see the architect of the
building. But, like the contractor, if he knew of such a room he refused any
information.

It was at that time Halsey came forward with his plan. I had seen Bailey
only once and that casually. He suggested that Jack make certain alterations
in his appearance, shaving off his small mustache and changing the way he
wore his hair, and buying some cheap clothing. In this disguise he could
probably find some work on the property, and look it over whenever he got
a chance.

"I told him you were half blind," Halsey said. "Half deaf too. I'm afraid
you were rather a shock to him."

"Then it was reciprocal," I retorted. "He had me scared out of my wits."

For of course it had been Jack Bailey, alias Alex, who had been our ghost.
Not only had he alarmed Louise—and himself, he admitted—on the circular
staircase, but he had dug the hole in the trunk-room wall, and later sent
Eliza into hysterics. The note Liddy had found in Gertrude's scrapbasket
was from him, and it was he who had shocked me into fainting by the clothes
chute and, with Gertrude's help, had carried me to Louise's room. Gertrude,
I learned, had watched all night beside me, in an extremity of anxiety.

That old Thomas had seen his master and thought he had seen his ghost,
there could be no doubt. Of that story of Thomas's, about seeing Jack Bailey
in the footpath between the club and Sunnyside the night Liddy and I heard
the noise on the circular staircase, that too was right. On the night before
Arnold Armstrong was murdered Bailey had made his first attempt to search
for the secret room. He secured Arnold's keys from his room at the club and
got into the house, armed with a golf stick for sounding the walls. He ran
against the hamper at the head of the stairs, caught his cuff link in it and
dropped the golf stick with a crash. He was glad enough to get away without
an alarm being raised, and he took the late train to town.

The oddest thing to me was that Jamieson had known for some time that
Alex was Jack Bailey. But the face of the pseudo gardener was very queer

indeed when that night in the cardroom the detective turned to him and said:

"How long are you and I going to play our little comedy, Mr. Bailey?"

Well, it is all over now. Paul Armstrong rests in Casanova churchyard, and this time there is no mistake. I went to the funeral, because I wanted to be sure he was really buried. And I looked at the step of the shaft where I had sat that night and wondered if it was all real. Sunnyside is for sale, but I shall not buy it. Little Lucien Armstrong is living with his stepgrandmother, and she is recovering gradually from troubles which had extended over the entire period of her second marriage. Anne Watson lies not far from the man she killed, and who as surely caused her death. And Thomas, the fourth victim of the conspiracy, is buried on the hill. With Nina Carrington's, five lives were sacrificed in the course of this grim conspiracy.

There will be two weddings before long, and Liddy has asked for my heliotrope to wear to the church. I knew she would. She has wanted it for three years, and she was quite ugly the time I spilled coffee on it. Otherwise we are very quiet, just the two of us. Liddy still clings to her ghost theory, and points to my wet and muddy shoes in the trunk room as proof. I am grayer than I was, I admit, but I haven't felt so well in a dozen years. Sometimes when I am bored I ring for Liddy, and we talk things over. When Warner married Rosie, Liddy sniffed and said what I took for faithfulness in Rosie had been nothing but mawkishness. I have not yet outlived Liddy's contempt because I gave them silver knives and forks as a wedding gift.

So we sit and talk, and sometimes Liddy threatens to leave and often I discharge her, but we stay together somehow. I am talking of renting a house next year, and Liddy says to be sure there is no ghost. To be perfectly frank, I never really lived until that summer. Time has passed since I began this story. My neighbors are packing up for another summer. Liddy is having the awnings put up, and the window boxes filled. But Liddy or no Liddy, I shall advertise tomorrow for a house in the country, and I don't care if it has a Circular Staircase.

The
Man in
Lower Ten

1

McKnight is gradually taking over the criminal end of the business. I never liked it, and since the strange case of the man in lower ten, I have been a bit squeamish. Take a case like that, where you can build up a network of clues that absolutely incriminate three entirely different people only one of whom can be guilty, and your faith in circumstantial evidence dies of overcrowding. I never see a shivering, white-faced wretch in the prisoners' dock that I do not hark back with shuddering horror to the strange events on the Pullman car Ontario, between Washington and Pittsburgh, on the night of September ninth last.

McKnight could tell the story a great deal better than I, although he cannot spell three consecutive words correctly. But, while he has imagination and humor, he is lazy.

"It didn't happen to me, anyhow," he protested, when I put it up to him. "And nobody cares for secondhand thrills. Besides, you want the unvarnished and ungarnished truth, and I'm no hand for that. I'm a lawyer."

So am I, although there have been times when my assumption in that particular has been disputed. I am unmarried, and just old enough to dance with the grown-up little sisters of the girls I used to know. I am fond of outdoors, prefer horses to the aforesaid grown-up little sisters, am without sentiment (*am* crossed out and *was* substituted—Ed.) and completely ruled and frequently routed by my housekeeper, an elderly widow.

In fact, of all the men of my acquaintance I was probably the most prosaic, the least adventurous, the one man in a hundred who would be likely to go without a deviation from the normal through the orderly procession of the seasons, summer suits to winter overcoats, golf to bridge.

So it was a queer freak of the demon Chance to perch on my unsusceptible thirty-year-old chest, tie me up with a crime, ticket me with a love affair, and start me on that sensational and not always respectable journey which ended so surprisingly less than three weeks later in the firm's private office. It had been the most remarkable period of my life. I would neither give it up nor live it again under any inducement, and yet all that I lost was some twenty yards off my drive!

It was really McKnight's turn to make the next trip. I had a tournament at Chevy Chase for Saturday, and a short yacht cruise planned for Sunday, and when a man has been grinding at tax laws for a week he needs relaxation. But McKnight begged off. It was not the first time he had shirked that summer in order to run down to Richmond, and I was surly about it. But this time he had a new excuse.

"I wouldn't be able to look after the business if I did go," he said. He has a sort of wide-eyed frankness that makes one ashamed to doubt him. "I'm always carsick crossing the mountains. It's a fact, Laurie. Seesawing over the peaks does it. Why, crossing the Allegheny Mountains has the Gulf Stream to Bermuda beaten to a frazzle."

So I gave him up finally and went home to pack. He came later in the evening with his car, the Cannonball, to take me to the station, and he brought the forged notes in the Bronson case.

"Guard them with your life," he warned me. "They are more precious than honor. Sew them in your undershirt, or wherever people keep valuables. I never keep any. I'll not be happy until I see Gentleman Andy doing the lockstep."

He sat down on my clean shirts, found my cigarettes and struck a match on the mahogany bedpost with one movement.

"Where's the Pirate?" he demanded. The Pirate is my housekeeper, Mrs. Klopton, a very worthy woman, so labeled—and libeled—because of a ferocious pair of eyes and what McKnight called a buccaneering nose. I quietly closed the door into the hall.

"Keep your voice down, Richey," I said. "She is looking for the evening paper to see if it is going to rain. She has my raincoat and an umbrella waiting in the hall."

The shirts being damaged beyond repair, he left them and went to the window. He stood there for some time, staring at the blackness that represented the wall of the house next door.

"It's raining now," he said over his shoulder, and closed the window and the shutters. Something in his voice made me glance up, but he was watching me, his hands idly in his pockets.

"Who lives next door?" he inquired in a perfunctory tone, after a pause. I was packing my razor.

"House is empty," I returned absently. "If the landlord would put it in some sort of shape—"

"Did you put those notes in your wallet?" he broke in.

"Yes." I was impatient. "Along with my certificate of birth, baptism and vaccination. Whoever wants them will have to steal my coat to get them."

"Well, I would move them, if I were you. Somebody in the next house was confoundedly anxious to see where you put them. Somebody right at that window opposite."

I scoffed at the idea, but nevertheless I moved the papers, putting them in my traveling bag, well down at the bottom. McKnight watched me uneasily.

"I have a hunch that you are going to have trouble," he said, as I locked the alligator bag. "Darned if I like starting anything important on Friday."

"You have a congenital dislike to start anything on any old day," I retorted, still sore from my lost Saturday. "And if you knew the owner of that house as

I do you would know that if there was anyone at that window he is paying rent for the privilege."

Mrs. Klopton rapped at the door and spoke discreetly from the hall.

"Did Mr. McKnight bring the evening paper?" she inquired.

"Sorry, but I didn't, Mrs. Klopton," McKnight called. "The Cubs won, three to nothing." He listened, grinning, as she moved away with little irritated rustles of her black silk dress.

I finished my packing, changed my collar and was ready to go. Then very cautiously we put out the light and opened the shutters. The window across was merely a deeper black in the darkness. It was closed and dirty. And yet, probably owing to Richey's suggestion, I had an uneasy sensation of eyes staring across at me. The next moment we were at the door, poised for flight.

"We'll have to run for it," I said in a whisper. "She's down there with a package of some sort, sandwiches probably. And she's threatened me with overshoes for a month. Ready now!"

I had a kaleidoscopic view of Mrs. Klopton in the lower hall, holding out an armful of such traveling impedimenta as she deemed essential, while beside her Euphemia, the colored housemaid, grinned over a white-wrapped box.

"Awfully sorry—no time—back Sunday," I panted over my shoulder. Then the door closed and the car was moving away.

McKnight bent forward and stared at the façade of the empty house next door as we passed. It was black, staring, mysterious, as empty buildings are apt to be.

"I'd like to hold a post-mortem on that corpse of a house," he said thoughtfully. "I've a notion to get out and take a look."

"Somebody after the brass pipes," I scoffed. "House has been empty for a year."

With one hand on the steering wheel McKnight held out the other for my cigarette case. "Perhaps," he said; "but I don't see what she would want with brass pipe."

"A woman." I laughed outright. "You have been looking too hard at the picture in the back of your watch, that's all. There's an experiment like that: if you stare long enough—"

But McKnight was sulky: he sat looking rigidly ahead, and he did not speak again until he brought the Cannonball to a stop at the station. Even then it was only a perfunctory remark. He went through the gate with me, and with five minutes to spare, we lounged and smoked in the train shed. My mind had slid away from my surroundings and had wandered to a polo pony that I couldn't afford and intended to buy anyhow. Then McKnight shook off his taciturnity.

"For heaven's sake, don't look so martyred," he burst out. "I know you've done all the traveling this summer. I know you're missing a game tomorrow. But don't be so damned patient. Confound it, I have to go to Richmond on Sunday. I want to see a girl."

"Oh, don't mind me," I observed politely. "Personally, I wouldn't change places with you. What's her name? North? South?"

"West," he snapped. "Don't try to be funny. And all I have to say, Blakeley, is that if you ever fall in love I hope you make an egregious ass of yourself."

Which, in view of what followed, came rather close to prophecy.

The trip to Pittsburgh was without incident. I played bridge with a furniture dealer from Grand Rapids, a sales agent for a Pittsburgh steel firm, and a young professor from an eastern college. I won three rubbers out of four, finished what cigarettes McKnight had left me, and went to bed at one o'clock. It was growing cooler, and the rain had ceased. Once toward morning I wakened with a start, for no apparent reason, and sat bolt upright. I had an uneasy feeling that someone had been looking at me, the same sensation I had experienced earlier in the evening at the window. But I could feel the bag with the notes between me and the window, and with my arm thrown over it for security I lapsed again into slumber. Later, when I tried to piece together the fragments of that journey, I remembered that my coat, which had been folded and placed beyond my restless tossing, had been rescued in the morning from a heterogeneous jumble of blankets, evening papers and cravat, had been shaken out with profanity and donned with wrath. At the time nothing occurred to me but the necessity of writing to the Pullman Company and asking them if they ever traveled in their own cars. I even formulated some of the letter.

"If they are built to scale, why not take a man of ordinary stature as your unit?" I wrote mentally. "I cannot fold together like the traveling cup from which I drink your abominable water."

I was more cheerful after I had had a cup of coffee in the Union Station. It was too early to attend to business, and I lounged in the restaurant and hid behind the morning papers. As I had expected, they had got hold of something. On the second page one of them stated that John Gilmore, of the steel company which bore his name, was recovering from his illness and had announced that he was seeing an attorney soon in connection with the Bronson case, which he intended to fight to a finish.

It did not name me, but I looked around apprehensively. There were no reporters yet in sight, and thankful to have escaped notice I paid for my breakfast and left. At the cab stand I chose the least dilapidated taxi I could find, and giving the driver the address of the Gilmore residence, in the East End, I got in.

I was just in time. As the cab turned and rolled off, a slim young man in a straw hat separated himself from a little group of men and hurried toward us.

"Hi! Wait a minute!" he called, breaking into a trot.

But the driver did not hear, or perhaps did not care to. We jogged comfortably along, to my relief, leaving the young man far behind. I avoid reporters on principle, having learned long ago that I am an easy mark for a clever interviewer.

It was perhaps nine o'clock when I left the station. Our way was along the boulevard that hugged the side of one of the city's great hills. Far below, to the left, lay the railroad tracks and the seventy times seven looming stacks of the mills. The white mist of the river, the grays and blacks of the smoke blended into a half-revealing haze, dotted here and there with fire. It was unlovely, tremendous. Whistler might have painted it with its pathos, its majesty, but he would have missed what made it infinitely suggestive—the rattle and roar of iron on iron, the rumble of wheels, the throbbing beat, against the ears, of fire and heat and brawn welding prosperity.

Something of this I voiced to the grim old millionaire who was responsible for at least part of it. He was propped up in bed in his East End home, listening to the market reports read by a nurse, and he smiled a little at my enthusiasm.

"I can't see much beauty in it myself," he said. "But it's our badge of prosperity. The full dinner pail here means a nose that looks like a flue. Pittsburgh without smoke wouldn't be Pittsburgh, any more than New York without night clubs would be New York. Sit down for a few minutes, Mr. Blakeley. Now, Miss Gardner, Westinghouse Electric."

The nurse resumed her reading in a monotonous voice. She read literally and without understanding, using initials and abbreviations as they came. But the shrewd old man followed her easily. Once, however, he stopped her.

"D-o, is ditto," he said gently, "not *do*."

As the nurse droned along, I found myself looking curiously at a photograph in a silver frame on the bedside table. It was a picture of a girl in white, with her hands clasped loosely before her. Against the dark background her figure stood out slim and young. Perhaps it was the rather grim environment, possibly it was my mood, but although as a general thing photographs of young girls make no appeal to me, this one did. I found my eyes straying back to it. By a little finesse I even made out the name written across the corner, "Alison."

Mr. Gilmore lay back among the pillows and listened to the nurse's listless voice. But he was watching me from under his heavy eyebrows, for when the reading was over, and we were alone, he indicated the picture with a gesture.

"I keep it there to remind myself that I am an old man," he said. "That's my granddaughter, Alison West."

I expressed the customary polite surprise, at which, finding me responsive, he told me his age with a chuckle of pride. More surprise, this time genuine. From that we went to what he ate for breakfast and did not eat for luncheon, and then to his intestines, which at seventy became a matter for thought. And so, in a wide circle, back to where we started, the picture.

"Her father was a scoundrel," he said, picking up the frame. "The happiest day of my life was when I knew he was safely dead in bed and not hanged. If the child looked like him, I—well, she doesn't. She's a Gilmore, every inch. Supposed to look like me."

"Very noticeably," I agreed soberly.

I had produced the notes by that time, and replacing the picture, Mr.

Gilmore gathered his spectacles from beside it. He went over the four notes methodically, examining each carefully and putting it down before he picked up the next. Then he leaned back and took off his glasses.

"Well," he said, "I guess Andy Bronson has outsmarted himself for once. There was a time when he borrowed money from me, and I borrowed money from him. But that's a good many years ago. I never saw these things before."

"So we thought. So the bank thought. That's how we came to it, of course." He chuckled dryly.

"They're pretty well done," he said. "Only Andy didn't know I'd put a small identifying mark on everything I signed for the past ten years."

"I suppose he thought you were dying. That's the bank's idea."

"Sure. He must have had them ready for a good while. Smart fellow, Andy. Too smart."

It was a clear case, and with some satisfaction I took his deposition and put it into my traveling bag with the forged notes. When I saw them again, almost three weeks later, they were unrecognizable, a mass of charred paper on a copper ash tray. In the interval other and bigger things had happened: the Bronson forgery case had shrunk beside the greater and more imminent mystery of the man in lower ten. And Alison West had come into the story and my life.

2

I LUNCHED ALONE at the Gilmore house, which was magnificent but gloomy, and went back to the city at once. The sun had lifted the mists, and a fresh summer wind had cleared away the smoke pall. The boulevard was full of cars flying countryward for the Saturday half-holiday, toward golf and tennis, green fields and babbling girls. I gritted my teeth and thought of McKnight at Richmond, visiting the lady with the geographical name. And then, for the first time, I associated John Gilmore's granddaughter with the "West" that McKnight had irritably flung at me.

I still carried my traveling bag, for McKnight's vision at the window of the empty house had not been without effect. I did not transfer the notes to my pocket, and if I had it would not have altered the situation later. Only the other day McKnight put this very thing up to me.

"I warned you," he reminded me. "I told you there were queer things coming, and to be on your guard. You ought to have taken your revolver."

"It would have been of exactly as much use as a bucket of snow in— Africa," I retorted. "If I had never closed my eyes, or if I had kept my finger on the trigger of a gun the result would have been the same. And the next time you want a little excitement with every variety of thrill thrown in, I can put you by way of it. You begin by getting the wrong berth in a Pullman car, and end—"

"Oh, I know how it ends," he finished shortly. "Don't you suppose the whole thing's written on my spinal marrow like What's-her-name and Calais?"

But I am wandering again. That is the difficulty with the nonprofessional storyteller: he yaws back and forth and can't keep in the wind; he drops his characters overboard when he hasn't any further use for them and drowns them; he forgets the coffeepot and the frying pan and all the other small essentials, and, if he carries a love affair, he mutters a fervent "Thank God" when he lands them, drenched with adventures, at the matrimonial dock at the end of the final chapter.

I put in a thoroughly unsatisfactory afternoon. Time dragged eternally. I dropped in at a movie, and bought some ties at a haberdasher's. I was bored but unexpectant. I had no premonition of what was to come. Nothing unusual had ever happened to me; friends of mine had sometimes sailed the high seas of adventure or skirted the coasts of chance, but all of the shipwrecks had occurred after a woman passenger had been taken on. So I had always said, no women. I repeated it to myself that evening almost savagely, when I found my thoughts straying back to the picture of John Gilmore's granddaughter. I was annoyed as I ate my solitary dinner at a downtown restaurant.

"Don't be a dope. Haven't you troubles enough," I reflected, "without looking for more? Aren't you comfortable as things are? Isn't your house in order? Do you want to sell a pony in order to have the library done over in pine or the living room by some fool of a decorator? Do you want somebody to count the empty bottles lying around every morning?"

Lay it to the long idle afternoon, to the new environment, to anything you like, but I began to think that perhaps I did. I was damned lonely. For the first time in my life its even course began to waver: the needle registered warning marks on the matrimonial seismograph, lines vague enough, but lines.

My alligator bag lay at my feet, still locked. While I waited for my coffee I leaned back and surveyed the people incuriously. There were the usual couples intent on each other. My new state of mind made me regard them with tolerance, but at the next table, where a man and a woman dined together, a different atmosphere prevailed. My attention was first caught by the woman's face. She had been speaking earnestly across the table, her profile turned to me. I had noticed casually her earnest manner, her somber clothes, and the great mass of odd, bronze-colored hair on her neck. But suddenly she glanced toward me and the utter hopelessness—almost tragedy—of her expression struck me with a shock. She half closed her eyes and drew a long breath, then she turned again to the man across the table.

Neither one was eating. The man sat low in his chair, his chin on his chest, ugly folds of thick flesh protruding over his collar. He was probably fifty, bald, grotesque, sullen, and yet not without a suggestion of power. But he had been drinking; as I looked, he raised an unsteady hand and summoned a waiter for another highball.

The young woman bent across the table and spoke again quickly. She had unconsciously raised her voice. Not beautiful, in her earnestness and stress she rather interested me. I had an idle inclination to advise the waiter to stop serving the man, and I wonder what would have happened if I had? Suppose Simon Harrington had not been intoxicated when he entered the Pullman car Ontario that night?

For they were about to make a journey, I gathered, and the young woman wished to go alone. I drank three cups of coffee, which accounted for my wakefulness later, and shamelessly watched the tableau before me. The woman's protest evidently went for nothing: across the table the man grunted monosyllabic replies and grew more and more lowering and sullen. Once, during a brief unexpected pianissimo in the music, her voice came to me sharply:

"If I could only see him in time!" she was saying. "He can't do such a thing. It's incredible."

In spite of my interest I would have forgotten the whole incident at once, erased it from my mind as one does the inessentials and clutterings of memory, had I not met them again, later that evening, in the Pennsylvania Station. The situation between them had not visibly altered: the same dogged determination showed in the man's face, but the young woman—daughter or wife? I wondered—kept her face turned away from me, and I could only suspect what white misery lay behind it.

There was no chance of a drawing room on the train: I bought my berth after waiting in a line of some eight or ten people. When, step by step, I had almost reached the window, a tall woman whom I had not noticed before spoke to me from my elbow. She had a ticket and money in her hand.

"Will you try to get me a lower when you buy yours?" she asked. "I have traveled for three nights in uppers."

I consented, of course; beyond that I hardly noticed the woman. I had a vague impression of height and a certain amount of stateliness, but the crowd was pushing behind me, and someone was standing on my foot. I managed to get two lowers finally, and, turning with the change and the berths, held out the tickets.

"Which will you have?" I asked. "Lower eleven or lower ten."

"It makes no difference," she said. "Thank you very much indeed."

At random, I gave her lower eleven, and called a porter to help her with her luggage. I followed them leisurely to the train shed, and ten minutes more saw us under way.

I looked into my car, but it presented the peculiarly unattractive appearance common to sleepers. Also, with travel as heavy as it was, they had obviously resurrected an ancient Pullman. The berths were designated by tags instead of numbers sewed to the curtains. The center aisle was a dingy path between them, and the only two unmade seats at the end of the car were piled high with suitcases. The perspiring porter was trying to be in six places at once: somebody has said that Pullman porters are black so they won't show the dirt, but they certainly show the heat.

Nine-fifteen was an outrageous hour to go to bed, especially since I sleep little or not at all on the train, so I made my way to the smoker and passed the time until nearly eleven with cigarettes and a magazine.

When I went back the car was very close. It was a warm night, and before turning in I stood a short time in the vestibule. The train had been stopping at frequent intervals, and, finding the brakeman, I asked the trouble.

It seemed there was a hotbox on the next car, and that not only were we late, but we were delaying the second section, just behind. I was beginning to feel pleasantly drowsy, and the air was growing cooler as we got into the mountains. I said good night to the brakeman and went back to my berth. To my surprise, lower ten was already occupied. A suitcase projected from beneath, a pair of shoes stood on the floor, and from behind the curtains came the heavy unmistakable breathing of deep slumber. I hunted out the porter and together we investigated.

"Are you asleep, sir?" asked the porter, leaning over .deferentially. No answer being forthcoming, he opened the curtains and looked in. Yes, the intruder was asleep—very much asleep—and an overwhelming odor of whisky proclaimed that he would probably remain asleep until morning. I was irritated. The car was full, and I was not disposed to take an upper in order to allow this drunken interloper to sleep comfortably in my berth.

"You'll have to get out of this," I said, shaking him angrily. But he merely grunted and turned over. As he did so, I saw his features for the first time. It was the quarrelsome man of the restaurant.

I was less disposed than ever to relinquish my claim, but the porter after a little quiet investigation offered a solution of the difficulty. "There's no one in lower nine," he suggested, pulling open the curtains just across. "It's likely nine's his berth, and he's made a mistake, owing to his condition. You'd better take nine, sir."

I did, with a firm resolution that if nine's rightful owner turned up later I should be just as unwakable as the man opposite. I undressed leisurely, making sure of the safety of the forged notes, and placing my grip as before between myself and the window.

Being a man of systematic habits I arranged my clothes carefully, putting my shoes out for the porter to polish and stowing my tie and belt in the little hammock swung for the purpose.

At last, with my pillows so arranged that I could see out comfortably, and with the unhygienic-looking blanket turned back—I have always a distrust of those much-used affairs—I prepared to wait gradually for sleep.

But sleep did not visit me. The train came to frequent grating stops, and I surmised the hotbox again. I am not a nervous man, but there was something chilling in the thought of the second section pounding along behind us. Once as I was dozing our locomotive whistled a shrill warning—"You keep back

where you belong," it screamed to my drowsy ears, and from somewhere behind came a chastened, "All right, I will."

I grew more and more wide awake. At Cresson I got up on my elbow
and blinked out at the station lights. Some passengers boarded the train there
and I heard a woman's low tones, a pleasant voice, rich and full. Then quiet
again. Every nerve was tense: time passed, perhaps ten minutes, possibly half
an hour. Then without the slightest warning as the train rounded a curve a
heavy body was thrown almost into my berth. The incident, trivial as it
seemed, was startling in its suddenness, for although my ears were painfully
strained and awake, I had heard no step outside. The next instant the curtain
hung limp again; still without a sound, my disturber had slipped away into
the gloom and darkness. In a frenzy of wakefulness I sat up, drew on a pair
of slippers and fumbled for my bathrobe.

From a berth across, probably lower ten, came that particularly annoying
snore which begins lightly, delicately and faintly soprano, goes down the
scale a note with every breath and, after keeping the listener tense with expectation, ends with an explosion that tears the very air. I was more and
more irritable: I sat on the edge of the berth and hoped the snorer would
choke to death.

He had considerable vitality, however; he withstood one shock after another
and survived to start again with new vigor. In desperation I found some cigarettes and one match, piled my blankets over my bag, and drawing the
curtains together as though the berth were still occupied, made my way to
the vestibule of the car.

I was not clad for dress parade. Is it because the male is so restricted to
gloom in his everyday attire that he blossoms into gaudy colors in his pajamas
and dressing gowns? It would take a Turk to feel at home before an audience
in my red and yellow bathrobe, a Christmas remembrance from Mrs.
Klopton, with slippers to match.

So, naturally, when I saw a feminine figure on the platform, my first instinct
was to dodge. The woman, however, was quicker than I; she gave me a startled
glance, wheeled and disappeared, with a flash of two bronze-colored braids,
into the next car. It was the woman of the restaurant.

Cigarette box in one hand, match in the other, I leaned against the uncertain frame of the door and gazed after her vanished figure. The mountain
air flapped my bathrobe around my bare ankles, my one match burned to
the end and went out, and still I stared. For I had seen on her expressive
face a haunting look that was horror, nothing less. Heaven knows, I am not
psychic. Emotions have to be written large before I can read them. But a
woman in trouble always appeals to me, and this woman was more than that.
She was in deadly fear.

If I had not been afraid of being ridiculous, I would have followed her.
But I fancied that the apparition of a man in a red and yellow bathrobe, with
an unkempt thatch of hair, walking up to her and assuring her he would
protect her would probably put her into hysterics. I had done that once before,

when the burglars had tried to break into the house, and had startled one of the maids into bed for a week. So I tried to assure myself that I had imagined the lady's distress—or caused it, perhaps—and to dismiss her from my mind. Perhaps she was merely anxious about the unpleasant gentleman of the restaurant. I thought smugly that I could have told her all about him: that he was sleeping the sleep of the just and the intoxicated in a berth that ought, by all that was fair and right, to have been mine, and that if I were tied to a man who snored like that I should have him anesthetized and his soft palate put where it would never again flap like a loose sail in the wind.

We passed Harrisburg as I stood there. It was starlight, and the great crests of the Alleghenies had given way to low hills. At intervals we passed smudges of gray-white, no doubt in daytime comfortable farms, which McKnight says is a good way of putting it, the farms being a lot more comfortable than the people on them.

I was growing drowsy: the woman with the bronze hair and the terrified face was fading in retrospect. It was colder, too, and I turned with a shiver to go in.

As I did so a bit of paper fluttered into the air and settled on my sleeve, like a butterfly on a gorgeous red and yellow blossom. I picked it up curiously and glanced at it. It was part of a telegram that had been torn into bits.

There were only parts of four words on the scrap, but it left me puzzled and thoughtful. It read, "—ower ten, car seve—." Lower ten, car seven, was my berth, the one I had bought and then found pre-empted.

3

No solution offering itself, I went back to my berth. The snorer across had apparently strangled, or turned over, and so after a time I dropped asleep, to be awakened by the early morning sunlight across my face.

I felt for my watch, yawning prodigiously. I reached under the pillow and failed to find it, but something scratched the back of my hand. I sat up irritably and nursed the wound, which was bleeding a little. Still drowsy, I felt more cautiously for what I imagined was a pin, but there was nothing there. Wide awake now, I reached for the bag, on the off chance that I had put my watch in it. I had drawn the satchel to me and had my hand on the lock before I realized that it was not my own.

Mine was of alligator hide. I had killed the beast in Florida, after the expenditure of enough money to have bought a house and enough energy to have built one. The bag I held in my hand was a black one—sealskin, I thought. The staggering thought of what the loss of my bag meant to me put my finger on the bell and kept it there until the porter came.

"Did you ring, sir?" he asked, poking his head through the curtains obsequiously. McKnight objects that nobody can poke his head through a curtain and be obsequious. But Pullman porters can and do.

"No," I snapped. "It rang itself. What in thunder do you mean by exchanging my bag for this one? You'll have to find it if you wake the entire car to do it. There are important papers in it."

"Porter," called a feminine voice from an upper berth near by. "Porter, am I to dangle here all day?"

"Let her dangle," I said savagely. "You find that bag of mine."

The porter frowned. Then he looked at me with injured dignity. "I brought in your overcoat, sir. You carried your own valise."

The fellow was right. In an excess of caution I had refused to relinquish my alligator bag, and had turned over my other traps to the porter. It was clear enough then. I was simply a victim of the usual sleeping-car robbery. I was in a lather of perspiration by that time: the lady down the car was still dangling and talking about it: still nearer a feminine voice was giving quick orders in French, presumably to a maid. The porter was on his knees, looking under the berth.

"Not there, sir," he said, dusting his knees. He was visibly more cheerful, having been absolved of responsibility. "Reckon it was taken while you was wanderin' around the car last night."

"I'll give you fifty dollars if you find it," I said. "A hundred. Reach up my shoes and I'll—"

I stopped abruptly. My eyes were fixed in stupefied amazement on the coat that lay folded at the foot of my berth. From the coat they traveled, dazed, to the soft-bosomed shirt beside it, and from there to the belt and necktie in the net hammock across the windows.

"A hundred!" the porter repeated, showing his teeth. But I caught him by the arm and pointed to the foot of the berth.

"What—what color's that coat?" I asked unsteadily.

"Gray, sir." His tone was one of gentle reproof.

"And—the trousers?"

He reached over and held up one creased leg. "Gray, too," he grinned.

"That's what I thought," I said. "As it happens my clothes were blue!"

The porter was amused; he dived under the curtains and brought up a pair of shoes. "Here they are, sir," he said, with a flourish. "Reckon you just forgot what you was wearing."

Now there are two things I always avoid in my dress, possibly an idiosyncrasy of my bachelor existence. These tabooed articles are red neckties and yellow shoes. And not only were the shoes the porter lifted from the floor of a gorgeous shade of yellow, but the tie that lay in the hammock was a gaudy red. It took a full minute for the real import of things to penetrate my dazed intelligence. Then I gave a vindictive kick at the offending shoes.

"They're not mine," I snarled. "They are some other fellow's. I'll sit here until I take root before I put them on. None of this stuff's mine."

"They're nice-lookin' clothes," the porter put in, eyeing the red tie with appreciation. "Ain't everybody would have left you anything."

"Call the conductor," I said shortly. Then a possible explanation occurred to me. "Oh, porter—what's the number of this berth?"

"Seven, sir. If you can't wear those shoes—"

"Seven!" In my relief I almost shouted it. "Why, then, it's simple enough. I'm in the wrong berth, that's all. My berth is nine. Only where the hell is the man who belongs here?"

"Likely in nine, sir." The darky was enjoying himself. "You and the other gentleman just got mixed in the night. That's all, sir." It was clear that he thought I had been drinking.

I drew a long breath. Of course that was the explanation. This was number seven's berth, that was his soft hat, this his umbrella, his coat, his bag. My rage turned to irritation at myself.

The porter went to the next berth and I could hear his softly insinuating voice. "Time to get up, sir. Are you awake? Time to get up."

There was no response from number nine. I guessed that he had opened the curtains and was looking in. Then he came back.

"Number nine's empty," he said.

"Empty! Do you mean my clothes aren't there?" I demanded. "What about my bag? Why don't you answer me?"

"You doan' give me time," he retorted. "There ain't nothin' there. But it's been slept in."

The disappointment was the greater for my few moments of hope. I sat up in a white fury and put on the clothes that had been left me. Then, still raging, I sat on the edge of the berth and put on the obnoxious yellow shoes. The porter, called to his duties, made little excursions back to me, to offer assistance and to chuckle at my discomfiture. He stood by, outwardly decorous but with little irritating grins of amusement around his mouth, when I finally emerged with the red tie in my hand.

"Bet the owner of those clothes didn't become them any more than you do," he said, as he plied the ubiquitous whisk broom.

"When I get the owner of these clothes," I retorted grimly, "he will need a shroud. Where's the conductor?"

The conductor was coming, he assured me; also that there was no bag answering the description of mine on the car. I slammed my way to the dressing room, washed, choked my fifteen and a half neck into a fifteen collar, and was back again in less than five minutes. The car as well as its occupants was gradually taking on a daylight appearance. I hobbled in, for one of the shoes was abominably tight, and found myself facing a young woman in blue with an unforgettable face. ("Three women already." McKnight says: "That's going some, even if you don't count the Gilmore nurse.") She stood, half turned toward me, one hand idly drooping, the other steadying her as she gazed out at the flying landscape. I had an instant impression that I had met her somewhere, under different circumstances; more cheerful ones, I thought, for the girl's dejection now was evident. Beside her and sitting down, a small dark woman, considerably older, was talking in a rapid undertone. The girl nodded indifferently now and then. I fancied, although I was not sure, that my appearance brought a startled look into her face. I sat down and, hands thrust deep into the other man's pockets, stared ruefully at the other man's shoes.

The stage was set. In a moment the curtain was going up on the first act of the play. For a while we would all say our little speeches and sing our little songs; and I, the villain, would hold center stage while the gallery hissed.

The porter was standing beside lower ten. He had reached in and was knocking valiantly. But his efforts met with no response. He winked at me over his shoulder; then he unfastened the curtains and bent forward. I saw him stiffen, heard his muttered exclamation, saw the bluish pallor that spread over his face and neck. As he retreated a step the interior of lower ten lay open to the day.

The man in it was on his back, the early morning sun striking full on his upturned face. But the light did not disturb him. A small stain of red dyed the front of his night clothes and trailed across the sheet: his half-open eyes were fixed, without seeing, on the shining wood above.

I grasped the porter's shaking shoulders and stared down to where the train imparted to the body a grisly suggestion of motion. "Good Lord," I gasped, "the man's been murdered!"

4

AFTERWARDS, when I tried to recall our discovery of the body in lower ten, I found that my most vivid impression was not that made by the revelation of the opened curtain. I had an instantaneous picture of a slender blue-clad girl who seemed to sense my words rather than hear them, of a hand that clutched desperately at the seat beside it. The girl in the aisle stood staring at me, perplexity and alarm fighting in her face.

With twitching hands the porter attempted to draw the curtains together. Then in a paralysis of shock he collapsed on the edge of my berth and sat there swaying. In my excitement I shook him.

"For God's sake keep your nerve, man," I said roughly. "You'll have every woman in the car in hysterics. And if you do, you'll wish you could change places with the man in there." He rolled his eyes.

A man near, who had been reading last night's paper, dropped it quickly and tiptoed toward us. He peered between the partly open curtains, closed them quietly and went back, ostentatiously solemn, to his seat. The very crackle with which he opened his paper added to the bursting curiosity of the car. For the passengers knew that something was amiss: I was conscious of a sudden tension.

With the curtains closed the porter was more himself; he wiped his lips with a handkerchief and stood erect.

"It's my last trip in *this* car," he remarked heavily. "There's something wrong with that berth. Last trip the woman in it took an overdose of some sleeping stuff and we found her, jes' like that, dead! And it ain't more'n three months now since there was twins born in that very spot. No, sir, it ain't natural."

At that moment a thin man with prominent eyes and a spare grayish goatee creaked up the aisle and paused beside me.

"Porter sick?" he inquired, taking in with a professional eye the porter's horror-struck face, my own excitement, and the slightly gaping curtains of lower ten. He reached for the darky's pulse and pulled out an old-fashioned gold watch.

"Hm! Only fifty! What's the matter? Had a shock?" He asked shrewdly.

"Yes," I answered for the porter. "We've both had one. If you are a doctor I wish you would look at the man in the berth across, lower ten. I'm afraid it's too late, but I'm not experienced in such matters."

Together we opened the curtains and the doctor bending down gave a comprehensive glance that took in the rolling head, the relaxed jaw, the ugly stain on the sheet. The examination needed only a moment. Death was written in the clear white of the nostrils, the colorless lips, the smoothing away of the unpleasant lines of the night before. With its new dignity the face was not unhandsome: the gray hair was still plentiful, the features strong and well cut.

The doctor straightened himself and turned to me. "Dead for some time," he said, running a professional finger over the stains. "These are dry and darkened, you see, and rigor mortis is well established. A friend of yours?"

"I don't know him at all," I replied. "Never saw him but once before."

"Then you don't know if he is traveling alone?"

"No, he was not—that is, I don't know anything about him," I corrected myself. It was my first blunder: the doctor glanced up at me quickly and then turned his attention again to the body. Like a flash there had come to me the vision of the woman with the bronze hair and the tragic face, whom I had surprised in the vestibule between the cars somewhere in the small hours of the morning. I had acted on my first impulse—the purely masculine one of shielding a woman.

The doctor had unfastened the coat of the striped pajamas and exposed the dead man's chest. On the left side was a small punctured wound of insignificant size.

"Very neatly done," the doctor said with appreciation. "Couldn't have done it better myself. Right through the intercostal space: no time even to grunt."

"Isn't the heart around there somewhere?" I asked. The medical man turned toward me and smiled austerely.

"That's where it belongs, just under that puncture, when it isn't gadding around in a man's throat or his boots."

I had a new respect for the doctor, for anyone indeed who could crack even a feeble joke under such circumstances, or who could run an impersonal finger over that wound and those stains. Odd how a healthy normal man holds the medical profession in half-contemptuous regard until he gets sick, or an emergency like this arises, and then turns meekly to the man who knows the ins and outs of his mortal tenement, takes his pills or his patronage, ties to him like a rudderless ship in a gale.

"Suicide, is it, doctor?" I asked.

He stood erect, after drawing the bedclothes over the face, and, taking off his glasses, wiped them slowly.

"No, it is not suicide," he announced decisively. "It is murder."

Of course, I had expected that, but the word itself brought a shiver. I was just a bit dizzy. Curious faces throughout the car were turned toward us, and I could hear the porter behind me breathing audibly. A stout woman in negligee came down the aisle and querulously confronted the porter. She wore a pink dressing jacket and carried portions of her clothing.

"Porter," she began, in the voice of the lady who had "dangled," "is there a rule of this company that will allow a woman to occupy the dressing room for one hour and make an elaborate toilet while respectable people haven't a place where they can put on their—"

She stopped suddenly and stared into lower ten. Her shining pink cheeks grew pasty, her jaw fell. I remember trying to think of something to say, and of saying nothing at all. Then she turned her eyes to the nondescript garments which hung from her arm and tottered back the way she had come. Slowly a little knot of men gathered around us, silent for the most part. The doctor was making a search of the berth when the conductor elbowed his way through followed by the inquisitive man, who had evidently summoned him. I had lost sight, for a time, of the girl in blue.

"Do it himself?" the conductor queried, after a businesslike glance at the body.

"No, he didn't," the doctor asserted. "There's no weapon here, and the window is closed. He couldn't have thrown it out, and he didn't swallow it. What on earth are you looking for, man?"

Someone was on the floor at our feet, face down, head peering under the berth. Now he got up without apology, revealing the man who had summoned the conductor. He was dusty, alert, cheerful, and he dragged up with him the dead man's suitcase. The sight of it brought back to me at once my own predicament.

"I don't know whether there's any connection or not, conductor," I said, "but I am a victim too, in less degree; I've been robbed of everything I possess, except a red and yellow bathrobe. I happened to be wearing the bathrobe, which was probably the reason the thief overlooked it."

There was a fresh murmur in the crowd. Somebody laughed nervously. The conductor was irritated.

"I can't bother with that now," he snarled. "The railroad company is responsible for transportation, not for clothes, jewelry and morals. If people happen to be robbed in the company's cars it's their affair. Why didn't you sleep in your clothes? I do."

I took an angry step forward. Then somebody touched my arm, and I unclenched my fist. I could understand the conductor's position, and also I realized that I had been guilty myself of contributory negligence.

"I'm not trying to make you responsible," I protested as amiably as I could, "and I believe the clothes the thief left are as good as my own. They are certainly newer. But my bag contained valuable papers, and it is to your interest as well as to mine to find the man who stole it."

"Why, of course," the conductor said shrewdly. "Find the man who skipped out with this gentleman's clothes, and you've probably got the murderer."

"I went to bed in lower nine," I said, my mind full again of lost papers, "and I wakened in number seven. I was up in the night prowling around, as I was unable to sleep, and I must have gone back to the wrong berth. Anyhow, until the porter wakened me this morning I knew nothing of my mistake. In the interval the thief—murderer, too, perhaps—must have come back, discovered my error, and taken advantage of it to further his escape."

The inquisitive man looked at me from between narrowed eyelids, ferret-like.

"Did anyone on the train suspect you of having valuable papers?" he inquired. The crowd was listening intently.

"Possibly. But why take my clothes?"

The doctor was investigating the murdered man's effects. The pockets of his trousers contained the usual miscellany of keys and small change, while in his hip pocket was found a small pearl-handled revolver of the type women usually keep around. A gold watch with a Masonic charm had slid down between the mattress and the window, while showy diamond cuff links still fastened the cuffs of his shirt. Taken as a whole, the personal belongings were those of a man of some means, but without any particular degree of breeding. The doctor heaped them together.

"Either robbery was not the motive," he reflected, "or the thief overlooked these things in his hurry."

The latter hypothesis seemed the more tenable when, after a thorough search, we found no pocketbook and less than a dollar in small change.

The suitcase gave no clue. It contained one empty leather-covered flask and a pint bottle, also empty, a change of body linen and some shirts with the laundry mark "S.H." In the leather tag on the handle was a card with the name Simon Harrington, Pittsburgh.

The conductor sat down on my unmade berth, across, and made an entry of the name and address. Then, on an old envelope, he wrote a few words and gave it to the porter, who disappeared.

"I guess that's all I can do," he said. "I've had enough trouble this trip to last for a year. They don't need a conductor on these trains any more. What they ought to have is a sheriff and a posse."

The porter from the next car came in and whispered to him. The conductor rose unhappily.

"Next car's caught the disease," he grumbled. "Doctor, a woman back there has fainted or something. Will you come back?"

The strange porter stood aside.

"Lady about the middle of the car," he said, "in black, sir, with queer-looking hair—sort of copper color, I think."

5

WITH THE DEPARTURE of the conductor and the doctor, the group around lower ten broke up, to re-form in smaller knots throughout the car. The porter remained on guard. With something of relief I sank into a seat. I wanted to think, to try to remember the details of the previous night. But my inquisitive acquaintance had other intentions. He came up and sat down beside me. Like the conductor, he had taken notes of the dead man's belongings, his name, address, clothing, and the general circumstances of the crime. Now with his little notebook open before him he prepared to enjoy the minor sensation of the robbery.

"And now for the second victim," he began cheerfully. "What is your name and address, please?"

I eyed him with suspicion.

"I have lost everything but my name and address," I parried. "What do you want them for? Publication?"

"Oh, no; dear, no!" he said, shocked at my misapprehension. "Merely for my own enlightenment. I like to gather data of this kind and draw my own conclusions. Most interesting and engrossing. Once or twice I have forestalled the results of police investigation—but entirely for my own amusement."

I nodded tolerantly. Most of us have hobbies; I knew a man once who carried his handkerchief up his sleeve and had a mania for old colored prints cut out of *Godey's Lady's Book*.

"I use that inductive method originated by Poe and followed since with such success by Conan Doyle. Have you ever read Gaboriau? Ah, you have missed a treat, indeed. And now, to get down to business, what is the name of our escaped thief and probable murderer?"

"How on earth do I know?" I demanded impatiently. "He didn't write it in blood anywhere, did he?"

The little man looked hurt and disappointed.

"Do you mean to say," he asked, "that the pockets of those clothes are entirely empty?"

The pockets! In the excitement I had forgotten entirely the leather bag which the porter now set at my feet, and I had not investigated the pockets at all. With the inquisitive man's pencil taking notes of everything I found, I emptied them on the opposite seat.

Upper left-hand waistcoat, two lead pencils and a fountain pen; lower right waistcoat, matchbox and a small stamp book; right-hand pocket coat, pair of gray suède gloves, new, size seven and a half; left-hand pocket, gunmetal cigarette case half full of Egyptian cigarettes. The trouser pockets contained a gold penknife, a small amount of money in bills and change, and a handkerchief with the initial "S" on it.

Further search through the coat discovered a case containing a car license made out to one Henry Pinckney Sullivan, and a small leather flask with gold mountings, filled with what seemed to be very fair whisky, and monogrammed H.P.S. was in the hip pocket of the trousers.

"His name evidently is Henry Pinckney Sullivan," said the cheerful follower of Gaboriau, as he wrote it down. "Address as yet unknown. Blond, probably. Have you noticed that it is almost always blond men who affect a very light gray, with a touch of red in the tie? Fact, I assure you. I kept a record once of the summer attire of men, and ninety per cent followed my rule. Dark men like you affect navy blue, or brown."

In spite of myself I was amused at the man's shrewdness.

"Yes; the suit he took was dark—a blue," I said.

He rubbed his hands and smiled at me delightedly.

"Then you wore black shoes, not tan," he said, with a glance at the aggressive ones I wore.

"Right again," I acknowledged. "Black low shoes and black socks. If you keep on you'll have a motive for the crime, and the murderer's present place of hiding. And if you come back to the smoker with me, I'll give you an opportunity to judge if he knew good whisky from bad."

I put the articles from the pockets back again and got up. "I wonder if there is a diner on?" I said. "I need something sustaining after all this."

I was conscious then of someone at my elbow. I turned to see the young woman whose face was so vaguely familiar. In the very act of speaking she drew back suddenly and colored.

"Oh, I beg your pardon," she said hurriedly, "I thought you were someone else." She was looking in a puzzled fashion at my coat. I felt all the cringing guilt of a man who has accidentally picked up the wrong umbrella: my borrowed collar sat tight on my neck.

"I'm sorry," I said idiotically. "I'm sorry, but there's nothing I can do about it, is there?" I have learned since that she has bright brown hair, which she wears brushed up into a pile of curls on top of her head, and dark-blue eyes with black lashes. Also—but what does it matter? One enjoys a picture as a whole: not as the sum of its parts.

She saw the flask then and her errand came back to her. "One of the ladies at the end of the car has fainted," she explained. "I thought perhaps some whisky—"

I picked up the flask at once and followed my guide down the aisle. Two or three women were working over the woman who had fainted. They had opened her collar and taken out her hairpins, whatever good that might do. The stout woman who had dangled was vigorously rubbing her wrists, with the idea, no doubt, of working up her pulse, and I saw that the unconscious woman was the one for whom I had secured lower eleven at the station.

I poured a little liquor in a bungling masculine fashion between her lips as she leaned back with closed eyes. She choked, coughed, and rallied somewhat.

"Poor thing," said the stout lady. "Such a good-looking person, too. I noticed her last night. She looked kind of upset."

The girl in blue was looking at us with wide, startled eyes. I saw her pale a little, saw the quick, apprehensive glance she threw at her traveling companion, the small woman I had noticed before. There was an exchange—almost a clash—of glances. The small woman frowned. That was all. I turned my attention again to my patient.

She had revived somewhat, and now she asked to have the window opened. The train had stopped again and the car was oppressively hot. People around were looking at their watches and grumbling over the delay. The doctor bustled in with a remark about its being his busy day. The amateur detective and the porter together mounted guard over lower ten. Outside, the heat rose in shimmering waves from the tracks: the very wood of the car was hot to touch. A Camberwell beauty darted through the open door and made its way, in erratic plunges, great wings waving, down the sunny aisle. All around lay the peace of harvested fields, the quiet of the country.

6

I WAS GROWING more and more irritable. The thought of what the loss of the notes meant was fast crowding the murder to the back of my mind. The forced inaction was intolerable.

The porter had reported no bag answering the description of mine on the train, but I was disposed to make my own investigation. I made a tour of the cars, scrutinizing every variety of hand luggage, ranging from luxurious English bags of solid leather to the pasteboard nondescripts of the day coaches. I was not alone in my quest, for the girl in blue was just ahead of me. Car by car she preceded me through the train, unconscious that I was behind her, looking at each passenger as she passed. I fancied the proceeding was distasteful, but that she had determined on a course and was carrying it through.

We reached the end of the train almost together—empty-handed, so to speak.

The girl went out to the observation platform. When she saw me she moved aside, and I stepped out beside her. Behind us the track curved sharply. The early sunshine threw the train, in long black shadow, over the hot earth. Forward somewhere they were hammering. The girl said nothing, but her profile was strained and anxious.

"I—if you have lost anything," I began, "I wish you would let me try to help. Not that my own success is anything to boast of."

She hardly glanced at me. It was not flattering.

"I have not been robbed, if that is what you mean," she replied quietly. "I'm rather puzzled, that's all."

There was nothing to say to that. I lifted my hat—the other fellow's hat—and turned to go back to my car. Two or three members of the train crew, including the conductor, were standing in the shadow talking. And at that moment from a farmhouse near came the swift clang of the breakfast bell, calling in the hands from barn and pasture. I turned back to the girl.

"We may be here for an hour," I said, "and there is no buffet car on. If I remember my youth, that bell means ham and eggs and country butter and coffee. If you care to run the risk—"

"I am not hungry," she said, "but perhaps a cup of coffee— Good heavens, I believe I *am* hungry!" she finished. "Only—" She glanced back of her.

"I can bring your companion," I suggested, without enthusiasm. But she shook her head.

"She is not hungry," she objected, "and she is very—well, I know she wouldn't come. Do you suppose we could make it if we run?"

"I haven't any idea," I said cheerfully. "Any old train would be better than this one, if it does leave us behind."

"Yes. Any train would be better than this one," she repeated gravely. I found myself watching her changing expression. I had spoken two dozen words to her and already I felt that I knew the lights and shades in her voice, I, who had always known how a woman rode a horse, and who never could have told the color of her hair.

I stepped down on the ties and turned to assist her, and together we walked back to where the conductor and the porter from our car were in close conversation. Instinctively my hand went to my usual cigarette pocket and came out empty. She saw the gesture.

"I have some here," she said, fumbling at her bag. "I don't usually smoke before breakfast, but the way things are—"

I had, however, found the gunmetal case by that time and produced it. But this commonplace action had an extraordinary result. The girl beside me stopped dead still and stood staring at it with fascinated eyes.

"Where did you get that?" she demanded, with a catch in her voice, her gaze fixed on the case.

"Then you haven't heard the rest of the story?" I asked, holding out the case. "It's frightfully bad luck for me, but it's certainly unusual. You see—"

At that moment the conductor and the porter ceased their colloquy. The conductor came directly toward me, tugging as he came at his bristling gray mustache.

"I would like to talk to you in the car," he said to me, with a curious glance at the young lady.

"Can't it wait?" I objected. "We are on our way to a cup of coffee and a slice of bacon. Be merciful, as you are powerful."

"I'm afraid the breakfast will have to wait," he replied. "I won't keep you long." There was a note of authority in his voice which I resented, but, after all, the circumstances were unusual.

"We'll have to defer that cup of coffee for a while," I said to the girl; "but don't despair; there's breakfast somewhere."

As we entered the car she stood aside, but I felt rather than saw that she followed us. I was surprised to see a half dozen men gathered around the berth in which I had wakened, number seven. It had not yet been made up.

Passing along the aisle I was conscious of a new expression on the faces of the passengers. The tall woman who had fainted was searching my face with narrowed eyes, while the stout woman of the kindly heart avoided my gaze and pretended to look out the window.

As we pushed our way through the group I fancied that it closed around me ominously. The conductor said nothing, but led the way without ceremony to the side of the berth.

"What's the matter?" I inquired. I was puzzled but not apprehensive. "Have you some of my things? I'd be thankful even for my shoes; these are damnably tight."

Nobody spoke, and I fell silent too. For one of the pillows had been turned over, and the under side of the white case was streaked with brownish stains. I think it was a perceptible time before I realized that the stains were blood, and that the faces around were filled with suspicion and distrust.

"Why, it—that looks like blood," I said vacuously. There was an odd pounding in my ears, and the conductor's voice came from far off.

"It *is* blood," he asserted grimly.

I looked around with a dizzy attempt at indifference. "Even if it is," I remonstrated, "surely you don't suppose for a moment that I know anything about it!"

The amateur detective elbowed his way in. He had a scrap of transparent paper in his hand, and a pencil.

"I would like permission to trace the stains," he began eagerly. "Also"—to me—"if you will kindly jab your finger with a pin—"

"If you don't keep out of this," the conductor said savagely, "I will do some jabbing myself. As for you, sir—" He turned to me. I was absolutely innocent, but I knew that I presented a typical picture of guilt. I was covered with cold sweat, and the pounding in my ears kept up dizzily. "As for you, sir—"

The irrepressible amateur detective made a quick pounce at the pillow and pushed back the cover. Before our incredulous eyes he drew out a narrow steel dirk which had been buried to the small cross that served as a head.

There was a chorus of voices around, a quick surging forward of the crowd. So that was what had scratched my hand! I buried the wound in my coat pocket.

"Well," I said, trying to speak naturally, "doesn't that prove what I have been telling you? The man who committed the murder belonged to this berth, and made an exchange in some way after the crime. How do you know he didn't change the tags so I would come back to this berth?" This was an inspiration; I was pleased with it. "That's what he did, he changed the tags," I reiterated.

There was a murmur of assent around. The doctor, who was standing beside me, put his hand on my arm. "If this gentleman committed this crime, and I for one feel sure he did not, then who is the fellow who got away? And why did he go?"

"We have only one man's word for that," the conductor growled. "I've traveled some in these cars myself, and no one ever changed berths with *me*."

Somebody on the edge of the group asserted that hereafter he would travel by daylight. I glanced up and caught the eye of the girl in blue.

"They are all mad," she said. Her tone was low, but I heard her distinctly. "Don't take them seriously enough to defend yourself."

"I am glad you think I didn't do it," I observed meekly, over the crowd. "Nothing else is of any importance."

The conductor had pulled out his notebook again. "Your name, please," he said gruffly.

"Lawrence Blakeley, Washington."

"Your occupation?"

"Attorney. A member of the firm of Blakeley and McKnight."

"Mr. Blakeley, you say you have occupied the wrong berth and have been robbed. Do you know anything of the man who did it?"

"Only from what he left behind," I answered. "These clothes—"

"They fit you," he said with quick suspicion. "Isn't that rather a coincidence? You are a large man."

"Good God," I retorted, stung into fury, "do I look like a man who would wear this kind of necktie? Do you suppose I carry purple and green barred silk handkerchiefs? Would any man in his senses wear a pair of shoes a full size too small?"

The conductor was inclined to hedge. "You will have to grant that I am in a peculiar position," he said. "I have only your word as to the exchange of berths, and you understand I am merely doing my duty. Are there any clues in the pockets?"

For the second time I emptied them of their contents, which he noticed. "Is that all?" he finished. "There was nothing else?"

"Nothing."

"That's not all, sir," broke in the porter, stepping forward. "There was a small black bag in the berth."

"That's so," I exclaimed. "I forgot the bag. I don't even know where it is."

The easily swayed crowd looked suspicious again. I have grown so accustomed to reading the faces of a jury, seeing them swing from doubt to belief, and back again to doubt, that I instinctively watched expressions. I saw that my forgetfulness had done me harm, that suspicion was aroused again.

The bag was found a couple of seats away, under somebody's raincoat—another dubious circumstance. Was I hiding it? It was brought to the berth and placed beside the conductor, who opened it at once.

It contained the usual traveling impedimenta—change of linen, collars, handkerchiefs, socks, a green tie and a safety razor. But the attention of the crowd riveted itself on a flat Russia leather wallet, around which a heavy gum band was wrapped, and which bore in gilt letters the name "Simon Harrington."

7

THE CONDUCTOR held it out to me, his face sternly accusing.

"Is this another coincidence?" he asked. "Did the man who left you his clothes and the barred silk handkerchief and the tight shoes leave you the murdered man's money too?"

The men standing around had drawn off a little, and I saw the absolute futility of any remonstrance. Have you ever seen a fly which, caught on a sheet of flypaper, finds itself more and more mired, and is finally quiet with the sticky stillness of despair?

Well, I was the fly. I had seen too much of circumstantial evidence to have any belief that the establishing of my identity would weigh much against the other incriminating details. To say the least, it meant imprisonment and trial, probably with all the notoriety and loss of prestige they would entail. A man thinks quickly at a time like that. All the possible consequences of the finding of that pocketbook flashed through my mind as I extended my hand to take it. Then I drew my hand back.

"I don't want it," I said. "Look inside. Maybe the other man took the money and left the wallet."

The conductor opened it, and again there was a curious surging forward of the crowd. To my intense disappointment the money was still there.

I stood blankly miserable while it was counted out: five one-hundred-dollar bills, six twenties, and some fives and ones that brought the total to six hundred fifty dollars.

The little man with the notebook insisted on taking the numbers of the notes, to the conductor's annoyance. It was immaterial to me. Small things had lost their power to irritate me. I was seeing myself in the prisoner's box, going through all the nerve-racking routine of a trial for murder, the challenging of the jury, the endless cross-examinations, the alternate hope and fear. I believe I have said before that I had no nerves, but for a few minutes I was as near as a man ever comes to physical and mental collapse.

I folded my arms and pulled myself together. I seemed to be the center of a hundred eyes, expressing every shade of doubt and distrust, but I tried not to flinch. Then someone created a diversion.

The amateur detective was busy again with the bag, investigating the make of the safety razor and the manufacturer's name on the green tie. Now, however, he paused and frowned, as though some pet theory had been upset.

Then from a corner of the bag he drew out and held up for our inspection some three inches of fine gold chain, one end of which was blackened and stained with blood.

The conductor held out his hand for it, but the little man was not ready to give it up. He turned to me.

"You say no watch was left you? Was there a piece of chain like that?"

"No chain at all," I said sulkily. "No jewelry of any kind, except plain gold buttons in the shirt I am wearing."

"Where are your glasses?" he threw at me suddenly.

Without thinking, I fumbled in my breast pocket. My glasses were not there, of course, and the little man smiled cynically and held out the chain.

"I saw you last night," he said. "You don't wear horn-rimmed spectacles to read. You use pince-nez with a fine chain like this and a hook over your ear. Rather unusual, isn't it?"

"If you mean that's a part of my chain, I don't believe it."

But he still held it out, and with a dozen or so suspicious eyes on me I had to take it.

"Very fine chains are much alike," I managed to say. "For all I know, this may be mine, but I don't know how it got into that bag. I never saw it until this morning after daylight."

"He admits that he had the bag," somebody said behind me. "If that's his chain—"

The little man, having made his point, sank into a seat near by and still holding the chain sat with closed eyes and pursed lips. It was evident to all the car that the solution of the mystery was a question of moments. Once he bent forward eagerly and putting the chain on the window sill, proceeded to go over it with a pocket magnifying glass, only to shake his head in disappointment. All the people around shook their heads too, although they had not the slightest idea what it was about.

The pounding in my ears began again. The group around me seemed to be suddenly motionless in the very act of moving. I remember that a freight train was rumbling by on the next track, and that the girl in blue was looking at me. Above the din I thought she said she must speak to me—something vital. Then suddenly the pounding grew louder and merged into a scream. With a grinding and splintering the car rose under my feet, and fell away into darkness.

8

HAVE YOU EVER been picked up out of your three-meals-a-day life, whirled around in a tornado of events, and landed in a situation so grotesque and yet so horrible that you laugh even while you are groaning, and straining at its hopelessness? McKnight says that is hysteria, and that no man worthy of the name ever admits to it.

Also, as McKnight says, it sounds like an old-fashioned movie, where, just as the revolving saw is about to cut the hero into stove lengths the second villain blows up the sawmill. The hero goes up through the roof and alights on the bank of a stream at the feet of his lady love, who is making daisy chains.

Nevertheless, when I was safe home again, with Mrs. Klopton brewing strange potions that came from the pharmacy and that smelled to heaven, I remember staggering to the door and closing it and then going back to bed and howling out the absurdity and the madness of the whole thing. And while I laughed my very soul was sick, for the girl was gone by that time, and I knew by all the loyalty that answers between men for honor that I would have to put her out of my mind.

And yet all the night that followed, filled as it was with the shrieking demons of pain, I saw her as I had seen her last, in the queer hat with the green ribbons. I told the doctor this guardedly the next morning, and he said it was the morphia, and that I was lucky not to have seen a row of devils with green tails.

I don't know anything about the wreck of September ninth last. Those who swallowed the details with their coffee and digested horrors with their morning bacon probably know a great deal more than I do. I remember very distinctly that the jumping and throbbing in my arm brought me back to a world that at first was nothing but sky and a heap of clouds that looked rather like the meringue on a blue charlotte russe. As the sense of hearing was slowly added to vision, I heard a woman near me sobbing that she had lost her hat, and that it had been a new one.

I think I dropped back into unconsciousness again, for the next thing I remember was of my blue patch of sky clouded with smoke, of a strange roaring and crackling, of a rain of fiery sparks on my face, and of somebody beating at me with feeble hands. I opened my eyes and closed them again. The girl in blue was bending over me, and with that imperviousness to big things and keenness to small that is the first effect of shock, I tried to be facetious, when a spark stung my cheek.

"You will have to rouse yourself!" she was repeating desperately. "You've been on fire twice already." A piece of striped ticking floated slowly over my head, and as the wind caught it its charred edges leaped into flame.

"Why not call the fire department?" I remarked idiotically. And then, as my arm gave an excruciating throb—"God, what's happened to my arm?"

The girl bent over and spoke slowly, distinctly, as one might speak to a deaf person or a child.

"Listen, Mr. Blakeley," she said earnestly. "You *must* rouse yourself. There has been a terrible accident. The second section ran into us and the freight train is burning. If we don't move, we'll catch fire. Do you hear me? Can you understand?"

Her voice and my arm were bringing me to my senses. "I hear," I said. "I—I'll sit up in a second. Are you hurt?"

"No, only bruised. Do you think you can walk?"

I drew up one foot after the other, gingerly.

"They seem to move all right," I remarked dubiously. "Would you mind telling me where the back of my head has gone? I can't help thinking it isn't there."

She made a quick exclamation. "It's pretty badly cut," she said. "You must have fallen on it."

I had got up on my uninjured elbow by that time, but the pain threw me back. "Don't look at the wreck," I entreated her. "It's no sight for a woman. If there is any way to tie up this arm, I might be able to do something. There may be people under those cars!"

"Then it is too late to help," she replied soberly.

Evidently the freight had set fire to the Pullmans. I was a few feet from the track, and a little shower of feathers, each carrying its fiery lamp, blew over us from some burning pillow. A part of the wreck collapsed with a crash. In a resolute endeavor to play a man's part in the tragedy going on all around, I got to my knees. Then I realized what I had not noticed before: the hand and wrist of the broken left arm were jammed through the handle of the black bag. I gasped and sat down suddenly.

"You mustn't do that," the girl insisted. I noticed now that she kept her back to the wreck, her eyes averted. "I tried to move it but I couldn't. Let me support the bag until we get back a few yards. Then you must lie down until we can get it cut off."

"Will it have to be cut off?" I asked as calmly as possible. There were red-hot stabs of agony clear to my neck, but we were moving slowly away from the track.

"Yes," she replied, with surprising coolness. "If I had a knife I could do it myself. You might sit here and lean against this fence."

By that time my returning faculties had realized that she was going to cut off the satchel, not the arm. The dizziness was leaving and I was gradually becoming myself.

"If you pull it might come." I suggested. "And with that weight gone, I think I will cease to be five feet eleven inches of baby."

She tried gently to loosen the handle, but it would not move, and at last with great drops of cold perspiration over me I had to give up.

"I'm afraid I can't stand it," I said. "But there's a knife somewhere around these clothes, and if I can find it, perhaps you can cut the leather."

As I gave her the knife she turned it over, examining it with a peculiar expression, bewilderment rather than surprise. But she said nothing. She set to work deftly, and in a few minutes the bag dropped free.

"That's better," I declared, sitting up. "Now, if you can pin my sleeve to my coat, it will support the arm so we can get away from here."

"The pin might give," she objected, "and the jerk would be terrible." She looked around, puzzled; then she got up, coming back in a minute with a craggled, partly scorched sheet. This she tore into a large square, and after she had folded it, she slipped it under the broken arm and tied it securely at the back of my neck.

The relief was immediate, and, picking up the sealskin bag with my right hand I walked slowly beside her, away from the track.

That is all I remember of the wreck, of the roaring of flames and shouting of men behind me, and a girl in a blue dress trying to steady me as I stumbled away from that particular bit of hell.

9

WE WERE STILL DAZED, I think, for we wandered on like two troubled children, our one idea at first to get as far away as we could from the horror behind us. We were both bareheaded, grimy, pallid through the grit. Now and then we met little groups of country folk hurrying to the track. They stared at us curiously, and some wanted to stop and question us. That way lay madness.

Only once the girl turned and looked behind her. The wreck was hidden, but the smoke cloud hung heavy and dense. For the first time I remembered that my companion had not been alone on the train.

"It's quiet here," I suggested. "If you will sit down on the bank I will go back and make some inquiries. I've been criminally thoughtless. Your traveling companion—"

She interrupted me, and something of her splendid poise was gone. "Please don't go back," she said. "I am afraid it would be of no use. And I don't want to be left alone."

Heaven knows, I did not want her to be alone. I was more than content to walk along beside her aimlessly for any length of time. Gradually, as she lost the exaltation of the moment, I was gaining my normal condition of mind. I was beginning to realize that I had lacked the morning grace of a shave, that I looked like some lost hope of yesterday, and that my left shoe pinched outrageously. A man does not rise triumphant above such handicaps. The girl, for all her disordered hair and the crumpled linen of her blouse, in spite of her missing hat and the broken strap of the large purse she had somehow recovered, still looked distressingly lovely.

"I won't leave you alone," I said manfully, and we stumbled on together. Thus far we had seen nobody from the wreck, but well up the lane we came across the tall dark woman who had occupied lower eleven. She was half crouching beside the road, her black hair about her shoulders, and an ugly bruise over her eye. She did not seem to know us, and refused to accompany us. We left her there at last, babbling incoherently and rolling in her hands a dozen pebbles she had gathered in the road.

The girl shuddered as we went on. Once she turned and glanced at my sling. "Does it hurt very much?" she asked.

"It's growing rather numb. But it might be worse," I answered mendaciously. If anything in this world could be worse, I had never experienced it.

And so we trudged on bareheaded under the summer sun, growing parched and dusty and weary, doggedly leaving behind us the pillar of smoke. I thought I knew of a trolley line somewhere in the direction we were going, or perhaps we could find a car to take us into Baltimore. The girl smiled when I suggested it.

"We will create a sensation, won't we?" she asked. "Isn't it queer—or perhaps it's my state of mind—but I keep wishing for a pair of gloves, when I haven't even a hat!"

When we reached the main road we sat down for a moment, and her hair, which had been coming loose for some time, fell over her shoulders in little curls that were most alluring. It seemed a pity to twist it up again, but when I suggested this, cautiously, she said it was troublesome and got in her eyes when it was loose. So she gathered it up, while I held a row of little shell combs and pins, and when it was done it was vastly becoming too. Funny about hair: a man never knows he has it until he begins to lose it, but it's different with a girl. Something of the unconventional situation began to dawn on her as she put in the last comb and patted some stray locks into place.

"I've not told you my name," she said abruptly. "I forgot that because I know who you are you know nothing about me. I am Alison West, and my home is in Richmond."

So that was it! This was the girl of the photograph on John Gilmore's bedside table. The girl McKnight expected to see in Richmond the next day, Sunday. She was on her way back to meet him! Well, what difference did it make anyhow? We had been thrown together by the merest chance. In an hour or two at the most we would be back in civilization and she would recall me, if she remembered at all, as an unshaved creature in a red cravat and yellow shoes, with a soiled Pullman sheet tied around my neck. I drew a deep breath.

"Just a twinge," I said, when she glanced up quickly. "It's very good of you to let me know, Miss West. I have been hearing delightful things about you for three months."

"From Richey McKnight?" She was frankly curious.

"Yes. From Richey McKnight," I assented. Was it any wonder McKnight was crazy about her? I dug my heels into the dust.

"I have been visiting near Cresson, in the mountains," she was saying. "The person you mentioned, Mrs. Curtis, was my hostess. We were on our way to Washington together." She spoke slowly, as if she wished to give the minimum of explanation. Across her face had come again the baffling expression of perplexity and trouble I had seen before.

"You were on your way home, I suppose? Richey spoke about seeing you." I floundered, finding it necessary to say something. She looked at me with level, direct eyes.

"No," she returned quietly. "I did not intend to go home. I—well, it doesn't matter; I am going home now."

A woman in a calico dress, with two children, each an exact duplicate of the other, had come quickly down the road. She took in the situation at a glance, and was explosively hospitable.

"You poor things," she said. "If you'll take the first road to the left over there, and turn in at the second pigsty, you will find breakfast on the table and a coffeepot on the stove. And there's plenty of soap and water too. Go right in and make yourselves at home."

We accepted the invitation and she hurried on toward the excitement and the railroad. I got up carefully and helped Miss West to her feet.

"At the second pigsty to the left," I repeated, "we will find the breakfast I promised you seven eternities ago. Forward to the pigsty!"

We said very little for the remainder of that walk. The shock was wearing off, and I had almost reached the limit of endurance. With every step the broken ends of the bone grated together. We found the farmhouse without difficulty, and I remember wondering if I could hold out to the end of the old stone walk that led between hedges to the door.

"Thank God," I said, with all the voice I could muster. "Behold the coffeepot!" And then I put down the grip and folded up like a jackknife on the porch floor.

When I came around something hot was trickling down my neck, and a despairing voice was saying, "Oh, I don't seem to be able to pour it into your mouth. Please open your eyes."

"But I don't want it in my eyes," I replied dreamily. "I haven't any idea what came over me. It was the shoes, I think: the left one is a red-hot torture." I was sitting by that time and looking across into her face.

Never before or since have I fainted, but I would do it joyfully a dozen times a day if I could wake again to the touch of soft fingers on my face, the hot ecstasy of coffee spilled by those fingers down my neck. There was a thrill in every tone of her voice that morning. Before long my loyalty to McKnight would step between me and the girl he loved. Life would develop new complexities, but in those early hours after the wreck, full of pain as they were, there was nothing of the suspicion and distrust that came later. Shorn of our gauds and baubles we were primitive man and woman together, our world for the hour the deserted farmhouse, the slope of wheatfield that led to the road, the woodland lot, the pasture.

We breakfasted together across the homely table. Our cheerfulness, at first sheer reaction, became less forced as we ate great slices of bread from the granny oven back of the house, and drank hot fluid that smelled like coffee and tasted like nothing that I have ever swallowed. Alison found cream in stone jars, sunk deep in the chill water of the springhouse. And there were eggs, great yellow-brown ones, a basket of them.

So like two children awakened from a nightmare we chattered over our food, we hunted mutual friends, we laughed together at my feeble witticisms, but we put the horror behind us resolutely. After all, it was the hat with the green ribbons that brought back the strangeness of the situation.

All along I had had the impression that she was deliberately putting out of her mind something that obtruded now and then. It brought with it a return of the puzzled expression I had surprised early in the day, before the wreck. I caught it once when, breakfast over, she was tightening the sling that held the broken arm. I had prolonged the morning meal as much as I could, but when the wooden clock with the pink roses on the dial pointed to half after ten, and the mother with the duplicate youngsters had not come back, she made the move I had dreaded.

"If we are to get into Baltimore at all we must start," she said rising. "You ought to see a doctor as soon as possible."

"Hush," I said warningly. "Don't mention the arm, please; it is asleep now. Don't wake it."

"If I only had a hat," she reflected. "It wouldn't need to be much of one, but—" She gave a little cry and darted to the corner. "Look," she said triumphantly, "the very thing! With the green streamers tied up in a bow, like this—do you suppose the child would mind? I can put five dollars or so here."

It was a queer affair of straw, that hat, with a round crown and a rim that flopped dismally. With a single movement she had turned it up at one side and fitted it to her head. Grotesque by itself, when she wore it it was a thing of joy.

Evidently the lack of head covering had troubled her, for she was elated at her find. She left me, scrawling a note of thanks and pinning it with a bill to the tablecloth, and ran upstairs to the mirror and the promised soap and water.

I did not see her when she came down. I had discovered a bench with a tin basin outside the kitchen door and was washing—in a helpless, one-sided way. I felt rather than saw that she was standing in the doorway, and I made a final plunge into the basin.

"How is it possible for a man with only a right hand to wash his left ear?" I asked from the roller towel. I was distinctly uncomfortable: men are more rigidly creatures of convention than women, whether they admit it or not. "There is so much soap on me still that if I laugh I will blow bubbles. Washing with rain water and homemade soap is like motoring on a slippery road. I've skidded quite a lot."

Then, having achieved a brilliant polish with the towel, I looked at her.

She was leaning against the frame of the door, her face perfectly colorless, her breath coming in slow, difficult respirations. The erratic hat was pinned in place, but it had slid rakishly to one side. When I realized that she was staring, not at me, but past me to the road along which we had come, I turned and followed her gaze. There was no one in sight: the lane stretched dust white in the sun—no moving figure on it, no sign of life.

10

THE SURPRISING CHANGE in her held me speechless. All the animation of the breakfast table was gone: there was no hint of the response with which before she had met my nonsensical sallies. She stood there, white-lipped and unsmiling, staring down the dusty road. One hand was clenched tight over some small object. Her eyes dropped to it from the distant road, and then closed with a quick indrawn breath.

Her color came back slowly. Whatever had caused the change, she said nothing. She was anxious to leave at once, almost impatient over my deliberate masculine way of getting my things together. Afterward I recalled that I had wanted to explore the barn for a horse and some sort of vehicle to take us to the trolley, and that she had refused to allow me to look. I remembered many things later that might have helped me, and did not. At the time, I was only completely bewildered. Save the wreck, the responsibility for which probably lay between Providence and the engineer of the second section, all the events of that strange morning were logically connected. They came from one cause and tended unerringly to one end. But the cause was still a complete mystery.

Not until we had left the house well behind did the girl's face relax its tense lines. I was watching her more closely than I had realized, for when we had gone a little way along the road she turned to me almost petulantly. "Please don't stare at me," she said. "I know that the hat is dreadful. Green always makes me look ghastly."

Perhaps it was the green. I was unaccountably relieved. "Do you know, a few minutes ago, you looked almost shocked. Did anything happen to scare you?"

She shook her head and glanced at me quickly, but I was gazing along the road. We were almost out of sight of the house now, and with every step away from it the girl was obviously relieved. Whatever she held in her hand, she never glanced at it. But she was conscious of it every second. She seemed to come to a decision about it while we were still in sight of the gate, for she murmured something and turned back alone, going swiftly, her feet stirring up small puffs of dust at every step. She fastened something to the gatepost; I could see the nervous haste with which she worked, and when she joined me again it was without explanation. But the clenched fingers were free now, and while she looked tired and worn, the strain had visibly relaxed.

We walked along slowly in the general direction of what promised to be a small town. Once a man with an empty farm wagon offered us a lift, but after a glance at the springless vehicle I declined.

"The ends of the bone think they are castanets as it is," I explained. "But the lady—"

The lady, however, declined and we went on together. Once, when the village was in sight, she got a pebble in her low shoe, and we sat down under a tree until she found the cause of the trouble.

"I don't know what I should have done without you," I blundered. "Moral support and all that. Do you know, my first conscious thought after the wreck was of relief that you had not been hurt?"

She was sitting beside me where a big chestnut tree shaded the road, and I surprised a look of misery on her face which certainly my words had not been meant to produce.

"And my first thought," she said slowly, "was regret that I hadn't been obliterated, blown out like a candle. Please don't look like that! I'm only talking."

But her lips were trembling, and I leaned over and patted her hand lightly where it rested on the grass beside me.

"Don't talk like a little idiot," I expostulated. "Perhaps after all your friends are safe. And you are."

"I had no friends on the train." Her voice was hard again, her tone final. She drew her hand from under mine, not quickly but decisively. A car was in sight, coming toward us. I waved and it stopped. We must have been a strange-looking pair, for the driver braked and stared curiously at us.

"Can you take us into Baltimore?" I asked. "We've been in a train wreck, and we both need attention."

He knew about the wreck, and he drove us carefully into the city. We said little in the car, but once she turned to me.

"I don't want my family to know about all this," she said. "They didn't know I was on that train. And Richey too. Please don't tell him either."

I promised, of course. Again, when we were almost in Baltimore, she asked to examine the gunmetal cigarette case and sat silent with it in her hands, while I told of the early morning's events on the Ontario.

"So you see," I finished, "this bag, everything I have on, belongs to a fellow named Sullivan. He probably left the train before the wreck, perhaps just after the murder."

"And so you think he did it?" Her eyes were on the cigarette case.

"Well," I said, "a man doesn't jump off a Pullman car in the middle of the night in another man's clothes unless he is trying to get away from something. Besides the dirk, there were the stains that you saw. And I have the murdered man's pocketbook in this bag right now. What does that look like?"

I colored when I saw the ghost of a smile hoving around the corners of her mouth. "That is," I finished, "if you care to believe that I am innocent."

"I do, of course."

That was when she opened her purse and fished for her compact, and when the little gilt leather bag fell out. It looked like a change purse, just one of the gadgets women carry. Anyhow, she didn't notice, and I picked it up and put it in my coat pocket. I felt somehow that it was safer there.

Afterward I wished I had let it lie unnoticed on the floor of that dirty little car, and even now when I see a woman carelessly dangling a similar trinket I am apt to shudder. There comes back to me the memory of a girl's puzzled eyes under the brim of a ridiculous hat, and the haunting suspicion of the sleepless nights that followed.

"Do you know that it is Sunday," she asked suddenly, "and that we are actually ragged?"

"Never mind that," I retorted with an attempt to be facetious. "All Baltimore is divided on Sunday into three parts: those who rise up and go to church, those who rise up and read the newspapers, and those who don't rise up. The first are somewhere between the creed and the sermon, and we needn't worry about the others."

"Don't treat me like a child," she said pettishly. "Don't try so hard to be cheerful. It's almost ghastly."

After that I subsided like a pricked balloon, and the remainder of the ride was made in silence. The information that she would go to friends in the city was a shock; it meant an earlier separation than I had planned for. But my arm was beginning again. In putting her into a taxi I struck it and gritted my teeth with pain. It was probably for that reason that I forgot to mention the little bag.

She leaned forward and held out her hand. "I may not have another chance to thank you," she said, "and I think I would better not try, anyhow. I can't tell you how grateful I am."

I muttered something about the gratitude being mine. Owing to the knock I was seeing two cabs, and two girls were holding out two hands.

"Remember," they were both saying, "you have never met me, Mr. Blakeley. And if you ever hear anything about me that is not pleasant, I want you to think the best you can of me. Don't forget."

The two girls were one now, with little flashes of white light playing all around. "I'm afraid that I shall think too well for my own good," I said unsteadily. And the taxi drove on.

11

I HAD MY ARM splinted temporarily in Baltimore and took the next train home. I was pretty far gone when I stumbled out of a cab almost into the scandalized arms of Mrs. Klopton. In fifteen minutes I was in bed, with that good woman piling on blankets and blistering me in unprotected places with hot-water bottles. And in an hour I had had a whiff of anesthetic and Doctor Williams had set the broken bone. I dropped asleep then, waking in the late twilight to a realization that I was at home again, without the papers that meant conviction for Andy Bronson, with a charge of murder hanging over my head, and with something more than an impression of the girl my best friend was in love with; a girl, moreover, who was almost as great an enigma as the crime itself.

"And I'm no hand at guessing riddles," I groaned half aloud. Mrs. Klopton came over promptly and put a cold cloth on my forehead.

"Euphemia," she said to the maid outside the door, "telephone the doctor that he is still rambling, but that he has switched from pigsties to riddles."

"There's nothing the matter with me, Mrs. Klopton," I rebelled. "I was only thinking out loud. Damn that cloth: it's trickling all over me!" I gave it a fling, and heard it land with a soggy thud on the floor.

"Thinking out loud is delirium," Mrs. Klopton said imperturbably. "A fresh cloth, Euphemia."

This time she held it on with a firm pressure that I was too weak to resist. I expostulated feebly that I was drowning, which she also laid to my mental excitement, and I finally dropped into a damp sleep. It was probably midnight when I roused again. I had been dreaming of the wreck, and it was inexpressibly comforting to feel the stability of my bed, and to realize the equal stability of Mrs. Klopton who sat, fully dressed, by the night light.

The room was like a furnace, and I saw that all the windows were closed and the curtains drawn.

"What the hell's the idea?" I demanded. "Get some air in here. I'm roasting."

She came over and stood stiffly by the bed.

"It ain't safe to open those windows," she said firmly. "You take your medicine and go to sleep again."

"Why isn't it safe?"

She weakened then.

"Because there are queer goings-on in that house next door," she said. "If you'll take the medicine, Mr. Lawrence, I'll tell you about them."

The queer goings-on, however, proved to be slightly disappointing. It seemed that after I left on Friday night a light was seen flitting fitfully through the empty house next door. Euphemia had seen it first and called Mrs. Klopton. Together they had watched it breathlessly until it disappeared on the lower floor.

"You should have been a writer of ghost stories," I said, giving my pillows a thump. "And so it was fitting flitfully!"

"That's what it was doing," she reiterated. "Fitting flitfully—I mean flitting fitfully—how you do throw me out, Mr. Lawrence! And what's more, it came again!"

"Oh, come now, Mrs. Klopton," I objected, "ghosts are like lightning; they never strike twice in the same night."

"You can ask Euphemia," she retorted with dignity. "Not more than an hour after there was a light there again. We saw it through the chinks of the shutters. Only—*this time it began at the lower floor and climbed!*"

"You oughtn't to tell ghost stories at night," came McKnight's voice from the doorway. "Really, Mrs. Klopton, I'm amazed at you." And to me: "You old duffer! I've got you to thank for the worst day of my life."

Mrs. Klopton gulped. Then realizing that the "old duffer" was meant for me, she took her medicine bottle and went out muttering.

"The Pirate's crazy about me, isn't she?" McKnight said to the closing door. Then he swung around and held out his hand.

"By Jove," he said, "I've been laying you out all day, lilies on the doorbell, black ties, everything. If you had had the sense of a ten-year-old child you'd have telephoned me."

"I never thought of it." I felt like a sap. "Upon my word, Rich, I hadn't an idea beyond getting away from that place. If you had seen what I saw—"

McKnight stopped me. "Seen it! Why, you lunatic, I've been digging for you all day in the wreck; I've lunched and dined on horrors. Give me something to rinse them down, can't you?"

He fished the key of the liquor closet from my desk and was mixing himself a stiff drink. Now that I saw him clearly he looked weary and grimy. I hated to tell him what I knew he was waiting to hear, but there was no use wading in by inches. I ducked and got it over.

"The notes are gone, Rich," I said, as quietly as I could. In spite of himself his face fell.

"I—of course I expected it," he said. "But Mrs. Klopton said over the telephone that you had brought home a bag and I hoped—well, God knows, we can't complain. You're here; damaged, but here." He lifted his glass. "Happy day, old man!"

"I'll have a drink myself," I said. "I need it. I have to tell you something. Rich—the notes were gone before the wreck!"

He wheeled and stared at me, the bottle in his hand. "Lost, strayed, or stolen?" he queried with forced lightness.

"Stolen, although I believe the theft was incidental to something else."

Mrs. Klopton came in at that moment, with an eggnog in her hand. She glanced at the clock, and, without addressing anyone in particular, intimated that it was time for self-respecting folks to be at home in bed. McKnight, who could never resist a fling at her, spoke to me in a stage whisper.

"Is she talking still, or again?" he asked, just before the door closed. There was a second's indecision with the knob, then, judging discretion the better part, Mrs. Klopton went away.

"Now, then," McKnight said, settling himself in the chair beside the bed, "spit it out. Not the wreck. I know all I want about that. But the theft. I can tell you beforehand that it was a woman."

I had crawled painfully out of bed, and was in the act of pouring the eggnog down the waste pipe of the washstand in the bathroom. I paused, with the glass in the air.

"A woman," I repeated, startled. "What makes you think that?"

"You don't know the first principles of a good detective yarn," he said scornfully. "You fell for a pretty woman on the train and she robbed you. Well, on with the dance: let joy be unconfined."

So I told the story. I had told it so many times that day that I did it automatically. And I told about the girl with the bronze hair, and my suspicions. But I did not mention Alison West. McKnight listened to the end without interruption. When I had finished he drew a long breath.

"Well!" he said. "That's something of a mess, isn't it? If you can only prove your mild and childlike disposition, they couldn't hold you for the murder—which is a regular grade B picture crime anyhow. But the notes— that's different. They are not burned anyhow. Your man wasn't on the train. Therefore, he wasn't in the wreck. If he didn't know what he was taking, as you seem to think, he probably reads the papers, and unless he is a fathead he's awake by this time to what he's got. He'll try to sell them to Bronson, probably."

"Or to us," I put in.

We said nothing for a few minutes. McKnight smoked a cigarette and stared at a photograph of Candida over the mantel. Candida is the best pony for a heavy mount in seven states.

"I didn't go to Richmond," he observed finally. The remark followed my own thoughts so closely that I started. "Alison West is not home yet from Seal Harbor."

Receiving no response, he lapsed again into thoughtful silence. Mrs. Klopton came in just as the clock struck one and made preparation for the night by putting a large gaudy comfortable into an armchair in the dressing room, with a smaller, stiff-backed chair for her feet. She was wonderfully attired in a dressing gown that was reminiscent, in parts, of all the ones she had given me for half dozen Christmases, and she had a purple veil wrapped around her head, to hide Heaven knows what deficiency. She examined the empty eggnog glass, inquired what the evening paper had said about the weather, and then stalked into the dressing room and prepared, with much ostentatious creaking, to sit up all night.

We fell silent again, while McKnight traced a rough outline of the berths on the white table cover, and puzzled it out slowly. It was something like this:

12	10*	8

AISLE

11	9	7

"You think he changed the tags on seven and nine, so that when you went back to bed you thought you were crawling into nine, when it was really seven, eh?"

"Probably—yes."

"Then toward morning, when everybody was asleep, your theory is that he changed the numbers again and left the train."

"I can't think of anything else," I replied wearily.

"Jove, what a game of bridge that fellow would play! It was like finessing an eight-spot and making a grand slam. They would scarcely have doubted your story had the tags been reversed in the morning. He certainly left you in a bad way; the stains, the stiletto, and the murdered man's pocketbook in your possession."

"Then you think this fellow Sullivan did it?"

"Of course," said McKnight confidently. "Unless you did it in your sleep. Look at the stains on his pillow, and the dirk stuck into it. And didn't he have the man Harrington's wallet in the bag?"

"Then why did he go off without it?" I persisted. "And where does the bronze-haired woman come in?"

"Probably the girl friend," McKnight retorted flippantly. "Else why her tears?"

"Then there is the piece of telegram. It said lower ten, car seven. It's extremely likely that she had it. That telegram was about me, Richey."

"I'm getting a headache," he said, putting out his cigarette. "All I'm certain of just now is that if there hadn't been a wreck, by this time you'd be sitting in an eight-by-ten cell, and the grand old state of Pennsylvania would be getting ready to hang you."

"But listen," I contended as he picked up his hat, "this fellow Sullivan is a fugitive, and he's a lot more likely to make advances to Bronson than to us. We'd better set a watch on him. It's our only chance."

"Not my watch," McKnight protested. "It's a family heirloom."

"You'd better go home," I said firmly. "Go home and go to bed. You're not funny and I'm still in the hell of a mess."

Mrs. Klopton's voice came drowsily from the next room, punctuated by a yawn. "I forgot to tell you," she called, with the suspicious lisp that characterizes her at night when she has taken out her teeth. "Somebody called up about noon today, Mr. Lawrence. It was long distance, and he said he would call again. The name was"—she yawned—"Sullivan."

Richey and I stared at each other.

"So he's going to sell us the notes, after all," Rich said softly. "He has a nerve, hasn't he?"

12

I HAD ALWAYS grinned at those cases of spontaneous combustion which, like fusing the component parts of a seidlitz powder, unite two people in a bubbling and ephemeral ecstasy. But surely there is possible, with but a single meeting, an attraction so great, a community of mind and interest so strong, that between that first meeting and the next the bond may grow into something stronger. This is especially true, I suppose, of people with imagination. Anyhow it is a nice question whether lovers begin to love when they are together, or when they are apart.

Not that I followed any such line of reasoning at the time. I would not admit my folly even to myself. But during the restless hours of that first night after the accident, when my back ached with lying on it and any other position was torture, I found my thoughts constantly going back to Alison West. I dropped into a doze, to dream of touching her fingers again, and awoke to find I had patted a teaspoonful of medicine out of Mrs. Klopton's indignant hand. What was it McKnight had said about making an ass of myself?

And that brought me back to Richey, and I imagine I groaned. There is no use expatiating on the friendship between two men who have gone together through college, have quarreled and made it up, fussed together over politics and debated creeds for years. Men don't need to be told, and women cannot understand. Nevertheless, I felt wretched that night.

Some things were mine, however, and I would keep them: the breakfast in the farmhouse, the queer hat, the pebble in her small shoe, and the little gilt bag. The bag! Why, it was in my pocket at that moment.

I got up painfully and found my coat. Yes, there it was. She would have missed it by now, and wondered what had happened to it. At least it gave me the chance to see her again, if only once. But it did not occur to me to open it. I slid it under my pillow and went to sleep almost happily.

McKnight came in about eleven the next morning. I heard his car at the curb, followed almost immediately by his slam at the front door and his usual clamor on the stairs. He had a bottle of Scotch under one arm and a carton of cigarettes under the other, and I heard Mrs. Klopton protesting.

"He oughtn't to smoke or drink, Mr. McKnight. You know that."

"Get out of my way, woman. What do you think he broke? His skull?" He was grinning when he came in.

"Well," he said cheerfully, "how did you sleep after keeping me up half the night?"

I slid my hand under the pillow. The little purse was well covered.

"Have it now, or wait till I get the cork out?" he rattled on.

"I don't want anything," I protested. "I wish you wouldn't be so damned cheerful, Rich." He stopped whistling to stare at me.

"'I am saddest when I sing!'" he quoted unctuously. "It's pure reaction, old boy. Yesterday the sky was low, I was digging for my best friend. Today he lies safe before me, his peevish self. Yesterday I thought the damned notes were burned: today I look forward to a good cross-country chase, and with luck we'll draw." His voice changed suddenly. "Yesterday she was in Seal Harbor. Today she's here."

"Here in Washington?" I asked, as naturally as I could.

"Yes. Going to stay a week or two."

He began to sing, and I put my hands to my ears.

"For God's sake, stop that racket, Rich! What's come over you?"

"Love," he said. "You ought to try it sometime. It's wonderful."

He came over and sat on the bed.

"I've taken to long country drives," he said dreamily, "and yesterday I ran over a sheep; nearly sent the car into a ditch. But there's a Providence that watches over fools and lovers. Just now I know darned well that I'm one, and I have a sneaking idea I'm both."

"You *are* both," I said with disgust. "If you can be rational for one moment, I wish you would tell me why that man Sullivan called me over the telephone yesterday morning."

"Kind of washes out the idea he's the killer, doesn't it? Or maybe he's trying to be smart. If he's got the notes—"

"Or he may only want his own clothes again!" I said fretfully. "Although how the hell he knows I've got them—"

"He's got yours, hasn't he? And the papers report you among the survivors."

The doctor interrupted us. As I may have said before, I think a lot of my doctor—when there is anything wrong with me. He is a young man, with an air of breezy self-confidence and good humor. He looked directly past the bottle, which is a very valuable accomplishment, and shook hands with McKnight until I could put the carton of cigarettes under the bedclothes. He had interdicted tobacco. Then he sat down beside the bed and felt around the bandages with hands as gentle as a baby's.

"Pretty good shape," he said. "How did you sleep?"

"Oh, occasionally," I replied. "I would like to sit up, doctor."

"Nonsense. Take a rest while you have an excuse for it. I wish to thunder I could stay in bed for a day or so. I was up all night."

"Have a drink," McKnight said, pushing over the bottle.

"Twins!" The doctor grinned.

"Then have two drinks."

But he refused.

"I wouldn't even wear a champagne-colored necktie during business hours," he explained. "By the way, I had another case from your wreck, Mr. Blakeley, yesterday afternoon. Under the tongue, please." He stuck a thermometer in my mouth.

I had a sudden terrible vision of the amateur detective coming to light, notebook, cheerful impertinence, and incriminating data. "A small man," I demanded, "gray hair—?"

"Keep your mouth closed," the doctor said peremptorily. "No. A woman with a fractured skull. Beautiful case. Van Kirk in Baltimore was up to his eyes and sent for me. Hemorrhage, right-sided paralysis, irregular pupils —all the trimmings. Worked for two hours."

"Did she recover?" McKnight put in. He was examining the doctor with a new awe.

"She lifted her right arm before I left," the doctor finished cheerily, "so the operation was a success. She may not live, of course."

"Good God!" McKnight shuddered. "And I thought you were just an ordinary mortal like the rest of us! Was she pretty?"

"Yes, and young. Had a wealth of bronze-colored hair too. I hated to cut it."

McKnight and I exchanged glances.

"Do you know her name?" I asked.

"No. The nurses said her clothes came from a Pittsburgh tailor."

"She's not conscious, I suppose?"

"No; she may be tomorrow, or in a week. Or never."

He looked at the thermometer, murmured something about liquid diet, avoiding my eye—Mrs. Klopton was broiling a chop at the time—and took his departure, humming cheerfully as he went downstairs. McKnight looked after him wistfully.

"Jove, I wish I had his constitution," he exclaimed. "Not a nerve in him. He ought to be flying a plane."

But I was serious.

"I have an idea," I said grimly, "that this small matter of the murder is going to come up again, and that I'll be in the devil of a fix if it does. If that woman is going to die, somebody ought to be around to take her deposition. She knows a lot, if she didn't do it herself. I wish you would go down to the telephone and get the hospital in Baltimore. Find out her name and if she's conscious."

McKnight went under protest. "I haven't much time," he said, looking at his watch. "I'm to meet Mrs. West and Alison at one. I want you to know them, Laurie. You would like the mother."

"Why not the daughter?" I inquired.

"Well," he said judicially, "you've always declared against the immaturity and romantic nonsense of young women—"

"I never said anything of the sort," I retorted. "Where did you get that idea?"

" 'There is more satisfaction to be had out of a good saddle horse!' " he quoted me. " 'More excitement out of a polo pony, and as for the eternal matrimonial chase, give me instead a good stubble, a fox, some decent hounds and a hunter, and I'll show you the real joys of the chase!' "

"For God's sake, go down to the telephone. You make my head ache," I said savagely.

I hardly know what prompted me to take out the gilt bag and look at it when he was gone. I only know I did so, with one eye on the door, for Mrs. Klopton has a ready eye and a noiseless shoe. But the house was quiet. Downstairs McKnight was flirting with the telephone central and there was an odor of boneset tea in the air. I think Mrs. Klopton was fascinated by the "boneset" in connection with the fractured arm.

Anyhow, I held up the bag and looked at it. It must have been unfastened, for the next instant something tumbled out of it. A necklace.

It was one of the barbaric affairs women were wearing, a pendant of cameos hanging from a slim chain. But the chain was broken. Three inches of it had been snapped off, and as well as I knew anything on earth, I knew that the bit of chain that the amateur detective had found, bloodstain and all, belonged just there.

And there was no one I could talk to about it, no one to tell me how hideously absurd it was, no one to give me a slap and tell me there are tons of fine gold chains made every year, or to point out the long arm of coincidence.

With my one useful hand I fumbled the thing back into the little bag and thrust it deep out of sight among the pillows. Then I lay back in a cold perspiration. What connection had Alison West with this crime? Why had she stared so at the gunmetal cigarette case that morning on the train? What had alarmed her at the farmhouse? What had she taken back to the gate? Why did she wish she had not escaped from the wreck? And last, in Heaven's name, how did a part of her necklace become worn off and covered with blood?

Downstairs McKnight was still at the telephone, and amusing himself with Mrs. Klopton in the interval of waiting.

"Why did he come home in a gray suit when he went away in a blue?" he repeated. "Well, wrecks are queer things, Mrs. Klopton. The suit may have turned gray with fright. Or perhaps wrecks do as queer stunts as lightning. Friend of mine once was struck by lightning; he and the caddy had taken refuge under a tree. After the flash, when they recovered consciousness, there was my friend in the caddy's clothes, and the caddy in his. And as my friend was a large man and the caddy a very small boy—"

McKnight's story was interrupted by the indignant slam of the dining-room door. He was obliged to wait some time, and even his eternal cheerfulness was ebbing when he finally got the hospital in Baltimore.

"Is Doctor Van Kirk there?" he asked. "Not there? Well, can you tell me how the patient is whom Doctor Williams, from Washington, operated on last night? Well, I'm glad of that. Is she conscious? Do you happen to know her name? Yes, I'll hold the line."

There was a long pause, then McKnight's voice:

"Hello— Yes? Thank you very much. Good-bye."

He came upstairs, two steps at a time.

"Look here," he said, bursting into the room, "there may be something in your theory, after all. The woman's name—she gave it before they operated —her name is Sullivan."

"What did I tell you?" I said, sitting up suddenly in bed. "She's probably the sister or wife of that fellow in lower seven."

"Well, I'll go over there someday soon. She's not conscious yet. In the meantime the only thing I can do is to keep an eye, through a detective, on the people who try to approach Bronson. One way or another those notes are going to turn up. Mark my words."

"Damn this arm," I said, paying for my energy with some excruciating throbs. "There's so much to be done, and here I am bandaged, splinted, and generally useless. It's plain hell."

"Don't forget that I am here," said McKnight pompously. "And another thing, when you feel this way just remember there are two less desirable places where you might be. One is jail, and the other is—" He strummed on an imaginary harp, with devotional eyes.

But McKnight's lightheartedness jarred on me that morning. I lay and frowned under my helplessness. When by chance I touched the little gilt bag it seemed to scorch my fingers. Richey, finding me unresponsive, left to keep his luncheon engagement with Alison West, and as he clattered down the stairs I turned my back to the morning sunshine and abandoned myself to misery. By what strain on her frayed nerves was Alison West keeping up? I wondered. Under the circumstances, would I dare to return the bag? Knowing that I had it, would she hate me for my knowledge? Or had I exaggerated the importance of the necklace, and in that case had she forgotten me already?

But McKnight had not gone, after all. I heard him coming back, his voice preceding him, and I groaned with irritation.

"Wake up!" he called. "Somebody's sent you a lot of flowers. Please hold the box, Mrs. Klopton; I'm going out to be run down by an automobile."

I roused to feeble interest. My brother's wife is punctilious about such things; all the new babies in the family have silver rattles, and all the sick people flowers.

McKnight pulled up an armful of roses, and held them out to me.

"Wonder who they're from?" he said, fumbling in the box for a card. "There's no name—yes, here's one."

He held it up and read it with exasperating slowness:

"Best wishes for an early recovery.

A COMPANION IN MISFORTUNE."

"Well, what do you know!" he exclaimed. "That's something you didn't tell me, Laurie."

"It was hardly worth mentioning," I said mendaciously, with my heart beating until I could hear it. "Just a nice girl who helped me away from the tracks."

He asked no questions. He merely grinned. Then he broke off a bud and fastened it in his buttonhole. I'm afraid I was not especially pleasant about it. They were her roses, and anyhow, they were meant for me. He left very soon, with an irritating final grin at the box.

"Good-bye, woman-hater," he jeered at me from the door.

So he wore one of the roses she had sent me to luncheon with her, and I lay back among my pillows and tried to remember that it was his game anyhow, and that I wasn't even drawing cards. To remember that, and to forget the broken necklace under my head.

13

I WAS IN THE HOUSE for a week. Much of that time I spent in composing and destroying letters of thanks to Alison West, and in growling at the doctor. McKnight dropped in daily, but he was less cheerful than usual. Now and then I caught him eying me as if he had something to say, but whatever it was he kept it to himself. Once during the week he went to Baltimore and saw the woman in the hospital there. From the description I had little difficulty in recognizing the young woman who had been with the murdered man in Pittsburgh. But she was still unconscious. An elderly aunt had appeared, a gaunt person in black who sat around like a buzzard on a fence, according to McKnight, and wept, a mixed figure, into a damp handkerchief.

On the last day of my imprisonment he stopped in to thrash out a case that was coming up in court the next day, and to play a game of double solitaire with me.

"Who won the ball game?" I asked.

"We were licked. Ask me something pleasant. Oh, by the way, Bronson's around again. I saw him today."

"I'm glad I'm not on his bond," I said pessimistically. "He'll clear out."

"Not he." McKnight pounced on my ace. "He's no fool. Don't you suppose he knows you took those notes to Pittsburgh? And he knows you escaped with your life and a broken arm from the wreck, and probably nothing else. A blind man on a dark night would know those notes are missing."

"Don't play so fast," I remonstrated. "I have only one arm to your two. Who is trailing Bronson? Did you try to get Johnson?"

"I asked for him but he had some work on hand."

"The murder's evidently a dead issue," I reflected. "No, I'm not joking. The wreck destroyed all the evidence. But I'm firmly convinced those notes will be offered, either to us or to Bronson, very soon. Johnson's a blackguard, but he's a good detective. He could make his fortune as a game dog. What's he doing?"

McKnight put down his cards, and rising, went to the window. As he held the curtain back his customary grin looked a little forced.

"To tell you the truth, Laurie," he said, "for the last two days he has been watching a well-known Washington attorney named Lawrence Blakeley. He's across the street now."

It took a moment for me to grasp what he meant.

"Why, it's ridiculous," I asserted. "What would they trail me for? Go over and tell Johnson to get out of there, or I'll pot at him with my revolver."

"You can tell him that yourself," McKnight paused and bent forward. "Hello, here's a visitor; little man with stringhalt."

"I won't see him," I said firmly. "I've been bothered enough with reporters."

We listened together to Mrs. Klopton's expostulating tones in the lower hall and the creak of the boards as she came heavily up the stairs. She had a piece of paper in her hand torn from a pocket account book, and on it was the name, "Mr. Wilson Budd Hotchkiss. Important business."

"Oh, well, show him up," I said resignedly. "You'd better put those cards away, Richey. I fancy it's the rector of the church around the corner."

But when the door opened to admit a curiously alert little man, adjusting his glasses with nervous fingers, my face must have shown my dismay.

It was the amateur detective of the Ontario!

I shook hands without enthusiasm. Here was the one survivor of the wrecked car who could do me any amount of harm. There was no hope that he had forgotten any of the incriminating details. In fact, he held in his hand the very notebook that contained them.

His manner was restrained, but it was evident he was highly excited. I introduced him to McKnight, who has the imagination I lack, and who placed him at once mentally.

"I only learned yesterday that you had been—er—saved," he said rapidly. "Terrible accident—unspeakable. Dream about it all night and think about it all day. Broken arm?"

"No. He just wears the splint to be different from other people," McKnight drawled lazily. I glared at him: there was nothing to be gained by antagonizing the little man.

"Yes, a fractured humerus, which isn't as funny as it sounds."

"Humerus—humorous! Pretty good," he cackled. "I must say you keep up your spirits pretty well, considering everything."

"You seem to have escaped injury," I parried. He was fumbling for something in his pockets.

"Yes, I escaped," he replied abstractedly. "Remarkable thing, too. I haven't a doubt I would have broken my neck, but I landed on—you'll never guess what! I landed head first on the very pillow that was under inspection at the time of the wreck. You remember, don't you? Where did I put that package?"

He found it finally and opened it on a table, displaying with some theatricalism a rectangular piece of muslin and a similar patch of striped ticking.

"You recognize it?" he said. "The stains, you see, and the hole made by the dirk. I tried to bring away the entire pillow, but they thought I was stealing it and made me give it up."

Richey touched the pieces gingerly. "By George," he said, "and you carry that around in your pocket! What if you should mistake it for your handkerchief?"

But Mr. Hotchkiss was not listening. He was standing bent somewhat forward, leaning over the table, and fixed me with his ferret-like eyes.

"Have you seen the evening papers, Mr. Blakeley?" he inquired.

I glanced to where they lay unopened, and shook my head.

"Then I have a disagreeable task," he said, with evident relish. "Of course, you had considered the matter of the man Harrington's death closed, after the wreck. I did myself. As far as I was concerned I meant to let it remain so. There were no other survivors, at least none that I knew of; and in spite of circumstances there were a number of points in your favor."

"Thank you," I put in with a sarcasm that was lost on him.

"I verified your identity, for instance, as soon as I recovered from the shock. Also I found on inquiring of your tailor that you invariably wore dark clothing."

McKnight came forward threateningly. "Who are you, anyhow?" he demanded. "And how is this any business of yours?"

Mr. Hotchkiss was entirely unruffled. "I have a minor position here," he said, reaching for a visiting card. "I am a very small patch on the seat of government, sir."

McKnight muttered something about certain offensive designs against the said patch and retired grumbling to the window. Our visitor was opening the paper with a tremendous expenditure of energy.

"Here it is. Listen." He read rapidly aloud:

"The Pittsburgh police have sent to Baltimore two detectives who are looking up the survivors of the ill-fated Washington Flier. It has transpired that Simon Harrington, the Wood Street merchant of that city, was not killed in the wreck, but was murdered in his berth the night preceding the accident. Shortly before the collision, John Flanders, the conductor of the Flier, sent this telegram to the chief of police:

"'Body of Simon Harrington found stabbed in his berth, lower ten, car Ontario, at six-thirty this morning.

JOHN FLANDERS, Conductor.'

"It is hoped that the survivors of the wrecked car Ontario will be found, to tell what they know of the discovery of the crime.

"Mr. John Gilmore, head of the steel company for which Mr. Harrington was purchasing agent, has signified his intention of sifting the matter to the bottom."

"So you see," Hotchkiss concluded, "there's trouble brewing. You and I are the only survivors of that unfortunate car."

I did not contradict him, but I knew of two others, at least: Alison West and the woman with the bronze-colored hair.

"Unless we can find the man who occupied lower seven," I suggested.

"I have already tried and failed. To find him would not clear you, of course, unless we could establish some connection between him and the murdered man. It is the only thing I see, however. I have learned this much," Hotchkiss concluded: "Lower seven was reserved from Cresson."

Cresson! Where Alison West and Mrs. Curtis had taken the train!

McKnight came forward and suddenly held out his hand. "Mr. Hotchkiss," he said, "I'm sorry if I have been offensive. I thought when you came in that, like the Irishman and the government, you were 'forninst' us. If you will put those cheerful relics out of sight somewhere, I should be glad to have you dine with me at the Incubator." (His name for his bachelor apartment.) "Compared with Johnson, you are the original resuscitator."

The strength of this was lost on Hotchkiss, but the invitation was clear. They went out together, and from my window I watched them get into McKnight's car. It was raining, and at the corner the Cannonball skidded. Across the street my detective, Johnson, looked after them with his crooked smile. As he turned up his collar he saw me and touched his hat.

I left the window and sat down in the growing dusk. So the occupant of lower seven had got on the car at Cresson, probably with Alison West and her companion. And there was someone she cared about enough to shield. I went irritably to the door and summoned Mrs. Klopton.

"You may throw out those roses," I said, without looking at her. "They're dead."

"They've been dead for three days," she retorted spitefully. "Euphemia said you threatened to discharge her if she touched them."

14

By Sunday evening, a week after the wreck, my forced inaction had goaded me to frenzy. The very sight of Johnson across the street or lurking, always within sight of the house, kept me constantly exasperated. It was on that day that things began to come to a focus, a burning glass of events that seemed to center on me.

I dined alone that evening in no cheerful frame of mind. There had been a polo game the day before and I had lent a pony, which is always a bad thing to do. And she had wrenched her shoulder, besides helping to lose the game. There was no one in town: the temperature was ninety and climbing, and my left hand persistently cramped under its bandage.

Mrs. Klopton herself saw me served, my bread buttered and cut in tidbits, my meat ready for my fork. She hovered around me maternally, obviously trying to cheer me.

"The paper says still warmer," she ventured. "The thermometer is ninety-two now."

"And this coffee is two hundred and fifty," I said, putting down my cup. "Where is Euphemia? I haven't seen her around, or heard a dish smash all day."

"Euphemia is in bed," Mrs. Klopton said dryly. "Is your meat cut small enough, Mr. Lawrence?" Mrs. Klopton can throw more mystery into an ordinary sentence than anyone else I know. She can say, "Are your sheets damp, sir?" And I can tell from her tone that the house across the street has been robbed, or that my left-hand neighbor has appendicitis. So now I looked up and asked the question she was waiting for.

"What's the matter with Euphemia?" I inquired idly.

"Frightened into her bed," Mrs. Klopton said in a stage whisper. "She's had three hot-water bottles and she hasn't done a thing all day but moan."

"She oughtn't to take hot-water bottles," I said in my severest tone. "One would make me moan. You needn't wait, I'll ring if I need anything."

Mrs. Klopton sailed to the door, where she stopped and wheeled indignantly. "I only hope you won't laugh on the wrong side of your face some morning, Mr. Lawrence," she declared, with Christian fortitude. "But I warn you, I am going to have the police watch that house next door."

I was half inclined to tell her that both it and we were under police surveillance at that moment. But I like Mrs. Klopton, in spite of the fact that I make her life a torment at times, so I refrained.

"Last night, when the paper said it was going to storm, I sent Euphemia to the roof to bring the rugs in. Eliza had slipped out, although it was her evening in. Euphemia went up to the roof—it was eleven o'clock—and soon I heard her running downstairs wailing. When she got to my room she just folded up on the floor. She said there was a black figure sitting on the parapet of the house next door—the empty house—and that when she appeared it rose and waved long black arms at her and spit like a cat."

I had finished my dinner and was trying to light a cigarette. "If there was anyone up there, which I doubt, they probably sneezed," I suggested. "But if you feel uneasy, I'll take a look around the roof tonight before I turn in. As far as Euphemia goes, I wouldn't be uneasy about her. Doesn't she always have an attack of some sort when Eliza rings in an extra evening on her?"

So I made a superficial examination of the window locks that night, visiting parts of the house I had not seen since I bought it. Then I went to the roof. Evidently it had not been intended for any purpose save to cover the house, for, unlike the houses around, there was no staircase. A ladder and a trap door led to it, and it required some nice balancing on my part to get up with my useless arm. I made it, however, and found this unexplored part of my domain rather attractive. It was cooler than downstairs, and I sat on the brick parapet and smoked my final cigarette. The roof of the empty house adjoined mine along the back wing, but investigation showed that the trap door across the low dividing wall was bolted underneath.

There was nothing out of the ordinary anywhere, and so I assured Mrs. Klopton. Needless to say, I did not tell her that I had left the trap door open, to see if it would improve the temperature of the house. I went to bed at midnight, merely because there was nothing else to do. I turned on the night lamp at the head of my bed, and picked up a volume of Shaw at random (it was *Arms and the Man*, and I remember thinking grimly that I was a good bit of a chocolate cream soldier myself), and prepared to go to sleep. Shaw always puts me to sleep. I have no apologies to make for what occurred that night, and not even an explanation that I am sure of. I did a foolish thing under impulse, and I have not been sorry.

It was something after two when the doorbell rang. It rang quickly, twice. I got up drowsily, for the maids and Mrs. Klopton always lock themselves beyond reach of the bell at night, and put on a dressing gown. The bell rang again on my way downstairs. I lit the hall light and opened the door. I was wide awake now, and I saw that it was Johnson. His bald head shone in the light, his crooked mouth was twisted in a smile.

"Good heavens, man," I said irritably. "Don't you ever go home and go to bed?"

He closed the vestibule door behind him and cavalierly turned out the light. Our dialogue was sharp, staccato.

"Have you a key to the empty house next door?" he demanded. "Somebody's in there."

"The houses are alike. The key to this door may fit. Did you see them go in?"

"No. There's a light moving up from room to room. I saw something like it last night, and I have been watching. The patrolman reported queer doings there a week or so ago. Have you got a gun?"

"Don't tell me you're watching me without one," I said ironically. "Yes, I have an automatic. Wait and I'll get it."

I brought it and Johnson planned the campaign, with his eyes on the house. He suggested that because of my familiarity with the roof, I go there and cut off escape in that direction. "I have Robison out there now, the patrolman on the beat," he said. "He'll watch below and you above, while I search the house. Be as quiet as possible."

I was rather amused. I put on some clothes and felt my way carefully up the stairs, the revolver swinging free in my pocket, my hand on the rail. At the foot of the ladder I stopped and looked up. Above me there was a gray rectangle of sky dotted with stars. It occurred to me that with my one serviceable hand holding the ladder I was hardly in a position to defend myself, and that I was about to hoist a body I am rather careful of into a danger I couldn't see and wasn't particularly keen about anyhow. I don't mind saying that the seconds it took me to scramble up the ladder were among the most unpleasant that I recall.

I got to the top, however, without incident. I could see fairly well after the darkness of the house beneath, but there was nothing suspicious in sight. The roofs, separated by two feet of brick wall, stretched around me, unbroken save by an occasional chimney. I went very softly over to the other trap, the one belonging to the suspected house. It was closed, but I imagined I could hear Johnson's footsteps ascending from below. Then even that was gone. A near-by clock struck three as I stood waiting. I examined my revolver then, for the first time, and found it was empty!

I had been rather skeptical until now. I had had the usual tolerant attitude of the man who is summoned from his bed to search for burglars, combined with the artificial courage of firearms. With the discovery of my empty gun I felt like a man on the top of a volcano in lively eruption. And suddenly I found myself staring incredulously at the trap door at my feet. I had examined it early in the evening and found it bolted. Did I imagine it, or had it raised about an inch? Wasn't it moving slowly as I looked? I am certainly no hero. I was startled into a panic. I had only one arm, and whoever was raising that trap door had two. My knees had a queer inclination to bend the wrong way.

Johnson's footsteps were distinct enough, but he was evidently far below. The trap, raised perhaps two inches now, remained stationary. There was no sound from beneath it. Once I thought I heard two or three gasping respirations; but I am not sure they were not my own. I wanted desperately to stand on one leg at a time and hold the other up out of focus of a possible revolver.

I did not see the hand appear. There was nothing, and then it was there, clutching the frame of the trap. I did the only thing I could think of; I put my foot on it!

There was not a sound from beneath. The next moment I was kneeling and had clutched the wrist just above the hand. After a second's struggle, the arm was still. With something real to race, I was myself again.

"Don't move, or I'll stand on the trap and break your arm," I panted. What else could I threaten? I couldn't shoot, I couldn't even fight. "Johnson!" I called.

And then I realized the thing that stayed with me for a month, the thing I cannot think of even now without a shudder. The hand lay small and strangely quiescent. Under my fingers an artery was beating feebly. The wrist was as slender as—I held the hand to the light. Then I let it drop.

"Good God," I muttered, and remained on my knees, staring at the spot where the hand had been. It was gone now: there was a faint rustle in the darkness below, and then silence.

I held up my own hand in the starlight and stared at the long scratch in the palm. "A woman!" I said to myself stupidly. "By all that's ridiculous, a woman!"

Johnson was striking matches below and swearing softly to himself. "How the devil do you get to the roof?" he called. "I think I've broken my nose!"

He found the ladder after a short search and stood at the bottom, looking up at me. "Well, I suppose you haven't seen him?" he inquired. "There are enough darned cubbyholes in this house to hide a patrol wagon load of thieves." He lighted a fresh match. "Hello, here's another door!"

By the sound of his diminishing footsteps I supposed it was a rear staircase. He came up again in ten minutes or so, this time with the policeman.

"He's gone all right," he said ruefully. "If you'd been attending to your business, Robison, you'd have watched the back door."

"I'm not twins." Robison was surly.

"Well," I broke in, as cheerfully as I could, "if you are through with this jolly little affair, and can get down my ladder without having my housekeeper ring the burglar alarm, I have some good whisky. How about it?"

They came without a second invitation across the roof, and with them safely away from the house I breathed more freely. Down in the den I fulfilled my promise, which Johnson drank to the toast, "Coming through the rye." He examined my gun rack with the eye of a connoisseur, and even when he was about to go he cast a loving eye back at the weapons.

"Ever been in the army?" he inquired.

"No," I said with a bitterness that he noticed but failed to comprehend. "I'm a chocolate cream soldier—you don't read Shaw, I suppose, Johnson?"

"Never heard of him," the detective said indifferently. "Well, good night, Mr. Blakeley. Much obliged." At the door he hesitated and coughed.

"I suppose you understand, Mr. Blakeley," he said awkwardly, "that this—er—surveillance is all in the day's work. I don't like it, but it's duty. Every man to his duty, sir."

"Sometime when you are in an open mood, Johnson," I returned, "you can explain why I am being watched at all."

15

ON MONDAY I went out for the first time. I did not go to the office. I wanted to walk. I thought fresh air and exercise would drive away the blue devils that had me by the throat. McKnight insisted on a long day in his car, but I refused.

"I don't know why not," he said sulkily. "I can't walk. I haven't walked two consecutive blocks in three years. Automobiles have made legs mere ornaments—and some not even that. We could have Johnson out there chasing us over the country at five dollars an hour!"

"He can chase us just as well at five miles an hour," I said. "But what gets me, McKnight, is why I am under surveillance at all. How do the police know I was accused of that thing?"

"The young lady who sent the flowers—she isn't likely to talk, is she?"

"No. That is, I don't think so." I groaned as I tried to throw a coat over my splinted arm. "Anyhow, she didn't tell," I finished with conviction, and McKnight laughed.

It had rained in the early morning, and Mrs. Klopton predicted more showers. In fact, so firm was her belief and so determined her eye that I took the umbrella she proffered me.

"Never mind," I said. "We can leave it next door; I have a story to tell you, Richey, and it requires proper setting."

McKnight was puzzled, but he followed me obediently round to the kitchen entrance of the empty house. It was unlocked, as I had expected. While we climbed to the upper floor I retailed the events of the previous night.

"It's the funniest thing I ever heard of," McKnight said, chuckling and staring up at the ladder and the trap. "What a vaudeville skit it would make! Only you ought not to have put your foot on her hand. They don't do it in the best circles."

I wheeled on him impatiently.

"You don't understand the situation at all, Richey!" I exclaimed. "What would you say if I tell you it was the hand of a lady? That is, it was small and delicate. Wore a ring or so, too."

"A lady!" he repeated. "Well, I'd say it was a damned compromising situation, and that the less you say of it the better. Look here, Lawrence, I think you dreamed it. You've been in the house too much. I take it all back: you do need exercise."

"She escaped through this door, I suppose," I said as patiently as I could. "Evidently down the back staircase. We might as well go down that way."

"According to the best precedents in these affairs, we should find a glove about here," he said as we started down. But he was more impressed than he cared to own. He examined the dusty steps carefully, and once a bit of loose plaster fell just behind him, he started like a nervous woman.

"What I can't understand is why you let her go," he said, stopping once, puzzled. "You're not usually quixotic."

"When we get out into the country, Rich," I replied gravely, "I am going to tell you another story, and if you don't tell me I'm a fool and a craven, on the strength of it, you are no friend of mine."

We stumbled through the twilight of the staircase into blackness of the shuttered kitchen. The house had the moldy smell of closed buildings: even on that warm September morning it was damp and chilly. As we stepped into the sunshine McKnight gave a shiver.

"Now that we are out," he said, "I don't mind telling you that I have been there before. Do you remember the night you left, and the face at the window?"

"When you speak of it, yes, I do."

"Well, I was curious about that thing," he went on, as we started up the street, "and I went back. The street door was unlocked, and I examined every room. I was Mrs. Klopton's ghost that carried a light, and clumb."

"Did you find anything?"

"Only a clean place rubbed on the window opposite your dressing room. Splendid view of an untidy interior. If that house is ever occupied, you'd better put opaque glass in that window of yours."

As we turned the corner I glanced back. Half a block behind us Johnson was moving our way slowly. When he saw me he stopped and proceeded with great deliberation to light a cigar. By hurrying, however, he caught the bus that we took, and stood unobtrusively on the rear platform. He looked fagged, and absent-mindedly paid our fares, to McKnight's delight.

"We'll give him a run for his money," he declared, as the vehicle moved countryward. "Driver, let us off at the muddiest lane you can find."

At one o'clock, after a six-mile ramble, we entered a small country hotel. We had seen nothing of Johnson for a half hour. At that time he was a quarter of a mile behind us and losing rapidly. Before we had finished our luncheon he staggered into the inn. One of his shoes was under his arm, and his whole appearance was deplorable. He was coated with mud, streaked with perspiration, and he limped as he walked. He chose a table not far from us and ordered Scotch. Beyond touching his hat he paid no attention to us.

"I'm just getting my second wind," McKnight declared. "How do you feel, Mr. Johnson? Six or eight miles more and we'll all enjoy our dinners."

Without replying Johnson put down the glass he had raised to his lips.

The fact was, however, that I was like Johnson. I was soft from my week's inaction, and I was pretty well done up. McKnight, who was a wellspring of vitality and high spirits, ordered a strange concoction, made of everything in the bar, and sent it over to the detective, but Johnson refused it.

"I hate that kind of person," McKnight said pettishly. "Kind of fellow that thinks you're going to poison his dog if you offer him a bone."

When we got back to the state road, with Johnson a draggled and drooping tail to the kite, I was in better spirits. I had told McKnight the story of the three hours just after the wreck. I had not named the girl, of course; she had my promise of secrecy. But I told him everything else. It was a relief to have a fresh mind on it: I had puzzled so much over the incident at the farmhouse and the necklace in the gold bag that I had lost perspective.

He had been interested, but inclined to be amused, until I came to the broken chain. Then he had whistled softly.

"But there are tons of fine gold chains made every year," he said. "Why in the world do you think that the—er—smeary piece came from that necklace?"

I had looked around. Johnson was far behind, scraping the mud off his shoes with a piece of wood.

"I have the short end of the chain in the sealskin bag," I reminded him. "When I couldn't sleep this morning I thought I would settle it, one way or the other. It was hell to go along the way I had been doing. And—there's no doubt about it, Rich. It's the same chain."

We walked along in silence until we caught the bus back to town.

"Well," he said finally, "you know the girl, of course, and I don't. But if you like her—and I think myself you're rather hard hit, old man—I wouldn't give a whoop about the chain in the gilt purse. It's just one of the little coincidences that hang people now and then. And as for last night—if she's the kind of girl you say she is, and you think she had anything to do with that—you're addled, that's all. You can depend on it, the lady of the empty house last week is the lady of last night. And your train acquaintance was in Cresson at that time."

Just before we got off the car, I reverted to the subject again. It was never far back in my mind.

"About this girl of the train, Rich," I said, with what I suppose was elaborate carelessness, "I don't want you to get a wrong impression. I am rather unlikely to see her again, but even if I do, I believe she is already engaged, or next thing to it. She practically said so."

He made no reply, but as I opened the door with my latchkey he stood looking up at me from the pavement with his quizzical smile.

"Love is like the measles," he orated. "The older you get it the worse the attack."

Johnson did not appear again that day. A small man in a raincoat took his place, and the next morning I made my initial trip to the office, the raincoat still on hand. I had a short conference with the bank officials at eleven. With the forged notes missing, their hands were more or less tied. But Bronson was under surveillance, and any attempt to sell the notes to him would probably result in their recovery.

There was nothing I could do. At noon I left the office and took a veterinarian to see Candida, the injured pony. By one o'clock my first day's duties had been performed, and a long Sahara of hot afternoon stretched ahead. McKnight, always glad to escape from the grind, suggested a movie and stage show, and in sheer boredom I consented. I could neither ride, drive nor golf, and my own company bored me to distraction.

"Coolest place in town these days," he declared. "Air-conditioned theater, breezy songs, airy costumes. And there's Johnson just behind—the coldest proposition in Washington."

He gravely bought three tickets and presented the detective with one. Then we went in. Having lived a normal, busy life, a movie in the afternoon is to me about on a par with ice cream for breakfast. After the picture a very stout woman in short pink skirts, with a smile that McKnight declared looked like a slash in a roll of butter, sang nasally, with a laborious kick at the end of each verse. Johnson, two rows ahead, went to sleep. McKnight prodded me with his elbow.

"Look at the first loge to the right," he said, in a stage whisper. "I want you to come over at the end of this act."

It was the first time I had seen her since I put her in the taxi at Baltimore. Outwardly I presume I was calm, for no one turned to stare at me, but every atom of me cried out at the sight of her. She was leaning, bent forward, lips slightly parted, gazing raptly at the Japanese conjurer who had replaced what McKnight disrespectfully called the Columns of Hercules. Compared with the draggled lady of the farmhouse, she was radiant.

For that first moment there was nothing but joy at the sight of her. McKnight's touch on my arm brought me back to reality.

"Come over and meet them," he said. "That's the cousin Miss West is visiting, Mrs. Dallas."

But I declined. After he went I sat there alone, painfully conscious that I was being pointed out and stared at from the box. The abominable Japanese gave way to yet more atrocious performing dogs.

"How many offers of marriage will the young lady in the box have?" The dog stopped sagely at "none," and then pulled out a card that said eight to wild shouts of glee by the audience.

After a little I glanced over. Mrs. Dallas was talking to McKnight, but Alison was looking straight at me. She was flushed but more calm than I, and she did not bow. I fumbled for my hat, but the next moment I saw that they were going and I sat still. When McKnight came back he was triumphant.

"I've made an engagement for you," he said. "Mrs. Dallas asked me to bring you to dinner tonight, and I said I knew you would fall all over yourself to go. You are requested to bring along the broken arm, and any other souvenirs of the wreck that you may possess."

"I'll do nothing of the sort," I declared, struggling against my inclination. "I can't even tie my necktie, and I have to have my food cut for me."

"Oh, that's all right," he said easily. "I'll send Stogie over to fix you up, and Mrs. Dal knows all about the arm. I told her."

(Stogie is his Filipino factotum, so called because he is lean, a yellowish brown in color, and because he claims to have been shipped into this country in a box.)

A newsreel was finishing the program. The house was dark and the music had stopped, as it does in the circus just before somebody risks his neck at so much a neck in the Dip of Death or the hundred-foot dive. Then, with a sort of shock, I heard a voice announcing:

"One of the worst railroad accidents in the history of the nation took place last week. Two miles before it occurred a news photographer snapped the first section of the Washington Flier, and was on hand shortly after to photograph the wreck itself."

I confess to a return of some of the sickening sensations of the wreck; people around me were leaning forward with tense faces. Then the voice was gone, and I saw a long level stretch of track, even the broken stone between the ties standing out distinctly. Far off under a cloud of smoke a small object was coming toward us and growing larger as it came.

Now it was roaring on us, a mammoth in size, with huge drivers and a colossal tender. The engine leaped aside, as if just in time to save us from destruction, with a glimpse of a stooping fireman and a grimy engineer. The long train of sleepers followed. From a forward vestibule a porter in a white coat waved his hand. The rest of the cars seemed still wrapped in slumber. With mixed sensations I saw my own car, Ontario, fly past, and then I rose to my feet and gripped McKnight's shoulder.

On the lowest step at the last car, one foot hanging free, was a man. His black derby hat was pulled well down to keep it from blowing away, and his coat was flying open in the wind. He was swung well out from the car, his free hand gripping a small valise, every muscle tense for a jump.

"Good God, that's my man!" I said hoarsely. "The train's slowing down and he's going to jump."

No one noticed me, apparently. The audience watched in silence. McKnight half rose. In his seat ahead Johnson stifled a yawn and turned to eye me.

I dropped into my chair limply, and tried to control my excitement. "The man on the last platform of the train," I said. "He was just about to leap; I'll swear that was my bag."

"Could you see his face?" McKnight asked in an undertone. "Would you know him again?"

"No. His hat was pulled down and his head was bent. I'm going back to find out where that picture was taken. They say two miles, but it may have been forty."

I did not look at the wreck itself. It nauseated me, and glancing at the loge I saw that Mrs. Dallas and Alison West had gone. In front of us Johnson had dropped his hat and was stooping for it.

"This way," I motioned to McKnight, and we wheeled into the narrow passage beside us, back of the boxes. At the end there was a door leading into the wings, and as we went boldly through I turned the key.

The final stage set was being struck, and no one paid any attention to us.

Luckily they were similarly indifferent to a banging at the door I had locked, a banging which I judged signified Johnson.

"I guess we've broken up his interference," McKnight chuckled.

Stage hands were hurrying in every direction; pieces of the side wall of the last drawing room menaced us, a switchboard behind us was singing like a teakettle. Everywhere we stepped we were in somebody's way. At last we were across, confronting a man in his shirt sleeves, who by dots and dashes of profanity seemed to be directing the chaos.

"Well?" he said, wheeling on us. "What can I do for you?"

"I would like to ask," I replied, "if you have any idea just where the last motion picture was taken."

"Broken board—picnickers—lake?"

"No. The Washington Flier."

He glanced at my bandaged arm.

"The announcement says two miles," McKnight put in, "but we should like to know whether it is railroad miles, automobile miles, or newsreel miles."

"Sorry I can't tell you," he replied, more civilly. "We get those pictures by contract. We don't take them ourselves."

"Where are the company's offices?"

"New York." He stepped forward and grasped a stage hand by the shoulder. "What in blazes are you doing with that chair in a kitchen set?"

I had not realized the extent of the shock, but now I dropped into a chair and wiped my forehead. The unexpected glimpse of Alison West, followed almost immediately by the revelation of the picture, had left me limp and unnerved. McKnight was looking at his watch.

"He says the newsreel people have an office downtown. We can make it if we go now."

He called a taxi, and we started in high gear. There was no sign of Johnson. "Upon my word," Richey said, "I feel lonely without him."

The people at the downtown office of the newsreel company were obliging but not helpful. The picture had been taken, they said, at M——, just two miles beyond the scene of the wreck. It was not much, but it was something to work on. I decided not to go home, but to send McKnight's Filipino for my clothes, and to dress at his apartment. I was determined, if possible, to make my next day's investigations without Johnson. In the meantime, even if it was for the last time, I would see Alison that night. I gave Stogie a note for Mrs. Klopton, and with my dinner clothes there came back the little gilt bag, as I had requested.

16

CERTAIN THINGS about the dinner at the Dallas house that night will always be obscure to me. I remember feeling ridiculous with only one arm in a white dinner jacket, with the rest of it hanging like a cape over my shoulder. And I remember Dallas talking interminably about fish while we ate caviar out of a hollowed block of ice.

I suppose Mrs. Dallas was there. She must have been. And there was a woman in yellow. I took her in to dinner, and I remember she loosened my lobster for me so I could get it. But the only real person at the table was a girl across from me in white, a young woman who was as brilliant as I was stupid, who never by any chance looked directly at me, and who appeared and disappeared across the candles and orchids in a sort of halo of radiance.

When the dinner had progressed from roast to salad, and the conversation had done the same thing—from politics to scandal—the yellow gown turned to me.

"We have been awfully good, haven't we, Mr. Blakeley?" she asked. "Although I am crazy to hear, I have not said 'wreck' once. I'm sure you must feel like the survivor of Waterloo, or something of the sort."

"If you want me to tell you about the wreck," I said, glancing across the table, "I'm sorry to be disappointing, but I don't remember anything."

"You are fortunate to be able to forget it." It was the first word Alison had spoken directly to me, and it went to my head.

"There are some things I have not forgotten," I said, over the candles. "I recall coming to myself some time after, and that a girl, a beautiful girl—"

"Ah!" said the lady in yellow, leaning forward breathlessly. Alison was staring at me coldly, but once started I had to stumble on.

"That a girl was trying to rouse me, and that she told me I had been on fire twice already." A shudder went around the table.

"But surely that isn't the end of the story," Mrs. Dallas put in aggrievedly. "Why, that's the most tantalizing thing I ever heard."

"I'm afraid that's all," I said. "She went her way and I went mine. If she recalls me at all, she probably thinks of me as a weak-kneed individual who faints like a woman when everything is over."

"What did I tell you?" Mrs. Dallas asserted triumphantly. "He fainted, did you hear? When everything was over! He hasn't begun to tell it."

I would have given a lot by that time if I had not mentioned the girl. But McKnight took it up there and carried on.

"Blakeley is a regular geyser," he said. "He never spouts until he reaches the boiling point. And by that same token, although he hasn't said much about the Lady of the Wreck, I think he is crazy about her. In fact, I am sure of it. He thinks he has locked his secret in the caves of his soul, but I call you to witness that he has it nailed to his face. Look at him!"

I squirmed miserably and tried to avoid the startled eyes of the girl across the table. I wanted to choke McKnight and murder the rest of the party.

"It isn't fair," I said as coolly as I could. "I have my fingers crossed; you are six against one."

"And to think that there was a murder on that very train," broke in the woman in yellow. "It was a perfect crescendo of horrors, wasn't it? And what became of the murdered man, Mr. Blakeley?"

McKnight had the sense to jump into the conversation and save my reply.

"I'm afraid we know that answer only too well," he said gravely.

The meal was over at last, and once in the drawing room it was clear we hung heavy on the hostess's hands. "It is so hard to get people for bridge in September," she wailed. "There is absolutely nobody in town. Seven is a dreadful number."

"It's a good poker number," her husband suggested.

The matter settled itself, however. I was hopeless, save as a dummy, and Alison said it was too hot for cards, and went out on a balcony that overlooked Sheridan Circle. With obvious relief Mrs. Dallas had the card table brought, and I was face to face with the minute I had dreaded and hoped for for a week.

Now that it had come it was more difficult than I had anticipated. I do not know if there was a moon, but there was the urban substitute for it, the street light. It threw the shadow of the balcony railing in long black bars against her white gown, and her face was in the light. I drew a chair close so that I could watch her.

"Do you know," I said, when she made no effort at speech, "that you are a much more formidable person tonight, in that gown, than you were the last time I saw you?"

The light was on her face. She was smiling faintly.

"That hat with the green ribbons!" she said. "I must send it back. I had almost forgotten."

"I have not forgotten anything." I pulled myself up short. This was hardly loyalty to Richey. His voice came through the window just then, and perhaps I was wrong but I thought she raised her head to listen.

"Look at this hand," he was saying. "Why bother? It's a lay-down."

"He's a dear, isn't he?" she said unexpectedly. "No matter how depressed and downhearted I am, I always cheer up when I see Rich."

"He's more than that," I returned warmly. "He's a great guy. If he wasn't so much that way, he would have a real career before him. He wanted to put on the doors of our offices, Blakeley and McKnight, P.B.H., which is Poor But Honest."

From my comparative poverty to the wealth of the girl beside me was a single mental leap. From that wealth to the grandfather who was responsible for it was another.

"I wonder if you know that I had been to Pittsburgh to see your grandfather when I met you?" I said.

"You?" She was surprised.

"Yes. And you remember the bag I told you was exchanged for the one you cut off my arm?" She nodded expectantly. "Well, in that valise were the forged Andy Bronson notes, and Mr. Gilmore's deposition that they were forged."

She was on her feet in an instant. "In that bag!" she cried. "Why didn't you tell me that before? Oh, it's so ridiculous, so—so hopeless. Why, I could—"

She stopped suddenly and sat down again. "I don't know that I am sorry, after all," she said after a pause. "Mr. Bronson was a friend of my father's for years. I suppose it was a bad thing for you, losing the papers?"

"Well, it wasn't a good thing," I conceded. "While we are on the subject of losing things, do you remember—do you know that I still have your little gilt purse?"

She did not reply at once. The shadow of a column was over her face, but I guessed that she was staring at me.

"You have it!"

"I picked it up in the car," I said, with a cheerfulness I did not feel. "On the way to Baltimore. Remember?"

I fumbled in my pocket and produced it, while she did not speak.

"I should have sent it to you before, I suppose, but as you know I've been laid up since the wreck."

We both saw McKnight at the same moment. He had pulled the curtains aside and was standing looking out at us. The tableau of give-and-take was unmistakable: the gilt purse, her outstretched hand, my own attitude. It was over in a second; then he came out and lounged on the balcony railing.

"They're mad at me in there," he said airily, "so I came out. I suppose the reason they call it bridge is because so many people get cross over it."

The heat broke up the card group soon after, and they all came out for the night breeze. I had no more words alone with Alison.

I went back to Richey's apartment for the night. We said almost nothing on the way home. There was a constraint between us for the first time that I could remember. It was too early for bed, and so we smoked in the living room and tried to talk of trivial things. After a time even those failed, and we sat silent. It was McKnight who finally broached the subject:

"So she wasn't at Seal Harbor at all."

"No."

"Do you know where she was, Laurie?"

"Somewhere near Cresson. She got the train there."

"And that was the purse—her purse—with the broken necklace in it?"

"Yes. You understand, don't you, Rich, that having given her my word, I couldn't tell you?"

"I understand a lot of things," he said, without bitterness.

We sat for some time and smoked. Then he got up and stretched himself.

"I'm off to bed, old man," he said. "Need any help with that game arm of yours?"

"No, thanks," I returned.

I heard him go into his room and lock the door. It was a bad hour for me. The first shadow between us, and the shadow of a girl at that.

17

McKnight is always a sympathizer with the early worm. It was late when he appeared. Perhaps, like myself, he had not slept well. But he was apparently cheerful enough, and he made a better breakfast than I did. It was one o'clock before we got to Baltimore. After a half hour's wait we took a local for M——, the station near which the motion picture had been taken.

We passed the scene of the wreck, McKnight with curiosity, I with a sickening sense of horror. Back in the fields was the little farmhouse where Alison West and I had intended getting coffee, and winding away from the track, maple trees shading it on each side, was the lane where we had stopped to rest, and where I had tried to comfort her.

We got out at M——, a small place with two or three houses and a general store. The station was a one-room affair, with a railed-off place at the end where a scale, a telegraph instrument, and a chair constituted the entire furnishing.

The station agent was a young man with a shrewd face. He stopped hammering a piece of wood over a hole in the floor to ask where we wanted to go.

"We're not going," said McKnight, "we're coming."

He offered a cigarette, and the agent took it with an inquiring glance, first at it and then at us.

"We want to ask you a few questions," began McKnight, perching himself on the railing and kicking the chair forward for me. "Or rather this gentleman does."

"Wait a minute," said the agent, glancing through the window. "There's a hen in that crate choking herself to death."

He was back in a minute, and took up his position near a sawdust-filled box that did duty as a cuspidor.

"Now fire away," he said.

"In the first place," I began, "do you remember the day the Washington Flier was wrecked below here?"

"Do I!" he said. "Did Jonah remember the whale?"

"Were you on the platform here when the first section passed?"

"I was."

"Do you recall seeing a man hanging to the platform of the last car?"

"There was no one hanging there when she passed here," he said with conviction. "I watched her out of sight."

"Did you see anything that morning of a man about my size, carrying a small bag, and wearing dark clothes and a derby hat?" I asked eagerly.

McKnight was trying to look unconcerned, but I was frankly anxious. It was clear that the man had jumped somewhere in the mile of track just beyond.

"Well, yes, I did." The agent cleared his throat. "When the smash came the operator at MX sent word along the wire, both ways. I got it here, and I was pretty near crazy, though I knew it wasn't any fault of mine."

"I was standing on the track looking down, for I couldn't leave the office, when a young fellow with light hair limped up to me and asked me what that smoke was over there.

" 'That's what's left of the Washington Flier,' I said, 'and I guess there's souls going up in that smoke.'

" 'Do you mean the first section?' he said, getting kind of greenish-yellow.

" 'That's what I mean,' I said; 'split to kindling wood because Rafferty, on the second section, didn't want to be late.'

"He put his hand out in front of him, and the bag fell with a bang.

" 'My God!' he said, and dropped right on the platform in a heap.

"I got him into the station and he came around, but he kept on groaning something awful. He'd sprained his ankle, and when he got a little better I drove him over in Carter's milk wagon to the Carter place, and I reckon he stayed there a spell."

"That's all, is it?" I asked.

"That's all—or no, there's something else. About noon that day one of the Carter twins came down with a note from him asking me to send a long-distance message to someone in Washington."

"To whom?" I asked eagerly.

"I reckon I've forgot the name, but the message was that this fellow—Sullivan was his name—was here, and if the man had escaped from the wreck would he come to see him."

"He wouldn't have sent that message to me," I said to McKnight, rather crestfallen. "He'd have every object in keeping out of my way."

"There might be reasons," McKnight observed judicially. "He might not have found the papers then."

"Was the name Blakeley?" I asked.

"It might have been. I can't say. But the man wasn't there, and there was a lot of noise. I couldn't hear well. Then in an hour or so down came the other twin to say the gentleman was taking on awful and didn't want the message sent."

"He's gone, of course?"

"Yes. Limped down here in about three days and took the noon train for the city."

It seemed a certainty now that our man, having hurt himself somewhat in his jump, had stayed quietly in the farmhouse until he was able to travel. But, to be positive, we decided to visit the Carter place.

I gave the station agent a five-dollar bill, which he rolled up with a couple of others and stuck in his pocket. I turned as we got to a bend in the road, and he was looking curiously after us.

It was not until we had climbed the hill and turned onto the road to the Carter place that I realized where we were going. Although we approached it from another direction, I knew the farmhouse at once. It was the one where Alison West and I had breakfasted nine days before. With the new restraint between us I did not tell McKnight. I wondered afterward if he had suspected it. I saw him looking hard at the gatepost which had figured in one of our mysteries, but he asked no questions. Afterward he grew almost taciturn, for him, and let me do most of the talking.

We opened the front gate of the Carter place and went slowly up the walk. Two ragged youngsters, alike even to freckles and squints, were playing in the yard.

"Is your mother around?" I asked.

"In the front room. Walk in," they answered in identical tones.

As we got to the porch we heard voices, and stopped. I knocked, but the people within, engaged in animated rather one-sided conversation, did not answer.

"'In the front room. Walk in,'" quoted McKnight, and did so.

In the stuffy farm parlor two people were sitting. One, a pleasant-faced woman with a checked apron, rose, somewhat embarrassed, to meet us. She did not know me, and I was thankful. But our attention was riveted on a little man who was sitting before a table, writing busily. It was Hotchkiss!

He got up when he saw us, and had the grace to look uncomfortable.

"Such an interesting case," he said nervously, "I took the liberty—"

"Look here," said McKnight suddenly, "did you make any inquiries at the station?"

"A few," he confessed. "I went to the movies last night—I felt the need of a little relaxation—and the sight of a picture there, a newsreel, started a fresh line of thought. Probably the same clue brought you gentlemen. I learned a good bit from the station agent."

"The son of a gun," said McKnight. "And you paid him, I suppose?"

"I gave him five dollars," was the apologetic answer.

Mrs. Carter, hearing sounds of strife in the yard, went out and Hotchkiss folded up his papers.

"I think the identity of the man is established," he said. "What number of hat do you wear, Mr. Blakeley?"

"Seven and a quarter," I replied.

"Well, it's only piling up evidence," he said cheerfully. "On the night of the murder you wore light-gray silk underclothing, with the second button of the shirt missing. Your hat had 'L.B.' in gilt letters inside, and there was a very minute hole in the toe of one black sock."

"Hush," McKnight protested. "If word gets to Mrs. Klopton that Mr. Blakeley was wrecked, or robbed, or whatever it was, with a button missing and a hole in one sock, she'll retire to the Old Ladies' Home. I've heard her threaten it."

Mr. Hotchkiss was without a sense of humor. He regarded McKnight gravely and went on:

"I've been up in the room where the man lay while he was unable to get away, and there is nothing there. But I found what may be a possible clue in the dust heap.

"Mrs. Carter tells me that in unpacking his grip the other day she took out of the coat of the pajamas some pieces of a telegram. As I figure it, the pajamas were his own. He probably had them on when he effected the exchange."

I nodded assent. All I had retained of my own clothing was the suit of pajamas I was wearing and my bathrobe.

"So the telegram was his, not yours. I have pieces here, but some are missing. I am not discouraged, however."

He spread out some bits of yellow papers, and we bent over them curiously. It was something like this:

> Man with p—— Get——
> Br——

We spelled it out slowly.

"Now," Hotchkiss announced, "I make it something like this: The 'p—' is one of two things, pistol—you remember the little pearl-handled affair belonging to the murdered man—or it is pocketbook. I am inclined to the latter view, as the pocketbook had been disturbed and the pistol had not."

I took the piece of paper from the table and scrawled four words on it.

"Now," I said, rearranging them, "it happens, Mr. Hotchkiss, that I found one of these pieces of the telegram on the train. I thought it had been dropped by someone else, you see, but that's immaterial. Arranged this way it almost makes sense. Fill out that 'p—' with the rest of the word, as I imagine it, and it makes 'papers,' and add this scrap and you have:

" 'Man with papers (in) lower ten, car seven. Get (them).' "

McKnight slapped Hotchkiss on the back.

"You're wonderful," he said. "Br— is Bronson, of course. It's almost too easy. You see, Mr. Blakeley here engaged lower ten, but found it occupied by the man who was later murdered there. The man who did the thing was a friend of Bronson's evidently, and in trying to get the papers we have the motive for the crime."

"There are still some things to be explained." Mr. Hotchkiss wiped his glasses and put them on. "For one thing, Mr. Blakeley, I am puzzled by that bit of chain."

I did not glance at McKnight. I felt that the hand with which I was gathering up the bits of torn paper was shaking. It seemed to me that this astute little man was going to drag Alison in in spite of me.

18

HOTCHKISS JOTTED DOWN the bits of telegram and rose.

"Well," he said, "we've done something. We've found where the murderer left the train, we know what day he went to Baltimore, and most important of all we have a motive for the crime."

"It seems rather ironic," said McKnight, getting up, "that a man should kill another man for certain papers he is supposed to be carrying, find he hasn't got them after all, decide to throw suspicion on another man by changing berths and getting out, bag and baggage, and then, by the merest fluke of chance take with him, in the bag he changed for his own, the very notes he was after. It was a bit of luck for him."

"Then why," put in Hotchkiss doubtfully, "why did he collapse when he heard of the wreck? And what about the telephone message the station agent sent? You remember they tried to countermand it, and with some excitement."

"We'll ask him those questions when we get him," McKnight said. We were on the unrailed front porch by that time, and Hotchkiss had put away his notebook. The mother of the twins followed us to the steps.

"Dear me," she exclaimed volubly, "and to think I was forgetting to tell you! I put the young man to bed with a spice poultice on his ankle. My mother always was a firm believer in spice poultices. It's wonderful what they will do in croup! And then I took the children and went down to see the wreck. It was Sunday, and the mister had gone to church; hasn't missed a day since he took the pledge nine years ago. And on the way I met two people, a man and a woman. They looked half dead, so I sent them right here for breakfast and some soap and water. I always say soap is better than liquor after a shock."

Hotchkiss was listening absently. McKnight was whistling under his breath, staring down across the field to where a break in the woods showed a half dozen telegraph poles, the line of the railroad.

"It must have been twelve o'clock when we got back. I wanted the children to see everything, because it isn't likely they'll ever see another wreck like that. Rows of—"

"About twelve o'clock," I broke in, "and what then?"

"The young man upstairs was awake," she went on, "and hammering at his door like all possessed. And it was locked on the outside!" She paused to enjoy her sensation.

"I would like to see that lock," Hotchkiss said promptly, but for some reason the woman demurred. "I'll bring the key down," she said and disappeared. When she returned she held out an ordinary door key of the cheapest variety.

"We had to break the lock," she volunteered, "and the key didn't turn up for two days. Then one of the twins found the turkey gobbler trying to swallow it. It has been washed since," she hastened to assure Hotchkiss, who showed an inclination to drop it.

"You don't think he locked the door himself and threw the key out the window?" the little man asked.

"He said he didn't. He was furious. He blamed it on the children, and it might have been Obadiah. He's the quiet kind, and you never know what he's about."

"He's about to strangle, isn't he," McKnight remarked lazily, "or *is* that Obadiah?"

Mrs. Carter picked the boy up and inverted him, talking amiably all the time. "He's always doing it," she said, giving him a shake. "Whenever we miss anything we look to see if Obadiah's black in the face." She gave him another shake, and the quarter I had given him shot out as if blown from a gun. Then we prepared to go back to the station.

From where I stood I could look into the cheery farm kitchen where Alison West and I had eaten our breakfast. I looked at the table with mixed emotions, and then gradually the meaning of something on it penetrated my mind. Still in its papers and evidently just opened was a hatbox, and protruding over the edge of the box was a streamer of vivid green ribbon.

On the plea that I wished to ask Mrs. Carter a few more questions I let the others go on. I watched them down the flagstone walk; saw McKnight stop and examine the gateposts and saw, too, the quick glance he threw back at the house. Then I turned to Mrs. Carter.

"I would like to speak to the young lady upstairs," I said.

She threw up her hands with a quick gesture of surrender. "I've done all I could!" she exclaimed. "She won't like it very well, but—she's in the room over the parlor."

I went eagerly up the ladderlike stairs, to the rag-carpeted hall. Two doors were open, showing interiors of four-poster beds and high bureaus. The door of the room over the parlor was almost closed. I hesitated in the hallway. After all, what right had I to intrude on her? But she settled my difficulty by throwing open the door and facing me.

"I'm awfully sorry," I stammered. "It has just occured to me that I am unpardonably rude. I saw the hat downstairs and I guessed—"

"The hat!" she said. "I might have known. Does Richey know I am here?"

"I don't think so." I turned to go down the stairs again. Then I halted. "The fact is," I said, in an attempt at justification, "I'm in rather a mess these days, and I'm apt to do irresponsible things. It is not impossible that I shall be arrested, in a day or so, for the murder of Simon Harrington."

She drew in her breath sharply. "Murder!" she echoed. "Then they have found you, after all?"

"I wouldn't worry," I said. "It's a nuisance, of course, but they can't convict me, you know. Almost all the witnesses are dead."

She was not deceived for a moment. She came over to me and stood, both hands on the rail of the stair. "I know just how serious it is," she said quietly. "My grandfather will not leave one stone unturned, and he can be terrible—terrible. But"—she looked directly into my eyes as I stood below her on the stairs—"the time may come soon when I can help you. I'm afraid I shan't want to; I'm a dreadful coward, Mr. Blakeley. But—I will." She tried to smile.

"Now look," I said, "you keep out of this. It's my trouble, not yours."

She shook her head. "I'm only as unhappy as I deserve to be," she said. And when I protested and took a step toward her she retreated, with her hands out before her.

"Why don't you ask me all the questions you're thinking?" she demanded, with a catch in her voice. "Oh, I know them. Or are you afraid to ask?"

I looked at her, at the lines around her eyes, at the drawn look about her mouth. Then I held out my hand. "Afraid!" I said, as she gave me hers. "There is nothing in God's green earth I am afraid of, save of trouble for you. I'll do anything to prevent that. And I don't want anything. Only—someday perhaps you'll come to me yourself and tell me the story."

The next moment I was out in the golden sunshine. The birds were singing carols of joy: I walked dizzily through rainbow-colored clouds, past the twins, cherubs now, swinging on the gate. It was a new world into which I stepped from the Carter farmhouse that morning. You see, I had kissed her!

19

McKNIGHT AND HOTCHKISS were sauntering slowly down the road as I caught up with them. As usual, the little man was busy with some abstruse mental problem.

"The idea is this," he was saying, his brows knitted in thought: "if a left-handed man, standing in the position of the man in the picture, should jump from a car, would he be likely to sprain his right ankle? When a right-handed man prepares for a leap of that kind, my theory is that he would hold on with his right hand, and alight at the proper time on his right foot. Of course—"

"I imagine, although I don't know," interrupted McKnight, "that a man either ambidextrous or one-armed, jumping from the Washington Flier, would be more likely to land on his head."

"Anyhow," I interposed, "what difference does it make whether Sullivan used one hand or the other? One pair of handcuffs will put both hands out of commission."

As usual when one of his pet theories was attacked, Hotchkiss looked aggrieved.

"My dear sir," he expostulated, "don't you understand what bearing this has on the case? How was the murdered man lying when he was found?"

"On his back," I said promptly, "head toward the engine."

"Very well," he retorted. "And what then? Your heart lies under your fifth intercostal space, and to reach it a right-handed blow would have struck either down or directly in.

"But, gentlemen, the point of entrance for the stiletto was below the heart, striking up! As Harrington lay with his head toward the engine, a person in the aisle must have used the left hand."

McKnight's eyes sought mine and he winked at me solemnly as I unostentatiously transferred the hat I was carrying to my right hand. Long training has largely counterbalanced heredity in my case, but I still pitch ball, play tennis, and carve with my left hand. But Hotchkiss was too busy with his theories to notice me.

We were only just in time for our train back to Baltimore, but McKnight took advantage of a second's delay to shake the station agent warmly by the hand.

"I want to express my admiration for you," he said beamingly. "Ability of your order is thrown away here. You should have been a city policeman, my friend."

The agent looked a trifle uncertain.

"The young lady was the one who told me to keep still," he said.

McKnight glanced at me, gave the agent's hand a final shake, and climbed on board. But I knew perfectly well that he had guessed the reason for my delay.

He was very silent on the way home. Hotchkiss, too, had little to say. He was reading over his notes intently, stopping now and then to make a penciled addition. Just before we left the train Richey turned to me. "I suppose it was the key to the door that she tied to the gate?"

"Probably. I didn't ask her."

"Curious, her locking that fellow in," he reflected.

"You can depend on it there was a good reason for it. And I wish you wouldn't be so suspicious of motives, Rich," I said warmly.

"Only yesterday you were the suspicious one," he retorted, and we lapsed into strained silence.

It was late when we got to Washington. One of Mrs. Klopton's small tyrannies was exacting punctuality at meals, and like several other things, I respected it. There are always some concessions that should be made in return for faithful service.

So, as my dinner hour of seven was long past, McKnight and I went to a little restaurant downtown where they have a very decent way of broiling a steak. Hotchkiss had departed, economically bent, for a small hotel where he lived on the American plan.

"I want to think some things over," he said in response to my invitation, "and, anyhow, there's no use eating out when I pay the same, dinner or no dinner, where I am stopping."

The day had been hot, and the first floor dining room was sultry in spite of the palms and fans that attempted to simulate the verdure and breezes of the country.

It was crowded, too, with a typical summer night crowd, and, after sitting for a few minutes in a sweltering corner, we got up and went to the smaller dining room upstairs. Here it was not so warm, and we settled ourselves comfortably by a window.

Over in a corner half a dozen boys on their way back to college were ragging a perspiring waiter, a proceeding so exactly to McKnight's taste that he insisted on going over to join them. But their table was full, and somehow that kind of fun had lost its point for both of us.

Not far from us a very stout middle-aged man, apoplectic with the heat, was elephantinely jolly for the benefit of a bored-looking girl across the table from him, and at the next table a newspaperwoman ate alone, the last edition propped against the water bottle before her, her hat, for coolness, on the corner of the table. It was a motley Bohemian crowd.

I looked over the room casually, while McKnight ordered the meal. Then my attention was attracted to a table not far from ours. Two people were sitting there, so deep in conversation that they did not notice us. The woman's face was hidden under her hat, as she traced the pattern of the cloth mechanically with her fork. But the man's features stood out clear in the light of the candles on the table. It was Andy Bronson!

"He shows the strain, doesn't he?" McKnight said, holding up the wine list as if he read from it. "Who's the woman?"

"Search me," I replied, in the same way.

When the steak came I still found myself gazing now and then at the abstracted couple near me. Evidently the subject of conversation was unpleasant. Bronson was eating little, the woman not at all. Finally he got up, pushed his chair back noisily, thrust a bill at the waiter and stalked out.

The woman sat still for a moment. Then with an apparent resolution to make the best of it she began slowly to eat the meal before her.

But the quarrel had taken away her appetite, for our steak was hardly ready to serve before she pushed her chair back a little and looked around the room.

I caught my first glimpse of her face then, and I confess it startled me. It was the tall, stately woman of the Ontario, the woman I had last seen cowering beside the road, rolling pebbles in her hand, blood streaming from a cut over her eye. I could see the scar now, a little affair about an inch long, gleaming red through its layers of powder.

And then, quite unexpectedly, she turned and looked directly at me. After a minute's uncertainty she bowed, letting her eyes rest on mine with a calmly insolent stare. She glanced at McKnight for a moment, then back to me. When she looked away again I breathed easier.

"Who is it?" asked McKnight under his breath.

"Ontario," I formed it with my lips rather than said it. McKnight's eyebrows went up and he looked with increased interest at the black-gowned figure.

I ate little after that. The situation was rather bad for me, I began to see. Here was a woman who could, if she wished, and had any motive for doing so, put me in jail under a capital charge. A word from her to the police, and polite surveillance would become active interference.

Then, too, she could say that she had seen me just after the wreck, with a young woman from the murdered man's car, and thus probably bring Alison West into the case.

It is not surprising, then, that I ate little. The woman across seemed in no hurry to go. She loitered over a demitasse, and that finished, sat with her elbow on the table, her chin in her hand, looking darkly at the changing groups in the room.

The fun at the table where the college boys sat began to grow a little noisy, the fat man, now a purplish shade, ambled away behind his slim companion, the newspaperwoman put on her businesslike hat and stalked out. Still the woman at the other table waited.

It was a relief when the meal was over. We got our hats and were about to leave the room when a waiter touched me on the arm.

"I beg your pardon, sir," he said, "but the lady at the table near the window, the lady in black, would like to speak to you."

I looked down between the rows of tables to where the woman sat alone, her chin still resting on her hand, her black eyes still insolently staring, this time at me.

"I'll have to go," I said to McKnight hurriedly. "She knows all about that affair and she'd be a bad enemy."

"I don't like her expression," McKnight observed, after a glance at her. "Better be careful, old man. I'm leaving."

20

I WENT OVER SLOWLY to where the woman sat alone. She smiled rather oddly as I drew near, and pointed to the chair Bronson had vacated.

"Sit down, Mr. Blakeley," she said. "I am going to take a few minutes of your valuable time."

"Certainly." I sat down opposite her and glanced at a clock on the wall. "I am sorry, but I have only a few mintues. If you—"

She laughed a little, not very pleasantly, and opening a small black fan waved it slowly.

"The fact is," she said, "I think we are about to make a bargain."

"A bargain?" I asked incredulously. "You have a second advantage of me. At least you know my name." I paused suggestively and she took the cue.

"I am Mrs. Conway," she said, and flicked a crumb off the table with an overmanicured finger.

The name was scarcely a surprise. I had already surmised that this might be the woman whom rumor credited as being Bronson's common-law wife. Rumor, I remembered, had said other things even less pleasant, but she was completely unscrupulous for one thing.

"We met last under less fortunate circumstances," she was saying. "I've been fit for nothing since that terrible day. And you—you had a broken arm, didn't you?"

"I still have it," I said, with a lame attempt at jocularity; "but to have escaped at all was a miracle. We have both a lot to be thankful for."

"I suppose we have," she said carelessly, "although sometimes I doubt it." She was looking somberly toward the door through which her late companion had made his exit.

"You sent for me—" I said.

"Yes, I sent for you." She roused herself and sat erect. "Now, Mr. Blakeley, have you found those papers?"

"The papers? What papers?" I parried. I needed time to think.

"Mr. Blakeley," she said quietly, "I think we can talk plainly. In the first place let me refresh your mind about a few things. The Pittsburgh police are looking for the survivors of the car Ontario. There are three that I know of, yourself, the young woman with whom you left the scene of the wreck, and myself. The wreck, you will admit, was a fortunate one for you."

I nodded without speaking.

"At the time of the collision you were in rather a hole," she went on, looking at me with a disagreeable smile. "You were, if I remember, accused of a rather atrocious crime. There was a lot of corroborative evidence, was there not? I seem to remember a dirk in your berth and the murdered man's pocketbook in your possession. Also a few other things that were—well, rather unpleasant."

I was thrown a bit off my guard.

"You remember also," I said quickly, "that a man disappeared from the car, taking my clothes, papers and everything."

"I remember that you *said* so." Her tone was quietly insulting, and I felt my face redden.

"You've missed one possibility," I said coldly, "and that is, the discovery of the man who left the train."

"You've found him?" She bent forward, and I regretted my hasty speech. "I knew it; I said so."

"We're going to find him," I asserted, with a confidence I did not feel.

"We can produce at any time proof that a man left the Flier as it slowed down a few miles beyond the wreck. And we can find him, I am positive."

"But you haven't found him yet?" She was clearly disappointed. "Well, that's that. Now for our bargain. I hope you'll admit I'm no fool."

I made no such admission, and she smiled mockingly.

"How flattering you are!" she said. "Very well. Now for the premises. You take to Pittsburgh four notes held by the Mechanics' National Bank, to have Mr. Gilmore, who is ill, declare his signature on them forged.

"On the journey back from Pittsburgh two things happen to you: you lose your clothing, your valise and your papers, including the notes, and you are accused of murder. In fact, Mr. Blakeley, the circumstances are most singular, and the evidence—well, almost conclusive."

I was completely at her mercy, but I lit a cigarette and surveyed her as calmly as I could.

"Now for the bargain." She leaned over and lowered her voice. "A fair exchange, you know. The minute you put those four notes in my hand—that minute the blow to my head has caused complete forgetfulness as to the events of that awful morning. I am the only witness, and I'll keep my mouth shut. Do you understand?"

My head was buzzing with the audacity of the idea.

"But," I said, to gain time, "I haven't the notes. I can't give you what I haven't got."

"You're still after Andy," she said sharply. "You expect to find them. And another thing," she added slowly, watching my face, "if you don't get them soon, Andy Bronson will have them. They've been offered to him already, but at a prohibitive price."

"But," I said, bewildered, "what is your object in coming to me? If Bronson will get them anyhow—"

She shut her fan with a click and her face was not particularly pleasant to look at.

"You *are* dense," she said insolently. "I want those papers for myself, not for Andy Bronson."

"Then the idea is," I said, ignoring her tone, "that you think you have me in a hole, and that if I find those papers and give them to you you will let me out. As I understand it, our friend Bronson, under those circumstances, also will be in a hole."

She nodded.

"The notes would be of no use to you for a limited length of time," I went on, watching her narrowly. "If they are not turned over to the prosecution within a reasonable time there will have to be a *nolle pros*—that is, the case will simply be dropped for lack of evidence."

"A week would answer, I think," she said slowly. "You will do it, then?"

I laughed, although I was not especially cheerful.

"No, I'll not do it. I expect to come across the notes any time now, and I expect just as certainly to use them against Bronson when I do get them."

She got up suddenly, pushing her chair back with a noisy grating sound that turned many eyes toward us.

"You're more of a fool than I thought you," she said coldly, and left me at the table.

21

I GOT MY HAT and went out in a very uncomfortable frame of mind. That she would inform the police at once of what she knew I never doubted, unless possibly she would give a day or two's grace in the hope that I would change my mind.

I reviewed the situation as I waited for a taxi. Two passed me going in the opposite direction, and in the first one I saw Bronson, his hat over his eyes, his arms folded, looking moodily ahead. Was it imagination? Or was the small man huddled in the cab just behind him our friend Hotchkiss?

As the taxi rolled on I found myself smiling. The alert little man was for all the world like a terrier, ever on the scent, and scouring about in every direction.

I found McKnight at his apartment, with his coat off, and working with enthusiasm and a manicure file over the horn of his car.

"It's the damnedest thing I ever ran across," he groaned, without looking up, as I came in. "The blankety-blank thing's gone on strike. The wiring's all right."

He punched it savagely, finally eliciting a faint throaty croak.

"Maybe it's just tired," I suggested. "The way you use it—"

But McKnight never sees any jokes but his own. He flung the horn clattering into a corner and collapsed sulkily into a chair.

"Now," I said, "if you're through manicuring that horn, I'll tell you about my talk with the lady in black."

"What's wrong?" asked McKnight languidly. "Police watching her too?"

"Not exactly. The fact is, Rich, there's hell to pay."

Stogie came in, bringing a few liquid additions to our comfort. When he went out I told my story.

"You must remember," I added, "that I had seen this woman before the morning of the wreck. She was buying her Pullman ticket when I did. Then the next morning, when the murder was discovered, she grew hysterical and I gave her some whisky. The third and last time I saw her until tonight was when she crouched beside the road after the wreck."

McKnight slid down in his chair until his weight rested on the small of his back, and put his feet on the coffee table.

"It is rather a facer," he said. "It's really too good a situation for a commonplace lawyer. It ought to be dramatized. You can't agree, of course; and by refusing you run the chance of jail, at least, and of having Alison brought into publicity, which is out of the question. You say she was at the Pullman window when you were?"

"Yes; I bought her ticket for her. Gave her lower eleven."

"And you took ten?"

"Lower ten."

McKnight straightened up and looked at me.

"Then she thought you were in lower ten."

"I suppose she did, if she thought at all."

"But listen, man." McKnight was growing excited. "What do you figure out of this? The Conway woman knows you have taken the notes to Pittsburgh. The probabilities are that she follows you there, on the chance of an opportunity to get them, either for Bronson or for herself.

"Nothing doing during the trip over or during the day in Pittsburgh; but she learns the number of your berth as you buy it at the Pullman ticket office in Pittsburgh, and she thinks she sees her chance. No one could have foreseen that that drunken fellow would have crawled into your berth.

"Now, I figure it out this way: She wanted those notes desperately—does still—not for Bronson, but to hold over his head for some purpose. In the night when everything's quiet she slips behind the curtains of lower ten, when the man's breathing shows he is asleep. Didn't you say he snored?"

"He did," I affirmed. "But I tell you—"

"Now keep still and listen. She gropes cautiously around in the darkness, finally discovering the wallet under the pillow. Can't you see it yourself?"

He was leaning forward excitedly, and I could almost see the gruesome tragedy he was depicting.

"She draws out the wallet. Then, perhaps, she remembers the alligator bag, and on the possibility that the notes are there, instead of in the pocketbook, she gropes around for it. Suddenly, the man awakes and clutches at the nearest object, perhaps her neck chain, which breaks. She drops the pocketbook and tries to escape, but he has caught her right hand.

"It is all in silence; the man is still stupidly drunk. But he holds her in a tight grip. Then the tragedy. She must get away. In a minute the car will be aroused. Such a woman on such an errand doesn't go without some sort of weapon, in this case a dagger, which unlike a revolver is noiseless.

"With a quick thrust—she's a big woman and a bold one—she strikes. Possibly Hotchkiss is right about the left-hand blow. Harrington may have held her right hand, or perhaps she held the dirk in her left hand as she groped with her right. Then, as the man falls back, and his grasp relaxes, she straightens and attempts to get away. The swaying of the car throws her almost into your berth, and, trembling with terror, she crouches behind the curtains of lower ten until everything is still. Then she goes noiselessly back to her berth."

I nodded.

"It seems to fit, partly at least," I said. "In the morning when she found that the crime had been not only fruitless, but that she had searched the wrong berth and killed the wrong man, when she saw me come out unhurt, just as she was bracing herself for the discovery of my dead body, then she went into hysterics. You remember I gave her some whisky.

"It really seems a tenable theory. But, like the Sullivan theory, there are one or two things that don't agree with the rest. For one thing, how did the remainder of that necklace get into Alison West's possession?"

"She may have picked it up on the floor. The Conway woman was wearing it."

"We'll admit that," I said; "and I'm sure I hope so. Then how did the murdered man's pocketbook get into the sealskin bag? And the dirk, how account for that, and the bloodstains?"

"Now, what's the use," asked McKnight aggrievedly, "of my building up beautiful theories for you to pull down? We'll take it to Hotchkiss. Maybe he can tell from the bloodstains if the murderer was male or female."

"Hotchkiss is no fool," I said warmly. "Under all his theories there's a good hard layer of common sense. And we must remember, Rich, that neither of our theories includes the woman at Doctor Van Kirk's hospital, that the pleasant picture you have just drawn doesn't account for Alison West's connection with the case, or for the bits of telegram in the Sullivan fellow's pajama pocket. You are like the man who put the clock together after taking it apart. You've got half the works left over."

"Oh, go home," said McKnight disgustedly. "I'm no Hotchkiss. What's the use of coming here and asking me things if you're so particular?"

With one of his quick changes of mood he picked up his guitar.

"Listen to this," he said. "It is a Hawaiian song about a fat lady, O, ignorant one! and how she fell off her mule."

But for all the lightness of the words, the voice that followed me down the stairs was anything but cheery.

"There was a Kanaka in Balu did dwell,
   Who had for his daughter a monstrous fat gal—"

he sang in his clear tenor. I paused on the lower floor and listened. He had stopped singing as abruptly as he had begun.

22

I HAD NOT BEEN HOME for thirty-six hours, since the morning of the preceding day. Johnson was not in sight, and I let myself in quietly with my latchkey. It was almost midnight, and I had hardly settled myself in the library when the bell rang and I was surprised to find Hotchkiss, much out of breath, in the vestibule.

"Why, come in, Mr. Hotchkiss," I said. "I thought you were going home to bed."

"So I was, so I was." He dropped into a chair beside my reading lamp and mopped his face. "And here it is almost midnight, and I'm wider awake than ever. I've seen Sullivan, Mr. Blakeley."

"You have!"

"I have," he said impressively.

"You were following Bronson at eight o'clock. Was that when it happened?"

"Something of the sort. When I left you at the door of the restaurant, I turned and almost ran into a plain-clothes man who'd been watching Bronson. Name's Arnold, and he knows me and my hobby. So he stopped me. Said he had been trailing Bronson all day and had had no time to eat. Bronson, it seems, isn't eating much these days. I at once jotted down the fact, because it argued that he was worried about the man with the notes."

"It might point to other things," I suggested. "Indigestion, you know."

Hotchkiss ignored me. "Well, Arnold had some reason for thinking that Bronson would try to give him the slip that night, so he asked me to stay around the private entrance there while he ran across the street and got something to eat. It seemed a fair presumption that, as he had gone there with a lady, they would dine leisurely and Arnold would have plenty of time to get back."

"What about your own dinner?" I asked curiously.

"Sir," he said pompously, "I have given you a wrong estimate of Wilson Budd Hotchkiss if you think that a question of dinner would even obtrude itself on his mind at such a time as this."

He was a frail little man, and tonight he looked pale with heat and over-exertion.

"Did you have any lunch?" I asked.

He was somewhat embarrassed at that.

"I—really, Mr. Blakeley, the events of the day were so engrossing—"

"Well," I said, "I'm not going to see you drop on the floor from exhaustion. Just wait a minute."

I went back to the pantry, only to be confronted with rows of locked doors and empty dishes. Downstairs in the basement kitchen, however, I found two unattractive-looking cold chops, some dry bread, and a piece of cake wrapped in a napkin, and from its surreptitious and generally hangdog appearance destined for the coachman in the stable at the rear. Trays there were none—everything but the chairs and tables seemed under lock and key, and there was neither napkin, knife nor fork to be found.

The luncheon was not attractive in appearance, but Hotchkiss ate his cold chops and gnawed at his crusts as though he had been famished, while he told his story.

"I had been there only a few minutes," he said, with a chop in one hand and the cake in the other, "when Bronson rushed out and cut across the street. He's a tall man, Mr. Blakeley, and I had hard work keeping close. It was a relief when he jumped into a passing taxi, although being well behind, it was a hard run for me to catch him. He had left the lady.

"Once in the taxi, he simply rode from one end of the city to the other and back again. I suppose he was passing the time, for I followed in another cab, and when I did once get a look at his face it made me—er—uncomfortable. He could have crushed me like a fly, sir."

I had brought him a glass of wine, and he was looking better. He stopped to finish it, declining with a wave of his hand to have it refilled, and continued:

"About nine o'clock or a little later he got out somewhere near Dupont Circle. He went along one of the residence streets there, turned to his left a square or two, and rang a bell. He had been admitted when I got there, but I guessed from the appearance of the place that it was a boardinghouse.

"I waited a few minutes and rang the bell. When a maid answered it, I asked for Mr. Sullivan. Of course there was no Mr. Sullivan there.

"I said I was sorry; that the man I was looking for was a new boarder. She was sure there was no such boarder in the house; the only new arrival was a man on the third floor. She thought his name was Stuart.

"'My friend has a cousin by that name,' I said. 'I'll just go up and see.'

"She wanted to show me up, but I said it was unnecessary. So after telling me it was the bedroom and sitting room on the third floor front, I went up.

"I met a couple of men on the stairs, but neither of them paid any attention to me. A boardinghouse is the easiest place in the world to enter."

"They're not always so easy to leave," I put in, to his evident irritation.

"When I got to the third story, I took out a bunch of keys and posted myself by a door near the ones the girl had indicated. I could hear voices in one of the front rooms, but could not understand what they said.

"There was no violent dispute, but a steady hum. Then Bronson jerked the door open. If he had stepped into the hall he would have seen me fitting a key into the door before me. But he spoke before he came out.

"'You're acting like a maniac,' he said. 'You know I can get those things some way; I'm not going to threaten you. It isn't necessary. You know me.'

"'It would be no use,' the other man said. 'I tell you, I haven't seen the notes for ten days.'

"'But you will,' Bronson said savagely. 'You're standing in your own way, that's all. If you're holding out expecting me to raise my figure, you're making a mistake. It's my last offer.'

"'I couldn't take it if it was for a million,' said the man inside the room. 'I'd do it, I expect, if I could. The best of us have our price.'

"Bronson slammed the door then, and flung past me down the hall.

"After a couple of minutes I knocked at the door, and a tall man about your size, Mr. Blakeley, opened it. He was very blond, with a smooth face and blue eyes—what I think you would call a handsome man.

"'I beg your pardon for disturbing you,' I said. 'Can you tell me which is Mr. Johnson's room? Mr. Francis Johnson?'

"'I don't know,' he said politely. 'I've only been here a few days.'

"I thanked him and left, but I had had a good look at him, and I think I'd know him readily anywhere."

I sat for a few minutes thinking it over. "But what did he mean by saying he hadn't seen the notes for ten days? And why was Bronson making the overtures?"

"I think he was lying," Hotchkiss reflected. "Bronson hasn't reached his figure."

"It's a big advance, Mr. Hotchkiss, and I appreciate what you have done more than I can tell you," I said. "And now, if you can locate any of my property in this fellow's room, we'll send him up for larceny, and at least have him where we can get at him. I'm going to Cresson tomorrow, to try to trace him a little from there. But I'll be back in a couple of days, and we'll begin to gather in these scattered threads."

Hotchkiss rubbed his hands together delightedly.

"That's it," he said. "That's what we want to do, Mr. Blakeley. We'll gather up the threads ourselves. If we let the police in too soon, they'll tangle it up again. I'm not vindictive by nature, but when a fellow like Sullivan not only commits a murder, but goes to all sorts of trouble to put the burden of guilt on an innocent man—I say hunt him down, sir!"

"You are convinced, of course, that Sullivan did it?"

"Who else?" He looked over his glasses at me with the air of a man whose mental attitude is unassailable.

"Well, listen to this," I said.

Then I told him at length of my encounter with Bronson in the restaurant, of the bargain proposed by Mrs. Conway, and finally of McKnight's new theory. But, although he was impressed, he was far from convinced.

"It's a very vivid piece of imagination," he said dryly, "but while it fits the evidence as far as it goes, it doesn't go far enough. How about the stains in lower seven, the stiletto and the wallet? Haven't we even got motive in that telegram from Bronson?"

"Yes," I admitted, "but that bit of chain—"

"Pooh," he said shortly. "Perhaps, like yourself, Sullivan wore glasses with a chain. Our not finding them does not prove they did not exist."

And there I made an error. Half confidences are always mistakes. I could not tell of the broken chain in Alison West's gilt purse.

It was one o'clock when Hotchkiss finally left. We had by that time arranged a definite course of action—Hotchkiss to search Sullivan's rooms and if possible find evidence to have him held for larceny, while I went to Cresson.

Strangely enough, however, when I entered the train the following morning, Hotchkiss was already there. He had bought a new notebook, and was sharpening a fresh pencil.

"I changed my plans, you see," he said, bustling his newspaper aside for me. "It is no discredit to your intelligence, Mr. Blakeley but you lack the professional eye, the analytical mind. You legal gentlemen call a spade a spade, although it may be a shovel."

> "A primrose by the river's brim
> A yellow primrose was to him,
> And nothing more!"

I quoted as the train pulled out.

23

I SLEPT MOST OF THE WAY to Cresson, to the disgust of the little man. Finally he struck up an acquaintance with a kindly faced old priest on his way home to his convent school, armed with a roll of dance music and surreptitious bundles that looked like boxes of candy. From scraps of conversation I gleaned that there had been mysterious occurrences at the convent, ending in the theft of what the reverend father called vaguely, "a quantity of undermuslins." I dropped asleep at that point, and when I roused a few moments later the conversation had progressed. Hotchkiss had a diagram on an envelope.

"With this window bolted, and that one inaccessible, and if, as you say, the garments were in a tub here at X, then, as you hold the key to the other door—I think you said the convent dog did not raise any disturbance? Pardon a personal question, but do you ever walk in your sleep?"

The priest looked bewildered.

"I'll tell you what to do," Hotchkiss said cheerfully, leaning forward, "look around a little yourself before you call in the police. Somnambulism is a queer thing. It's a question whether we are most ourselves sleeping or waking. Ever think of that? Live a saintly life all day, prayers and matins and all that, and the subconscious mind hikes you out of bed at night to steal undermuslins! Subliminal theft, so to speak. Better examine the roof."

I dozed again. When I wakened Hotchkiss sat alone, and the priest, from a corner, was staring at him dazedly over his breviary.

It was raining when we reached Cresson, a wind-driven rain that had forced the agent at the newsstand to close himself in, and that beat back from the rails in parallel lines of white spray. Hotchkiss talked chiefly with the agent and later led the way up the main street. He was completely oblivious of the weather, of the threatening dusk, and of our generally draggled condition. *My* draggled condition, I should say, for he improved every moment, his eyes brighter, his ruddy face ruddier, his collar newer and glossier. Sometime, when it does not encircle the little man's neck, I shall test that collar with a match.

I was growing steadily more depressed. I loathed my errand and its necessity. I had always held that a man who played the spy on a woman was beneath contempt. Then, too, I admit I was afraid of what I might learn. For a time, however, this promised to be a negligible quantity. The streets of the straggling little mountain town had been clean-washed of humanity by the downpour. Windows and doors were inhospitably shut, and from around an occasional drawn shade came narrow strips of light that merely emphasized our gloom. When Hotchkiss's umbrella turned inside out, I stopped.

"I don't know where you are going," I snarled, "and I don't care. But I'm going to get under cover inside of ten seconds. I'm not amphibious."

I ducked into the next shelter, which happened to be the yawning entrance to a garage, and shook myself dog-fashion. Hotchkiss wiped his collar with his handkerchief. It emerged gleaming and unwilted.

"This will do as well as any place," he said, raising his voice above the rattle of the rain. "Got to make a beginning."

I sat down on the usual chair without a back, just inside the door, and stared out at the darkening street. The whole affair had an air of unreality. Now that I was there, I doubted the necessity, or the value, of the journey. I was wet and uncomfortable. Around me, with Cresson as a center, stretched an irregular circumference of mountain, with possibly a ten-mile radius, and in it I was to find the residence of a woman whose first name I did not know, and a man who so far had been a purely chimerical person.

Hotchkiss had penetrated the steaming interior of the cave, which seemed to be a combination of garage and livery stable; for from somewhere in the rear came the usual pungent odors and occasional thud of horses' feet. When he came back he was rubbing his hands together.

"Sullivan was staying at the Curtis place," he said cheerfully. "That's about seven miles up in the hills. Mr. Peck—this is Mr. Peck—says he knows him. It's clearing, isn't it?"

"It is not," I said irritably.

Hotchkiss ignored this.

"There's only one difficulty," he explained. "The mountain roads are bad in weather like this. I'm afraid we'll have to take a horse and trap."

"Buggy," said Mr. Peck succinctly.

I got up.

"Now listen," I said. "I'm waiting until morning. Even a horse in weather like this—"

But Hotchkiss continued to ignore me. It appeared that the local doctor's horse was available, as the doctor was out of town, and before I knew it the rig was ready. In the interval Hotchkiss told me what he knew.

"Six Curtises in the town and vicinity," he said. "Sort of family name around here. One of them is telegraph operator at the station. Person we are

looking for is—or was—a wealthy widow, and Sullivan's her brother. Both supposed to have been killed on the Flier."

"Her brother," I repeated stupidly.

"You see," Hotchkiss went on, "three people in one party took the train
here that night: Miss West, Mrs. Curtis, and Sullivan. The two women had
the drawing room, and Sullivan had lower seven. What we want to find out
is just who these people were, where they came from, if Bronson knew them,
and how Miss West became entangled with them. She may have been engaged to Sullivan, for one thing."

I fell into gloom after that. The roan was led unwillingly into the weather,
Hotchkiss and I in eclipse behind a rubber apron which reached our chins.
Mr. Peck stood in the doorway and called directions to us. "You can't miss
it," he finished. "Got the name over the gate anyhow, 'The Laurels.' The
servants are still there, leastways we didn't bring them down." He even took
a step into the rain as Hotchkiss picked up the lines. "If you're going to
settle the estate," he bawled, "don't forget us, Peck and Peck. A half bushel
of name and a bushel of service."

Hotchkiss could not drive. Born a clerk, he guided the roan much as he
would drive a bad pen. And the roan spattered through puddles and splashed
ink—mud, that is—until I was in a frenzy of irritation.

"What are we going to say when we get there?" I asked after I had finally
taken the reins in my one useful hand. "Get out there at midnight and tell
the servants we have come to ask a few questions about the family? It's an
idiotic trip anyhow. I wish to God I had stayed at home."

The roan fell just then, and we had to crawl out and help him up. By the
time we had partly unharnessed him our matches were gone, and the small
bicycle lamp on the buggy was wavering only too certainly. We were covered
with mud, panting with exertion, and even Hotchkiss showed a disposition
to be surly. The rain, which had lessened for a time, came on again, the
lightning flashes doing more than anything else to reveal our isolated position.

Another mile saw us, if possible, more despondent. The water in our
clothes had had time to penetrate: the roan had sprained his shoulder, and
drew us along in a series of convulsive jerks. And then through the rain-
spattered window of the blanket I saw a light. It was a small light, rather
yellow, and it lasted perhaps thirty seconds. Hotchkiss missed it, and was
inclined to doubt me. But in a couple of minutes the roan hobbled to the
side of the road and stopped, and I made out a break in the pines and an
arched gate.

It was a small gate, too narrow for the buggy. I pulled the horse into as
much shelter as possible under the trees, and we got out. Hotchkiss tied the
beast and we left him there, head down against the driving rain, drooping
and dejected. Then we went toward the house.

It was a long walk. The path bent and twisted, and now and then we lost
it. We were climbing as we went. Oddly there were no lights ahead, although

it was only ten o'clock or so. Hotchkiss kept a little ahead of me, knocking into trees now and then, but finding the path in half the time I should have taken. Once, as I felt my way around a tree in the blackness, I put my hand unexpectedly on his shoulder, and felt a shudder go down my back.

"What do you expect me to do?" he protested, when I remonstrated. "Hang out a red lantern? What was that? Listen."

We both stood peering into the gloom. The sharp patter of the rain on leaves had ceased, and from just ahead there came back to us the stealthy padding of feet in wet soil. My hand closed on Hotchkiss's shoulder and we listened together, warily. The steps were close by, unmistakable. The next flash of lightning showed nothing moving. The house was in full view now, dark and uninviting, looming huge above a terrace, with an Italian garden at the side. Then the blackness came again. Somebody's teeth were chattering. I accused Hotchkiss but he denied it.

"Although I'm not very comfortable, I'll admit," he confessed. "There was something breathing right at my elbow here a moment ago."

"Nonsense!" I took his elbow and steered him in what I made out to be the direction of the steps of the Italian garden. "I saw a deer just ahead by the last flash; that's what you heard. By Jove, I hear wheels."

We paused to listen and Hotchkiss put his hand on something close to us. "Here's your deer," he said. "Iron."

As we neared the house the sense of surveillance we had had in the park gradually left us. Stumbling over flower beds, running afoul of a sundial, groping our way savagely along hedges and thorny banks, we reached the steps finally and climbed the terrace.

It was then that Hotchkiss fell over one of the two large urns which, with tall boxwood trees in them, mounted guard at each side of the door. He didn't make any attempt to get up. He sat in a puddle on the stone floor of the terrace and clutched his leg and swore softly in Government English.

The occasional relief of the lightning was gone. I could not see an outline of the house before me. We had no matches, and an instant's investigation showed that the windows were boarded and the house closed. Hotchkiss, still recumbent, was ascertaining the damage and tenderly peeling down his stocking.

"Upon my soul," he said finally, "I don't know whether this moisture is blood or rain. I think I've broken a bone."

"Blood is thicker than water," I suggested. "Is it sticky? See if you can move your toes."

There was a pause. Hotchkiss moved his toes. By that time I had found a knocker and was making the night hideous. But there was no response save the wind that blew sodden leaves derisively in our faces. Once Hotchkiss declared he heard a window sash lifted, but renewed violence with the knocker produced no effect.

"There's only one thing to do," I said finally. "I'll go back and try to bring the buggy up for you. You can't walk, can you?"

Hotchkiss sat back in his puddle and said he didn't think he could stir, but for me to go back to town and leave him, that he didn't have any family dependent on him, and that if he was going to have pneumonia he had probably got it already. I left him there, and started back to get the horse.

If possible, it was worse than before. There was no lightning, and only by a miracle did I find the little gate again. I drew a long breath of relief, followed by another equally long of dismay. For I had found the hitching strap and there was nothing at the end of it. In a lull of the wind I seemed to hear far off the eager thud of stable-bound feet. So for the second time I climbed the slope to the Laurels, and on the way I thought of many things to say.

I struck the house at a new angle, for I found a veranda, destitute of chairs and furnishings, but dry and evidently roofed. It was better than the terrace, and so by groping along the wall I tried to make my way to Hotchkiss. That was how I found the open window. I had passed perhaps six, all closed, and to have my hand grope for the next one and to find instead the soft drapery of the inner curtain was startling, to say the least.

I found Hotchkiss at last around an angle of the stone wall, and told him that the horse was gone. He was disconcerted, but not abashed; maintaining that it was a new kind of knot that couldn't slip and that the horse must have chewed the halter through! He was less enthusiastic than I had expected about the window.

"It looks uncommonly like a trap," he said. "I tell you there was someone in the park below when we were coming up. Man has a sixth sense that scientists ignore—a sense of the nearness of things. And all the time you have been gone, someone has been watching me."

"Couldn't see you," I maintained. "I can't see you now. And your sense of contiguity didn't tell you about that flower crock."

In the end of course he consented to go with me. He was very lame, and I helped him around to the open window. He was full of moral courage, the little man: it was only the physical in him that quailed. And as we groped along, he insisted on going through the window first.

"If it is a trap," he whispered, "I have two arms to your one, and besides, as I said before, life holds much for you. As for me, the government would merely lose an indifferent employee."

When he found I was going first he was rather hurt, but I did not wait for his protests. I swung my feet over the sill and dropped. I made a clutch at the window frame with my good hand when I found no floor under my feet, but I was too late. I dropped probably ten feet and landed with a crash that seemed to split my eardrums. I was thoroughly shaken, but in some miraculous way the bandaged arm had escaped injury.

"For Heaven's sake," Hotchkiss was calling from above, "have you broken your back?"

"No," I returned, as steadily as I could, "merely driven it up through my skull. This is a staircase. I'm coming up to open another window."

It was eerie work, but I accomplished it finally, discovering, not without mishap, a room filled with more tables than I had ever dreamed of and tables that seemed to waylay and strike at me. When I had got a window open, Hotchkiss crawled through, and we were at last under shelter.

Our first thought was for a light. The same laborious investigation that had landed us where we were revealed that the house was lighted by electricity, and that the plant was not in operation. By accident I stumbled across a tabouret with smoking materials, and found a half dozen matches. The first one showed us the magnitude of the room we stood in, and revealed also a brass candlestick almost four feet high, supporting a candle of similar colossal proportions. It was Hotchkiss who discovered that it had been recently lighted. He held the match to it and peered at it over his glasses.

"Within ten minutes," he announced impressively, "this candle has been burning. Look at the wax! And the wick! Both soft."

"Perhaps it's the damp weather," I ventured, moving a little nearer to the circle of light. A gust of wind came in just then, and the flame turned over on its side and threatened demise. There was something almost ridiculous in the haste with which we put down the window and nursed the flicker to life.

The peculiarly ghostlike appearance of the room added to the uncanniness of the situation. The furniture was swathed in white covers for the winter. Even the pictures wore shrouds. And in a niche between two windows a figure on a pedestal, similarly wrapped and one arm extended under its winding sheet, made a most lifelike ghost. If any ghost can be lifelike.

In the light of the candle we surveyed each other, and we were objects for mirth. Hotchkiss was taking off his sodden shoes and preparing to make himself comfortable, while I hung my muddy raincoat over the ghost in the corner. Thus habited, he presented a rakish but distinctly more comfortable appearance.

"When these people built," Hotchkiss said, surveying the huge dimensions of the room, "they must have bought a mountain and built all over it. What a room!"

It seemed to be a living room, although Hotchkiss remarked that it was much more like a dead one. It was probably fifty feet long and twenty-five feet wide. It was very high too, with a domed ceiling, and a gallery ran around the entire room, about fifteen feet above the floor. The candlelight did not penetrate beyond the dim outlines of the gallery rail, but I fancied the wall there hung with smaller pictures.

Hotchkiss had discovered a fire laid in the enormous fireplace, and in a few minutes we were steaming before a cheerful blaze. Within the radius of its light and heat we were comfortable again. But the brightness merely emphasized the gloom of the ghostly corners. We talked in subdued tones, and I smoked some Turkish cigarettes I found in a table drawer. We had decided to stay all night, there being nothing else to do. I suggested a game of double-dummy bridge, but did not urge it when my companion asked me if it resembled euchre. Gradually, as the ecclesiastical candle paled in the firelight, we grew drowsy. I drew a divan into the cheerful area and stretched myself out for sleep. Hotchkiss, who said the pain in his leg made him wakeful, sat wide-eyed by the fire, smoking a pipe.

I have no idea how much time had passed when something threw itself violently on my chest. I roused with a start and leaped to my feet, and a large Angora cat fell with a thump on the floor. The fire was still bright and there was an odor of scorched leather through the room, from Hotchkiss's shoes. The little detective was sound asleep, his dead pipe in his fingers. The cat sat back on its haunches and wailed.

The curtain at the door into the hallway bellied slowly into the room and fell again. The cat looked toward it and opened its mouth for another howl. I thrust at it with my foot, but it refused to move. Hotchkiss stirred uneasily, and his pipe clattered to the floor.

The cat was standing at my feet, staring behind me. The tip of its tail waved threateningly, but when I wheeled I saw nothing.

I took the candle and made a circuit of the room. Behind the curtain that had moved the door was securely closed. The windows were shut and locked, and everywhere the silence was absolute. The cat followed me majestically. I stooped and stroked its head, but it persisted in its uncanny watching of the corners of the room.

When I went back to my divan, after putting a fresh log on the fire, I was reassured. I took the precaution, and smiled at myself for doing it, to put the fire tongs within reach of my hand. But the cat would not let me sleep. After a time I decided it wanted water, and I started out in search of some, carrying the candle without the stand. I wandered through several rooms, all closed and dismantled, before I found a small lavatory opening off a billiard room. The cat lapped steadily, and I filled a glass to take back with me. The candle flickered in a sickly fashion which threatened to leave me there lost in the wanderings of the many hallways, and from somewhere there came an occasional violent puff of wind. The cat stuck by my feet, with the hair on its back rising menacingly. I don't like cats; there is something psychic about them.

Hotchkiss was still asleep when I got back to the big room. I moved his boots back from the fire and trimmed the candle. Then, with sleep gone from me, I lay back on my divan and reflected on many things: on my idiocy in coming; on Alison West and the fact that only a week before she had been a guest in this very house; on Richey and the constraint that had come between us. From that I drifted back to Alison, and to the barrier my comparative poverty would be, even granting everything else was right.

The emptiness, the stillness were oppressive. Once I heard footsteps moving, rhythmical steps that neither hurried nor dragged, and seemed to mount endless staircases without coming any closer. I realized finally that I had not quite turned off the tap, and that the lavatory, which I had circled to reach, must be quite close.

The cat lay by the fire, its nose on its folded paws, content in the warmth and companionship. I watched it idly. Now and then the green wood hissed in the fire, but the cat never batted an eye. Through an unshuttered window the lightning flashed. Suddenly the cat looked up. It lifted its head and stared directly at the gallery above. Then it blinked, and stared again. Not until it had got up on its feet, eyes still riveted on the balcony, tail waving at the tip, the hair on its back a bristling brush, did I glance casually over my head.

From among the shadows a face gazed down at me, a face that seemed a fitting tenant of the ghostly room below. I saw it faintly but unmistakably. While I stared at it with startled eyes, the apparition disappeared. The rail was there, the Bokhara rug still swung from it, but the gallery was empty.

The cat threw back its head and wailed again.

24

I JUMPED UP and seized the fire tongs. The cat's wail had roused Hotchkiss, who was wide awake at once. He took in my offensive attitude, the tongs, the direction of my gaze, and needed nothing more. As he picked up the candle and darted out into the hall I followed him. He made directly for the staircase, and part way up he turned off to the right through a small door. We were on the gallery itself; below us the fire gleamed cheerfully, the cat was not in sight. There was no sign of my ghostly visitant, but as we stood there the Bokhara rug without warning slid over the railing and fell to the floor below.

"Man or woman?" Hotchkiss inquired in his most professional tone.

"Neither—that is, I don't know. I didn't notice anything but the eyes," I muttered. "They were looking a hole in me. If you'd seen that cat you would realize my state of mind. That was a traditional graveyard yowl."

"I don't think you saw anything at all," he lied cheerfully. "You dozed off, and the rest is the natural result of our general situation."

Nevertheless, he examined the Bokhara carefully when we went down, and when I finally went to sleep he was reading the only book in sight, somebody or other on bridge. The first rays of daylight were coming mistily into the room when he roused me. He had his finger on his lips, and he whispered sibilantly while I tried to draw on my distorted boots.

"I think we have him," he said triumphantly. "I've been looking around some, and I can tell you this much. Just before we came in through the window last night another man came. Only he did not drop as you did. He swung over the stair railing, and then slid down. The rail is scratched. He was long enough ahead of us to go into the dining room and get a decanter out of the sideboard. He poured the liquor into a glass, left the decanter there,

and took the whisky into the library across the hall. Then he broke into a
desk, using a paper knife for a jimmy."

"Good Lord, Hotchkiss!" I exclaimed. "It may have been Sullivan himself!
Confound your theories—he's getting farther away every minute."

"It was Sullivan," Hotchkiss returned imperturbably. "And he hasn't gone.
His boots are by the library fire."

"He probably had a dozen pairs where he could get them," I scoffed. "And
while you and I sat and slept, the very man we want to get our hands on
leered at us over that railing."

"Softly, softly, my friend," Hotchkiss said, as I stamped into my other shoe.
"I did not say he was gone. Don't jump at conclusions. It is fatal to reasoning.
As a matter of fact, he didn't relish a night on the mountains any more than
we did. After he had unintentionally frightened you almost into paralysis,
what would my gentleman naturally do? Go out in the storm again? Not
if I know the Sullivan type. He went upstairs, well up near the roof, locked
himself in and went to bed."

"And he's there now?"

"He is there now."

We had no weapons. I am aware that the traditional hero is always armed,
and that Hotchkiss as the low comedian should have had a revolver that
misfired. As a fact, we had nothing of the sort. Hotchkiss now carried the
fire tongs, but my sense of humor was too strong for me. I declined the poker.

"All we want is a little peaceable conversation with him," I demurred.
"We can't brain him first and converse with him afterward. And anyhow,
while I can't put my finger on the place, I think your theory is weak. If he
wouldn't run a hundred miles through fire and water to get away from us,
then he is not the man we want."

Hotchkiss, however, was certain. He had found the room and listened outside the door to the sleeper's heavy breathing, and so we climbed past luxurious suites, revealed in the deepening daylight, past long vistas of hall and
boudoir. And we were both badly winded when we got there. It was a tower
room, reached by narrow stairs, and well above the roof level. Hotchkiss was
glowing.

"It is partly good luck, but not all," he panted in a whisper. "If we had
persisted in the search last night he would have taken alarm and fled. Now
we have him. Are you ready?"

He gave a mighty rap at the door with the fire tongs, and stood expectant.
Certainly he was right; someone moved within.

"Hello! Hello there!" Hotchkiss bawled. "You might as well come out.
We won't hurt you, if you come peaceably."

"Tell him we represent the law," I prompted. "That's the customary thing,
you know."

But at that moment a bullet came squarely through the door and flattened
itself with a sharp *pst* against the wall of the tower staircase. We ducked
unanimously, dropped back out of range, and Hotchkiss retaliated with a

spirited bang at the door with the tongs. This brought another bullet. It was a ridiculous situation. Under the circumstances no doubt we should have retired, at least until we had armed ourselves, but Hotchkiss had no end of fighting spirit and as for me, my blood was up.

"Break the lock," I suggested, and Hotchkiss, standing at the side, out of range, retaliated for every bullet by a smashing blow with the tongs. The shots ceased after a half dozen, and the door was giving slowly. One of us each side of the door, we were ready for almost any kind of desperate resistance. As it swung open Hotchkiss poised with the tongs; I stood, bent forward, my arm drawn back for a blow.

Nothing happened.

There was not a sound. Finally, at the risk of losing an eye which I justly value, I peered around and into the room. There was no desperado there: only a fresh-faced, trembling-lipped country girl, sitting on the edge of her bed, with a quilt around her shoulders and the empty revolver at her feet.

We were victorious, but no conquered army ever beat such a retreat as ours down the tower stairs, and into the refuge of the living room. There, with the door closed, sprawled on the divan, I went from one spasm of mirth into another, becoming sane at intervals, and suffering relapse again every time I saw Hotchkiss's disgruntled countenance. He was pacing the room, the tongs still in his hand, his mouth pursed with irritation. Finally he stopped in front of me and compelled my attention.

"When you have finished cackling," he said with dignity, "I wish to justify my position. Do you think the young woman upstairs put a pair of number eight boots to dry in the library last night? Do you think she poured the whisky out of that decanter?"

"They've been known to do it," I put in, but his eye silenced me.

"Moreover, if she had been the person who peered at you over the gallery railing last night, don't you suppose, with her belligerent disposition, she could have filled you as full of lead as a window weight?"

"I do," I assented. "It wasn't that scared little maid. I grant you that. Then who was it?"

Hotchkiss felt certain that it had been Sullivan, but I was not sure. Why would he have crawled like a thief into his own house? If he had crossed the park, as seemed probable, when we did, he had not made any attempt to use the knocker. I gave it up finally, and made an effort to conciliate the young woman in the tower.

We had heard no sound since our spectacular entrance into her room. I was distinctly uncomfortable as, alone this time, I climbed to the tower staircase. Reasoning from before, she would probably throw a chair at me. I stopped at the foot of the staircase and called.

"Hello up there," I said, in as debonnair a manner as I could summon. "Good morning. Wie geht es bei Ihnen?"

No reply.

"Bon jour, mademoiselle," I tried again. This time there was a movement of some sort from above, but nothing fell on me.

"I—we want to apologize for rousing you so unexpectedly this morning," I went on. "The fact is, we wanted to talk to you, and you were hard to waken. We are travelers, lost in your mountains, and we crave a breakfast and an audience."

She came to the door then. I could feel that she was investigating the top of my head from above. "Is Mr. Sullivan with you?" she asked. It was the first word from her, and she was not sure of her voice.

"No. We are alone. If you will come down and look at us you will find us two perfectly harmless people, whose horse departed without leave last night and left us at your gate."

She relaxed somewhat then and came down a step or two. "I was afraid I'd killed somebody," she said. "The housekeeper left yesterday, and the other servants went with her."

When she saw that I was comparatively young and lacked the earmarks of the highwayman, she was apparently relieved. She was inclined to fight shy of Hotchkiss, however, for some reason. She gave us a breakfast of sorts, for there was little in the house, and afterward we telephoned to the town for a vehicle. While Hotchkiss examined scratches and replaced the Bokhara rug, I engaged her in conversation.

"Can you tell me," I asked, "who is managing the estate since Mrs. Curtis was killed?"

"No one," she returned shortly. "Not that I know of, anyhow."

"Has any member of the family been here since the accident?"

"No, sir. There was only the two of them, and some think Mr. Sullivan was killed as well as his sister."

"You don't?"

"No," with conviction.

"Why?"

She wheeled on me with quick suspicion.

"Are you a detective?" she demanded.

"No."

"You told that other man to say you represented the law."

"I am a lawyer. Some of them misrepresent the law, but I—"

She broke in impatiently.

"A sheriff's officer?"

"No. Look here, my dear girl, I am all that I should be. You'll have to believe that. And I'm in a bad position through no fault of my own. I want you to answer some questions. If you'll help me, I'll do what I can for you. Do you live near here?"

Her chin quivered. It was the first sign of weakness she had shown.

"My home is in Pittsburgh," she said, "and I haven't enough money to get there. They hadn't paid any wages for two months. They didn't pay anybody."

"Very well," I returned. "I'll send you back to Pittsburgh, Pullman included, if you will tell me some things I want to know."

She agreed eagerly. Outside the window Hotchkiss was bending over, examining footprints in the drive.

"Now," I began, "there has been a Miss West staying here?"

"Yes."

"Mr. Sullivan was attentive to her?"

"Yes. She was the granddaughter of a wealthy man in Pittsburgh. My aunt has been in his family for twenty years. Mrs. Curtis wanted her brother to marry Miss West."

"Do you think she was engaged to him?" I could not keep the excitement out of my voice.

"No. There were reasons—" She stopped abruptly.

"Do you know anything of the family? Where did they come from?"

"They came from somewhere in the South. I have heard Mrs. Curtis say her mother was a Cuban. I don't know much about them, but Mr. Sullivan had a wicked temper, though he didn't look it. Folks say big light-haired people are easygoing, but I don't believe it, sir."

"How long was Miss West here?"

"Two weeks."

I hesitated about further questioning. Critical as my position was, I could not pry deeper into Alison West's affairs. If she had got into the hands of adventurers, as Sullivan and his sister appeared to have been, she was safely away from them again. But something of the situation in the car Ontario was forming itself in my mind. The incident at the farmhouse lacked only motive to be complete. Was Sullivan, after all, a rascal or a criminal? Was the murderer Sullivan or Mrs. Conway? The lady or the tiger again.

Jennie was speaking.

"I hope Miss West was not hurt?" she asked. "We liked her, all of us. She was not like Mrs. Curtis."

I wanted to say that she was not like anybody in the world. Instead— "She escaped with some bruises," I said.

She glanced at my arm. "You were on the train?"

"Yes."

She waited for more questions but, none coming, she went to the door. Then she closed it softly and came back.

"Mrs. Curtis is dead? You are sure of it?" she asked.

"She was killed instantly, I believe. The body was not recovered. But I have reason to believe that Mr. Sullivan is living."

"I knew it," she said. "I think he was here the night before last. That's why I went to the tower room. I believe he would kill me if he could." As nearly as her round and comely face could express it Jennie's expression was tragic at that moment. I made a quick resolution, and acted on it at once.

"You are not entirely frank with me, Jennie," I protested. "And I am going to tell you more than I have. We're talking at cross purposes and getting nowhere.

"I was on the wrecked train, in the same car with Mrs. Curtis, Miss West and Mr. Sullivan. During the night there was a crime committed in that car and Mr. Sullivan disappeared. But he left behind him a chain of circumstantial evidence that involved me completely, so that I may at any time be arrested."

Apparently she did not comprehend for a moment. Then, as if the meaning of my words had just dawned on her, she looked up and gasped:

"You mean Mr. Sullivan committed the crime himself?"

"I think he did."

"What was it?"

"It was murder," I said deliberately.

Her hands clenched involuntarily, and she shrank back. "A woman?" She could scarcely form the words.

"No, a man; a Mr. Simon Harrington, of Pittsburgh."

Her effort to retain her self-control was pitiful. Then she broke down and cried; her head on the back of a tall chair.

"It was my fault," she said wretchedly, "my fault. I shouldn't have sent them the word."

After a few minutes she grew quiet. She seemed to hesitate over something, and finally determined to say it.

"You will understand better, sir, when I say that I lived for a while with the Harrington family. Mr. Harrington was Mr. Sullivan's wife's father!"

25

SO IT HAD BEEN the tiger, not the lady! Well, I had held to that theory all through. Jennie suddenly became a valuable person. If necessary she could prove the connection between Sullivan and the murdered man, and show a motive for the crime. I was triumphant when Hotchkiss came in. When the girl had produced a photograph of Mrs. Sullivan, and I had recognized the bronze-haired girl of the train, we were both well satisfied. Which goes to prove the ephemeral nature of most human contentments.

Jennie either had nothing more to say, or feared she had said too much. She was evidently uneasy before Hotchkiss. I told her that Mrs. Sullivan was recovering in a Baltimore hospital, but she already knew it from some source, and merely nodded. She made a few preparations for leaving, while Hotchkiss and I compared notes, and then, with the cat in her arms, she climbed into the car which had been sent from the town. I sat with her, and on the way down she told me a little, not much.

"If you see Mrs. Sullivan," she advised, "and she is conscious, she probably thinks that both her husband and her father were killed in the wreck. She will be in a bad way, sir."

"You mean that she still cares about her husband?"

The cat crawled over onto my knee, and rubbed its head against my hand invitingly. Jennie stared at the undulating line of the mountain crests, a colossal surf against a blue ocean of sky. "Yes, she cares," she said softly. "Women are made like that. They say they are cats, but Peter there in your lap wouldn't come back and lick your hand if you kicked him. If—if you have to tell her the truth, be as gentle as you can, sir. She has been good to me. That's why I have played the spy here all summer. It's a thankless thing, spying on people."

"It is that," I agreed soberly.

Hotchkiss and I arrived in Washington late that evening, and rather than arouse the household I went to the club. I was at the office early the next morning and admitted myself. McKnight rarely appeared before half after ten, and our modest office force sometime after nine. I looked over my previous day's mail and waited, with such patience as I possessed, for McKnight. In the interval I called up Mrs. Klopton and announced that I would dine at home that night. What my household subsists on during my numerous absences I have never discovered. Tea, probably, and crackers. Diligent search, when I have made a midnight arrival, never reveals anything more substantial. Possibly I imagine it, but the announcement that I am about to make a journey always seems to create a general atmosphere of depression throughout the house, as though Euphemia and Eliza, and Thomas, the handyman, were already subsisting in imagination on Mrs. Klopton's meager fare.

So I called her up and announced my arrival. There was something unusual in her tone, as though her throat was tense with indignation. Always shrill, her elderly voice rasped my ear painfully through the receiver.

"I have changed the butcher, Mr. Lawrence," she announced portentously. "The last roast was a pound short and his mutton chops—any self-respecting sheep would refuse to acknowledge them."

As I said before I can always tell when, from the voice in which Mrs. Klopton conveys the most indifferent matters, something of real significance has occurred. Also through long habit, I have learned how quickest to bring her to the point.

"You are pessimistic this morning," I returned. "What's the matter, Mrs. Klopton? You haven't used that tone since Euphemia gave that pie to the iceman. What is it now? Somebody poison the dog?"

She cleared her throat.

"The house has been broken into, Mr. Lawrence," she said. "I have lived in the best families, and never have I stood by and seen what I saw yesterday —every bureau drawer opened, and my—my most private belongings—" She choked.

"Did you notify the police?" I asked sharply.

"Police!" she sniffed. "Police! It was the police that did it, two detectives with a search warrant. I wouldn't dare tell you over the telephone what one of them said when he found the whisky and rock candy for my cough."

"Did they take anything?" I demanded, every nerve on edge.

"They took the cough medicine," she returned indignantly, "and they said—"

"Confound the cough medicine!" I was frantic. "Did they take anything else? Were they in my dressing room?"

"Yes. I threatened to sue them, and I told them what you would do when you came back. But they wouldn't listen. They took away that black sealskin bag you brought home from Pittsburgh with you."

I knew then that my hours of freedom were numbered. To have found Sullivan and then, in support of my case against him, to have produced the bag, minus the bit of chain, had been my intention. But the police now had the bag, and, beyond knowing something of Sullivan's history, I was practically no nearer his discovery than before. Hotchkiss hoped he had his man in the house off Dupont Circle, but on the very night he had seen him Jennie claimed that Sullivan had tried to enter the Laurels. Then suppose we found Sullivan and proved the satchel and its contents his? Since the police had the bit of chain it might mean involving Alison in the story. I sat down and faced the situation. There was no escape. I figured it out despondingly.

Against me was the evidence of the survivors of the Ontario that I had been accused of the murder at the time. There had been bloodstains on my pillow and a hidden dagger under it. Into the bargain, in my possession had been found a traveling bag containing the dead man's pocketbook.

In my favor of course was McKnight's theory against Mrs. Conway. She had a motive for wanting the notes, she believed I was in lower ten, and she had collapsed at the discovery of Harrington's dead body in the morning.

Against both of these theories was I to accuse a purely chimerical person named Sullivan, who was not seen by any of the survivors save one, Alison, whom I could not bring into the case? I could find a motive for his murdering his father-in-law, whom, according to the girl of the Laurels, he hated. But again I would have to drag her in. And I had agreed not to do so.

What was more, not one of the theories explained the telegram and the broken necklace.

Outside, the office force was arriving. They were comfortably ignorant of my presence, and over the transom floated scraps of dialogue and the stenographer's gurgling laugh. McKnight had a relative who was reading law with him in the intervals between calling up the young women of his acquaintance. He came in singing, and the office boy joined in with the uncertainty of voice of fifteen. I smiled grimly. I was too busy with my own troubles to find any joy in opening the door and startling them into silence. I even heard, without resentment, Blobs of the uncertain voice inquire when "Blake" would be back.

I hoped McKnight would arrive before the arrest occurred. There were many things to arrange. But when at last I telephoned I found he had been gone for more than an hour. Clearly he was not coming directly to the office, and with such resignation as I could muster I paced the floor and waited.

I felt more alone than I have ever felt in my life. "Born an orphan," as Richey said, I have made my own way, carved out myself such success as had been mine. I had built up my house of life on the props of law and order, and now some unknown hand had withdrawn the supports and I stood among ruins.

I suppose it is the maternal in a woman that makes a man turn to her when everything else fails. The eternal boy in him goes to have his wounded pride bandaged, his tattered self-respect repaired. If he loves the woman, he wants her to kiss the hurt.

The longing to see Alison, always with me, was stronger than I was that morning. It might be that I would not see her again. I had nothing to say to her save one thing and that, under the cloud that hung over me, I did not dare to say. But I wanted to see her, to touch her hand, as only a lonely man can crave it, I wanted the comfort of her, the peace that lay in her presence. And so, with every step outside the door a threat, I telephoned to her.

She was gone! The disappointment was great, for my need was great. In a fury of revolt against the scheme of things, I heard that she had started home to Richmond, but that she might still be caught at the station.

To see her had by that time become an obsession. I picked up my hat, threw open the door and oblivious of the shock to the office force of my presence, followed so immediately by my exit, I dashed out to the elevator. As I went down in one cage I caught a glimpse of Johnson and two other men going up in the next. I hardly gave them a thought. There was no taxi in sight, and I jumped on a passing streetcar. Let come what might, arrest, prison, disgrace, I was going to see Alison.

I saw her. I flung into the station and saw that it was empty. At least she was not there, so I hurried out to the gates. I saw her then, a familiar figure in blue. But she was not alone. Bending over her, talking earnestly with all his boyish heart in his face, was Richey.

Neither of them saw me, and I was glad of it. After all, it had been Mc-Knight's game first. I turned on my heel and made my way as well as I could out of the station. Before I lost them I turned once and looked toward them, standing apart from the crowd, absorbed in each other. They were the only two people on earth I cared about, and I left them there together. Then I went back miserably to the office and waited to be arrested.

26

STRANGELY ENOUGH, I was not disturbed that day. McKnight did not appear at all. I sat at my desk and transacted routine business all afternoon, working with feverish energy. Like a man on the verge of a critical illness or a hazardous journey I cleared up my correspondence, paid bills until I had writer's cramp from signing checks, read over my will, and paid up my life insurance, made to the benefit of an elderly sister of my mother's.

I no longer dreaded arrest. After that morning in the station I felt that anything would be a relief from the tension. I went home with perfect openness, courting the warrant that I knew was waiting, but I was not molested. The delay puzzled me. The early part of the evening was uneventful. I read until late, with occasional lapses when my book lay on my knees and I smoked and thought. Mrs. Klopton closed the house with ostentatious caution about eleven, and hung around waiting to enlarge on the outrageousness of the police search. I did not encourage her.

"One would think," she concluded pompously, one foot in the hall, "that you were something you oughtn't to be, Mr. Lawrence. They acted as though you had committed a crime."

"I'm not sure that I didn't, Mrs. Klopton," I said wearily. "Somebody did, and the general verdict seems to point my way."

She stared at me in speechless indignation. Then she flounced out. She came back once to say that the paper predicted cooler weather and that she had put a blanket on my bed, but to her disappointment I refused to reopen the subject.

At half past eleven McKnight and Hotchkiss came in. Rich has a habit of stopping his car in front of the house and honking until someone comes out. He has a code of signals with the horn, which I never remember. Two long and a short blast mean, I believe, "Send out a box of cigarettes," and six short blasts, which sound like a police call, mean "Can you lend me some money?" Tonight I knew something was up, for he got out and rang the doorbell.

They came into the library, and Hotchkiss wiped his collar until it gleamed. McKnight was aggressively cheerful.

"Not pinched yet!" he exclaimed. "What do you think of that for luck? You always were a fortunate devil, Lawrence."

"Yes," I assented, with some bitterness, "I hardly know how to contain myself for joy sometimes. I suppose you know"—to Hotchkiss—"that the police were here while we were at Cresson, and that they found the bag that I brought from the wreck?"

"Things are coming to a head," he said. "Unless a little plan that I have in mind—" He hesitated.

"I hope so, I'm pretty nearly finished," I said wearily.

"Don't be a damned fool," said McKnight. "Although jail can't be so bad. Plenty of fellows get the habit and keep going back and going back." He looked at his watch, and I fancied his cheerfulness was strained. Hotchkiss was nervously fumbling my book.

"Did you ever read *The Purloined Letter*, Mr. Blakeley?" he inquired.

"Probably, years ago," I said. "Poe, isn't it?"

He was choked at my indifference. "It is a masterpiece," he said, with enthusiasm. "I reread it today."

"And what happened?"

"Then I inspected the rooms in the house of Dupont Circle. I made some discoveries, Mr. Blakeley. For one thing, our man there is left-handed." He looked around for our approval. "There was a small cushion on the dresser, and the scarfpins in it had been stuck in with the left hand."

"Somebody may have twisted the cushion," I objected, but he looked hurt and I desisted.

"There is only one discrepancy," he admitted, "but it troubles me. According to that woman at the farmhouse our man wore very gaudy pajamas, while I found here only the most severely plain ones."

McKnight winked at me furtively.

"I am convinced of one thing," Hotchkiss went on, clearing his throat: "the notes are not in that room. Either he carries them with him or he has sold them."

A sound on the street made both my visitors listen sharply. Whatever it was it passed on, however. I was growing curious and the restraint was telling on McKnight. He has no talent for secrecy. In the interval we discussed the strange occurrence at Cresson, which lost nothing by Hotchkiss's dry narration.

"And so," he concluded, "the woman in the Baltimore hospital is the wife of Henry Sullivan and the daughter of the man he murdered. No wonder he collapsed when he heard of the wreck."

"Joy, probably," McKnight put in. "Is that clock right, Lawrence? Never mind, it doesn't matter. By the way, Mrs. Conway dropped in the office yesterday while you were away."

"What! What did she want?"

"Said she had heard great things of us, and wanted us to handle her case against the railroad."

"I would like to know what she's really after," I reflected. "Is she trying to reach me through you?"

Richey's flippancy is often a cloak for deeper feeling. He dropped it now. "Yes," he said, "she's after the notes, of course. Matter of fact I felt sorry for her. She stood by the door with her face white, and told me contemptuously that I could save you from a murder charge and wouldn't do it. She made me feel like a cur. I was just as guilty as if I could have obliged her.

She hinted that there were reasons and she laid my attitude to beastly motives."

"Nonsense," I said, as easily as I could. Hotchkiss had gone to the window. "She was excited. There are no 'reasons,' whatever she means."

Richey put his hand on my shoulder. "We've been together too long to let any 'reasons' or 'unreasons' come between us, old man," he said, and grinned down at me.

Hotchkiss, who had been silent, here came forward in his most impressive manner. He put his hands under his coattails and coughed.

"Mr. Blakeley," he began, "by Mr. McKnight's advice we have arranged a little interview here tonight. If all has gone as I planned, Mr. Henry Pinckney Sullivan is by this time under arrest. Within a very few minutes he will be here."

"I wanted to talk to him before he was locked up," Richey explained. "He's clever enough to be worth knowing, and, besides, I'm not so cocksure of his guilt as our friend here, the Patch on the Seat of Government. No murderer worthy of the name needs six different motives for the same crime, beginning with robbery, and ending with an unpleasant father-in-law."

We were all silent for a while. McKnight stationed himself at a window, and Hotchkiss paced the floor expectantly. "I'm rather proud of the way things are working out," he chirruped. "While the police have been guarding houses and standing with their mouths open waiting for clues to fall in and choke them, we have pieced together, bit by bit, a foolproof case that—"

The doorbell rang, followed immediately by sounds of footsteps in the hall. McKnight threw the door open, and Hotchkiss flung out his arm in a gesture of superb eloquence.

"Well, here's your man!" he stated.

Through the open doorway came a tall, blond fellow, clad in light gray, wearing tan shoes, and followed closely by an officer.

"I brought him here as you suggested, Mr. McKnight," said the constable.

But McKnight was doubled over the library table in silent convulsions of mirth, and I was almost as bad. Little Hotchkiss stood up, his important attitude finally changing to one of chagrin, while the blond man ceased to look angry, and became sheepish.

It was Stuart, our confidential clerk for the last half dozen years!

McKnight sat up and wiped his eyes.

"Stuart," he said sternly, "there are two very serious things we have learned about you. First, you jab your scarfpins into your cushion with your left hand, which is most reprehensible; and second, you wear tailored solid-colored pajamas."

Stuart was bewildered. He looked from McKnight to me, and then at the crestfallen Hotchkiss.

"I haven't any idea what it's all about," he said. "I was arrested as I reached my boardinghouse tonight after the theater, and brought directly here. I told the officer it was a mistake."

Poor Hotchkiss tried bravely to justify the fiasco.

"You can't deny," he contended, "that Mr. Andrew Bronson followed you to your rooms last Monday evening."

Stuart looked at us and flushed.

"No, I don't deny it," he said, "but there was nothing criminal about it, on my part at least. Mr. Bronson has been trying to induce me to secure the forged notes for him. There was nothing doing, of course."

"And you were not on the wrecked Washington Flier?" persisted Hotchkiss. But McKnight interfered.

"There is no use trying to pin the other fellow's identity on Stuart, Mr. Hotchkiss," he protested. "He has been our confidential clerk for six years, and he hasn't been away from the office a day for a year. I am afraid that the beautiful fabric we have pieced out of all these scraps is going to be a crazy quilt." His tone was facetious, but I could detect the undercurrent of real disappointment.

I paid the constable for his trouble, and he departed. Stuart, still rather indignant, left to go back to Dupont Circle. He shook hands with McKnight and myself magnanimously, but he hurled a look of utter hatred at Hotchkiss, sunk crestfallen in his chair.

"As far as I can see," said McKnight dryly, "we're exactly as far along as we were the day we met at the Carter place. We're not a step nearer to finding our man."

"We have one thing that may be of value," I suggested. "He is the husband of a bronze-haired woman at Van Kirk's Hospital in Baltimore, and it is just possible we may trace him through her. I hope we are not going to lose your valuable co-operation, Mr. Hotchkiss?" I asked.

He roused at that feeble interest. "I—of course not, if you still care to have me. I was wondering about the man who just went out—Stuart, you say? I told his landlady tonight that he wouldn't need the room again. I hope she hasn't rented it to somebody else."

We cheered him as best we could, and I suggested that we go to Baltimore the next day and try to find the real Sullivan through his wife. He left sometime after midnight, and Richey and I were alone.

He drew a chair near the lamp and lighted a cigarette, and for a time we were silent. I was in the shadow, and I sat back and watched him. It was not surprising, I thought, that she cared for him. Women had always loved him, perhaps because he always loved them. There was no disloyalty in the thought. It was his nature to give and crave affection. Only I was different. I had never really cared about a girl before, and my life had been entirely loveless. I had fought a lonely battle always. Once before, in college, we had both laid ourselves and our callow devotions at the feet of the same girl. Her name was Dorothy—I had forgotten the rest—but I remembered the sequel. In a spirit of quixotic youth I had relinquished my claim in favor of Richey and gone cheerfully on my way, elevated by my heroic sacrifice to a somber, white-hot martyrdom. As is often the case, McKnight's first words showed our parallel lines of thought.

"I say, Laurie," he asked, "do you remember Dorothy Browne?" *Browne*, that was it!

"Dorothy Browne?" I repeated. "Oh—why, yes, I recall her now. Why?"

"Nothing," he said. "I was thinking about her. That's all. You remember you were crazy about her, and dropped back because she preferred me?"

"I got out," I said with dignity, "because you declared you would shoot yourself if she didn't go with you to something or other!"

"Yes, I recall now!" he mimicked. He tossed his cigarette in the general direction of the hearth and got up. We were both a little self-conscious, and he stood with his back to me, fingering a Japanese vase on the mantel.

"I was thinking," he began, turning the vase around, "that if you feel pretty well again and ready to take hold, I'd like to go away for a week or so. Things are fairly well cleaned up at the office."

"Do you mean you are going to Richmond?" I asked, after a scarcely perceptible pause. He turned and faced me, with his hands thrust in his pockets.

"No. That's off, Laurie. The Seiberts are going for a week's cruise along the coast. The hot weather has played hob with me and the cruise means seven days' breeze and bridge."

I lighted a cigarette and offered him the box, but he refused. He was looking haggard and suddenly tired. I couldn't think of anything to say, and neither evidently could he. The matter between us lay too deep for speech.

"How's the pony?" he asked.

"Martin says a month and she will be all right," I returned in the same tone. He picked up his hat, but he had something more to say. He blurted it out finally, halfway to the door.

"The Seiberts are not going for a couple of days," he said, "and if you want a day or so off to go down to Richmond yourself "

"Perhaps I *shall*," I returned, as indifferently as I could. "Not going, yet, are you?"

"Yes. It's late." He drew in his breath as if he had something more to say, but the impulse passed. "Well, good night," he said from the doorway.

"Good night, old man."

The next moment the outer door slammed and I heard the engine of his car throbbing in the street. Then the quiet settled down around me again, and there in the lamplight I dreamed dreams. I was going to see her.

I made my escape the next morning through the stable back of the house, and then by devious dark and winding ways to the office. There after a conference with Blobs, whose features fairly jerked with excitement, I double-locked the door of my private office and finished off some imperative work. By ten o'clock I was free, and for the twentieth time I consulted my train schedule. At five minutes after ten, with McKnight not yet in sight, Blobs knocked at the door—the double rap we had agreed upon—and on being admitted slipped in and quietly closed the door behind him. His eyes were glistening with excitement, and a purple dab of typewriter ink gave him a peculiarly villainous and stealthy expression.

"They're here," he said, "two of 'em, and that crazy Stuart wasn't on, and said you were somewhere in the building."

A door slammed outside, followed by steps on the uncarpeted outer office.

"This way," said Blobs, in a husky undertone, and darting into a lavatory threw open a door that I had always supposed locked. Thence into a back hall piled high with boxes and past the presses of a bookbindery to the freight elevator.

Greatly to Blobs's disappointment there was no pursuit. I was exhilarated but out of breath when we emerged into an alleyway, and the sharp daylight shone on Blobs's excited face.

"Great sport, isn't it?" I panted, dropping a dollar into his palm, inked to correspond with his face. "Regular walkaway in the hundred-yard dash."

"Gimme two dollars more and I'll drop 'em down the elevator shaft," he suggested ferociously. I left him there with his bloodthirsty schemes and started for the station. I had a tendency to look behind me now and then, but I reached the station unnoticed. The afternoon was hot, the train rolled slowly along, stopping to pant at sweltering stations, from whose roofs the heat rose in waves. But I noticed these things objectively, not subjectively, for at the end of the journey was a girl with blue eyes and bright brown hair, hair that could hang loose around her shoulders or be twisted up into little coils of delight.

27

I TELEPHONED as soon as I reached my hotel, and I had not known how much I had hoped from seeing her until I learned that she was out of town. I hung up the receiver, almost dizzy with disappointment, and it was fully five minutes before I thought of calling up again and asking if she was within telephone reach. It seemed she was down on the bay staying with the Samuel Forbeses.

Sammy Forbes! It was a name to conjure with just then. In the old days at college I had rather flouted him, but now I was ready to take him to my heart. I remembered that he had always meant well, anyhow, and that he was explosively generous. I called him up.

"By the fumes of gasoline!" he said, when I told him who I was. "Blakeley, the Fount of Wisdom against Woman! Blakeley, the Great Unkissed! Welcome to our city!"

Whereupon he proceeded to urge me to come down to the Shack, and to say that I was an agreeable surprise because four times in two hours youths had called up to ask if Alison West was stopping with him, and to suggest that they had a vacant day or two.

"Oh—Miss West!" I shouted politely. There was a buzzing on the line. "Is she there?"

Sam had no suspicions. Was not I, in his mind, always the Great Un-kissed?—which sounds like the Great Unwashed and is even more of a re-proach. He asked me down promptly, as I had hoped, and thrust aside my objections.

"Nonsense," he said. "Bring yourself. The lady that keeps my boarding-house is calling me to insist. You remember Dorothy, don't you, Dorothy Browne? She says unless you have lost your figure you can wear my clothes all right. All you need here is a bathing suit for daytime and a dinner coat for evening."

"It sounds cool," I temporized. "If you are sure I won't put you out—very well, Sam, since you and your wife are good enough. I have a couple of days free. Give my love to Dorothy until I can do it myself."

Sam met me himself and drove me out to the Shack, which proved to be a substantial house overlooking the water. On the way he confided to me that lots of married men thought they were contented when they were merely resigned, but that it was the only life, and that Sam Junior could swim like a duck. Incidentally he said that Alison was his wife's cousin, their respective grandmothers having at proper intervals married the same man, and that Alison would lose her good looks if she was not careful.

"I say she's worried, and I stick to it," he said, as he prepared to get out of the car. "You know her, and she's the kind of girl you think you can read like a book. But you can't; don't fool yourself. Take a good look at her at dinner, Blake. You won't lose your head like the other fellows. And then tell me what's wrong with her. We're mighty fond of Allie."

He went ponderously up the steps, for Sam had put on weight since I knew him. At the door he turned around. "Do you happen to know the MacLures at Seal Harbor?" he asked irrelevantly, but Mrs. Sam came into the hall just then, both hands out to greet me, and, whatever Forbes had meant to say, he did not pick up the subject again.

"We are having tea in here," Dorothy said gaily, indicating the door behind her. "Tea by courtesy, because I think tea is the only beverage that isn't represented. And then we must dress, for this is hop night at the club."

"Which is as great a misnomer as the tea," Sam put in. "It's bridge night, and the only hops are in the beer."

He was still gurgling over this as he took me upstairs. He showed me my room himself, and then began the fruitless search for evening raiment that kept me home that night from the club. For I couldn't wear Sam's clothes. That was clear, after a perspiring séance of a half hour.

"I won't do it, Sam," I said, when I had draped his dress coat on me toga fashion. "Who am I to have clothing to spare like this, when many a poor chap hasn't even a cellar door to cover him? I won't do it. I'm selfish, but not that selfish."

"Lord," he said, wiping his face, "how you've kept your figure! I can't wear a belt any more; got to have suspenders."

He reflected over his grievance for some time, sitting on the side of the bed. "You *could* go as you are," he said finally. "We do it all the time, only tonight happens to be the annual something or other, and—" He trailed off into silence, trying to buckle my belt around him. "A good six inches," he sighed. "I never get into a car any more that I don't expect to hear a spring snap. Well, Allie isn't going either. She turned down Granger this afternoon, the Annapolis fellow you met on the stairs—pigeon-breasted chap—and she always gets a headache on those occasions."

He got up heavily and went to the door. "Granger is leaving," he said. "I may be able to get his dinner coat for you. How well do you know her?" he asked, with his hand on the knob.

"If you mean Dolly—"

"Alison."

"Fairly well," I said cautiously. "Not as well as I would like to. I dined with her last week in Washington. And—I knew her before that."

Forbes touched the bell instead of going out, and told the servant who answered to see if Mr. Granger's suitcase had gone. If not, to bring it across the hall. Then he came back to his former position on the bed.

"You see, we feel responsible for Allie—near relation and all that," he began pompously. "And we can't talk to the people here at the house—all the men are in love with her, and all the women are jealous. Then there's a lot of money, too, or will be."

"Damn the money!" I muttered. "That is—nothing, Sam. Razor slipped."

"I can tell you," he went on, "because you don't lose your head over every pretty face, although Allie is more than that, of course. But about a month ago she went to Seal Harbor to visit Janet MacLure. Know her?"

"No."

"She came home to Richmond yesterday, and then came down here— Allie, I mean. And yesterday afternoon Dolly had a letter from Janet saying that she was disappointed not to have had Alison there, that she had promised them a two weeks' visit! What do you make of that? And that isn't the worst. Allie herself wasn't in the room, but there were eight other women, and because Dolly had atropine in her eyes to get some glasses fitted and couldn't see anything nearer than across the room, someone read the letter aloud to her, and the whole story is out. One of the cats told Granger and the boy proposed to Allie today, to show her he didn't care a tinker's damn where she had been."

"Good boy!" I said, with enthusiasm. I liked the Granger fellow, since he was out of the running. But Sam was looking at me with suspicion.

"Blake," he said, "if I didn't know you for what you are, I'd say you were interested there yourself."

Being so near her, under the same roof with even the tie of a dubious secret between us, was making me heady. I pushed Forbes toward the door.

"I interested!" I retorted, holding him by the shoulders. "There isn't a word in your vocabulary to fit my condition. I am an island in a sunlit sea of emotion, Sam, a—an empty place surrounded by longing—a—"

"An empty place surrounded by longing!" he retorted. "You want your dinner, that's what's the matter with you."

I shut the door on him then. He seemed suddenly sordid. Dinner! I thought. Although, as a matter of fact, I made a very fair meal when, Granger's suitcase *not* having gone, in his coat and some other man's trousers I was finally fit for the amenities. Alison did not come down to dinner, so it was clear she would not go to the clubhouse dance. I pleaded my injured arm and a fictitious, vaguely located sprain from the wreck as an excuse for remaining at home. Sam regaled the table with accounts of my distrust of women, my one love affair—with Dorothy; to which I responded, as was expected, that only my failure there had kept me single all these years, and that if Sam would be mysteriously missing during the bathing hour tomorrow, and so on.

And when the endless meal was over, and yards of veils had been tied over pretty heads and some eight ensembles with their abject complements had been packed into three automobiles and a trap, I drew a long breath and faced about. I had just then only one object in life, to find Alison, to assure her of my absolute faith and confidence in her, and to offer my help and my poor self, if she would let me, in her service.

She was not easy to find. I searched the lower floor, the verandas and the grounds, circumspectly. Then I ran into a little English girl who turned out to be her maid, and who also was searching. She was concerned because her mistress had had no dinner, and because the tray of food she carried would soon be cold. I took the tray from her, on the glimpse of something white on the shore, and that was how I found her again.

She was sitting on an overturned boat, her chin in her hands, and staring out to sea. The soft tide of the bay lapped almost at her feet, and the draperies of her white gown melted hazily into the sands. She looked like a wraith, a despondent phantom of the sea, although the adjective is redundant. Nobody ever thinks of a cheerful phantom. Strangely enough considering her evident depression, she was whistling softly to herself, over and over, some dreary little minor air that sounded like a dirge. She glanced up quickly when I made a misstep and my dishes jingled. All considered the tray was out of the picture: the sea, the misty starlight, the girl, even the sad little whistle that stopped now and then to go bravely on again. And then I came, accompanied by a tray of little silver dishes that jingled and an unmistakable odor of broiled chicken.

"Oh!" she said quickly; and then, "Oh! I thought you were Jenkins."

"*Timeo Danaos*—what's the rest of it?" I asked, tendering my offering. "You didn't have any dinner, you know." I sat down beside her. "See, I'll be the table. What was the old fairy tale? 'Little goat bleat: little table appear!' I'm perfectly willing to be the goat too."

She was laughing rather shakily.

"We never *do* meet like other people, do we?" she asked. "We really ought to shake hands and say how are you."

"I don't want to meet you like other people, and I suppose you always think of me as wearing the other fellow's clothes," I said. "I'm doing it again: I don't seem to be able to help it. These are Granger's that I have on now."

She threw back her head and laughed again, cheerfully this time.

"It's so ridiculous," she said, "and you have never seen me when I wasn't eating! It's too prosaic!"

"Which reminds me that the chicken is getting cold, and the ice warm," I suggested. "At the time I thought there could be no place better than the farmhouse kitchen, but this is. I ordered all this for something I want to say to you—the sea, the sand, the stars."

"How alliterative you are!" she said, trying to be flippant. "You are not to say anything until I have had my supper. Look how the things are spilled around!"

But she ate nothing, after all, and pretty soon I put the tray down in the sand. I said little. There was no hurry. We were together, and time meant nothing against that agelong wash of the sea. The air blew her hair in small damp curls against her face, and little by little the tide retreated, leaving our boat an oasis in a waste of gray sand.

> "If seven maids with seven mops
> 　　swept it for half a year,
> Do you suppose, the walrus said,
> 　　that they could get it clear?"

she threw at me once when she must have known I was going to speak. I held her hand, and as long as I merely held it she let it lie warm in mine. But when I raised it to my lips and kissed the soft open palm she drew it away without displeasure.

"Not that, please," she protested, and fell to whistling softly again, her chin in her hands. "I can't sing," she said, to break an awkward pause, "and so when I'm fidgety or have something on my mind I whistle. I hope you don't dislike it?"

"I love it," I asserted warmly. I did; when she pursed her lips like that I was mad to kiss them.

"I saw you at the station," she said suddenly. "You were in a hurry to go." I didn't say anything, and after a pause she drew a long breath. "Men are queer, aren't they?" she said, and fell to whistling again.

After a while she sat up as if she had made a resolution. "I am going to confess something," she announced suddenly. "You said, you know, that you had ordered all this for something you wanted to say to me. But the fact is, I fixed it all. Came here, I mean, because I knew you would come, and I had something to tell you. It was such a miserable thing that I needed the accessories to help me out."

"I don't want to hear anything that bothers you to tell," I assured her. "I didn't come here to force your confidence, Alison. I came because I couldn't help it." She did not object to my use of her name.

"Have you found your papers?" she asked, looking directly at me for almost the first time.

"Not yet. We hope to."

"The police have not interfered with you?"

"They haven't had any opportunity," I equivocated. "You needn't distress yourself about that, anyhow."

"But I do. I wonder why you still believe in me? Nobody else does."

"I wonder," I repeated, "why I do!"

"If you produced Harry Sullivan," she was saying, partly to herself, "and if you could connect him with Andy Bronson, and get a full account of why he was on the train and all that, it would help, wouldn't it?"

I acknowledged that it would. Now that the whole truth was almost in my possession I was stricken with the old cowardice. I did not want to know what she might tell me. The yellow line on the horizon, where the moon was coming up, was a broken bit of golden chain, my heel in the sand was again pressed on a woman's yielding fingers. I pulled myself together with a jerk.

"In order that what you might tell may help me, if it will," I said constrainedly, "it would be necessary perhaps that you tell it to the police. Since they have found the end of the necklace—"

"The end of the necklace?" she repeated slowly. "What about the end of the necklace?"

I stared at her. "Don't you remember"—I leaned forward—"the end of the cameo necklace, the part that was broken off, and was found in the black sealskin bag, stained with blood?"

"Blood?" she said dully. "You mean that *you* found the broken end? And then you had my little purse and you saw the necklace in it, and you must have thought—"

"I didn't think anything," I hastened to assure her. "I tell you, Alison, I never thought of anything but that you were unhappy, and that I had no right to help you. God knows, I thought you didn't want me to help you."

She held out her hand to me and I took it between both of mine. No word of love had passed between us, but I felt that she knew and understood. It was one of the moments that come seldom in a lifetime and then only in great crises, a moment of perfect understanding and trust.

Then she drew her hand away and sat, erect and determined, her fingers laced in her lap. As she talked the moon came up slowly and threw its bright pathway across the water. Back of us, in the trees beyond the sea wall, a sleepy bird chirruped drowsily, and a wave larger and bolder than its brothers sped up the sand, bringing the moon's silver to our very feet. I bent toward her.

"I am going to ask just one question."

"Anything you like." Her voice was almost dreary.

"Was it because of anything you are going to tell me that you refused Richey?"

She drew her breath in sharply.

"No," she said, without looking at me. "No. That was not the reason."

28

SHE TOLD HER story evenly, with her eyes on the water. Only now and then, when I, too, sat looking seaward, I thought she glanced at me furtively. And once, in the middle of it, she stopped altogether.

"You don't realize it, probably," she protested, "but you rather scare me. Your face is dreadful."

"I'll turn my back if it will help any," I said. "But if you expect me to look anything but murderous, you don't know what I am going through. That's all."

The story of her meeting with the Curtis woman was brief enough. They had met in Rome first, where Alison and her mother had taken a villa for a year. Mrs. Curtis had hovered on the ragged edges of society there, pleading the poverty of the South since the war as a reason for not going out more. There was talk of a brother, but Alison had not seen him and after a scandal which implicated Mrs. Curtis and a young attaché of the Austrian embassy Alison had been forbidden to see her.

"The women had never liked her, anyhow," she said. "She did unconventional things, and they are very conventional there. And they said she did not always pay her gambling debts. I thought they didn't like her because she was poor and popular with men. Then we came home and I almost forgot her, but last spring when Mother was not well—she had taken Grandfather to the Riviera, and it always uses her up—we went to Virginia Hot Springs and we met them there, the brother too this time. His name was Sullivan, Henry Pinckney Sullivan."

"I know. Go on."

"Mother had a nurse, so I was alone a great deal, and they were very kind to me. I saw a lot of them. The brother rather attracted me, partly because he didn't make love to me. He even seemed to avoid me, and I was piqued. I had been spoiled, I suppose. Most of the other men I knew had—"

"I know that too," I said bitterly, and moved away from her a trifle. I was brutal, but the whole story was a long torture. I think she knew what I was suffering, for she showed no resentment.

"It was early and there were few people around—none that I cared about. Mother and the nurse played cribbage eternally, until I felt as though the little pegs were driven into my brain. And when Mrs. Curtis arranged drives and picnics, I slipped away and went. I suppose you won't believe me, but I had never done that kind of thing before, and I—well, I've paid up, I think."

"What sort of looking chap was Sullivan?" I demanded. I had got up and was pacing back and forward on the sand. I remember kicking savagely at a bit of water-soaked board that lay in my way.

"As large as you are, but fair, and even more erect. He was supposed to be handsome."

I drew my shoulders up sharply. I am straight enough, but I was fairly sagging with jealous rage.

"When Mother began to get around somebody told her that I had been going about with Mrs. Curtis and her brother, and we had a dreadful time. I was dragged home like a bad child. Did anybody ever do that to you?"

"Nobody ever cared. I was born an orphan," I said, with a cheerless attempt at levity. "Go on."

"If Mrs. Curtis knew, she never said anything. She wrote me charming letters and in the summer, when they went to Cresson, she asked me to visit her there. I was too proud to let her know that I couldn't go where I wanted, and so I sent Polly, my maid, to her aunt's in the country, pretended to go to Seal Harbor, and really went to Cresson. You see, I warned you it would be an unpleasant story."

I went over and stood in front of her. All the accumulated jealousy of the past few weeks had been fired by what she told me. If Sullivan had come across the sands just then I think I would have strangled him with my hands, out of pure hate.

"Did you marry him?" I demanded. My voice sounded hoarse and strange in my ears. "That's all I want to know. Did you marry him?"

"No."

I drew a long breath.

"But you cared about him?"

She hesitated.

"No," she said finally. "I did not care about him."

I sat down on the edge of the boat and mopped my hot face. I was heartily ashamed of myself, and mingled with my abasement was a great relief. If she had not married him and had not cared for him, nothing else was of any importance.

"I was sorry, of course, the moment the train had started. But I had wired I was coming and I couldn't go back. Then when I got there, the place was charming. There were no neighbors, but we fished and rode and motored, and—it was moonlight, like this."

I put my hand over both of hers, clasped in her lap. "I know," I acknowledged repentantly, "and people do queer things when it is moonlight. The moon has got me tonight, Alison. If I am a boor, remember that, won't you?"

Her fingers lay quiet under mine. "And so," she went on with a little sigh, "I began to think perhaps I cared. But all the time I felt that there was something not quite right. Now and then Mrs. Curtis would say or do something that gave me a queer start, as if she had dropped a mask for a moment. And there was trouble with the servants. They were almost insolent. I couldn't understand. I don't know when it dawned on me that old Baron Cavalcanti in Rome had been right when he said they were not my kind of people. But I wanted to get away, wanted it desperately."

"Of course they were not your kind," I said dryly. "The man was married. The girl Jennie, a housemaid, was a spy in Mrs. Sullivan's employ. Not only that but the man he murdered, Harrington, was his wife's father. And I'll see him hang by the neck yet if it takes every energy and every penny I possess."

I could have told her more gently, have broken the shock for her. I have never been proud of that evening on the sand. I was alternately a boor and a ruffian, like a hurt youngster who passes the blow that has hurt him on to his playmate, that both may bawl together. And now Alison sat, white and cold, without speech.

"Married?" she said finally, in a small voice. "Why, I don't think it is possible, is it? I was on my way to Baltimore to marry him myself when the wreck came."

"But you said you didn't care for him!" I protested, my heavy masculine mind unable to jump the gaps in her story. And then without any warning I realized she was crying. She shook off my hand and fumbled for her handkerchief, and failing to find it accepted the one I thrust into her fingers.

Then little by little she told me, a sordid story of a motor trip in the mountains without Mrs. Curtis, of a lost road and a broken car, and a rainy night when she and Sullivan tramped eternally and did not get home. And of Mrs. Curtis, when they got home at dawn, suddenly grown conventional and deeply shocked.

But here she looked at me frankly.

"It was silly, of course, in this day and age. But she was southern and—well, I suppose I was still infatuated. I wasn't really normal again until I got into that dreadful train."

She began to realize then what she was doing, she explained. She made up her mind she wouldn't marry him. She was all set for a scene with him the next morning. And then he simply disappeared.

"It was the most incredible relief," she said, and began to cry again.

"Please don't," I protested unsteadily. "I won't be responsible if you keep on like this. I may forget that I have a capital charge hanging over my head, and that I may be arrested at any moment."

That brought her out of the handkerchief at once. "I meant to be so helpful," she said, "and I've thought of nothing but myself! There are some things I meant to tell you. If Jennie was what you say, then I understand why she came to me just before I left. She had been packing my things and she must have seen what condition I was in, for she came over to me when I was getting my wraps on to leave, and said, 'Don't do it, Miss West, I beg you don't do it. You'll be sorry ever after.' And just then Mrs. Curtis came in and Jennie slipped out."

"That was all?"

"No. As we went through the station the telegraph operator gave Harry a message. He read it on the platform, and it excited him terribly. He took his sister aside and they talked together. He was white with either fear or anger, I don't know which. Then, when we boarded the train, a woman in black, with beautiful hair, who was standing on the car platform, touched him on the arm and then drew back. He looked at her and glanced away again, but she acted as if he had struck her."

"Then what?" The situation was growing clearer.

"Mrs. Curtis and I had the drawing room. I had a dreadful night, just sleeping a little now and then. I dreaded to see daylight come. Then when we found Harry had disappeared in the night, Mrs. Curtis was in a frenzy. Later on, I saw his cigarette case in your hand. I had given it to him. You wore his clothes. The murder was discovered and you were accused of it! What could I do? And then afterward, when I found him asleep at the farmhouse, I was panic-stricken. I locked him in and ran. I didn't know why he did it, but he had killed that man."

Someone was calling Alison through a megaphone from the veranda. It sounded like Sam. "All-ee!" he called. "All-ee! We're home. Come on up." Neither of us listened.

"I wonder," I reflected, "if you would be willing to repeat a part of that story—just from the telegram on—to a couple of detectives, say on Monday. If you would tell that, and how the end of your necklace got into the sealskin bag—"

"My necklace!" she repeated. "But it isn't mine. I picked it up in the car."

"All-ee!" Sam again. "I see you down there. I'm making a julep!"

Alison turned and called through her hands. "Coming in a moment, Sam," she said, and rose. "It must be very late: they're back. We'd better go back to the house."

"Don't," I begged her. "Juleps and Sam will go on forever, and I have you such a little time. I suppose I am only one of a dozen or so, but—you are the only girl in the world for me. I suppose you know that."

Sam was whistling, an irritating bird call, over and over. She pursed her red lips and answered him in kind. It was more than I could endure.

"Sam or no Sam," I said firmly, "I am going to kiss you!"

But Sam's voice came strident through the megaphone. "Be good, you two," he bellowed, "I've got the binoculars!" And so, under fire, so to speak, we walked sedately back to the house. My pulses were throbbing. The little swish of her long dress beside me on the grass was pain and ecstasy. I had but to put out my hand to touch her, and I hadn't the courage to do it.

Sam, armed with megaphone and field glasses, bent over the rail and watched us with gleeful malignity.

"Home early, aren't you?" Alison called, when we reached the steps.

"Left my partner in a two-bid original, and she broke up the game," he said cheerfully. "Lost forty dollars. Come on in."

Three hours later I went up to bed. I had not seen Alison alone again. The noise was at its height below and I glanced down into the garden, still bright in the moonlight. Leaning against a tree and staring interestedly into the billiard room was Johnson.

29

THAT WAS SATURDAY NIGHT, two weeks after the wreck. The previous five days had been full of swift-moving events: the woman in the house next door, the picture in the theater of a man about to leap from the doomed train, the dinner at the Dallas home, and Richey's discovery that Alison was the girl in the case. In quick succession had come our visit to the Carter place, the finding of the rest of the telegram, my seeing Alison there, and the strange interview with Mrs. Conway. The Cresson trip stood out in my memory for its seriocomic horrors and its one real thrill. Then the discovery by the police of the sealskin bag and the bit of chain, Hotchkiss triumphantly producing Stuart for Sullivan and his subsequent discomfiture, McKnight at the station with Alison, and later the confession that he was out of the running.

And yet, when I thought it all over, the entire week and its events were two sides of a triangle that was narrowing rapidly to an apex, a point. And the said apex was at that moment in the drive below my window, resting his long legs by sitting on a carriage block, and smoking a pipe that probably made the night hideous. The sense of the ridiculous is very close to the sense of tragedy. I opened my screen and whistled, and Johnson looked up and grinned. We said nothing. I held up a handful of cigars, he extended his hat, and when I finally went to sleep it was to a soothing breeze that wafted in salt air and a faint aroma of good tobacco. I was thoroughly tired, but I slept restlessly, to be roused about dawn by a light rap at the door. Opening it I found Forbes, in a pair of trousers and a pajama coat. He was as pleasant as most fleshy people are when they have to get up at night, and he said the telephone had been ringing for an hour, and he didn't know why somebody else in the blankety-blank house couldn't have heard it. *He* wouldn't get to sleep until noon.

As he was palpably asleep on his feet, I left him grumbling and went to the telephone. It proved to be Richey, who had found me by the simple expedient of tracing Alison, and he was jubilant.

"You'll have to come back," he said. "Got a railroad schedule there?"

"I don't sleep with one in my pocket," I retorted, "but if you'll hold the line I'll call out the window to Johnson. He's probably got one."

"Johnson!" I could hear the laugh with which McKnight comprehended the situation. He was still chuckling when I came back.

"Train to Richmond at six-thirty A.M.," I said. "What time is it now?"

"Four. Listen, Laurie. We've got him. Do you hear? Through the woman at Baltimore. Then the other woman, the lady of the restaurant"—he was obviously avoiding names—"is playing our cards for us. No, I don't know why, and I don't care. But you be at my place tonight at eight o'clock. If you can't shake Johnson, bring him, damn him."

To this day I believe the Sam Forbeses have not recovered from the surprise of my unexpected arrival, my one appearance at dinner in Granger's clothes, and the note on my dresser which informed them the next morning that I had folded my tents like the Arabs and silently stolen away. For at half after five Johnson and I, the former as uninquisitive as ever, were on our way through the dust to the station, three miles away, and by four that afternoon we were in Washington. The journey had been uneventful. Johnson relaxed under the influence of my tobacco, and spoke at some length on the latest improvements in electric chairs. I remember, too, that he mentioned the curious anomaly that permits a man about to be hanged to eat a hearty meal. I did not enjoy my dinner that night.

Before we got into Washington I had made arrangements with Johnson to surrender myself at two the following afternoon. Also I had wired to Alison, asking her if she would do what I had asked the night before. Johnson saw me home, and rather casually left me there.

Mrs. Klopton received me with dignified reserve. The very tone in which she asked me when I would have dinner told me that something was wrong.

"What is it, Mrs. Klopton?" I demanded finally, when she had informed me, in a patient and long-suffering tone, that she felt worn out and thought she needed a rest.

"When I lived with Mr. Justice Springer," she began acidly, her mending basket in her hands, "it was an orderly, well-conducted household. You can ask any of the neighbors. Meals were cooked and, what's more, they were *eaten*; there was none of this 'here today and gone the next' business."

"Nonsense," I observed. "You're tired, that's all, Mrs. Klopton. And I wish you would go out; I need a bath."

She did not move.

"That's *not* all," she said with dignity, from the doorway. "Women coming and going here, women whose shoes I am not fit—I mean, women who are not fit to touch my shoes—coming here as insolent as you please and asking for you."

"Good God!" I exclaimed. "What did you tell them—her, whichever it was?"

"Told her you were sick in a hospital and wouldn't be out for a month," she said triumphantly. "And when she said she thought she'd come in and wait for you I slammed the door on her."

"What time was she here?"

"Late last night. And she had a light-haired man across the street. If she thought I didn't see him she don't know me." Then she closed the door and left me to my bath and my reflections.

At five minutes before eight I was at Richey's apartment, where I found Hotchkiss and McKnight. They were bending over a table, on which lay McKnight's total armament, a pair of pistols, an elephant gun, and an old cavalry saber.

"Draw up a chair and help yourself," he said, pointing to the arsenal. "This is for the benefit of our friend Hotchkiss here, who says he is a small man and fond of life."

Hotchkiss, who had been trying to get the wrong end of a cartridge into the barrel of one of the revolvers, straightened himself and mopped his face.

"We have desperate people to handle," he said pompously, "and we may need desperate means."

But they were serious enough, both of them, under it all, and when they had told me what they planned I was serious, too.

"You're compounding a felony," I remonstrated, when they had explained. "I'm not eager to be locked away, but if you intend to offer her the stolen notes in exchange for Sullivan—"

"We haven't got either of them, you know," McKnight remonstrated, "and we won't have if we don't start. Come along, Fido" to Hotchkiss.

The plan was simplicity itself. According to Hotchkiss, Sullivan was to meet Andy Bronson at Mrs. Conway's apartment at eight-thirty that night, with the notes. He was to be paid there and the papers destroyed. "But just before that interesting finale," McKnight ended, "we will walk in, take the notes, grab Sullivan, and give the police a jolt that will put them out for the count."

I suppose not one of us, slewing around corners in the car that night, had the faintest doubt that we were on the right track, or that Fate, scurvy enough before, was playing into our hands at last. Little Hotchkiss was in a state of fever. He alternately twitched and examined the revolver, and a fear that the two movements might be synchronous kept me uneasy. He produced and dilated on the scrap of pillow slip from the wreck, and showed me the stiletto, with its point in cotton batting for safekeeping. And in the intervals he implored Richey not to make such fine calculations at the corners.

We were all grave enough and very quiet, however, when we reached the large building where Mrs. Conway had her apartment. McKnight left the engine going, in case we might have to make a quick getaway, and Hotchkiss gave a final look at the revolver. I had no weapon. Somehow it all seemed melodramatic to the verge of farce. In the doorway Hotchkiss was a half dozen feet ahead and Richey fell back beside me. He dropped his affectation of gaiety, and I thought he looked tired.

"Same old Sam, I suppose?" he asked.

"Same, only more of him."

"I suppose Alison was there? How is she?" he inquired irrelevantly.

"Very well. I didn't see her this morning." Hotchkiss was waiting near the elevator, and McKnight put his hand on my arm. "Now look here, old man," he said, "I've got two arms and a gun, and you've got one arm and nothing but. If Hotchkiss is right, and there's a row, you crawl under a table."

"The hell I will!" I declared scornfully.

We crowded out of the elevator at the fourth floor, and found ourselves in a rather theatrical hallway of draperies and armor. It was very quiet. We stood uncertainly after the car had gone, and looked at the two or three doors in sight. They were heavy, covered with metal, and soundproof. From somewhere above there came the metallic sound of a radio in full blast, and through the open window we could hear—or feel—the throb of Richey's car.

"Well, Sherlock," McKnight said, "what's the next move in the game? Is it our jump or theirs? You brought us here."

None of us knew what to do next. No sound of conversation penetrated the heavy doors. We waited uneasily for some minutes, and Hotchkiss looked at his watch. Then he put it to his ear.

"Good gracious!" he exclaimed, his head cocked on one side. "I believe it has stopped. I'm afraid we are late."

We *were* late. My watch and Hotchkiss's agreed at nine o'clock, and with the discovery that our man might have come and gone our zest for the adventure began to flag. McKnight motioned us away from the door and rang the bell. There was no response, no sound within. He rang it twice, the second time long and vigorously, without result. Then he turned and looked at us.

"I don't half like this," he said. "That woman is in; you heard me ask the elevator boy. For two cents I'd—"

I had seen it when he did. The door was ajar about an inch, and a narrow wedge of rose-colored light showed beyond. I pushed the door a little and listened. Then with both men at my heels I stepped into the private corridor of the apartment and looked around. It was a square reception hall, with rugs on the floor, a tall mahogany rack for hats, and a couple of chairs. A lamp with a rose shade and a desk light over a writing table made it bright and cheerful. It was empty.

None of us was comfortable. The place was full of feminine trifles that made us feel the weakness of our position. Some such instinct made McKnight suggest division.

"We look like an invading army," he said. "If she's here alone we'll scare her into a fit. One of us could take a look around and—"

"What was that? Didn't you hear something?"

The sound, whatever it had been, was not repeated. We went awkwardly out into the hall, very uncomfortable, all of us, and flipped a coin. The choice fell to me, which was right enough, for the affair was primarily mine.

"Wait just inside the door," I directed, "and if Sullivan comes, or anybody that answers his description, grab him without ceremony and ask him questions afterwards."

The apartment, save the hall, was unlighted. By one of those freaks of arrangement possible only in the modern flat I found the kitchen first, and was struck a smart and unexpected blow by a swinging door. I carried a handful of matches, and by the time I had passed through a butler's pantry and a refrigerator room I was completely lost in the darkness. Until then the situation had been merely uncomfortable. Suddenly it became grisly. From somewhere near came a long-sustained groan, followed almost instantly by the crash of something—glass or china—on the floor.

I struck a fresh match, and found myself in a narrow rear hallway. Behind me was the door by which I must have come. With a keen desire to get back to the place I had started from I opened the door and attempted to cross the room. I thought I had kept my sense of direction, but I crashed without warning into what, from the resulting jangle, was a dining table probably laid for dinner. I cursed my stupidity in getting into such a situation, and cursed my nerves for making my hand shake when I tried to strike a match. The groan had not been repeated.

I braced myself against the table and struck the match sharply against the sole of my shoe. It flickered faintly and went out. And then, without the slightest warning, another dish went off the table. It fell with a thousand splinterings; the very air seemed broken into crashing waves of sound. I stood still, braced against the table, holding the red end of the dying match, and listened. I had not long to wait. The groan came again, and I recognized it, the cry of a dog in straits. I breathed again.

"Come, old fellow," I said. "Come on, old man. Let's have a look at you."

I could hear the thud of his tail on the floor, but he did not move. He only whimpered. There is something companionable in the presence of a dog, and I fancied this dog in trouble. Slowly I began to work my way around the table toward him.

"Good boy," I said, as he whimpered. "We'll find the light, which ought to be somewhere or other around here, and then—"

I stumbled over something, and I drew back my foot almost instantly. "Did I step on you, old boy?" I exclaimed, and bent to pat him. I remember straightening suddenly and hearing the dog pad softly toward me around the table. I recall even that I had put the matches down and could not find them. Then, with a bursting horror of the room and its contents, of the gibbering dark around me, I turned and made for the door by which I had entered.

I could not find it. I felt along endless wainscoting, past miles of wall. The dog was beside me, I think, but to my excited mind he was part and parcel now of the thing under the table. And when after aeons of search I found a knob and stumbled into the reception hall, I was as nearly in a panic as any man could be.

I was myself again in a second, and by the light from the hall I led the way back to the tragedy I had stumbled on. Andy Bronson still sat at the table, his elbows propped on it, his cigarette still lighted, burning a hole in the cloth. Partly under the table lay Mrs. Conway, face down. The dog stood over her and wagged his tail.

McKnight pointed silently to a large copper ash tray, filled with ashes and charred bits of paper.

"The notes, probably," he said ruefully. "He got them after all and burned them before her. It was more than she could stand. She stabbed him first and then herself."

Hotchkiss got up and took off his hat. "They are dead," he announced solemnly, and took his notebook out of his hatband.

McKnight and I did the only thing we could think of—drove Hotchkiss and the dog out of the room, and closed and locked the door. "It's a matter for the police," McKnight said flatly. "I suppose you've got an officer tied to you somewhere, Lawrence? You usually have."

We left Hotchkiss in charge and went downstairs. It was McKnight who first saw Johnson, leaning against a park railing across the street, and called him over. We told him in a few words what we had found, and he grinned at me cheerfully.

"After while, in a few weeks or months, Mr. Blakeley," he said, "when you get tired of monkeying around with the bloodstain and fingerprint specialist upstairs, you come to me. I've had that fellow you want under surveillance for ten days."

30

AT TEN MINUTES before two the following day, Monday, I arrived at my office. I had spent the morning putting my affairs in shape, and in a trip to the stable. The afternoon would see me either a free man or a prisoner for an indefinite length of time, and in spite of Johnson's promise to produce Sullivan I was more prepared for the latter than the former.

Blobs was watching for me outside the door, and it was clear that he was in a state of excitement bordering on delirium. He did nothing, however, save to tip me a wink that meant "as man to man, I'm for you." I was too much engrossed either to reprove him or return the courtesy, but I heard him follow me down the hall to the small room where we keep outgrown lawbooks, typewriter supplies and, incidentally, our coats and hats. I was wondering vaguely if I would ever hang my hat on its nail again when the door closed behind me. It shut firmly without any particular amount of sound, and I was left in the dark. I groped my way to it, irritably, to find it locked on the outside. I shook it frantically, and was rewarded by a sibilant whisper through the keyhole.

"Keep quiet," Blobs was saying huskily. "You're in deadly danger. The police are waiting in your office, three of 'em. I'm goin' to lock the whole bunch in and throw the key out the window."

"Come back here, you young devil!" I called furiously, but I could hear him speeding down the corridor, and the slam of the outer office door by which he always announced his presence. And so I stood there in that ridiculous closet, hot with the heat of a steaming September day, musty with the smell of old leather bindings, littered with broken overshoes and handleless umbrellas. I was apoplectic with rage, and it seemed an hour before Blobs came back.

He came without haste, strutting with new dignity, and paused outside my prison door.

"Well, I guess that will hold them for a while," he remarked comfortably, and proceeded to turn the key. "I've got 'em fastened up like sardines in a can," he explained, working with the lock. "Gee whiz, you'd ought to hear 'em!" When he got his breath after the shaking I gave him he began to splutter. "How'd I know?" he demanded sulkily. "You nearly broke your neck gettin' away the other time. And I haven't got the key anyhow. It's lost."

"Where's it lost?" I demanded, with another gesture toward his coat collar.

"Down the elevator shaft." There was a gleam of indignant satisfaction through his tears of rage and humiliation.

And so, while he hunted the key in the debris at the bottom of the shaft, I quieted his prisoners with the assurance that the lock had slipped, and that they would be free as soon as we could find the janitor with a passkey. Stuart went down finally and discovered Blobs, with the key in his pocket, telling the engineer how he had tried to save me from arrest and failed. When Stuart came up he was almost cheerful, but Blobs did not appear again that day.

Simultaneous with the finding of the key came Hotchkiss, and we went in together. I shook hands with two men who, with Hotchkiss, made a not very animated group. The taller one, an oldish man, lean and hard, announced his errand at once.

"A Pittsburgh warrant?" I inquired, unlocking my cigar drawer.

"Yes. Allegheny County has assumed jurisdiction, the exact locality where the crime was committed being in doubt." He seemed to be the spokesman. The other, shorter and rotund, kept an amiable silence. "We hope you will see the wisdom of waiving extradition," he went on. "It will save time."

"I'll come, of course," I agreed. "The sooner the better. But I want you to give me an hour here, gentlemen, I think we can interest you. Have a cigar?"

The lean man took a cigar. The rotund man took three, putting two in his pocket.

"How about the catch of that door?" he inquired jovially. "Any danger of it going off again?" Really, considering the circumstances, they were remarkably cheerful. Hotchkiss, however, was not. He paced the floor uneasily, his hands under his coattails. The arrival of McKnight created a diversion. He carried a long package and a corkscrew, and shook hands with the police and opened the bottle with almost a single gesture.

"I always want something to cheer me on these occasions," he said. "Where's the water, Blakeley? Everybody ready?" Then in French he toasted the two detectives.

"To your eternal discomfiture," he said, bowing ceremoniously. "May you go home and never come back! If you take Monsieur Blakeley with you, I hope you choke."

The lean man nodded gravely. "Prosit," he said. But the fat one leaned back and laughed consumedly.

Hotchkiss finished a mental synopsis of his position, and put down his glass. "Gentlemen," he said pompously, "within five minutes the man you want will be here, a murderer caught in a net of evidence so fine that a mosquito could not get through."

The detectives glanced at each other solemnly. Had they not in their possession a sealskin bag containing a wallet and a bit of gold chain which, by putting the crime on me, would leave a gap big enough for Sullivan himself to crawl through?

"Why don't you say your little speech before Johnson brings the other man, Lawrence?" McKnight inquired. "They won't believe you, but it will help them to understand what is coming."

"You understand, of course," the lean man put in gravely, "that what you say may be used against you."

"I'll take the risk," I answered impatiently.

It took some time to tell the story of my worse than useless trip to Pittsburgh and its sequel. They listened gravely, without interruption.

"Mr. Hotchkiss here," I finished, "believes that the man Sullivan, whom we are momentarily expecting, committed the crime. Mr. McKnight is inclined to implicate Mrs. Conway, who stabbed Bronson and then herself last night. As for myself, I am open to conviction."

"I hope not," said the stout detective quizzically. And then Alison was announced. My impulse to go out and meet her was forestalled by the detectives, who rose when I did. McKnight therefore brought her in, and I met her at the door.

"I have put you to a great deal of trouble," I said, when I saw her glance around the room. "I wish I could have saved you from it."

"Why shouldn't I come?" she replied, looking up at me. "I am the cause of most of it, I am afraid. Mrs. Dallas is going to wait in the outer office."

I presented Hotchkiss and the two detectives, who eyed her with interest.

In her poise, her beauty, even in her smart suit and hat I fancy she represented a new type to them. They remained standing until she sat down.

"I have brought the necklace," she began, holding out a white-wrapped
box, "as you asked me to."

I passed it, unopened, to the detectives. "The necklace from which was
broken the fragment you found in the sealskin bag," I explained. "Miss West
found it on the floor of the car, near lower ten."

"When did you find it?" asked the lean detective, bending forward.

"In the morning, not long before the wreck."

"Did you ever see it before?"

"I'm not certain," she replied. "I have seen one very much like it." Her
tone was troubled. She glanced at me as if for help, but I was powerless.

"Where?" The detective was watching her closely.

At that moment there came an interruption. The door opened without
ceremony and Johnson ushered in a tall blond man, a stranger to all of us.
I glanced at Alison; she was pale, but composed and scornful. She met the
newcomer's eyes full, and caught unawares he took a hasty backward step.

"Sit down, Mr. Sullivan," McKnight beamed cordially. "Have a cigar? I
beg your pardon, Alison, do you mind this smoke? Will you have a cigarette
yourself?"

"Not now, thanks," she said composedly. Sullivan had had a second to
sound his bearings.

"No—no, thanks," he mumbled. "If you will be good enough to explain—"

"But that's what you're to do," McKnight said cheerfully, pulling up a
chair. "You've got the most attractive audience you could ask. These two
gentlemen are detectives from Pittsburgh, and we are all curious to know the
finer details of what happened on the car Ontario two weeks ago, the night
your father-in-law was murdered." Sullivan gripped the arms of his chair. "We
are not prejudiced, either. The gentlemen from Pittsburgh are betting on
Mr. Blakeley, over there. Mr. Hotchkiss, the gentleman by the radiator, is
ready to place ten-to-one odds on you. And some of us have still other theories."

"Gentlemen," Sullivan said slowly, "I give you my word of honor that I
did not kill Simon Harrington, and that I do not know who did."

"Fiddlededee!" cried Hotchkiss, bustling forward. "Why, I can tell you—"
But McKnight pushed him firmly into a chair and held him there.

"I am ready to plead guilty to the larceny," Sullivan went on. "I took Mr.
Blakeley's clothes, I admit. If I can reimburse him in any way for the inconvenience—"

The stout detective was listening with his mouth open. "Do you mean to
say," he demanded, "that you got into Mr. Blakeley's berth, as he contends,
took his clothes and forged notes and left the train before the wreck?"

"Yes."

"The notes, then?"

"I gave them to Bronson yesterday. Much good they did him!" bitterly.

We were all silent for a moment. The two detectives were adjusting them-selves with difficulty to a new point of view. Sullivan was looking dejectedly at the floor, his hands hanging loose between his knees. I was watching Alison. From where I stood, behind her, I could almost touch the soft hair behind her ear.

"I have no intention of pressing any charge against you," I said with forced civility, for my hands were itching to get at him, "if you will give us a clear account of what happened on the Ontario that night."

Sullivan raised his handsome, haggard head and looked around at me. "I've seen you before, haven't I?" he asked. "Weren't you at the Laurels a few days—or nights—ago? The cat, you remember, and the rug that slipped?"

"I remember," I said shortly. He glanced from me to Alison and quickly away.

"The truth can't hurt me," he said, "but it's devilish unpleasant. Alison, you know all this. You'd better go out."

His use of her name crazed me. I stepped in front of her and stood over him. "You will not bring Miss West into the conversation," I threatened, "and she will stay if she wishes."

"Oh, very well," he said with assumed indifference.

Hotchkiss just then escaped from Richey's grasp and crossed the room. "Did you ever wear glasses?" he asked eagerly.

"Never." Sullivan glanced with some contempt at mine.

"I'd better begin by going back a little," he went on sullenly. "I suppose you know I was married to Ida Harrington about five years ago. She was a good girl, and I thought a lot of her. But her father opposed the marriage. He'd never liked me, and he refused to make any sort of settlement.

"I'd thought of course that there would be money, and it was a bad day when I found out I'd made a mistake. My sister was wild with disappoint-ment. We were pretty hard up, my sister and I."

I was watching Alison. Her hands were tightly clasped in her lap, and she was staring out the window at the cheerless roof below. She had set her lips a little, but that was all.

"You understand, of course, that I'm not defending myself," went on the sullen voice. "The day came when old Harrington put us both out of the house and I threatened—I suppose you know that, too—I threatened to kill him.

"My sister and I had hard times after that. We lived on the Continent for a while. I was at Monte Carlo and she was in Italy. She met a young lady there, the granddaughter of a steel manufacturer and an heiress, and she sent for me. When I got to Rome the girl was gone. Last winter I was all in. I'd been social secretary to an Englishman, a wholesale grocer with a new title, but we had a row and I came home. I went out to the Heaton boys' ranch in Wyoming and met Bronson there. He lent me money, and I've been doing his dirty work ever since."

Sullivan got up then and walked slowly forward and back as he talked, his eyes on the faded pattern of the office rug.

"If you want to live in hell," he said savagely, "put yourself in another man's power. Bronson got into trouble, forging John Gilmore's name to those notes, and in some way he learned that a man was bringing the papers back to Washington on the Flier. He even learned the number of his berth, and the night before the wreck, just as I was boarding the train, I got a telegram."

Hotchkiss stepped forward once more importantly.

"Which read, I think: 'Man with papers in lower ten, car seven. Get them.'"

Sullivan looked at the little man with sulky blue eyes.

"It was something like that, anyhow. But it was a nasty business, and it made matters worse that he didn't care that a telegram which must pass through a half dozen hands was more or less incriminating to me.

"Then, to add to the unpleasantness of my position, just after we boarded the train—I was accompanying my sister and this young lady, Miss West— a woman touched me on the sleeve, and I turned to face my wife!

"That took away my last bit of nerve. I told my sister, and you can understand she was in a bad way too. We knew what it meant. Ida had heard that I was going—"

He stopped and glanced uneasily at Alison.

"Go on," she said coldly. "It is too late to protect me. The time to have done that was when I was your guest."

"Well," he went on, his eyes turned carefully away from my face, which must have presented certainly anything but a pleasant sight, "Miss West was going to do me the honor to marry me and—"

I made a move toward him, and one of the detectives got up and stood between us.

"You must remember, Mr. Blakeley, that you are forcing this story from this man. These details are unpleasant but important. You were going to marry this young lady," he said, turning to Sullivan, "although you already had a wife living?"

"It was my sister's plan. We were in a bad way for money, and if I could marry secretly a wealthy girl and go to Europe it was unlikely that Ida— that is, Mrs. Sullivan—would hear of it.

"So it was more than a shock to see my wife on the train, and to realize from her face that she knew what was going on. I don't know yet, unless some of the servants—well, never mind that.

"It meant that the whole thing had gone up. Old Harrington had carried a gun for me for years, and the same train wouldn't hold both of us. Of course I thought he was in the coach just behind ours."

Hotchkiss was leaning forward now, his eyes narrowed, his thin lips drawn to a line.

"Are you left-handed, Mr. Sullivan?" he asked.

Sullivan stopped in surprise.

"No," he said gruffly. "Can't do anything with my left hand." Hotchkiss subsided, crestfallen but alert. "I tore up that cursed telegram, but I was afraid to throw the scraps away. Then I looked around for lower ten. It was almost exactly across. My berth was lower seven, and it was of course a bit of exceptional luck for me that the car was number seven."

"Did you tell your sister of the telegram from Bronson?" I asked.

"No. It would do no good, and she was in a bad way without that to make her worse."

"Your sister was killed, I think." The shorter detective took a small package from his pocket and held it in his hand, snapping the rubber band which held it.

"Yes, she was killed," Sullivan said soberly. "What I say now can do her no harm."

He stopped to push back the heavy hair that dropped over his forehead, and went on more connectedly:

"It was late, after midnight, and we went at once to our berths. I undressed, and then I lay there for an hour, wondering how I was going to get the notes. Someone in lower nine was restless and wide awake, but finally became quiet.

"The man in lower ten was sleeping heavily. I could hear his breathing, and it seemed to be only a question of getting across and behind the curtains of his berth without being seen. After that, it was a mere matter of quiet searching.

"The car became very still. I was about to try for the other berth when someone brushed softly past and I lay back again.

"Finally, however, when things had been quiet for a time I got up, and after looking along the aisle I slipped behind the curtains of lower ten. You understand, Mr. Blakeley, that I thought you were in lower ten, with the notes."

I nodded curtly.

"I'm not trying to defend myself," he went on. "I was ready to steal the notes—I had to. But murder!"

He wiped his forehead with his handkerchief.

"Well, I slipped across and behind the curtains. It was very still. The man in ten didn't move, although my heart was thumping until I thought he would hear it.

"I felt around cautiously. It was perfectly dark, and I came across a bit of chain, about as long as my finger. It seemed a queer thing to find there, and it was sticky too."

He shuddered, and I could see Alison's hands clenching and unclenching with the strain.

"All at once, it struck me that the man was strangely silent, and I think I lost my nerve. Anyhow I drew the curtains open a little, and let the light fall on my hands. They were red, blood-red."

He leaned one hand on the back of the chair and was silent for a moment, as though he lived over again the awful events of that more than awful night.

The stout detective had let his cigar go out. He was still drawing at it nervously. Richey had picked up a paperweight and was tossing it from hand to hand; when it slipped and fell to the floor, a startled shudder passed through the room.

"There was something glittering in there," Sullivan resumed, "and on impulse I picked it up. Then I dropped the curtains and stumbled back to my own berth."

"Where you wiped your hands on the bedclothes and stuck the dirk under the pillow." Hotchkiss was seeing his carefully built structure crumbling to pieces, and he looked chagrined.

"I suppose I did. I'm not very clear about what happened then. But when I rallied a little I saw a Russia leather wallet lying in the aisle almost at my feet, and like a fool I stuck it with the bit of chain into my bag.

"I sat there, shivering, for what seemed hours. It was still perfectly quiet, except for someone snoring. I thought that would drive me crazy.

"The more I thought of it the worse things looked. The telegram was the first thing against me. It would put the police on my track at once when it was discovered that the man in lower ten had been killed.

"Then I remembered the notes, and I took out the wallet and opened it."

He stopped for a minute, as if the recalling of the next occurrence was almost beyond him.

"I took out the wallet," he said simply, "and opening it held it to the light. In gilt letters was the name 'Simon Harrington.'"

The detectives were leaning forward now, their eyes on his face.

"Things seemed to whirl around for a while. I sat there almost paralyzed, wondering what this new development meant for me. My wife, I knew, would swear I had killed her father. Nobody would be likely to believe the truth.

"Do you believe me now?" He looked around at us defiantly. "I am telling the absolute truth, and not one of you believes me!

"After a bit the man in lower nine got up and walked along the aisle toward the smoking compartment. I heard him go, and leaning from my berth watched him out of sight.

"It was then I got the idea of changing berths with him, getting into his clothes, and leaving the train. I give you my word I had no idea of throwing suspicion on him."

Alison looked scornfully incredulous, but I felt that the man was telling the truth.

"I changed the numbers of the berths, and it worked well. I got into the other man's berth, and he came back to mine. The rest was easy. I dressed in his clothes—luckily, they fitted—and jumped the train as it slowed down not far from Baltimore, just before the wreck."

"There is something else you must clear up," I said. "Why did you try to telephone me from M——, and why did you change your mind about the message?"

He looked astounded.

"You knew I was in M——?" he stammered.

"Yes, we traced you. What about the message?"

"Well, it was this way: of course I didn't know your name, Mr. Blakeley. The telegram said, 'Man with papers in lower ten, car seven,' and after I had made what I considered my escape, I began to think I had left the man in my berth in a bad way.

"He would probably be accused of the crime. So, although when the wreck occurred I supposed everyone connected with the affair had been killed, there was a chance that you had survived. I've not been of much account, but I didn't want a man to swing because I'd left him in my place. Besides, I began to have a theory of my own.

"As we entered the car a tall dark woman passed us with a glass of water in her hand, and I vaguely remembered her. She was amazingly like Blanche Conway, Andy Bronson's mistress.

"If she too thought the man with the notes was in lower ten it explained a lot, including that piece of a woman's necklace. She was a fury, Blanche Conway, capable of anything."

"Then why did you countermand the message?" I asked curiously.

"When I got to the Carter house, and got to bed—I had sprained my ankle in the jump—I went through the alligator bag I had taken from lower nine. When I found your name I sent the first message. Then, soon after, I came across the notes. It seemed too good to be true, and I was crazy for fear the message had gone.

"At first I was going to send them to Bronson. Then I began to see what the possession of the notes meant to me. It meant power over Bronson, money, influence, everything. He was a devil, that man."

"Well, he's at home now," said McKnight, and we were glad to laugh and relieve the tension.

Alison put her hand over her eyes, as if to shut out the sight of the man she had so nearly married, and I furtively touched the soft hair at the back of her neck.

"When I was able to walk," went on the sullen voice, "I came at once to Washington. I tried to sell the notes to Bronson, but he was almost at the end of his rope. Not even my threat to send them back to you, Mr. Blakeley, could make him meet my figure. He didn't have the money."

McKnight was triumphant.

"I think you gentlemen will see reason in my theory now," he said. "Mrs. Conway wanted the notes to force a legal marriage, I suppose?"

"Sure. She'd been after that for years."

The detective with the small package carefully rolled off the rubber band and unwrapped it. I held my breath as he took out first the Russia leather wallet.

"These things, Mr. Blakeley, we found in the sealskin bag Mr. Sullivan says he left you. This wallet, Mr. Sullivan—is this the one you found on the floor of the car?"

Sullivan opened it, and, glancing at the name inside, "Simon Harrington," nodded affirmatively.

"And this," went on the detective—"this is a piece of gold chain?"

"It seems to be," said Sullivan, recoiling at the bloodstained end.

"This I believe is the dagger or whatever you call it." He held it up, and Alison gave a faint cry of astonishment and dismay. Sullivan's face grew ghastly and he sat down weakly on the nearest chair.

The detective looked at him shrewdly, then at Alison's agitated face.

"Where have you seen this dagger before, young lady?" he asked, kindly enough.

"Oh, don't ask me!" she gasped breathlessly, her eyes turned on Sullivan. "It's—it's too terrible!"

"Tell him," I advised, leaning over to her. "It will be found out later, anyhow."

"Ask him," she said, nodding toward Sullivan.

The detective unwrapped the small box Alison had brought, disclosing the trampled necklace and broken chain. With clumsy fingers he spread it on the table and fitted into place the bit of chain. There could be no doubt that it belonged there.

"Where did you find that chain?" Sullivan asked hoarsely looking for the first time at Alison.

"On the floor, near the murdered man's berth."

"Now, Mr. Sullivan," said the detective civilly, "I believe you can tell us, in the light of these two exhibits, who really did murder Simon Harrington."

Sullivan looked again at the dagger, a sharp little bit of steel with a Florentine handle. Then he picked up the locket and pressed a hidden spring under one of the cameos. Inside, very neatly engraved, was the name and a date.

"Gentlemen," he said, his face ghastly, "it is of no use for me to attempt a denial. The dagger and necklace belonged to my sister, Alice Curtis."

31

HOTCHKISS WAS THE FIRST to break the tension. "Mr. Sullivan," he asked suddenly, "was your sister left-handed?"

"Yes."

Hotchkiss put away his notebook and looked around with an air of triumphant vindication. It gave us a chance to smile and look relieved. After all, Mrs. Curtis was dead. It was the happiest solution of the unhappy affair. McKnight brought Sullivan some whisky, and he braced up a little.

"I learned through the papers that my wife was in a Baltimore hospital, and yesterday I ventured there to see her. I felt if she would help me to keep straight, with her father and my sister both dead, we might be happy together.

"I understand now what puzzled me then. It seemed that my sister went into the next car and tried to make my wife promise not to interfere. But Ida—Mrs. Sullivan—was firm, of course. She said her father had papers, certificates and so on, that would stop the marriage at once.

"She said also that her father was in our car, and that there would be the mischief to pay in the morning. It was probably when my sister tried to get the papers that he wakened, and she had to do—what she did."

It was over. Save for a technicality or two, I was a free man. Alison rose quietly and prepared to go; the men stood to let her pass, save Sullivan who sat crouched in his chair, his face buried in his hands. Hotchkiss, who had been tapping the desk with his pencil, looked up abruptly and pointed the pencil at me.

"If all this is true, and I believe it is,—then who was in the house next door, Blakeley, the night you and Mr. Johnson searched? You remember, you said it was a woman's hand at the trap door."

I glanced hastily at Johnson, whose face was impassive. He had his hand on the knob of the door and he opened it before he spoke.

"There were a number of scratches on Mrs. Conway's right hand," he observed to the room in general. "Her wrist was bandaged and badly bruised."

He went out then, but he turned as he closed the door and threw at me a glance of half-amused, half-contemptuous tolerance.

McKnight saw Alison, with Mrs. Dallas, to their car and came back again. The gathering in the office was breaking up. Sullivan, looking worn and half sick, was standing by the window and staring at the broken necklace in his hand. When he saw me watching him he put it on the desk and picked up his hat.

"If I can't do anything more—" He hesitated.

"I think you have done about enough," I replied grimly, and he went out.

I believe that Richey and Hotchkiss led me somewhere to dinner and that, for fear I would be lonely without him, they sent for Johnson! And I recall a spirited discussion in which Hotchkiss told the detective that he could manage certain cases, but that he lacked induction. Richey and I were mainly silent. My thoughts would slip ahead to that hour, later in the evening, when I meant to see Alison again. At home once more, I dressed in frantic haste, and was so particular about my tie that Mrs. Klopton gave up in despair.

"I wish, until your arm is better, that you would buy the kind that hooks on," she protested, almost tearfully. "I'm sure they look very nice, Mr. Lawrence. My late husband always—"

"That's a lover's knot you've tied this time," I snarled, and, jerking open the bow knot she had so painfully executed, looked out the window for Johnson—until I recalled that he no longer belonged in my perspective. I ended by driving frantically to the club and getting George to do it.

I was late, of course. The drawing room and library at the Dallas home were empty. I could hear billiard balls rolling somewhere, and I turned the other way. I found Alison at last on the balcony, sitting much as she had that night on the beach, her chin in her hands, her eyes fixed unseeingly on the trees and lights of the square across. She was even whistling a little, softly. But this time the plaintiveness was gone. It was a tender little tune. She did not move as I stood beside her looking down. And now, when the moment had come, all the thousand and one things I had been waiting to say forsook me, precipitately beat a retreat, and left me unsupported. The arc-moon sent little fugitive lights over her hair, her eyes, her gown.

"Don't do that," I said unsteadily. "You know what I want to do when you whistle!"

She glanced up at me, and she did not stop. She *did not stop!* She went on whistling softly, a bit tremulously. And straightway I forgot the street, the chance of passers-by, the voices in the house behind us. "The world doesn't hold anyone but you," I said. "I'm mad about you, Alison. I suppose I'm not quite sane, but here goes!"

I kissed her. And she kissed me.

A boy was whistling on the pavement below. I let her go at last and sat back where I could see her.

"I haven't done this the way I intended to at all," I confessed. "In books they get things all settled, and then kiss the lady."

"Settled?" she inquired.

"Oh, about getting married and that sort of thing," I explained with elaborate carelessness. "We could go down to Bermuda or Jamaica, say in December. How about it?"

She drew her hand away and faced me squarely.

"I believe you are afraid," she declared. "I refuse to marry you unless you propose properly. Everybody does it. And it is a woman's privilege. She wants to have that to look back to."

"Very well," I consented, with an exaggerated sigh. "If you will promise not to think I look like an idiot I shall do it."

I looked down at her. "It is a terrible thing," I said, "to love a girl the way I love you, and to have only one arm!" Then I closed the door.

From across the street there came a sharp crescendo whistle, and a vaguely familiar figure separated itself from the park railing.

"Say," he called cheerfully, "shall I throw the key down the elevator shaft?"

*The
Case of
Jennie Brice*

1

WE HAVE JUST HAD another flood, bad enough, but only a foot or two of water on the first floor. Yesterday we got the mud shoveled out of the cellar and found Peter, the spaniel Mr. Ladley left when he "went away." The flood, and the fact that it was Mr. Ladley's dog whose body was found half buried in the basement fruit closet, brought back to me the strange events of the other flood five years ago, when the water reached more than halfway to the second story and brought with it to some, mystery and sudden death, and to me the worst case of "shingles" I have ever seen.

My name is Pitman in this narrative. It is not really Pitman, but that does well enough. I belong to an old Pittsburgh family. I was born on Penn Avenue, when that was the best part of town, and I lived until I was fifteen very close to what is now the Pittsburgh Club. It was a dwelling then. I have forgotten who lived there.

I was a girl in 'seventy-seven during the railroad riots, and I recall our driving in the family carriage over to one of the Allegheny hills, and seeing the yards burning and the sound of shooting from across the river. It was the next year that I ran away from school to marry Mr. Pitman, and I have not known my family since. We were never reconciled, although I came back to Pittsburgh after twenty years of wandering. Mr. Pitman was dead. The old city called me, and I came. I had a hundred dollars or so, and I took a house in lower Allegheny where, because they are partly inundated every spring rents are cheap, and I kept boarders. My house was always orderly and clean, and although the neighborhood had a bad name a good many theatrical people stopped with me. Five minutes across the bridge and they were in the theater district. Allegheny at that time was still an independent city. But since then it has allied itself with Pittsburgh. It is now the North Side.

I was glad to get back. I worked hard, but I made my rent and my living, and a little over. Now and then on summer evenings I went to one of the parks and sitting on a bench watched the children playing around, and looked at my sister's house, closed for the summer. It is a very large house; her butler once had his wife boarding with me—a nice little woman.

It is curious to recall that at that time five years ago I had never seen my niece, Lida Harvey, and then to think that only the day before yesterday she came in her car as far as she dared, and then sat there waving to me, while the police patrol brought across in a skiff a basket of provisions she had sent me.

I wonder what she would have thought had she known that the elderly

271

woman in a calico wrapper with an old overcoat over it and wearing a pair of rubber boots was her full aunt!

The flood and the sight of Lida both brought back the case of Jennie Brice. For even then Lida and Mr. Howell were interested in each other.

This is April. The flood I am writing about five years ago was earlier, in March. It had been a long hard winter, with ice gorges in all the upper valley. Then in early March there came a thaw. The gorges broke up and began to come down, filling the rivers with crushing grinding ice.

There are three rivers at Pittsburgh, the Allegheny and the Monongahela uniting there at the Point to form the Ohio. And all three were covered with broken ice, logs, and all sorts of debris from the upper valleys.

A warning was sent out from the weather bureau, and I got my carpets ready to lift that morning. That was on the fourth of March, a Sunday. Mr. Ladley and his wife, Jennie Brice, had the parlor bedroom and the room behind it. Mrs. Ladley, or Miss Brice as she preferred to be known, had a small part at a local theater which kept a permanent stock company. Her husband was in the same business, but he was not working that season. It was the wife who paid the bills, and a lot of quarreling they did about it.

I knocked at the door at ten o'clock, and Mr. Ladley opened it. He was a short man, rather stout and getting bald, and he always had a cigarette in his mouth. Even yet, the parlor smells of them in damp weather.

"What do you want?" he asked sharply, holding the door open about an inch.

"The water's coming up very fast, Mr. Ladley," I said. "It's up to the swinging shelf in the cellar now. I'd like to take up the carpet and move the piano."

"Come back in an hour or so," he snapped, and tried to close the door. But I had got my toe in the crack.

"I'll have to have the piano moved, Mr. Ladley," I said. "You'd better put off what you're doing."

I thought he was probably writing. He spent most of the day writing, using the washstand as a desk, and it kept me busy with oxalic acid taking ink spots out of the splasher and the towels. He was writing a play, and talked a lot about the Shuberts having promised to star him in it when it was finished.

"Hell!" he said, and turning spoke to somebody in the room.

"We can go into the back room," I heard him say, and he closed the door. When he opened it again the room was empty. I called in Terry, the Irishman who does odd jobs for me now and then, and we both got to work at the tacks in the carpet, Terry working by the window and I by the door into the back parlor, which the Ladleys used as a bedroom.

That was how I happened to hear what I afterward told the police.

Someone, a man but not Mr. Ladley, was talking. Mrs. Ladley broke in. "I won't do it!" she said flatly. "Why should I help him? He doesn't help me. He loafs here all day, smoking and sleeping, and sits up all night drinking and keeping me awake."

The voice went on again, as if in reply to this, and I heard a rattle of glasses as if they were pouring drinks. They always had whisky, even when they were behind with their board.

"That's all very well," Mrs. Ladley said. I could always hear her, since she had the theatrical sort of voice which carries. "But what about the prying she-devil that runs the house?"

"Hush, for God's sake!" broke in Mr. Ladley, and after that they spoke in whispers. Even with my ear against the panel I could not catch a word.

The men came just then to move the piano, and by the time we had taken it and the furniture upstairs the water was over the kitchen floor, and creeping forward into the hall. I had never seen the river come up so fast. By noon the yard was full of floating ice, and at three that afternoon the police skiff was on the front street, and I was wading around in rubber boots, taking the pictures off the walls.

I was too busy to see who the Ladleys' visitor was, and he had gone when I remembered him again. The Ladleys took the second-story front, which was empty, and Mr. Reynolds who was in the silk department in a store across the river had the room just behind.

I put up a coal stove in a back room next the bathroom, and managed to cook the dinner there. I was washing up the dishes when Mr. Reynolds came in. As it was Sunday he was in his slippers, and he had the colored supplement of a morning paper in his hand.

"What's the matter with the Ladleys?" he asked. "I can't read for their quarreling."

"Booze, probably," I said. "When you've lived in the flood district as long as I have, Mr. Reynolds, you'll know that the rising of the river is a signal for every man in the vicinity to stop work and get tight. The fuller the river, the fuller the male population."

"Then this flood will likely make 'em drink themselves to death!" he said. "It's a lulu."

"It's the neighborhood's annual debauch. The women are busy keeping the babies from getting drowned in the cellars, or they'd get full too. Since it's come this far I hope it will come farther, so the landlord will have to paper the parlor."

That was at three o'clock. At four Mr. Ladley went down the stairs, and I heard him getting into a skiff in the lower hall. There were boats going back and forth all the time, carrying crowds of curious people, and taking the flood sufferers to the corner grocery, where they were lowering groceries in a basket on a rope from an upper window.

I had been making tea when I heard Mr. Ladley go out. I fixed a tray with a cup of it and some crackers and took it to their door. I had never liked Mrs. Ladley, but it was chilly in the house with the gas shut off and the lower floor full of ice water. And it is hard enough to keep boarders in the flood district.

She did not answer to my knock, so I opened the door and went in. She was at the window, looking after him, and the brown valise which figured in the case later was open on the floor. Over the foot of the bed was the black and white dress with the red collar.

When I spoke to her she turned around quickly. She was a tall woman, about twenty-eight, with very white teeth and yellow hair, which she parted a little to one side and drew down over her ears. She had a sullen face and large well-shaped hands, with her nails long and very pointed.

"The she-devil has brought you some tea," I said. "Where shall she put it?"

"She-devil!" she repeated, raising her eyebrows. "It's a very thoughtful she-devil. Who called you that?"

But what with the sight of the valise and the fear that they might be leaving, I thought it best not to quarrel. She had left the window, and going to her dressing table had picked up her nail file.

"Never mind," I said. "I hope you are not going away. These floods don't last, and they're really a benefit. Plenty of the people around here rely on them every year to wash out their cellars."

"No, I'm not going away," she replied lazily. "I'm taking that dress to Miss Hope at the theater. She is going to wear it in *Charlie's Aunt* next week. She hasn't half enough of a wardrobe to play leads in stock. Look at this thumbnail, broken to the quick!"

If I had only looked to see which thumb it was! But I was putting the tea tray on the washstand and moving Mr. Ladley's papers to find room for it. Peter, the spaniel, begged for a lump of sugar and I gave it to him.

"Where is Mr. Ladley?" I asked.

"Gone out to see the river."

"I hope he'll be careful. There's a drowning or two every year in these floods."

"Then I hope he won't," she said calmly. "Do you know what I was doing when you came in? I was looking after his boat and hoping it had a hole in it."

"You won't feel that way tomorrow, Mrs. Ladley," I protested, shocked. "You're just nervous and worn out. Most men have their ugly times. Many a time I wished Mr. Pitman was gone—until he went. Then I'd have given a good bit to have him back again."

She was standing in front of the dresser fixing her hair. She turned and looked at me over her shoulder.

"Probably Mr. Pitman was a man," she said. "My husband is a fiend, a devil."

Well, a good many women have said that to me at different times. But just let me say such a thing to them, or repeat their own words to them the next day, and they would fly at me in a fury. So I said nothing, and put the cream into her tea.

I never saw her again.

2

THERE IS NOT MUCH SLEEPING done in the flood district during a spring flood. The gas and electric lights were shut off, and I gave Mr. Reynolds and the Ladleys each a lamp. I sat in the back room I had made into a temporary kitchen, with a candle and with a bedquilt around my shoulders. The water rose fast in the lower hall, but by midnight at the seventh step it stopped rising and stood still. I always have a skiff during the flood season, and as the water rose I tied it to one spindle of the staircase after another.

I made myself a cup of tea, and at one o'clock I stretched out on a sofa for a few hours' sleep. I think I had been sleeping only an hour or so when someone touched me on the shoulder and I started up. It was Mr. Reynolds, partly dressed.

"Someone has been in the house, Mrs. Pitman," he said. "They went away just now in the boat."

"Perhaps it was Peter," I suggested drowsily. "That dog is always wandering around at night."

"Not unless Peter can row a boat," said Mr. Reynolds dryly.

I got up, being already fully dressed, and taking the candle we went to the staircase. I noticed it was a minute or so after two o'clock as we left the room. The boat was gone, not untied, but cut loose. The end of the rope was still fastened to the stair rail. I sat down on the stairs and looked at Mr. Reynolds.

"It's gone!" I said. "If the house catches fire we'll have to drown."

"It's rather curious, when you consider it." We both spoke softly, not to disturb the Ladleys. "I've been awake, and I heard no boat come in. Yet, if no one came in a boat, and came from the street, they would have had to swim in."

I felt queer and creepy. The street door was open, of course, and there was some light outside. It gave me a strange feeling to sit there in the darkness on the stairs, with the arch of the front door like the entrance to a cavern, and see now and then a chunk of ice slide into view, turn around in the eddy, and pass on. It was bitter cold too, and the wind was rising.

"I'll go through the house," said Mr. Reynolds. "There's likely nothing worse the matter than some drunken mill hand on a vacation while the mills are underwater. But I'd better look."

He left me, and I sat there alone in the darkness. I had a presentiment of something wrong, but I tried to think it was only discomfort and the cold. The water, driven in by the wind, swirled at my feet. And something dark floated in and lodged on the step below. I reached down and touched it. It was a dead kitten. I had never known a dead cat to bring me anything but bad luck, and here was one washed in at my very feet.

Mr. Reynolds came back soon, and reported the house quiet and in order. "But I found Peter shut up in one of the third-floor rooms," he said, "and let him out. Did you put him there?"

I had not, and said so; but as the dog went everywhere, and the door might have blown shut, we did not attach much importance to that at the time.

Well, the skiff was gone, and there was no use worrying about it until morning. I went back to the sofa to keep warm, but I left my candle lighted and my door open. I did not sleep. The dead cat was on my mind, and as if it were not bad enough to have it washed in at my feet, about four in the morning Peter, prowling uneasily, discovered it and brought it in and put it on my couch, wet and stiff, poor little thing!

I looked at the clock. It was a quarter after four, and except for the occasional crunch of one ice cake hitting another in the yard everything was quiet. And then I heard the stealthy sound of oars in the lower hall.

I am not a brave woman. I lay there, hoping Mr. Reynolds would hear and open his door. But he was sleeping soundly. Peter snarled and ran out into the hall, and the next moment I heard Mr. Ladley speaking. "Down, Peter," he said. "Down. Go and lie down."

I took my candle and went out into the hall. Mr. Ladley was stooping over the boat, trying to tie it to the staircase. The rope was short, having been cut, and he was having trouble. Perhaps it was the candlelight, but he looked ghost-white and haggard.

"I borrowed your boat, Mrs. Pitman," he said, civilly enough. "Mrs. Ladley was not well, and I went to the drugstore."

"You've been more than two hours going to the drugstore," I said.

He muttered something about not finding any open at first, and went into his room. He closed and locked the door behind him, and although Peter whined and scratched he did not let him in.

He looked so agitated that I thought I had been harsh, and that perhaps she was really ill. I knocked at the door and asked if I could do anything. But he only called "No" curtly through the door, and asked me to take that infernal dog away.

I went back to the sofa and tried to sleep, for the water had dropped an inch or so on the stairs and I knew the danger was over. Peter came shivering at dawn and got on the sofa with me. I put an end of the quilt over him, and he stopped shivering after a time and went to sleep.

The dog was company. I lay there, wide awake, thinking about Mr. Pitman's death; and how I had come, by degrees, to be keeping a cheap boardinghouse in the flood district, and to having to take impudence from everybody who chose to rent a room from me, and to being called a she-devil. From that I got to thinking again about the Ladleys, and how she had said he was a fiend, and to doubting about his having gone out for medicine for her. I dozed off again at daylight, and being worn out I slept heavily.

At seven o'clock Mr. Reynolds came to the door, dressed for the store. He was a tall man of about fifty, neat and orderly in his habits, and he always remembered that I had seen better days, and treated me as a lady.

"Never mind about breakfast for me this morning, Mrs. Pitman," he said. "I'll get a cup of coffee at the other end of the bridge. I'll take the boat and send it back with Terry."

He turned and went along the hall and down to the boat. I heard him push off from the stairs with an oar and row out into the street. Peter followed him to the stairs.

At a quarter after seven Mr. Ladley came out and called to me: "Just bring in a cup of coffee and some toast," he said. "Enough for one."

He went back and slammed his door, and I made his coffee. I steeped a cup of tea for Mrs. Ladley at the same time. He opened the door just wide enough for the tray, and took it without so much as a "thank you." He had a cigarette in his mouth as usual, and I could see a fire in the grate and smell something like scorching cloth.

"I hope Mrs. Ladley is better," I said, getting my foot in the crack of the door so he could not quite close it. It smelled to me as if he had accidentally set fire to something with his cigarette, and I tried to see into the room.

"What about Mrs. Ladley?" he snapped.

"You said she was ill last night."

"Oh, yes! Well, she wasn't very sick. She's better."

"Shall I bring her some tea?"

"Take your foot away!" he ordered. "No. She doesn't want tea. She's not here."

"Not here!"

"Good heavens!" he snarled. "Is her going away anything to make such a fuss about? The Lord knows I'd be glad to get out of this infernal pig-wallow myself."

"If you mean my house—" I began.

But he had pulled himself together and was more polite when he answered. "I mean the neighborhood. Your house is all that could be desired for the money. If we don't have linen sheets and double cream, at least we're paying muslin and milk prices."

Either my nose was growing accustomed to the odor or it was dying away. I took my foot away from the door. "When did Mrs. Ladley leave?" I asked.

"This morning, very early. I rowed her to Federal Street."

"You couldn't have had much sleep," I said dryly. For he looked horrible. There were lines around his eyes, which were red, and his lips looked dry and cracked.

"She's not in the piece this week at the theater," he said, licking his lips and looking past me, not at me. "She'll be back by Saturday."

I did not believe him. I do not think he imagined I did. He shut the door in my face, and it caught poor Peter by the nose. The dog ran off howling, but although Mr. Ladley had been as fond of the animal as it was in his nature to be fond of anything he paid no attention. As I started down the hall after him, I saw what Peter had been carrying—a slipper of Mrs. Ladley's. It was soaked with water. Evidently Peter had found it floating at the foot of the stairs.

Although the idea of murder had not entered my head at that time, the slipper gave me a turn. I picked it up and looked at it, a black one with a beaded toe, short in the vamp and high heeled, the sort most actresses wear. Then I went back and knocked at the door of the front room again.

"What the devil do you want now?" he called from beyond the door.

"Here's a slipper of Mrs. Ladley's," I said. "Peter found it floating in the lower hall."

He opened the door wide and let me in. The room was in tolerable order, much better than when Mrs. Ladley was about. He looked at the slipper, but he did not touch it. "I don't think that's hers," he said.

"I've seen her wear it a hundred times."

"Well, she'll never wear it again." And then seeing me stare he added: "It's ruined with the water. Throw it out. And by the way I'm sorry, but I set fire to one of the pillow slips—dropped asleep, and my cigarette did the rest. Just put it on the bill."

He pointed to the bed. One of the pillows had no slip, and the ticking cover had a scorch or two on it. I went over and looked at it.

"The pillow will have to be paid for too, Mr. Ladley," I said. "And there's a sign nailed on the door that forbids smoking in bed. If you are going to set fire to things I shall have to charge extra."

"Really!" he jeered, looking at me with his cold fishy eyes. "Is there any sign on the door saying that boarders are charged extra for seven feet of filthy river in the bedrooms?"

I was never a match for him, and I make it a principle never to bandy words with my boarders. I took the pillow and the slipper and went out. The telephone was ringing on the stair landing. It was the theater, asking for Miss Brice.

"She has gone away," I said.

"What do you mean? Moved away?"

"Gone for a few days' vacation," I replied. "She isn't playing this week, is she?"

"Wait a moment," said the voice. There was a hum of conversation from the other end, and then another man came to the telephone.

"Can you find out where Miss Brice has gone?"

"I'll see."

I went to Ladley's door and knocked. Mr. Ladley opened it a crack and answered from just beyond.

"The theater is asking where Mrs. Ladley is."

"Tell them I don't know," he snarled, and shut the door. I took his message to the telephone.

Whoever it was swore and hung up the receiver.

All the morning I was uneasy, I hardly knew why. Peter felt it as I did.

There was no sound from the Ladleys' room, and the house was quiet, except for the lapping water on the stairs and the police patrol going back and forth.

At eleven o'clock a boy in the neighborhood, paddling on a raft, fell into the water and was drowned. I watched the police boat go past carrying his little cold body, and after that I was good for nothing. I went and sat with Peter on the stairs. The dog's conduct had been strange all morning. He had sat just above the water, looking at it and whimpering. Perhaps he was expecting another kitten, or—

It is hard to say how ideas first enter one's mind. But the notion that Mr. Ladley had killed his wife and thrown her body into the water came to me as I sat there. All at once I seemed to see it all: the quarreling the day before, the night trip in the boat, the water-soaked slipper, his haggard face that morning, even the way the spaniel sat and stared at the flood.

Terry brought the boat back at half past eleven, towing it behind another. "Well," I said, from the stairs, "I hope you've had a pleasant morning."

"What doing?" he asked, not looking at me.

"Rowing about the streets. You've had that boat for hours."

He tied it up without a word to me, but he spoke to the dog. "Good morning, Peter," he said. "It's nice weather for fishes, ain't it?"

He picked out a bit of floating wood from the water, and showing it to the dog, flung it into the parlor. Peter went after it with a splash. He was pretty fat, and when he came back I heard him wheezing. But what he brought back was not the stick of wood. It was the knife I use for cutting bread. It had been on a shelf in the room where I had slept the night before, and now Peter brought it out of the flood where its wooden handle had kept it afloat. The blade was broken off short.

It is not unusual to find one's household goods floating around during floodtime. More than once I've lost a chair, and seen it after the water had gone down, new scrubbed and painted, in Molly Maguire's kitchen next door. And perhaps now and then a bit of luck would come to me, a dog kennel or a chicken house or a kitchen table, or even as happened once a month-old baby in a wooden cradle which lodged against my back fence and had come forty miles, as it turned out, with no worse mishap than a cold in its head.

But the knife was different. I had put it on the mantel over the stove I was using upstairs the night before, and I hadn't touched it since. As I sat staring at it, Terry took it from Peter and handed it to me.

"Better give me a penny, Mrs. Pitman," he said in his impudent Irish way. "I hate to give you a knife. It may cut our friendship."

I reached over to hit him a clout on the head, but I did not. The sunlight was coming in through the window at the top of the stairs and shining on the rope that was tied to the banister. The end of the rope was covered with stains, brown with a glint of red in them.

I got up shivering. "You can get the meat at the butcher's, Terry," I said, "and come back for me in a half hour." Then I turned and went upstairs, weak in the knees, to put on my hat and coat. I had made up my mind that there had been murder done.

3

I LOOKED AT MY CLOCK as I went downstairs. It was just twelve-thirty. I thought of telephoning for Mr. Reynolds to meet me, but it was his lunch hour, and besides I was afraid to telephone from the house while Mr. Ladley was in it.

Peter had been whining again. When I came down the stairs he had stopped whimpering and was wagging his tail. A strange boat had put into the hallway and was coming back.

"Now, old boy!" somebody was saying from the boat. "Steady, old chap! I've got something for you."

A little man, elderly and alert, was standing up in the boat, poling it along with an oar. Peter gave vent to joyful yelps. The elderly gentleman brought his boat to a stop at the foot of the stairs, and reaching down into a tub at his feet held up a large piece of raw liver. Peter almost went crazy, and I remembered suddenly that I had forgotten to feed the poor beast for more than a day.

"Would you like it?" asked the gentleman. Peter sat up, as he had been taught to do, and barked. The gentleman reached down again, got a wooden platter from a stack of them at his feet, and placing the liver on it put it on the step. The whole thing was so neat and businesslike that I could only stare.

"That's a well-trained dog, madam," said the elderly gentleman, beaming at Peter over his glasses. "You should not have neglected him."

"The flood put him out of my mind," I explained, humbly enough, for I was ashamed.

"Exactly. Do you know how many starving dogs and cats I have found this morning?" He took a notebook out of his pocket and glanced at it. "Forty-eight dogs. Forty-eight, madam! And ninety-three cats! I have found them marooned in trees, clinging to fences, floating on barrels, and I have found them in comfortable houses where there was no excuse for their neglect. Well, I must be moving on. I have the report of a cat with a new litter in the loft of a stable near here."

He wiped his hands carefully on a fresh paper napkin, of which also a heap rested on one of the seats of the boat, and picked up an oar, smiling benevolently at Peter. Then suddenly he bent over and looked at the stained rope end, tied to the stair rail.

"What's that?" he said.

"That's what I'm going to find out," I replied. I glanced up at the Ladleys' door, but it was closed.

The little man dropped his oar, and fumbling in his pockets pulled out a small magnifying glass. He bent over, holding to the rail, and inspected the stains with the glass. I had taken a fancy to him at once, and in spite of my excitement I had to smile a little.

"Humph!" he said, and looked up at me. "That's blood. Why did you *cut* the boat loose?"

"I didn't," I said. "If that is blood, I want to know how it got there. That was a new rope last night." I glanced at the Ladleys' door again, and he followed my eyes.

"I wonder," he said, raising his voice a little, "if I come into your kitchen, if you will allow me to fry a little of that liver. There's a wretched Maltese in a tree at the corner of Fourth Street that won't touch it raw."

I saw that he wanted to talk to me, so I turned around and led the way to the temporary kitchen I had made.

"Now," he said briskly, when he had closed the door, "there's something wrong here. Perhaps if you tell me I can help. If I can't it will do you good to talk about it. My name's Holcombe, retired merchant. Apply to First National Bank for references."

"I'm not sure there *is* anything wrong," I began. "I guess I'm only nervous, and thinking little things are big ones. There's nothing to tell."

"Nonsense. I come down the street in my boat. A white-faced gentleman with a cigarette looks out from a window when I stop at the door, and ducks back when I glance up. I come in and find a pet dog, obviously overfed at ordinary times, whining with hunger on the stairs. As I prepare to feed him a pale woman comes down, trying to put a right-hand glove on her left hand, and with her jacket wrong side out. What am I to think?"

I started and looked at my coat. He was right. And when as I tried to take it off he helped me, and even patted me on the shoulder—what with his kindness, and the long morning alone worrying and the sleepless night—I began to cry. He had a clean handkerchief in my hand before I had time to think of one.

"That's it," he said. "It will do you good, only don't make a noise about it. If it's a husband on the annual flood spree, don't worry, madam. They always come around in time to whitewash the cellars."

"It isn't a husband," I sniffled.

"Tell me about it," he said. There was something so kindly in his face, and it was so long since I had had a bit of human sympathy, that I almost broke down again.

I sat there, with a crowd of children paddling on a raft outside the window, and Molly Maguire next door hauling the morning's milk up in a pail fastened to a rope, her doorway being too narrow to admit the milkman's boat, and I told him the whole story.

"Humph!" he exclaimed, when I had finished. "It's curious, but—you can't prove a murder unless you can produce a body."

"When the river goes down we'll find the body," I said, shivering. "It's in the parlor."

"Then why doesn't he try to get away?"

"He is ready to go now. He only went back when your boat came in."

Mr. Holcombe went to the door, and flinging it open peered into the lower hall. He was too late. His boat was gone, tub of liver, pile of wooden platters and all!

We hurried to the room the Ladleys had occupied. It was empty. From the window as we looked out we could see the boat, almost a square away. It had stopped where, the street being higher, a doorstep rose above the flood. On the step was sitting a forlorn yellow puppy. As we stared Mr. Ladley stopped the boat, looked back at us, bent over, placed a piece of liver on a platter and reached it over to the dog. Then rising in the boat he bowed, with his hat over his heart, in our direction, sat down calmly and rowed around the corner out of sight.

Mr. Holcombe was in a frenzy of rage. He jumped up and down, shaking his fist out the window after the retreating boat. He ran down the staircase, only to come back and look out the window again. The police boat was not in sight, but the Maguire children had worked their raft around to the street and were under the window. He leaned out and called to them.

"A quarter each, boys," he said, "if you'll take me on that raft to the nearest pavement."

"Money first," said the oldest boy, holding his cap.

But Mr. Holcombe did not wait. He swung out over the window sill, holding by his hands, and lit fairly in the center of the raft.

"Don't touch anything in that room until I come back," he called to me, and jerking the pole from one of the boys propelled the raft with amazing speed down the street.

The liver on the stove was burning. There was a smell of scorching through the rooms and a sort of bluish haze smoke. I hurried back and took it off. By the time I had cleaned the pan Mr. Holcombe was back again, in his own boat. He had found it at the end of the next street, where the flood ceased, but no sign of Ladley anywhere. He had not seen the police boat.

"Perhaps that is just as well," he said philosophically. "We can't go to the police with a wet slipper and a bloodstained rope and accuse a man of murder. We have to have a body."

"He killed her," I said obstinately. "She told me yesterday he was a fiend. He killed her and threw the body in the water."

"Very likely. But he didn't throw it here."

In spite of that, however, he went over all the lower hall with his boat, feeling every foot of the floor with an oar, and finally at the back end he looked up at me as I stood on the stairs.

"There's something here," he said.

I went cold all over and had to clutch the railing. But when Terry had come, and the two of them brought the thing to the surface, it was only the dining-room rug, which I had rolled up and forgotten to carry upstairs!

At half past one Mr. Holcombe wrote a note and sent it off with Terry, and borrowing my boots, which had been Mr. Pitman's, investigated the dining room and kitchen from a floating plank. The doors were too narrow to admit the boat. But he found nothing more important than a rolling pin. He was apparently not at all depressed by his failure. He came back drenched to the skin about three, and asked permission to search the Ladleys' bedroom.

"I have a friend coming pretty soon, Mrs. Pitman," he said, "a young newspaperman named Howell. He's a nice boy, and if there is anything to this I'd like him to have it for his paper. He and I have been having some arguments about circumstantial evidence too, and I know he'd like to work on this."

I gave him a pair of Mr. Pitman's socks, for his own were saturated, and while he was changing them the telephone rang. It was the theater again, asking for Jennie Brice.

"You are certain she is out of the city?" someone asked, the same voice as in the morning.

"Her husband says so."

"Ask him to come to the phone."

"He is not here."

"When do you expect him back?"

"I'm not sure he is coming back."

"Look here," said the voice angrily, "can't you give me any satisfaction? Or don't you care to?"

"I've told you all I know."

"You don't know where she is?"

"No, sir."

"She didn't say she was coming back to rehearse for next week's piece?"

"Her husband said she went away for a few days' rest. He left here about noon and hasn't come back. That's all I know, except that they owe me three weeks' rent I'd like to get hold of."

The owner of the voice hung up the receiver with a snap, and left me pondering. It seemed to me that Mr. Ladley had been very reckless. Did he expect anyone to believe that Jennie Brice had gone for a vacation without notifying the theater? Especially when she was to rehearse that week? I thought it curious, to say the least. I went back and told Mr. Holcombe, who put it down in his notebook, and together we went to the Ladleys' room.

The room was in better order than usual, as I have said. The bed was made—which was out of the ordinary, for Jennie Brice never made a bed—but made the way a man makes one, with the blankets wrinkled and crooked beneath and the white counterpane pulled smoothly over the top, showing every hump. I showed Mr. Holcombe the splasher, dotted with ink as usual.

"I'll take it off and soak it in milk," I said. "It's his fountain pen. When the ink doesn't run he shakes it, and—"

"Where's the clock?" said Mr. Holcombe, stopping in front of the mantel with his notebook in his hand.

"The clock?"

I turned and looked. My onyx clock was gone from the mantelshelf.

Perhaps it seems strange, but from the moment I missed that clock my rage at Mr. Ladley increased to a fury. It was all I had had left of my former gentility. When times were hard and I got behind with the rent, as happened now and then, more than once I'd been tempted to sell the clock, or to pawn it. But I had never done so. Its ticking had kept me company on many a lonely night, and its elegance had helped me to keep my pride and to retain the respect of my neighbors. For in the flood district onyx clocks are not plentiful. Mrs. Bryan, the saloonkeeper's wife, had one and I had another. That is, I *had* had.

I stood staring at the mark in the dust of the mantelshelf, which Mr. Holcombe was measuring with a pocket tape measure.

"You are sure you didn't take it away yourself, Mrs. Pitman?" he asked.

"Sure? Why, I could hardly lift it," I said.

He was looking carefully at the oblong of dust where the clock had stood. "The key is gone too," he said, busily making entries in his notebook. "What was the maker's name?"

"I don't think I ever noticed."

He turned to me angrily. "Why didn't you notice?" he snapped. "Good God, woman, do you only use your eyes to cry with? How can you wind a clock, time after time, and not know the maker's name? It proves my contention; the average witness is totally unreliable."

"Not at all," I snapped back. "I am ordinarily both accurate and observing."

"Indeed!" he said, putting his hands behind him. "Then perhaps you can tell me the color of the pencil I have been writing with."

"Certainly. Red." Most pencils are red, and I thought this was safe.

But he held out his right hand with a flourish. "I've been writing with a fountain pen," he said in deep disgust, and turned his back on me.

But the next moment he had run to the washstand and pulled it out from the wall. Behind it where it had fallen lay a towel, covered with stains as if someone had wiped bloody hands on it. He held it up, his face working with excitement. I could only cover my eyes.

"This looks better," he said, and began making a quick search of the room, running from one piece of furniture to another, pulling out bureau drawers, drawing the bed out from the wall, and crawling along the baseboard with a lighted match in his hand. He gave a shout of triumph finally, and reappeared from behind the bed with the broken end of my knife in his hand.

"Very clumsy," he said. "*Very* clumsy. Peter the dog could have done better."

I had been examining the wallpaper about the washstand. Among the ink spots were one or two reddish ones that made me shiver. And seeing a scrap of note paper stuck between the baseboard and the wall, I dug it out with a hairpin and threw it into the grate, to be burned later. It was by the merest chance there was no fire there. The next moment Mr. Holcombe was on his knees by the fireplace reaching for the scrap.

"*Never* do that, under such circumstances," he snapped, fishing among the ashes. "You might throw valuable—Hello, Howell!"

I turned and saw a young man in the doorway, smiling, his hat in his hand. Even at that first glance I liked Mr. Howell, and later, when everyone was against him and many curious things were developing, I stood by him through everything, and even helped him to the thing he wanted more than anything else in the world. But that of course was later.

"What's the trouble, Holcombe?" he asked. "Hitting the trail again?"

"A very curious thing that I just happened on," said Mr. Holcombe. "Mrs. Pitman, this is Mr. Howell, of whom I spoke. Sit down, Howell, and let me read you something."

With the crumpled paper still unopened in his hand, Mr. Holcombe took his notebook and read aloud what he had written. I have it before me now:

" 'Dog meat, two dollars, boat hire'—that's not it. Here. 'Yesterday, Sunday, March the 4th, Mrs. Pitman, landlady at 42 Union Street, heard two of her boarders quarreling, a man and his wife. Man's name, Philip Ladley. Wife's name, Jennie Ladley, known as Jennie Brice at the Liberty Stock Company, where she has been playing small parts.' "

Mr. Howell nodded. "I've heard of her," he said. "Not much of an actress, I believe."

" 'The husband also was an actor, out of work, and employing his leisure time in writing a play.' "

"Everybody's doing it," said Mr. Howell idly.

"The Shuberts were to star him in this," I put in. "He said that the climax at the end of the second act—"

Mr. Holcombe shut his notebook with a snap. "After we have finished gossiping," he said, "I'll go on."

" 'Employing his leisure time in writing a play—' " quoted Mr. Howell.

"Exactly. 'The husband and wife were not on good terms. They quarreled frequently. On Sunday they fought all day, and Mrs. Ladley told Mrs. Pitman she was married to a fiend. At four o'clock Sunday afternoon, Philip Ladley went out, returning about five. Mrs. Pitman carried their supper to them at six, and both ate heartily. She did not see Mrs. Ladley at the time, but heard her in the next room. They were apparently reconciled. Mrs. Pitman reports Mr. Ladley in high good humor. If the quarrel recommenced during the night the other boarder, named Reynolds, in the next room heard nothing. Mrs. Pitman was up and down until one o'clock, when she dozed off. She heard no unusual sound.

" 'At approximately two o'clock in the morning, however, this Reynolds came to her room and said he had heard someone in a boat in the lower hall. He and Mrs. Pitman investigated. The boat which Mrs. Pitman uses during a flood and which she had tied to the stair rail was gone, having been cut loose, not untied. Everything else was quiet, except that Mrs. Ladley's dog had been shut in a third-story room.

" 'At a quarter after four that morning Mrs. Pitman, thoroughly awake, heard the boat returning and going to the stairs met Ladley coming in. He muttered something about having gone for medicine for his wife and went to his room, shutting the dog out. This is worth attention, for the dog ordinarily slept in their room.' "

"What sort of dog?" asked Mr. Howell. He had been listening attentively.

"A cocker spaniel. 'The rest of the night, or early morning, was quiet. At a quarter after seven Ladley asked for coffee and toast for one, and on Mrs. Pitman remarking this, said that his wife was not playing this week and had gone for a few days' vacation, having left early in the morning.' Remember, during the night he had been out for medicine for her. Now she was able to travel, and in fact had already started."

Mr. Howell was frowning at the floor. "If he was doing anything wrong he was doing it very badly," he said.

"This is where I entered the case," said Mr. Holcombe. "I rowed into the lower hall this morning to feed the dog, Peter, who was whining on the staircase. Mrs. Pitman was coming down, pale and agitated over the fact that the dog shortly before had found floating in the parlor downstairs a slipper belonging to Mrs. Ladley, and, later, a knife with a broken blade. She maintains that she had the knife last night upstairs, that it was not broken, and that it was taken from a shelf in her room while she dozed. The question is, then: Why was the knife taken? Who took it? And why? Has this man made away with his wife, or has he not?"

Mr. Howell looked at me and smiled. "Mr. Holcombe and I are old enemies," he said. "Mr. Holcombe believes that circumstantial evidence may probably hang a man. I do not." And to Mr. Holcombe: "So, having found a wet slipper and a broken knife, you are prepared for murder and sudden death!"

"I have more evidence," Mr. Holcombe said eagerly, and proceeded to tell what we had found in the room. Mr. Howell listened, smiling to himself, but at the mention of the onyx clock he got up and went to the mantel.

"By Jove!" he said, and stood looking at the mark in the dust. "Are you sure the clock was here yesterday?"

"I wound it night before last and put the key underneath. Yesterday, before they moved up, I wound it again."

"The key is gone also. Well, what of it, Holcombe? Did he brain her with the clock? Or choke her with the key?"

Mr. Holcombe was looking at his notebook. "To summarize," he said, "we have here as clues indicating a crime the rope, the broken knife, the slipper, the towel, and the clock. Besides, this scrap of paper may contain some information." He opened it and sat gazing at it in his palm. Then, "Is this Ladley's writing?" he asked me in a curious voice.

"Yes."

I glanced at the slip. Mr. Holcombe had just read from his notebook: "'Rope, knife, slipper, towel, clock.'"

The slip I had found behind the washstand said: "Rope, knife, shoe, towel. Horn—" The rest of the last word was torn off.

Mr. Howell was staring at the mantel. "Clock!" he repeated.

4

IT WAS AFTER FOUR when Mr. Holcombe had finished going over the room. I offered to make both the gentlemen some tea, for Mr. Pitman had been an Englishman and I had got into the habit of having a cup in the afternoon, with a cracker or a bit of bread. But they refused. Mr. Howell said he had promised to meet a lady, and to bring her through the flooded district in a boat. He shook hands with me and smiled at Mr. Holcombe.

"You will have to restrain his enthusiasm, Mrs. Pitman," he said. "He is a bloodhound on the scent. If his baying gets on your nerves just send for me." He went down the stairs and stepped into the boat. "Remember, Holcombe," he called, "every well-constituted murder has two things, a motive and a corpse. You haven't either, only a mass of piffling details—"

"If everybody waited until he saw flames, instead of relying on the testimony of the smoke," Mr. Holcombe said tartly, "what would the fire loss be?"

Mr. Howell poled his boat to the front door, and sitting down prepared to row out.

"You are warned, Mrs. Pitman," he called to me. "If he doesn't find a body to fit the clues, he's quite capable of making one to fill the demand."

"Horn—" said Mr. Holcombe, looking at the slip again. "The tail of the 'n' is torn off—evidently only part of a word. Hornet, Horning, Horner— Mrs. Pitman, will you go with me to the police station?"

I was more than anxious to go. In fact I could not bear the idea of staying alone in the house, with heaven only knows what concealed in the depths of that muddy flood. I got on my wraps again and Mr. Holcombe rowed me out. Peter plunged into the water to follow, and had to be sent back. He sat on the lower step and whined. Mr. Holcombe threw him another piece of liver, but he did not touch it.

We rowed to the corner of Robinson Street and Federal—it was before Federal Street was raised above the flood level—and left the boat in charge of a boy there. From there we walked to the police station. On the way Mr. Holcombe questioned me closely about the events of the morning, and I recalled the incident of the burned pillow slip. He made a note of it at once, and grew very thoughtful.

He left me at the police station, however. "I'd rather not appear in this, Mrs. Pitman," he said apologetically, "and I think better along my own lines.

Not that I have anything against the police. They've done some splendid work. But this case takes imagination, and the police department deals with facts. We have no facts yet. What we need, of course, is to have the man detained until we are sure of our case."

He lifted his hat and turned away, and I went slowly up the steps to the police station. Living as I had in a neighborhood where the police, like the poor, are always with us, and where the visit of the patrol car is one of those familiar sights which no amount of repetition enabled any of us to treat with contempt, I was uncomfortable until I remembered that my grandfather had been one of the first mayors of the city. And that, if the police had been at my house more than once, the entire neighborhood would testify that my boarders were usually orderly.

At the door someone touched me on the arm. It was Mr. Holcombe again.

"I have been thinking it over," he said, "and I believe you'd better not mention the piece of paper you found behind the washstand. They might say the whole thing is a hoax."

"Very well," I agreed, and went in.

The police sergeant in charge knew me at once, having stopped at my house more than once in floodtime for a cup of hot coffee.

"Sit down, Mrs. Pitman," he said. "I suppose you are still making the best coffee and doughnuts in the city of Allegheny? Well, what's the trouble in your district? Want an injunction against the river for trespass?"

"The river has brought me a good bit of trouble," I said. "I'm worried, Mr. Sergeant. I think a woman from my house has been murdered, but I don't know."

"Murdered," he said, and drew up his chair. "Tell me about it."

I told him everything, while he sat back with his eyes half closed and his fingers beating a tattoo on the arm of his chair.

When I finished he got up and went into an inner room. He came back in a moment.

"I want you to come in and tell that to the chief," he said, and led the way.

All told, I repeated my story three times that afternoon, to the sergeant, to the chief of police, and the third time to both of them and two detectives. The second time the chief made notes of what I said.

"Know this man Ladley?" he asked the others. None of them did, but they all knew of Jennie Brice, and some of them had seen her in the theater.

"Get the theater, Tom," the chief said to one of the detectives.

Luckily, what he learned over the telephone from the theater corroborated my story. Jennie Brice was not in the cast that week, but should have reported that morning (Monday) to rehearse the next week's play. No message had been received from her, and a substitute had been put in her place.

The chief hung up the receiver and turned to me. "You are sure about the clock, Mrs. Pitman?" he asked. "It was there when they moved upstairs to the room?"

"Yes, sir."

"You're certain you will not find it on the parlor mantel when the water goes down?"

"The mantels are uncovered now. It's not there."

"You think Ladley has gone for good?"

"Yes, sir."

"He'd be a fool to try to run away, unless—Graves, you'd better get hold of the fellow, and keep him until either the woman or a body is found. The river is falling. In a couple of days we'll know if she is around the premises anywhere."

Before I left I described Jennie Brice for them carefully. Asked what she probably wore, if she had gone away as her husband said, I had no idea. She had a lot of clothes, and dressed very well. But I recalled that I had seen, lying on the bed, the black and white dress with the red collar. And they took that down, as well as the brown valise.

The chief rose and opened the door for me himself. "If she actually left town at the time you mention," he said, "she ought not to be hard to find. There are not many trains before seven in the morning, and most of them are locals."

"And if she did not, if he— Do you think she is in the house—or the cellar?"

"Not unless Ladley is more of a fool than I think he is," he said, smiling. "Personally, I believe she has gone away, as he says she did. But if she hasn't, he probably took the body with him when he said he was getting medicine, and dropped it in the current somewhere. But we must go slow with all this. There's no use shouting 'wolf' yet."

"But—the towel?"

"He may have cut himself shaving. It *has* been done."

"And the knife?"

He shrugged his shoulders good-naturedly.

"I've seen a perfectly good knife spoiled opening a bottle of pickles."

"But the slipper? And the clock?"

"My good woman, enough shoes and slippers are forgotten in the bottoms of cupboards year after year in floodtime, and are found floating around the streets, to make all the old-clothes men in town happy. I have seen almost everything floating about during one of these annual floods."

"I dare say you never saw an onyx clock floating around," I replied a little sharply. I had no sense of humor that day. He stopped smiling at once and stood tugging at his mustache.

"No," he admitted. "An onyx clock sinks, that's true. That's a very nice point, that onyx clock. He may be trying to sell it, or perhaps—" He did not finish.

I went back immediately, only stopping at the market to get meat for Mr. Reynolds's supper. It was after half past five and dusk was coming on. I got a boat and was rowed directly home. Peter was not at the foot of the steps. I paid the boatman and let him go, and turned to go up the stairs. Someone was speaking in the hall above.

I have read somewhere that no two voices are exactly alike, just as no two violins ever produce precisely the same sound. I think it is what they call the timbre that is different. I have for instance never heard a voice like Mr. Pitman's, although Mr. Harry Lauder's in a phonograph resembles it. And voices have always done for me what odors do for some people, revived forgotten scenes and old memories. But the memory the voice at the head of the stairs brought back was not very old, although I had forgotten it. I seemed to hear again all at once the lapping of the water Sunday morning as it began to come in over the doorsill, the sound of Terry ripping up the parlor carpet, and Mrs. Ladley calling me a she-devil in the next room in reply to this very voice.

But when I got to the top of the stairs it was only Mr. Howell, who had brought his visitor to the flood district, and on getting her splashed with muddy water had brought her to my house for a towel and a cake of soap.

I lighted the lamp in the hall, and Mr. Howell introduced the girl. She was a pretty girl, slim and young, and she had taken her wetting good-naturedly.

"I know we are intruders, Mrs. Pitman," she said, holding out her hand. "Especially now, when you're in trouble."

"I have told Miss Harvey a little," Mr. Howell said, "and I promised to show her Peter, but he's not here."

I think I had known it was my sister's child from the moment I lighted the lamp. There was something of Alma in her, not Alma's hardness or haughtiness but Alma's dark-blue eyes with black lashes and Alma's nose. Alma was always the beauty of the family. What with the day's excitement, and seeing Alma's child like this in my house, I felt things going round and clutched at the stair rail. Mr. Howell caught me.

"Why, Mrs. Pitman!" he said. "What's the matter?"

I got myself in hand in a moment and smiled at the girl.

"Nothing at all," I said. "Indigestion, most likely. Too much tea the last day or two, and not enough solid food. I've been too anxious to eat."

Lida—for she was that to me at once, although I had never seen her before— Lida was all sympathy and sweetness. She actually asked me to go with her to a restaurant and have a real dinner. I could imagine Alma, had she known! But I excused myself.

"I have to cook something for Mr. Reynolds," I said, "and I'm better now anyhow, thank you. Mr. Howell, may I speak to you for a moment?"

He followed me along the back hall, which was dusk.

"I have remembered something I had forgotten, Mr. Howell," I said. "On Sunday morning the Ladleys had a visitor."

"Yes?"

"They had very few visitors."

"I see."

"I did not see him, but I heard his voice." Mr. Howell did not move, but I fancied he drew his breath in quickly. "It sounded—it was not by any chance *you?*"

"I? A newspaperman who goes to bed at three A.M. on Sunday morning, up and about at ten!"

"I didn't say what time it was," I said sharply.

But at that moment Lida called from the front hall.

"I think I hear Peter," she said. "He is shut in somewhere, whining."

We went forward at once. She was right. Peter was scratching at the door of Mr. Ladley's room, although I had left the door closed and Peter in the hall. I let him out and he crawled to me on three legs, whimpering. Mr. Howell bent over him and felt the fourth.

"Poor little beast!" he said. "His leg is broken!"

He made a splint for the dog, and with Lida helping they put him to bed in a clothes basket in my upstairs kitchen. It was easy to see how things lay with Mr. Howell. He was all eyes for her. He made excuses to touch her hand or her arm, little caressing touches that made her color heighten. And with it all there was a sort of hopelessness in his manner, as if he knew how far the girl was out of his reach. Knowing Alma and her pride, I knew better than they how hopeless it was.

I was not so sure about Lida. I wondered if she was in love with the boy, or only in love with love. She was very young, as I had been. God help her, if as I had, she sacrificed everything to discover too late that she was only in love with love.

5

MR. REYNOLDS did not come home to dinner after all. The water had got into the basement at the store, he telephoned, one of the floodgates in a sewer having leaked, and they were moving some of the departments to an upper floor. I had expected to have him in the house that evening, and now I was left alone again.

But as it happened I was not alone. Mr. Graves, one of the city detectives, came at half past six and went carefully over the Ladleys' room. I showed him the towel and the slipper and the broken knife, and where we had found the blade. He was noncommittal, and left in a half hour taking the articles with him in a newspaper.

At seven the doorbell rang. I went down as far as I could on the staircase, and I saw a boat outside the front door, with the boatman and a woman in it. I called to them to bring the boat back along the hall, and I had a queer feeling that it might be Mrs. Ladley and that I'd been making a fool of myself all day for nothing. But it was not Mrs. Ladley.

"Is this number forty-two?" asked the woman, as the boat came back.

"Yes."

"Does Mr. Ladley live here?"

"Yes. But he is not here now."

"Are you Mrs. Pittock?"

"Pitman, yes."

The boat bumped against the stairs, and the woman got out. She was as tall as Mrs. Ladley, and when I saw her in the light from the upper hall I knew her instantly. It was Temple Hope, the leading woman from the Liberty Theater.

"I would like to talk to you, Mrs. Pitman," she said. "Where can we go?"

I led the way back to my room, and when she had followed me in she turned and shut the door.

"Now then," she said without any preliminary, "where is Jennie Brice?"

"I don't know, Miss Hope," I answered.

We looked at each other for a minute, and each of us saw what the other suspected.

"He's killed her!" she exclaimed. "She was afraid he would do it, and he has."

"Killed her and thrown her into the river," I said. "That's what I think, and he'll go free at that. It seems there isn't any murder when there isn't any corpse."

"Nonsense! If he has done that, the river will give her up, eventually."

"The river doesn't always give them up," I retorted. "Not in floodtime anyhow. Or when they are found it is months later, and you can't prove anything."

She had only a little time, being due at the theater soon, but she sat down and told me the story she told afterward on the stand.

She had known Jennie Brice for years, they having been together in the chorus as long before as *Nadjy*.

"She was married then to a fellow on the vaudeville circuit," Miss Hope said. "He left her about that time, and she took up with Ladley. I don't think they were ever married."

"What!" I said, jumping to my feet. "And they came to a respectable house like this! There's never been a breath of scandal about this house, Miss Hope, and if this comes out I'm ruined."

"Well, perhaps they were married," she said. "Anyhow, they were always quarreling. And when he wasn't playing it was worse. She used to come to my hotel and cry her eyes out."

"I knew you were friends," I said. "Almost the last thing she said to me was about the black and white dress of hers you were to borrow for the piece this week."

"Black and white dress? I borrow one of Jennie Brice's dresses!" exclaimed Miss Hope. "I should think not. I have plenty of my own."

That puzzled me, for she had said it, that was sure. And then I remembered I had not seen the dress in the room that day, and I went in to look for it. It was gone. I came back and told Miss Hope.

"A black and white dress! Did it have a red collar?" she asked.

"Yes."

"Then I remember it. She wore a small black hat with a red quill with that dress. You might look for the hat."

She followed me back to the room and stood in the doorway while I searched. The hat was gone too.

"Perhaps after all he's telling the truth," she said thoughtfully. "Her fur coat isn't in the closet, is it?"

It was gone too. It is strange that all day I had never thought of looking over her clothes and seeing what was missing. I hadn't known all she had, of course, but I had seen her all winter in her fur coat and admired it. It was a striped fur, brown and gray, and very unusual. But with the coat missing and a dress and hat gone it began to look as if I had been making a fool of myself, and stirring up a tempest in a teacup. Miss Hope was as puzzled as I was.

"Anyhow, if he didn't kill her," she said, "it isn't because he didn't want to. Only last week she had hysterics in my dressing room and said he threatened to poison her. It was all Mr. Bronson, the business manager, and I could do to quiet her."

She looked at her watch and exclaimed that she was late and would have to hurry. I saw her down to her boat. The river had been falling rapidly for the last hour or two, and I heard the boat scrape as it went over the door sill. I did not know whether to be glad that the water was going down and I could live like a Christian again or to be sorry for fear of what we might find in the mud that was always left.

Peter was lying where I had put him, on a folded blanket laid in a clothes basket. I went back to him and sat down beside the basket.

"Peter!" I said. "Poor old Peter! Who did this to you? Who hurt you?" He looked at me and whined, as if he wanted to tell me if only he could.

"Was it Mr. Ladley?" I asked, and the poor thing cowered close to his bed and shivered. I wondered if it had been he, and if it had why he had come back. Perhaps he had remembered the towel. Perhaps he would come again and spend the night there. I was like Peter. I cowered and shivered at the very thought.

At nine o'clock I heard a boat at the door. It had stuck there, and its occupant was scolding furiously at the boatman. Soon after I heard splashing, and I knew that whoever it was was wading back to the stairs through the foot and a half or so of water still in the hall. I ran back to my room and locked myself in, and then stood armed with the stove-lid lifter, in case it should be Ladley and he should break the door in.

The steps came up the stairs, and Peter barked furiously. It seemed to me that this was to be my end, killed like a rat in a trap and thrown out the window, to float like my kitchen chair into Mollie Maguire's kitchen, or to be found lying in the ooze of the yard after the river had gone down.

The steps hesitated at the top of the stairs, and turned back along the hall. Peter redoubled his noise; he never barked for Mr. Reynolds or the Ladleys.

I stood still, hardly able to breathe. The door was thin, and the lock loose. One good blow, and—

The door knob turned, and I screamed. I recall that the light turned black, and that is all I *do* remember until I came to a half hour later, and saw Mr. Holcombe stooping over me. The door, with the lock broken, was standing open.

I tried to move, and then I saw that my feet were propped up on the edge of Peter's basket.

"Better leave them up," Mr. Holcombe said. "It sends the blood back to the head. Half the damfool people in the world stick a pillow under a fainting woman's shoulders. How are you now?"

"All right," I said feebly. "I thought you were Mr. Ladley."

He helped me up, and I sat in a chair and tried to keep my lips from shaking. And then I saw that Mr. Holcombe had brought a suitcase with him, and had set it inside the door.

"You're safe from him, until he gets bail anyhow," he said. "They picked him up as he was boarding a Pennsylvania train bound east."

"For murder?" I asked.

"As a suspicious character," he replied grimly. "That does as well as anything for a time." He sat down opposite me, and looked at me intently.

"Mrs. Pitman," he said, "did you ever hear the story of the horse that wandered out of a village and could not be found?"

I shook my head.

"Well, the best wit of the village failed to locate the horse. But one day the village idiot walked into town leading the missing animal by the bridle. When they asked him how he had done it, he said: 'Well, I just thought what I'd do if I was a horse, and then I went and did it.'"

"I see," I said, humoring him.

"You *don't* see. Now, what are we trying to do?"

"We're trying to find a body. Do you intend to become a corpse?"

He leaned over and tapped on the table between us. "We are trying to prove a crime, and I intend for the time to be the criminal."

He looked so curious, bent forward and glaring at me from under his bushy eyebrows, and with his shoes on his knee—he had taken them off to wade to the stairs—and his trousers rolled up, that I wondered if he was entirely sane. But Mr. Holcombe, eccentric as he might be, was sane enough.

"Not really a criminal?" I asked feebly.

"As really as lies in me. Listen, Mrs. Pitman. I want to put myself in Ladley's place for a day or two, live as he lived, do what he did, even think as he thought if I can. I am going to sleep in his room tonight, with your permission."

I could not see any reason for objecting, although I thought it silly and useless. I led the way to the front room, Mr. Holcombe following with his shoes and suitcase. I lighted a lamp, and he stood looking around him.

"I see you have been here since we left this afternoon," he said.

"Twice," I replied. "First with Mr. Graves, and later—"

The words died on my tongue. Someone had been in the room since my last visit there.

"He has been here!" I gasped. "I left the room in tolerable order. Look at it!"

"When were you here last?"

"At seven-thirty, or thereabouts."

"Where were you between seven-thirty and eight-thirty?"

"In the kitchen with Peter." I told him then about the dog, and about finding him shut in the room.

The washstand was pulled out. The sheets of Mr. Ladley's manuscript, usually an orderly pile, were half on the floor. The bed coverings had been jerked off and flung over the back of a chair.

Peter, imprisoned, might have moved the washstand and upset the manuscript. But Peter had never put the bedclothes over the chair, or broken his own leg.

"Humph!" he said, and getting out his notebook he made an exact memorandum of what I had told him, and of the condition of the room. That done, he turned to me.

"Mrs. Pitman," he said, "I'll thank you to call me Mr. Ladley for the next day or so. I am an actor out of employment, forty-one years of age, short, stout, and bald, married to a woman I would like to be quit of, and I am writing myself a play in which the Shuberts intend to star me, or in which I intend the Shuberts to star me."

"Very well, Mr. Ladley," I said, trying to enter into the spirit of the thing and, God knows, seeing no humor in it. "Then you'll like your soda from the icebox?"

"Soda? For what?"

"For your whisky and soda, before you go to bed, sir."

"Oh, certainly, yes. Bring the soda. And—just a moment, Mrs. Pitman. Mr. Holcombe is a total abstainer, and has always been so. It is Ladley, not Holcombe, who takes this abominable stuff."

I said I quite understood, but that Mr. Ladley could skip a night if he so wished. But the little gentleman would not hear to it, and when I brought the soda he poured himself a double portion. He stood looking at it with his face screwed up, as if the very odor revolted him.

"The chances are," he said, "that Ladley—that I—having a nasty piece of work to do during the night would—will take a larger drink than usual." He raised the glass, only to put it down. "Don't forget," he said, "to put a large knife where you left the one last night. I'm sorry the water has gone down, but I shall imagine it still at the seventh step. Good night, Mrs. Pitman."

"Good night, Mr. Ladley," I said, smiling, "and remember, you are three weeks in arrears with your rent."

His eyes twinkled through his spectacles. "I shall imagine it paid," he said.

I went out, and I heard him close the door behind me. Then through the door I heard a great sputtering and coughing, and I knew he had got the whisky down somehow. I put the knife out, as he had asked me to, and went to bed. I was ready to drop. Not even the knowledge that an imaginary Mr. Ladley was about to commit an imaginary crime in the house that night could keep me awake.

Mr. Reynolds came in at eleven o'clock. I was roused when he banged his door. That was all I knew until morning. The sun on my face wakened me. Peter, in his basket, lifted his head as I moved, and thumped his tail against his pillow in greeting. I put on a wrapper, and called Mr. Reynolds by knocking at his door. Then I went on to the front room. The door was closed, and someone beyond was groaning. My heart stood still, and then raced on. I opened the door and looked in.

Mr. Holcombe was on the bed, fully dressed. He had a wet towel tied around his head, and his face looked swollen and puffy. He opened one eye and looked at me.

"What a night!" he groaned.

"What happened! What did you find?"

He groaned again. "Find!" he said. "Nothing, except that there was something wrong with that whisky. It poisoned me. I haven't been out of the house!"

So for that day at least Mr. Ladley became Mr. Holcombe again, and as such accepted ice in quantities, a mustard plaster over his stomach, and considerable nursing. By evening he was better, but although he clearly intended to stay on he said nothing about changing his identity again, and I was glad enough. The very name of Ladley was horrible to me.

The river went down almost entirely that day, although there was still considerable water in the cellars. It takes time to get rid of that. The lower floors showed nothing suspicious. The papers were ruined, of course, the doors warped and sprung, and the floors coated with mud and debris. Terry came in the afternoon, and together we hung the dining-room rug out to dry in the sun.

As I was coming in I looked over at the Maguire yard. Molly Maguire was there, and all her children around her, gaping. Molly was hanging out a sodden fur coat that had once been striped, brown and gray.

I went over after breakfast and claimed the coat as belonging to Mrs. Ladley. But she refused to give it up. There is a sort of unwritten law concerning the salvage of flood articles, and I had to leave the coat, as I had my kitchen chair. But it was Mrs. Ladley's, beyond a doubt.

I shuddered when I thought how it had probably got into the water. And yet it was curious too, for if she had had it on how did it get loose to go floating around Molly Maguire's yard? And if she had not worn it, how did it get in the water?

6

THE NEWSPAPERS from that time on were full of the Ladley case, with its curious solution and many surprises. It was considered unique in many ways. Mr. Pitman had always read all the murder trials, and used to talk about the *corpus delicti* and writs of *habeas corpus*, *corpus* being the legal way, I believe, of spelling corpse. But I came out of the Ladley trial—for it came to trial ultimately—with only one point of law that I was sure of: that was, that it is mighty hard to prove a man a murderer unless you can show what he killed.

And that was the weakness in the Ladley case. There was a body, but it could not be identified.

The police held Mr. Ladley for a day or two and then, nothing appearing, they let him go. Mr. Holcombe, who was still occupying the second-floor front, almost wept with rage and despair when he read the news in the papers. He was still working on the case in his curious way, wandering along the wharves at night, and writing letters all over the country to learn about Philip Ladley's previous life and his wife's. But he did not seem to get anywhere.

The press all over the country had been full of the Jennie Brice disappearance. For disappearance it proved to be. So far as could be learned she had not left the city that night or since, and as she was a striking-looking woman, very blonde, as I have said, with a full voice and a languid manner, she could hardly have taken refuge anywhere without being discovered. The morning after her disappearance a young woman, tall like Jennie Brice and fair, had been seen in the Union Station. But as she was accompanied by a young man who bought her magazines and papers and bade her an excited farewell, sending his love to various members of a family, and promising to feed the canary, this was not seriously considered. A sort of general alarm went over the country. When she was younger she had been pretty well known at the Broadway theaters in New York. One way or another, the Liberty Theater got a lot of free advertising from the case, and I believe Miss Hope's salary was raised.

The police communicated with Jennie Brice's people. She had a sister in Olean, New York, but she had not heard from her. The sister wrote, I heard later, that Jennie had been unhappy with Philip Ladley and afraid he would kill her. And Miss Hope told the same story. But there was no *corpus*, as the lawyers say, and finally the police had to free Mr. Ladley.

Beyond making an attempt to get bail, and failing, he had done nothing. Asked about his wife, he merely shrugged his shoulders and said she had left him and would turn up all right. He was unconcerned, smoked cigarettes all day, ate and slept well, and looked better since he had had nothing to drink. And two or three days after the arrest he sent for the manuscript of his play.

Mr. Howell came for it on the Thursday of that week.

I was on my knees scrubbing the parlor floor when he rang the bell. I let him in, and it seemed to me that he looked tired and pale.

"Well, Mrs. Pitman," he said, smiling, "what did you find in the cellar when the water went down?"

"I'm glad to say that I didn't find what I feared, Mr. Howell."

"Not even the onyx clock?"

"Not even the clock," I replied. "And I feel as if I'd lost a friend. A clock is a lot of company."

"Do you know what I think?" he said, looking at me closely. "I think you put that clock away yourself in the excitement and have forgotten all about it."

"Nonsense."

"Think hard." He was very much in earnest. "You knew the water was rising and the Ladleys would have to be moved up to the second-floor front, where the clock stood. You went in there and looked around to see if the room was ready, and you saw the clock. And knowing that the Ladleys quarreled now and then, and were apt to throw things—"

"Nothing but a soap dish, and that only once."

"—you took the clock to the attic and put it, say, in an old trunk."

"I did nothing of the sort. I went in, as you say, and I put up an old splasher because of the way he throws ink about. Then I wound the clock, put the key under it, and went out."

"And the key is gone too!" he said thoughtfully. "I wish I could find that clock, Mrs. Pitman."

"So do I."

"Ladley went out Sunday afternoon about three, didn't he, and got back at five?"

I turned and looked at him. "Yes, Mr. Howell," I said. "Perhaps *you* know something about that."

"I?" He changed color. Twenty years of dunning boarders has made me pretty sharp at reading faces, and he looked as uncomfortable as if he owed me money. "I!" I knew then that I had been right about the voice. It had been his.

"You!" I retorted. "You were here Sunday morning and spent some time with the Ladleys. I'm the old she-devil. I notice you didn't tell your friend Mr. Holcombe about having been here on Sunday."

He was quick to recover. "I'll tell you all about it, Mrs. Pitman," he said smilingly. "You see, all my life I have wanted an onyx clock. It has been my ambition, my Great Desire. Leaving the house that Sunday morning and hearing the ticking of the clock, I recognized that it was an onyx clock, clambered from my boat through an upper window and so reached it. The clock showed fight, but after stunning it with a chair—"

"Exactly!" I said. "Then the thing Mrs. Ladley said she would not do was probably to wind the clock?"

He dropped his bantering manner at once. "Mrs. Pitman," he said, "I don't know what you heard or did not hear. But I want you to give me a little time before you tell anybody that I was here that Sunday morning. And in return I'll find your clock."

I hesitated, but however put out he was he didn't look like a criminal. Besides he was a friend of my niece's, and blood is thicker even than flood-water.

"There was nothing wrong about my being here," he went on, "but I don't want it known. Don't spoil a good story, Mrs. Pitman."

I did not quite understand that, although those who followed the trial carefully may do so. Poor Mr. Howell! I am sure he believed that it was only a good story. He got the description of my onyx clock and wrote it down, and I gave him the manuscript for Mr. Ladley. That was the last I saw of him for some time.

That Thursday proved to be an exciting day. Late in the afternoon Terry, digging the mud out of the cellar, came across my missing gray false front near the coal vault and brought it up, grinning. And just before six Mr. Graves, the detective, rang the bell and then let himself in. I found him in the lower hall looking around.

"Well, Mrs. Pitman," he said, "has our friend come back yet?"

"She was no friend of mine."

"Not she. Ladley. He'll be out this evening, and he'll probably be around for his clothes."

I felt my knees waver, as they always did when he was spoken of.

"He may want to stay here," said Mr. Graves. "In fact, I think that's just what he will want."

"Not here," I protested. "The very thought of him makes me quake."

"If he comes here, better take him in. I want to know where he is."

I tried to say that I wouldn't have him, but the old habit of the ward asserted itself. From taking a bottle of beer or a slice of pie to telling one where one might or might not live, the police were autocrats in that neighborhood. And respectable woman that I am, my neighbors' fears of the front office have infected me.

"All right, Mr. Graves," I said.

He pushed the parlor door open and looked in, whistling. "This is the place, isn't it?"

"Yes. But it was upstairs that he—"

"I know. Tall woman, Mrs. Ladley?"

"Tall and blonde. Very airy in her manner."

He nodded and still stood looking in and whistling. "Never heard her speak of a town named Horner, did you?"

"Horner? No."

"I see." He turned and wandered out again into the hall, still whistling.

At the door he stopped and turned, however. "Look anything like this?" he asked, and held out one of his hands, with a small kodak picture on the palm.

It was a snapshot of a children's frolic in a village street, with some on-lookers in the background. Around one of the heads had been drawn a circle in pencil. I took it to the gas jet and looked at it closely. It was a tall woman with a hat on, not unlike Jennie Brice. She was looking over the crowd, and I could see only her face, and that in shadow. I shook my head.

"I thought not," he said. "We have a lot of stage pictures of her, but what with false hair and their being retouched beyond recognition they don't amount to much." He started out, and stopped on the doorstep to light a cigar.

"Take him on if he comes," he said. "And keep your eyes open. Feed him well and he won't kill you!"

I had plenty to think of when I was cooking Mr. Reynolds's supper: the chance that I might have Mr. Ladley again, and the woman at Horner. For it had come to me like a flash as Mr. Graves left that the "Horn—" on the paper slip might have been "Horner."

7

AFTER ALL there was nothing sensational about Mr. Ladley's return. He came at eight o'clock that night, fresh-shaved and with his hair cut, and, al-though he had a latchkey he rang the doorbell. I knew his ring, and I thought it no harm to carry an old razor of Mr. Pitman's with the blade open and folded back on the handle, the way the colored people use them, in my left hand.

But I saw at once that he meant no mischief.

"Good evening," he said, and put out his hand. I jumped back, until I saw there was nothing in it and that he only meant to shake hands. I didn't do it. I might have to take him in and make his bed and cook his meals, but I did not have to shake hands with him.

"You too!" he said, looking at me with what I suppose he meant to be a reproachful look. But he could no more put an expression of that sort in his eyes than a fish could. "I suppose, then, there is no use asking if I may have my old room? The front room. I won't need two."

I didn't want him, and he must have seen it. But I took him. "You may have it, as far as I'm concerned," I said. "But you'll have to let the paper-hanger in tomorrow."

"Assuredly." He came into the hall and stood looking around him, and I fancied he drew a breath of relief. "It isn't much yet," he said, "but it's better to look at than six feet of muddy water."

"Or than stone walls," I said.

He looked at me and smiled. "Or than stone walls," he repeated, and went into his room.

So I had him again, and if I gave him only the dull knives and locked up the bread knife the moment I had finished with it, who can blame me? I took all the precaution I could think of, had Terry put an extra bolt on every door, and hid the rat poison and the carbolic acid in the cellar.

Peter would not go near him. He hobbled around on his three legs, with the splint beating a sort of tattoo on the floor, but he stayed back in the kitchen with me, or in the yard.

It was Sunday night or early Monday morning that Jennie Brice disappeared. On Thursday evening her husband came back. On Friday the body of a woman was washed ashore at Beaver, down the Ohio River, but turned out to be that of a stewardess who had fallen overboard from one of the Cincinnati packets. Mr. Ladley himself showed me the article in the morning paper when I took in his breakfast.

"Public hysteria has killed a man before this," he said, when I had read it. "Suppose that woman had been mangled, or the screw of the steamer had cut her head off! How many people do you suppose would have been willing to swear that it was my—was Mrs. Ladley?"

"Even without a head I'd know Mrs. Ladley," I retorted.

He shrugged his shoulders. "Let's trust she's still alive, for my sake," he said. "But I'm glad anyhow that this woman has a head. You'll allow me to be glad, won't you?"

"You can be anything you want, as far as I'm concerned," I snapped, and went out.

Mr. Holcombe still retained the second-story front room. I think, although he said nothing more about it, that he was still "playing horse." He wrote a good bit at the washstand, and, from the loose sheets of manuscript he left I believe actually tried to begin a play. But mostly he wandered along the water front or stood on one or another of the bridges, looking at the water and thinking. It is certain that he tried to keep in the part by smoking cigarettes, but he hated them and usually ended by throwing the cigarette away and lighting an old pipe he carried.

On that Thursday evening he came home and sat down to supper with Mr. Reynolds. He ate little and seemed much excited. The talk ran on crime, as it always did when he was around, and Mr. Holcombe quoted Spencer a great deal, Herbert Spencer. Mr. Reynolds was impressed, not knowing much beyond silks and the National League.

"Spencer," Mr. Holcombe would say, "Spencer shows that every occurrence is the inevitable result of what has gone before, and carries in its train an equally inevitable series of results. Try to interrupt this chain in the smallest degree, and what follows? Chaos, my dear sir, chaos."

"We see that at the store," Mr. Reynolds would say. "Accustom a lot of women to a silk sale on Fridays and then make it toothbrushes. That's chaos, all right."

Well, Mr. Holcombe came in that night about ten o'clock and I told him Ladley was back. He was almost wild with excitement, wanted to have the back parlor so he could watch him through the keyhole, and was terribly upset when I told him there was no keyhole, that the door fastened with a thumb bolt. On learning that the room was to be papered the next morning he grew calmer, however, and got the paperhanger's address from me. He went out just after that.

Friday, as I say, was very quiet. Mr. Ladley moved to the back parlor to let the paperhanger in the front room, smoked and fussed with his papers all day, and Mr. Holcombe stayed in his room, which was unusual. In the afternoon Molly Maguire put on the striped fur coat and walked slowly past the house so that I would be sure to see her. Beyond slamming the window I gave her no satisfaction.

At four o'clock Mr. Holcombe came to my kitchen, rubbing his hands together. He had a pasteboard tube in his hand about a foot long, with an arrangement of small mirrors in it. He said it was modeled after the periscope that is used on a submarine, and that he and the paperhanger had fixed a place for it between his floor and the ceiling of Mr. Ladley's room, so that the chandelier would hide it from below. He thought he could watch Mr. Ladley through it; and as it turned out, he could.

"I want to find his weak moment," he said excitedly. "I want to know what he does when the door is closed and he can take off his mask. And I want to know if he sleeps with a light."

"If he does," I replied, "I hope you'll let me know, Mr. Holcombe. The gas bills are a horror to me as it is. I think he kept it on last night. I turned off all the other lights and went to the cellar. The meter was going around."

"Fine!" he said. "Every murderer fears the dark. And our friend of the parlor bedroom is a murderer, Mrs. Pitman. Whether he hangs or not he's a murderer."

The periscope was installed that day and worked amazingly well. Plaster is always falling in those old houses, especially after a flood. Mr. Holcombe had cut a hole in the floor boards of his room upstairs, and the paperhanger had done so in the ceiling below. It was not noticeable from below, having a paper flap which stayed pretty well in place until it was pushed down. It all seemed rather silly to me, but I went into Mr. Holcombe's room with him to try it out, and I distinctly saw the paperhanger take a cigarette from Mr. Ladley's box and put it in his pocket. Just after that Mr. Ladley sauntered into the room and looked at the new paper. I could both see and hear him. It was rather weird.

"God, what a wallpaper!" he said.

He did not look at the ceiling at all.

8

THAT WAS FRIDAY AFTERNOON. All that evening, and most of Saturday and Sunday, Mr. Holcombe sat on the floor with his eye to the reflecting mirror and his notebook beside him. I have it before me.

On the first page is the "dog meat—two dollars" entry. On the next, the description of what occurred on Sunday night, March fourth, and Monday morning the fifth. Following that came a copy, made with a carbon sheet, of the torn paper found behind the washstand:

And then came the entries for Friday, Saturday, and Sunday. Friday evening:

6:30—Eating hearty supper, brought from delicatessen.

7:00—Lights cigarette and paces floor. Notice that when Mrs. P. knocks he goes to desk and pretends to be writing.

8:00—Is examining book. Looks like a railway guide.

8:30—It is a steamship guide.

8:45—Tailor's boy brings box. Gives boy fifty cents. Query: Where does he get money, now that J.B. is gone?

9:00—Tries on new suit, brown.

9:30—Has been spending a quarter of an hour on his knees looking behind furniture and examining baseboard.

10:00—He has the key to the onyx clock. Has hidden it twice, once up the chimney flue, once behind baseboard.

10:15—He has just thrown key or similar small article out window into yard.

11:00—Has gone to bed. Light burning. Shall sleep here on floor.

11:30—He cannot sleep. Is up walking the floor and smoking.

2:00 A.M.—Saturday. Disturbance below. He had had nightmare and was calling "Jennie!" He got up, took a drink, and is now reading.

8:00 A.M.—Must have slept. He is shaving.

12:00 M.—Nothing this morning. He wrote for four hours, sometimes reading aloud what he had written.

2:00 P.M.—He has a visitor, a man. Cannot hear all, only a word now and then. "Llewellyn is the very man." "Devil of a risk—" "We'll see you through." "Lost the slip—"

Then more clearly: "Didn't go to the hotel. She went to a private house." "Eliza Shaeffer."

Who went to a private house? Jennie Brice?

2:30—Cannot hear at all. Are whispering. The visitor has given Ladley roll of bills.

4:00—Followed the visitor, a tall man with a pointed beard. He went to the Liberty Theater. Found it was Bronson, business manager there. Who is Llewellyn, and who is Eliza Shaeffer?

4:15—Had Mrs. P. bring telephone book. Six Llewellyns in the book, no Eliza Shaeffer. Ladley appears more cheerful since Bronson's visit. He has bought all the evening papers and is searching for something. Has not found it.

7:00—Ate well again. Have asked Mrs. P. to take my place here while I interview the six Llewellyns.

11:00—Mrs. P. reports a quiet evening. He read and smoked. Has gone to bed. Light burning. Saw five Llewellyns. None of them knew Bronson or Ladley. Sixth—a lawyer—out at revival meeting. Went to the church and walked home with him. He knows something. Acknowledged he knew Bronson. Had met Ladley. Did not believe Mrs. Ladley dead. Regretted I had not been to the meeting. Good sermon. Asked me for a dollar for missions.

9:00 A.M.—Sunday. Ladley in bad shape. Apparently been drinking all night. Cannot eat. Sent out early for papers and has searched them all. Found entry on second page, stared at it, then flung the paper away. Have sent out for same paper.

10:00 A.M.—Paper says: "Body of woman washed ashore yesterday at Sewickley. Much mutilated by flood debris." Ladley in bed, staring at ceiling. Wonder if he sees tube? He is ghastly.

That is the last entry in the notebook for that day: Mr. Holcombe called me in great excitement shortly after ten and showed me the item. Neither of us doubted for a moment that it was Jennie Brice who had been found. He started for Sewickley that same afternoon, and he probably communicated with the police before he left. For once or twice I saw Mr. Graves, the detective, sauntering past the house.

Mr. Ladley ate no dinner. He went out at four, and I had Mr. Reynolds follow him. But they were both back in a half hour. Mr. Reynolds reported that Mr. Ladley had bought some headache tablets and some bromide powders to make him sleep.

Mr. Holcombe came back that evening. He thought the body was that of Jennie Brice, but the head was gone. He was much depressed, and did not immediately go back to the periscope. I asked if the head had been cut off or taken off by a steamer. He was afraid the latter, as a hand was gone too.

It was about eleven o'clock that night that the doorbell rang. It was Mr. Graves, with a small man behind him. I knew the man; he lived in a shanty-boat not far from my house, a curious affair with shelves full of dishes and tinware. In the spring he would be towed up the Monongahcla a hundred miles or so and float down, tying up at different landings and selling his wares. Timothy Senft was his name. We called him Tim.

Mr. Graves motioned me to be quiet. Both of us knew that behind the parlor door Ladley was probably listening.

"Sorry to get you up, Mrs. Pitman," said Mr. Graves, "but this man says he has bought beer here today. That won't do, Mrs. Pitman."

"Beer! I haven't such a thing in the house. Come in and look," I snapped. And the two of them went back to the kitchen.

"Now," said Mr. Graves, when I had shut the door, "where's the dog's-meat man?"

"Upstairs."

"Bring him quietly."

I got Mr. Holcombe and he came eagerly, notebook and all. "Ah!" he said, when he saw Tim. "So you've turned up!"

"Yes, sir."

"It seems, Mr. Dog's—Mr. Holcombe," said Mr. Graves, "that you are right, partly anyhow. Tim here did help a man with a boat that night—"

"Threw him a rope, sir," Tim broke in. "He'd got out in the current, and what with the ice and his not knowing much about a boat he'd have kept on to New Orleans if I hadn't caught him, or to Kingdom Come."

"Exactly. And what time did you say this was?"

"Between three and four last Sunday night, or Monday morning. He said he couldn't sleep and went out in a boat, meaning to keep in close to shore. But he got drawn out in the current."

"Where did you see him first?"

"By the Ninth Street bridge."

"Did you hail him?"

"He saw my light and hailed me. I was making fast to a coal barge after one of my ropes had busted."

"You threw the line to him there?"

"No, sir. He tried to work in to shore. I ran along River Avenue to below the Sixth Street bridge. He got pretty close in there and I threw him a rope. He was about done up."

"Would you know him again?"

"Yes, sir. He gave me five dollars, and said to say nothing about it. He didn't want anybody to know he had been such a fool."

They took him quietly upstairs then and let him look through the periscope. He identified Mr. Ladley absolutely.

When Tim and Mr. Graves had gone, Mr. Holcombe and I were left alone in the kitchen. Mr. Holcombe leaned over and patted Peter as he lay in his basket.

"We've got him, old boy," he said. "The chain is just about complete. He'll never kick you again."

But Mr. Holcombe was wrong, not about kicking Peter, although I don't believe Mr. Ladley ever did that again, but in thinking we had him.

I washed that next morning, Monday, but all the time I was rubbing and starching and hanging out my mind was with Jennie Brice. The sight of Molly Maguire, next door, at the window, rubbing and brushing at the fur coat, only made things worse.

At noon when the Maguire youngsters came home from school I bribed Tommy, the youngest, into the kitchen with the promise of a doughnut.

"I see your mother has a new fur coat," I said, with the plate of doughnuts just beyond his reach.

"Yes'm."

"She didn't buy it?"

"Sure she didn't buy it. Say, Mrs. Pitman, gimme that doughnut."

"Oh, so the coat washed in?"

"No'm. Pop found it down by the Point, on a cake of ice. He thought it was a dog and rowed out for it."

Well, I hadn't wanted the coat, as far as that goes. I'd managed well enough without furs for twenty years or more. But it was a satisfaction to know that it had not floated into Mrs. Maguire's kitchen and spread itself at her feet, as one may say. However, that was not the question, after all. The real issue was that if it was Jennie Brice's coat, and was found across the river on a cake of ice, then one of two things was certain. Either Jennie Brice's body wrapped in the coat had been thrown into the water, out in the current, or she herself, hoping to incriminate her husband, had flung her coat into the river.

I told Mr. Holcombe, and he interviewed Joe Maguire that afternoon. The upshot of it was that Tommy had been correctly informed. Joe had witnesses who had lined up to see him rescue a dog, and had beheld his return in triumph with a wet and soggy fur coat. At three o'clock Mrs. Maguire, instructed by Mr. Graves, brought the coat to me for identification, turning it about for my inspection but refusing to take her hands off it.

"If her husband says to me that he wants it back, well and good," she said, "but I don't give it up to nobody but him. Some folks I know of would be glad enough to have it."

I was certain it was Jennie Brice's coat, but the maker's name had been ripped out. With Molly holding one arm and I the other, we took it to Mr. Ladley's door and knocked. He opened it, grumbling.

"I have asked you not to interrupt me," he said, with his pen in his hand. Then his eyes fell on the coat. "What's that?" he asked, changing color.

"I think it's Mrs. Ladley's fur coat," I said.

He stood there looking at it and thinking. Then: "It can't be hers," he said. "She wore hers when she went away."

"Perhaps she dropped it in the water."

He looked at me and smiled. "And why would she do that?" he asked mockingly. "Was it out of fashion?"

"That's Mrs. Ladley's coat," I persisted, but Molly Maguire jerked it from me and started away. He stood there looking at me and smiling in his nasty way.

"This excitement is telling on you, Mrs. Pitman," he said coolly. "You're too emotional for detective work." Then he went in and shut the door.

When I went downstairs Molly Maguire was waiting in the kitchen, and had the audacity to ask me if I thought the coat needed a new lining!

It was on Monday evening that the strangest event in years happened to me. I went to my sister's house! And the fact that I was admitted at a side entrance made it even stranger. It happened in this way:

Supper was over, and I was cleaning up, when an automobile came to the door. It was Alma's car. The chauffeur gave me a note:

Dear Mrs. Pitman—I am not at all well, and very anxious. Will you come to see me at once? My mother is out to dinner and I am alone. The car will bring you.

> Cordially,
> Lida Harvey.

I put on my best dress at once and got into the limousine. Half the neighborhood was out watching. I leaned back in the upholstered seat, fairly quivering with excitement. This was Alma's car. That was Alma's cardcase. The little clock had her monogram on it. Everything about it reminded me of Alma, a trifle showy but good to look at. And I was going to her house!

I was not taken to the main entrance, but to a side door. The queer dreamlike feeling was still there. In this back hall, separated from the more conspicuous part of the house, there were even pieces of furniture from our old home, and my father's picture in an oval gilt frame hung over my head. I had not seen a picture of him for twenty years. I went over and touched it gently.

"Father, father!" I said.

Under it was the tall hall chair that I had climbed over as a child, and had stood on many times to see myself in the mirror above. The chair was newly finished and looked the better for its age. I glanced in the old glass. The chair had stood time better than I. I was a middle-aged woman, lined with poverty and care, shabby, prematurely gray, a little hard. I had thought father an old man when that picture was taken, and now I was even older. "Father!" I whispered again, and fell to crying in the dimly lighted hall.

Lida sent for me at once. I had only time to dry my eyes and straighten my hat. Had I met Alma on the stairs I would have passed her without a word. She would not have known me. But I saw no one.

Lida was in bed. She was lying there with a rose-shaded lamp beside her and a great bowl of spring flowers on a little stand at her elbow. She sat up when I went in and had a maid place a chair for me beside the bed. She looked very childish, with her hair spread over the pillow and her slim young arms and throat bare.

"I'm so glad you came," she said, and would not be satisfied until the light was just right for my eyes, and my coat unfastened and thrown open.

"I'm not really sick," she informed me. "I'm just tired and nervous and—and unhappy, Mrs. Pitman."

"I'm sorry," I said. I wanted to lean over and pat her hand, to draw the covers around her and mother her a little. I had had no one to mother for so long. But I could not. She would have thought it queer and presumptuous —or, no, not that. She was too sweet to have thought that.

"Mrs. Pitman," she said suddenly, "who was this Jennie Brice?"

"She was an actress. She and her husband lived at my house."

"I never saw her acting: was she—was she beautiful?"

"Well," I said slowly, "I never thought of that. She was handsome, in a large way."

"Was she young?"

"Yes. Twenty-eight or so."

"That isn't very young," she said, looking relieved. "But I don't think men like very young women. Do you?"

"I know one who does," I said, smiling. But she sat up in bed suddenly and looked at me with her clear childish eyes.

"I don't want him to like me," she flashed. "I want him to hate me."

"Tut, tut! You want nothing of the sort."

"Mrs. Pitman," she said, "I sent for you because I'm nearly crazy. Mr. Howell was a friend of that woman. He has acted like a maniac since she disappeared. He doesn't come to see me, he has given up his work on the paper, and I saw him today on the street—he looks like a ghost."

That put me to thinking.

"He might have been a friend," I admitted. "Although, as far as I know, he was never at the house but once, and then he saw both of them."

"When was that?"

"Sunday morning, the day before she disappeared. They were arguing about something."

She was looking at me attentively. "You know more than you are telling me, Mrs. Pitman," she said. "Do you think Jennie Brice is dead, and that Mr. Howell knows who did it?"

"I think she is dead, and I think possibly Mr. Howell suspects who did it. He doesn't know, or he would have told the police."

"You don't think he was in love with her, do you?"

"I'm certain of that," I said. "He is very much in love with a foolish girl, who ought to have more faith in him than she has."

She colored a little and smiled at that, but the next moment she was sitting forward, tense and questioning again.

"If that's true, Mrs. Pitman," she said, "who was the woman he met Monday morning at daylight and took across the bridge to Pittsburgh? I believe it was Jennie Brice. If it wasn't, who was it?"

"I don't believe he took any woman across the bridge at that hour. Who says he did?"

"Uncle Jim saw him. He had been playing cards all night at one of the clubs, and was walking home. He says he met Mr. Howell face to face, and spoke to him. The woman was tall, but he couldn't see her face. Uncle Jim sent for him a day or two later, and he refused to explain. Then they forbade him the house. Mother objected to him anyhow and he only came on sufferance. He's a college man. His family is all right too. But he has no money at all except what he earns. And now—"

I had had some young newspapermen staying with me, and I knew what they got. They were nice boys, but they made about twenty-five dollars a week. I'm afraid I smiled a little as I looked around the room, with its pale-gray walls, its toilet table spread with ivory and gold, and the maid in attendance in her black dress and white apron, collar and cuffs. Even the little nightgown Lida was wearing would have taken a week's salary or more. She saw my smile.

"It was to be his chance," she said. "If he made good he was to have something better. My uncle Jim owns the paper and he promised me to help him. But—"

So Jim was running a newspaper. That was a curious career for Jim to choose. Jim, who was twice expelled from school, and who could never write a letter without a dictionary beside him! I had a pang when I heard his name again, after all the years. For I had written to Jim from Oklahoma after Mr. Pitman died, asking for money to bury him, and had never even had a reply.

"And you haven't seen him since?" I inquired.

"Once. I didn't hear from him, and I called him up. We met in the park. He said everything was all right, but he couldn't tell me anything just then. The next day he resigned from the paper and went away. Mrs. Pitman, it's driving me crazy! For they have found a body and they think it's hers. If it is, and he was with her—"

"Don't be a foolish girl," I protested. "If he was with Jennie Brice, she's still living, and if he was not with Jennie Brice—"

"If it wasn't Jennie Brice, then I have a right to know who it was," she declared. "He was not like himself at all when I met him. He said such queer things. He talked about an onyx clock, and said he had been made a fool of, and that no matter what came out I was always to remember that he had done what he did for the best. And that—that he cared for me more than for anything else in this world or the next."

"That wasn't so foolish." I couldn't help it. I leaned over and drew the blanket up over her bare white shoulder. "You won't help anything or anybody by taking cold, my dear," I said. "Call your maid and have her put a bed jacket on you."

I left soon after. There was little I could do. But I comforted her as best I could, and said good night. My heart was heavy as I went downstairs. For, twist things as I might, it was clear that in some way the Howell boy was mixed up in the Brice case. Poor little troubled Lida! Poor distracted boy!

I had a curious experience downstairs. I had reached the foot of the staircase and was turning to go back along the hall to the side entrance, when I came face to face with Isaac, the old colored man who had driven the family carriage when I was a child, and whom I had seen at intervals since I came back, pottering around Alma's house. The old man was bent and feeble. He came slowly down the hall with a bunch of keys in his hand. I had seen him do the same thing many times.

He stopped when he saw me and I shrank back from the light, but he had seen me. "Miss Bess!" he said. "Foh Gawd's sake, Miss Bess!"

"You are making a mistake, my friend," I said, quivering. "I am not Miss Bess!"

He came close to me and stared into my face. And from that he looked at my cloth gloves, at my old coat, and he shook his white head. "I sure thought you was Miss Bess," he said, and made no further effort to detain me. He led the way back to the door where the car waited, his head shaking with the palsy of age, and muttering as he went. He opened the door with his best manner, and stood aside.

"Good night, ma'am," he quavered.

I had tears in my eyes. I tried to keep them back. "Good night," I said. "Good night, *Ikkie*."

It had slipped out, my baby name for old Isaac.

"Miss Bess!" he cried. "Oh, praise Gawd, it's Miss Bess again!"

He caught my arm and pulled me back into the hall, and there he held me, crying over me, muttering praises for my return, begging me to come back, recalling little tender things out of the past which almost killed me to hear again.

But I had made my bed and must lie in it. I forced him to swear silence about my visit. I made him promise not to reveal my identity to Lida, and I told him—Heaven forgive me—that I was well and prosperous and happy.

Dear old Isaac! I would not let him come to see me, but the next day there came a basket with six bottles of wine, and an old daguerreotype of my mother which had been his great treasure. Nor was that basket the last.

Perhaps he followed me home that night. Certainly he discovered where I lived.

9

THE CORONER held an inquest over the headless body the next day, Tuesday. Mr. Graves telephoned me in the morning, and I went to the morgue with him.

I do not like the morgue, although some of my neighbors pay it weekly visits. It is by way of excursion, like the nickelodeons or watching the circus put up its tents. I have heard them threaten the children that if they misbehaved they would not be taken to the morgue that week.

But I failed to identify the body. How could I? It had been a tall woman, probably five feet eight, and I thought the nails looked like those of Jennie Brice. The thumbnail of one was broken short off, and I told Mr. Graves about her speaking of a broken nail. But he shrugged his shoulders and said nothing.

There was a curious scar over the heart, and he was making a sketch of it. It reached from the center of the chest for about six inches across the left breast, a narrow thin line that one could hardly see. It was shaped like this:

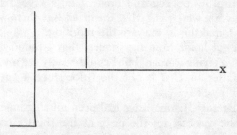

I felt sure that Jennie Brice had had no such scar, and Mr. Graves thought as I did. Temple Hope, called to the inquest, said she had never heard of one, and Mr. Ladley himself at the inquest swore that his wife had had nothing of the sort. I was watching him, and I did not think he was lying. Yet the hand was very like Jennie Brice's. It was all bewildering.

Mr. Ladley's testimony at the inquest was disappointing. He was cool and collected, said he had no reason to believe that his wife was dead and less reason to think she had been drowned. She had left him in a rage, and if she found out that by hiding she was putting him in an unpleasant position she would probably hide indefinitely.

To the disappointment of everybody the identity of the woman remained a mystery. No one with such a scar was missing. A small woman of my own age, a Mrs. Murray whose daughter, a stenographer, had disappeared, attended the inquest. But her daughter had had no such scar, and had worn her nails short because of using the typewriter. Alice Murray was the missing girl's name. Her mother sat beside me, and cried most of the time.

One thing was brought out at the inquest. The body had been thrown into the river after death. There was no water in the lungs. The verdict was "death at the hands of some person or persons unknown."

Mr. Holcombe was not satisfied. In some way or other he had got permission to attend the autopsy, and had brought away a tracing of the scar. All the way home in the streetcar he stared at the drawing, holding first one eye shut and then the other. But, like the coroner, he got nowhere. He folded the paper and put it in his notebook.

"None the less, Mrs. Pitman," he said, "that is the body of Jennie Brice. Her husband killed her, probably by strangling her. He took the body out in the boat and dropped it into the swollen river above the Ninth Street bridge."

"Why do you think he strangled her?"

"There was no mark on the body, and no poison was found."

"Then if he strangled her, where did the blood in the room come from?"

"I didn't limit myself to strangulation," he said irritably. "He may have cut her throat."

"Or brained her with my onyx clock," I added, with a sigh. For I missed the clock more and more.

He went down in his pockets and brought up a key. "I'd forgotten this," he said. "It shows you were right, that the clock was there when the Ladleys took the room. I found this in the yard this morning."

It was when I got home from the inquest that I found old Isaac's basket waiting. I am not a crying woman, but I could hardly see my mother's picture for tears. Well, after all, that is not the Brice story. I am not writing the sordid tragedy of my life.

That was on Tuesday. Jennie Brice had been missing nine days. In all that time, although she was cast for the piece at the theater that week, no one there had heard from her. Her relatives had had no word. She had gone away, if she had gone, on a cold March night in a striped black and white dress with a red collar and a red and black hat, but without her fur coat, which she had worn all winter. She had gone very early in the morning, or during the night. How had she gone? Mr. Ladley said he had rowed her to Federal Street at half after six and had brought the boat back. After they had quarreled violently all night, and when she was leaving him, wouldn't he have allowed her to take herself away? Besides, the police had found no trace of her on any early train. And then at daylight, between five and six, my own brother had seen a woman with young Howell, a woman who might have been Jennie Brice. But if it was, why did Mr. Howell not say so?

Mr. Ladley claimed she was hiding, to make trouble for him. But Jennie Brice was not that sort of woman. There was something big about her, something which is found often in large women, a lack of spite. She was not petty or malicious. Her faults, like her virtues, were for all to see.

In spite of the failure to identify the body Mr. Ladley was arrested that night, Tuesday, and this time it was for murder. I know now that the police were taking long chances. They had no strong motive for the crime. As Mr. Holcombe said, they had provocation but not motive, which is different. They had opportunity, and they had a lot of straggling links of clues, which in the total made a fair chain of circumstantial evidence. But that was all.

That is the way the case stood on Tuesday night, March the thirteenth.

Mr. Ladley was taken away at nine o'clock. He was perfectly cool, asked me to help him pack a suitcase, and whistling while it was being done. He requested to be allowed to walk to the jail, and went quietly, with a detective on one side and I think a sheriff's officer on the other.

Just before he left, he asked for a word or two with me, and when he paid his bill up to date and gave me an extra dollar for taking care of Peter I was almost overcome. He took the manuscript of his play with him, and I remember his asking if he could have any typing done in the jail. I had never seen a man arrested for murder before, but I think he was probably the coolest suspect the officers had ever seen. They hardly knew what to make of it.

Mr. Reynolds and I had a cup of tea after all the excitement, and were sitting at the dining-room table drinking it when the bell rang. It was Mr. Howell. He half staggered into the hall when I opened the door, and was for going into the parlor bedroom without a word.

"Mr. Ladley's gone, if you want him," I said. I thought his face cleared.

"Gone!" he said. "Where?"

"To jail."

He did not reply at once. He stood there, tapping the palm of one hand with the forefinger of the other. He was dirty and unshaved. His clothes looked as if he had been sleeping in them.

"So they've got him!" he muttered finally, and turning was about to go out the front door without another word. But I caught his arm.

"You're sick, Mr. Howell," I said. "You'd better not go out just yet."

"Oh, I'm all right." He took his handkerchief out and wiped his face. I saw that his hands were shaking.

"Come back and have a cup of tea and a slice of homemade bread."

He hesitated and looked at his watch. "I'll do it, Mrs. Pitman," he said. "I suppose I'd better throw a little fuel into this engine of mine. It's been going hard for several days."

He ate like a wolf. I cut half a loaf into slices for him, and he drank the rest of the tea. Mr. Reynolds creaked up to bed and left him still eating, and me still cutting and spreading. Now that I had a chance to see him, I was shocked. The rims of his eyes were red, his collar was dirty, and his hair hung over his forehead. But when he finally sat back and looked at me his color was better.

"So they've canned him!" he said.

"High time, too," said I.

He leaned forward and put both his elbows on the table. "Mrs. Pitman," he said earnestly, "I don't like him any more than you do. But he never killed that woman."

"Somebody killed her."

"How do you know? How do you know she's dead?"

Well, I didn't, of course. I only felt it.

"The police haven't even proved a crime. They can't hold a man for a supposititious murder."

"Perhaps they can't but they're doing it," I retorted. "If the woman's alive she won't let him hang."

"I'm not so sure of that," he said heavily, and got up. He looked in the little mirror over the sideboard and brushed back his hair. "I look bad enough," he said, "but I feel worse. Well, you've saved my life, Mrs. Pitman. Thank you."

"How is my—how is Miss Harvey?" I asked, as we started out. He turned and smiled at me in his boyish way.

"The best ever!" he said. "I haven't seen her for days, and it seems like centuries. She's the only girl in the world for me, Mrs. Pitman, although I—" He stopped and drew a long breath. "She is beautiful, isn't she?"

"Very beautiful," I answered. "Her mother was always—"

"Her mother!" He looked at me curiously.

"I knew her mother years ago," I said, putting the best face on my mistake that I could.

"Then I'll remember you to her, if she ever allows me to see her again. Just now I'm *persona non grata.*"

"If you'll do the kindly thing, Mr. Howell," I said, "you'll forget me to her."

He looked into my eyes and then thrust out his hand.

"All right," he said. "I'll not ask any questions. I guess there are some curious stories hidden in these old houses."

Peter hobbled to the front door with him. He had not gone as far as the parlor once while Mr. Ladley was in the house.

They had had a sale of spring flowers at the store that day, and Mr. Reynolds had brought me a pot of white tulips. That night I hung my mother's picture over the mantel in the dining room, and put the tulips beneath it. It gave me a feeling of comfort; I had never seen my mother's grave, or put flowers on it.

10

I HAVE SAID BEFORE that I do not know anything about the law. I believe that the Ladley case was unusual in several ways. Mr. Ladley had once been well known in New York among the people who frequent the theaters, and Jennie Brice was even better known. A good many lawyers, I believe, said that the police had not a leg to stand on, and I know the case was watched with much interest by the legal profession. People wrote letters to the newspapers, protesting against Mr. Ladley's being held. And I believe that the district attorney, in taking him before the grand jury, hardly hoped to secure an indictment.

But he did, to his own surprise, I fancy, and the trial was set for May. In the meantime, however, many curious things had happened.

In the first place, the week following Mr. Ladley's arrest my rooms were filled up with eight or ten members of a touring company from the Gaiety Theater, very cheerful and jolly and well behaved. Three men, I think, and the rest girls. One of the men was named John Bellows, and it turned out that he had known Jennie Brice very well.

From the moment he learned this Mr. Holcombe hardly left him. He walked to the theater with him and waited to walk home again. He took him out to restaurants and for long walks or rides in the mornings, and on the last night of their stay, Saturday, they got gloriously drunk together—Mr. Holcombe, no doubt, in his character of Ladley—and came reeling in at three in the morning, singing. Mr. Holcombe was very sick the next day, but by Monday he was all right, and he called me into the room.

"We've got him, Mrs. Pitman," he said, looking mottled but cheerful. "As sure as God made little fishes we've got him." That was all he would say. It seemed he was going to New York, and might be gone for a month. "I've no family," he said, "and enough money to keep me. If I find my relaxation in hunting down criminals, it's a harmless and cheap amusement, and it's my own business."

He went away that night, and I must admit I missed him. I rented the parlor bedroom the next day to a schoolteacher, and I found the periscope affair very handy. I could see just how much gas she used, and although the notice on each door forbids cooking and washing in rooms, I found she was doing both: making coffee and boiling an egg in the morning, and rubbing out stockings and handkerchiefs in her washbowl. I'd much rather have men as boarders than women. The women are always lighting alcohol lamps on the bureau, and wanting the bed turned into a cozy corner so they can see their gentlemen friends in their rooms.

Well, with Mr. Holcombe gone, and Mr. Reynolds busy all day and half the night getting out the summer silks and preparing for remnant day, and with Mr. Ladley in jail and Lida out of the city—for I saw in the papers that she was not well, and her mother had taken her to Bermuda—I had a good bit of time on my hands. And so I got in the habit of thinking things over and trying to draw conclusions, as I had seen Mr. Holcombe do. I would sit down and write things out as they had happened, and study them, and especially I worried over how we could have found a slip of paper in Mr. Ladley's room with a list, almost exact, of the things we had discovered there.

I used to read it over, "rope, knife, shoe, towel, Horn—" and get more and more bewildered. "Horn—might have been a town, or it might not have been. There was a town called Horner, according to Mr. Graves, but apparently he had made nothing of it. Was it a town that was meant?

The dictionary gave only a few words beginning with "horn"—hornet, hornblende, hornpipe, and horny, none of which was of any assistance. And then one morning I happened to see in the personal column of one of the newspapers that a woman named Eliza Shaeffer of Horner had day-old Buff Orpington and Plymouth Rock chicks for sale, and it started me to puzzling again. Perhaps it had been Horner, and possibly this very Eliza Shaeffer—

I suppose my lack of experience was in my favor, for, after all, Eliza Shaeffer is a common enough name, and the "Horn" might have stood for hornswoggle for all I knew. The story of the man who thought of what he would do if he were a horse came back to me, and for an hour or so I tried to think I was Jennie Brice, wanting to get away and hide from my rascal of a husband. But I made no headway. I would never have gone to Horner, or to any small town, if I had wanted to hide. I think I should have gone around the corner and taken a room in my own neighborhood, or have lost myself in some large city.

It was that same day that, since I did not go to Horner, Horner came to me. The bell rang about three o'clock, and I answered it myself. For with times hard and only two or three roomers all winter I had not had a servant, except Terry to do odd jobs, for some months.

There stood a fresh-faced young girl holding a covered basket.

"Are you Mrs. Pitman?" she asked.

"I don't need anything today," I said, trying to shut the door. And at that minute something in the basket cheeped. Young women selling poultry are not common in our neighborhood. "What have you there?" I asked more agreeably.

"Chicks, day-old chicks, but I'm not trying to sell you any. I—may I come in?"

It was dawning on me then that perhaps this was Eliza Shaeffer. I led her back to the dining room, with Peter sniffing at the basket.

"My name is Shaeffer," she said. "I've seen your name in the papers, and I believe I know something about Jennie Brice."

Eliza Shaeffer's story was curious. She said that she was postmistress at Horner, and lived with her mother on a farm a mile out of the town, driving in and out each day in a buggy.

On Monday afternoon, March fifth, a woman had alighted at the station from a train and had eaten lunch at the hotel. She told the clerk she was on the road selling corsets, and was much disappointed to find no store of any size in the town. The woman, who had registered as Mrs. Jane Bellows, said she was tired and would like to rest for a day or two on a farm. She was told to see Eliza Shaeffer at the post office and, as a result, drove out with her to the farm after the last mail came in that evening.

Asked to describe her, the girl said she was over medium height, light-haired, quick in her movements, and wore a black and white striped dress with a red collar and hat to match. She carried a small brown valise which Miss Shaeffer presumed contained her samples.

Mrs. Shaeffer had made her welcome, although they did not usually take boarders until June. She had not eaten much supper, and that night she had asked for pen and ink and had written a letter. The letter was not mailed until Wednesday. All of Tuesday Mrs. Bellows had spent in her room, and Mrs. Shaeffer had driven to the village in the afternoon with word that she had been crying all day, and bought some headache medicine for her.

On Wednesday morning, however, she had appeared at breakfast, eaten heartily, and had asked Miss Shaeffer to take her letter to the post office. It was addressed to Mr. Ellis Howell, in care of a Pittsburgh newspaper.

That night when Miss Eliza went home, about half past eight, the woman was gone. She had paid for her room and had been driven as far as Thornville, where all trace of her had been lost. On account of the disappearance of Jennie Brice being published shortly after that, Eliza and her mother had driven to Thornville, but the station agent there was surly. They had learned nothing about the woman.

Since that time, three men had made inquiries about the woman in question. One had a Vandyke beard. The second from the description I fancied must have been Mr. Graves. The third without doubt was young Howell. Eliza Shaeffer said that this last man had seemed half frantic. I brought her photographs of Jennie Brice in a couple of plays. She said there was a resemblance, but that it ended there. Only of course, as Mr. Graves had said, by the time an actress gets her photograph retouched to suit her it doesn't particularly resemble her. And unless I had known Jennie Brice myself I should hardly have recognized the pictures.

Well, in spite of all that, there seemed no doubt that Jennie Brice had been living three days after her disappearance, and that would clear Mr. Ladley. But what had Mr. Howell to do with it all? Why had he not told the police of the letter from Horner? Or about the woman on the bridge? Why had Mr. Bronson, who was likely the man with the pointed beard, said nothing about having traced Jennie Brice to Horner?

I did as I thought Mr. Holcombe would have wished me to do. I wrote down on a clean sheet of note paper all that Eliza Shaeffer said, the description of the black and white dress, the woman's height, and the rest. Then I took her to the courthouse, chicks and all, and she told her story there to one of the assistant district attorneys.

The young man was interested, but not convinced. He had her story taken down, and she signed it. He was smiling as he bowed us out. I turned in the doorway.

"This will free Mr. Ladley, I suppose?" I asked.

"Not just yet," he said pleasantly. "This makes just eleven places where Jennie Brice spent the first three days after her death."

"But I can positively identify the dress."

"My good woman, that dress has been described, to the last stilted arch and colonial volute, in every newspaper in the United States!"

That evening the newspapers announced that during a conference at the jail between Mr. Ladley and James Bronson, business manager at the Liberty Theater, Mr. Ladley had attacked Mr. Bronson with a chair and almost brained him.

11

ELIZA SHAEFFER went back to Horner, after delivering her chicks somewhere in the city, and things went on as before. The trial was set for May. The district attorney's office had all the material we had found in the house that Monday afternoon, the stained towel, the broken knife and its blade, the slipper that had been floating in the parlor, and the rope that had fastened my boat to the staircase. Somewhere—wherever they keep such things—was the headless body of a woman with a hand missing and with a curious scar across the left breast. The slip of paper which I had found behind the baseboard, however, was still in Mr. Holcombe's possession, nor had he mentioned it to the police.

Mr. Holcombe had not come back. He wrote me twice asking me to hold his room, once from New York and once from Chicago. To the second letter he added a postscript:

Have not found what I wanted, but am getting warm. If any news, address me at Des Moines, Iowa, General Delivery.   H.

It was nearly the end of April when I saw Lida again. I had seen by the newspapers that she and her mother were coming home. I wondered if she had heard from young Howell, for I had not, and I wondered too if she would send for me again.

But she came herself, on foot, late one afternoon, and the schoolteacher being out I took her into the parlor bedroom. She looked thinner than before and rather white. My heart ached for her.

"I've been away," she explained. "I thought you might wonder why you didn't hear from me. But, you see, my mother—" She stopped and flushed. "I would have written you from Bermuda, but my mother watched my correspondence, so I couldn't."

No. I knew she couldn't. Alma had once found a letter of mine to Mr. Pitman. Very little escaped Alma.

"I wondered if you have heard anything?" she asked.

"I have heard nothing. Mr. Howell was here once, just after I saw you. I didn't believe he is in the city."

"Perhaps not, although— Mrs. Pitman, I believe he is in the city, hiding."

"Hiding? Why?"

"I don't know. But last night I thought I saw him below my window. I opened the window, so if he was there, he could see me. But he moved on without a word. Later whoever it was came back. I put out my light and watched. Someone stood there in the shadow until after two this morning. Part of the time he was looking up."

"Don't you think, had it been Howell, he would have spoken when he saw you?"

She shook her head. "He's in trouble," she said. "He hasn't heard from me, and he thinks I don't care any more. Just look at me, Mrs. Pitman! Do I look as if I don't care?"

She looked half killed, poor lamb.

"He may be out of town, searching for a better position," I tried to comfort her. "He wants to have something to offer more than himself."

"I only want him," she said, looking at me frankly. "I don't know why I tell you all this, but you're so kind, and I have to talk to someone."

She sat there, in the cozy corner the schoolteacher had made with a portiere and some cushions, and I saw she was about ready to break down and cry. I went over to her and took her hand, for she was my own niece, although she didn't suspect it, and I had never had a child of my own.

But after all I could not help her much. I could only assure her that he would come back and explain everything, and that he was all right, and that the last time I had seen him he had spoken of her, and had said she was "the best ever." My heart fairly yearned over the girl, and I think she felt it. For she kissed me shyly when she was leaving.

With the newspaper files before me it is not hard to give the details of that sensational trial. It commenced on Monday, the seventh of May, but it was late Wednesday when the jury was finally selected. I was at the courthouse early on Thursday, and so was Mr. Reynolds.

The district attorney made a short speech. "We propose, gentlemen, to prove that the prisoner, Philip Ladley, murdered his wife," he said in part. "We will show first that a crime was committed. Then we will show a motive for this crime. And finally we expect to show that the body washed ashore at Sewickley is the body of the murdered woman, and thus establish beyond doubt the prisoner's guilt."

Mr. Ladley listened with attention. He wore the brown suit, and looked well and cheerful. He was much more like a spectator than a prisoner, and he was not so nervous as I was.

Of that first day I don't recall much. I was called early in the day. The district attorney questioned me.

"Your name?"

"Elizabeth Marie Pitman."

"Your occupation?"

"I keep a boardinghouse at 42 Union Street."

"You know the prisoner?"

"Yes. He was a boarder in my house."

"For how long?"

"From December first. He and his wife came at that time."

"Was his wife the actress, Jennie Brice?"

"Yes, sir."

"Were they living together at your house the night of March fourth?"

"Yes, sir."

"In what part of the house?"

"They rented the double parlors downstairs, but on account of the flood I moved them upstairs to the second-floor front."

"That was on Sunday? You moved them on Sunday?"

"Yes, sir."

"At what time did you retire that night?"

"Not at all. The water was very high. I lay down dressed at one o'clock, and dropped into a doze."

"How long did you sleep?"

"An hour or so. Mr. Reynolds, a boarder, roused me to say he had heard someone rowing a boat in the lower hall."

"Do you keep a boat around during floodtimes?"

"Yes, sir."

"What did you do when Mr. Reynolds roused you?"

"I went to the top of the stairs. My boat was gone."

"Was the boat secured?"

"Yes, sir. By a rope. Anyhow there was no current in the hall."

"What did you do then?"

"I waited a time and went back to my room."

"What examination of the house did you make, if any?"

"Mr. Reynolds looked around."

"What did he find?"

"He found Peter, the Ladleys' dog, shut in a room on the third floor."

"Was there anything unusual about that?"

"I had never known it to happen before."

"State what happened later."

"I did not go to sleep again. At a quarter after four I heard the boat come back. I took a candle and went to the stairs. It was Mr. Ladley. He said he had been out getting medicine for his wife."

"Did you see him tie up the boat?"

"Yes."

"Did you observe any stains on the rope?"

"I did not notice any."

"What was the prisoner's manner at that time?"

"I thought he was surly."

"Now, Mrs. Pitman, tell us about the following morning."

"I saw Mr. Ladley at a quarter before seven. He said to bring breakfast for one. His wife had gone away. I asked if she was not ill and he said no, that she had gone away early, that he had rowed her to Federal Street, and that she would be back Saturday. It was shortly after that when the dog Peter brought in one of Mrs. Ladley's slippers, water-soaked."

"You recognized the slipper?"

"Positively. I had seen it often."

"What did you do with it?"

"I took it to Mr. Ladley."

"What did he say?"

"He said at first that it was not hers. Then he said if it was she would never wear it again. Then he added, because it was ruined."

"Did he offer any statement as to where his wife was?"

"No, sir. Not at that time. Before, he had said she had gone away for a few days."

"Tell the jury about the broken knife."

"The dog found it floating in the parlor with the blade broken off."

"You had not left it downstairs?"

"No, sir. I had used it upstairs the night before, and left it on a mantel of the room I was using as a temporary kitchen."

"Was the door of this room locked?"

"No. It was standing open."

"Were you asleep in this room?"

"Yes. For some hours."

"You heard no one come in?"

"No one until Mr. Reynolds roused me."

"Where did you find the blade?"

"Behind the bed in Mr. Ladley's room."

"What else did you find in the room?"

"A bloodstained towel behind the washstand. Also my onyx clock was missing."

"Where was the clock when the Ladleys were moved up into this room?"

"On the mantel. I wound it just before they came upstairs."

"When you saw Mrs. Ladley on Sunday did she say she was going away?"

"No, sir."

"Did you see any preparation for a journey?"

"The black and white dress was laid out on the bed, and a small bag. She said she was taking the dress to the theater to lend to Miss Hope."

"Is that all she said?"

"No. She said she'd been wishing her husband would drown; that he was a fiend.

I could see that my testimony had made an impression. I tried not to look at Mr. Ladley, but it was difficult. When I did he looked relaxed, and once he even smiled at me. It was all a most unpleasant experience, and it was not over.

12

THE SLIPPER, the rope, the towel, and the knife and blade were produced in court, and I identified them all. They made a noticeable impression on the jury. Then Mr. Llewellyn, the lawyer for the defense, cross-examined me.

"Is it not true, Mrs. Pitman," he said, "that many articles, particularly shoes and slippers, are found floating around during a flood?"

"Yes," I admitted.

"Now, you say the dog found this slipper floating in the hall and brought it to you. Are you sure this slipper belonged to Jennie Brice?"

"She wore it. I presume it belonged to her."

"Ahem. Now, Mrs. Pitman, after the Ladleys had been moved to the upper floor, did you search their bedroom and the connecting room downstairs?"

"No, sir."

"Ah. Then how do you know that this slipper was not left on the floor or in a closet?"

"It is possible, but not likely. Anyhow, it was not the slipper alone. It was the other things *and* the slipper. It was—"

"Exactly. Now, Mrs. Pitman, this knife. Can you identify it positively?"

"I can."

"But isn't it true that this is a very common sort of knife? One that nearly every housewife has in her possession?"

"Yes, sir. But that knife handle has three notches in it. I put the notches there myself."

"Before this presumed crime?"

"Yes, sir."

"For what purpose?"

"My neighbors were constantly borrowing things. It was a means of identification."

"Then this knife is yours?"

"Yes."

"Tell again where you left it the night before it was found floating downstairs."

"On a shelf over the stove."

"Could the dog have reached it there?"

"Not without standing on a hot stove."

"Is it not possible that Mr. Ladley, unable to untie the boat, borrowed your knife to cut the boat's painter?"

"No painter was cut that I heard about. The paperhanger—"

"No, no. The boat's painter—the rope."

"Oh! Well, he might have. He never said."

"Now then, this towel, Mrs. Pitman. Did not the prisoner, on the following day, tell you that he had cut his wrist in freeing the boat, and ask you for some court plaster?"

"He did not," I said firmly.

"You have not seen a scar on his wrist?"

"No." I glanced at Mr. Ladley: he was smiling again, as if amused. It made me angry. "And what's more," I flashed, "if he has a cut on his wrist, he put it there himself, to account for the towel."

I was sorry the next moment that I had said it, but it was too late. The counsel for the defense moved to exclude the answer and I received a caution that I deserved. Then:

"You saw Mr. Ladley when he brought your boat back?"

"Yes."

"What time was that?"

"A quarter after four Monday morning."

"Did he come in quietly, like a man trying to avoid attention?"

"Not particularly. It would have been of no use. The dog was barking."

"What did he say?"

"That he had been out for medicine. That his wife was sick."

"Do you know a pharmacist named Alexander, Jonathan Alexander?"

"There is such a one, but I don't know him."

I was excused, and Mr. Reynolds was called. He had heard no quarreling that Sunday night; had even heard Mrs. Ladley laughing. This was about nine o'clock. Yes, they had fought in the afternoon. He had not overheard any words, but their voices were quarrelsome, and once he heard a chair or some article of furniture overthrown. Was awakened about two by footsteps on the stairs, followed by the sound of oars in the lower hall. He told his story plainly and simply. Under cross-examination admitted that he was fond of detective stories and had tried to write one himself; that he had said at the store that he would like to see that "conceited ass" swing, referring to the prisoner; that he had sent flowers to Jennie Brice at the theater, and had made a few advances to her, without success.

My head was going around. I don't know yet how the police learned it all, but by the time poor Mr. Reynolds left the stand half the people there believed that he had been in love with Jennie Brice, that she had spurned his advances, and that there was more to the story than any of them had suspected.

Miss Hope's story held without any alteration under the cross-examination. She was perfectly at ease, looked handsome and well dressed, and could not be shaken. She told how Jennie Brice had been in fear of her life and had asked her, only the week before she disappeared, to allow her to go home with her Miss Hope. She told of the attack of hysteria in her dressing room, and that the missing woman had said that her husband would kill her someday. There was much wrangling over her testimony, and I believe at least a part of it was not allowed to go to the jury. But I am not a lawyer, and I repeat what I recall.

"Did she say that he had attacked her?"

"Yes, more than once. She was a large woman, fairly muscular, and had always held her own."

"Did she say that these attacks came when he had been drinking?"

"I believe he was worse then."

"Did she give any reason for her husband's attitude to her?"

"She said he wanted to marry another woman."

There was a small sensation at this. If proved, it established a motive.

"Did she know who the other woman was?"

"I believe not. She was away most of the day, and he put in his time as he liked."

"Did Miss Brice ever mention the nature of the threats he made against her?"

"No, I think not."

"Have you examined the body washed ashore at Sewickley?"

"Yes," in a low voice.

"Is it the body of Jennie Brice?"

"I cannot say."

"Does the remaining hand look like the hand of Jennie Brice?"

"Very much. The nails are filed to points, as she wore hers."

"Did you ever know of Jennie Brice having a scar on her breast?"

"No, but that would be easily concealed."

"Just what do you mean?"

"Many actresses conceal defects. She could have worn flesh-colored plaster and covered it with powder. Also, such a scar would not necessarily be seen."

"Explain that."

"Most of Jennie Brice's décolleté gowns were cut to a point. That would conceal such a scar."

Miss Hope was excused, and Jennie Brice's sister from Olean was called. She was a smaller woman than Jennie Brice had been, very lady-like in her manner. She said she was married and living in Olean. She had not seen her sister for several years, but had heard from her often. The witness had discouraged the marriage to the prisoner.

"Why?"

"She had had bad luck before."

"She had been married before?"

"Yes, to a man named John Bellows. They were in vaudeville together, on the Keith Circuit. They were known as the Pair of Bellows."

I sat up at this, for John Bellows had boarded at my house.

"Mr. Bellows is dead?"

"I think not. She divorced him."

"Did you know of any scar on your sister's body?"

"I never heard of one."

"Have you seen the body found at Sewickley?"

"Yes," faintly.

"Can you identify it?"

"No, sir."

A flurry was caused during the afternoon by Timothy Senft. He testified to what I already knew, that between three and four on Monday morning, during the height of the flood, he had seen from his shanty-boat a small skiff caught in the current near the Ninth Street bridge. He had shouted encouragingly to the man in the boat, running out a way on the ice to make him hear. He had told him to row with the current, and to try to steer in toward shore. He had followed close to the riverbank in his own boat. Below Sixth Street the other boat was within rope-throwing distance. He had pulled it in, and had towed it well back out of the current. The man in the boat was the prisoner. Asked if the prisoner gave any explanation—yes, he said he couldn't sleep, and had thought to tire himself rowing. He had been caught in the current before he knew it. He himself saw nothing suspicious in or about the boat. As they passed the police patrol boat, the prisoner had called to ask if there was much distress, and expressed regret when told there was.

Tim was excused. He had made a profound impression. I would not have given a dollar for Mr. Ladley's chance with the jury, at that time.

13

THE PROSECUTION produced many witnesses during the next two days: Shanty-boat Tim's story withstood the most vigorous cross-examination. After him, Mr. Bronson from the theater corroborated Miss Hope's story of Jennie Brice's attack of hysteria in the dressing room, and told of taking her home that night.

He was a poor witness, nervous and halting. He weighed each word before he said it, and he made a generally unfavorable impression. I thought he was holding something back. In view of what Mr. Pitman would have called the denouement, his attitude is easily explained. But I was puzzled then.

So far the prosecution had touched but lightly on the possible motive for a crime, the other woman. But on the third day, to my surprise, a Mrs. Agnes Murray was called. It was the Mrs. Murray I had seen at the morgue.

I have lost the clipping of that day's trial, but I remember her testimony perfectly.

She was a widow, living above a small millinery shop on Federal Street, Allegheny. She had one daughter, Alice, who did stenography and typing as a means of livelihood. She had no office, and worked at home. Many of the small stores in the neighborhood employed her to send out their bills. There was a card at the street entrance beside the shop, and now and then strangers brought her work.

Early in December the prisoner had brought her the manuscript of a play to type, and from that time on he came frequently, sometimes every day, bringing a few sheets of manuscript at a time. Sometimes he came without any manuscript, and would sit and talk while he smoked a cigarette. They had thought him unmarried.

On Wednesday, February twenty-eighth, Alice Murray had disappeared.

She had taken some of her clothing, not all, and had left a note. The witness read the note aloud in a trembling voice:

> Dear Mother: When you get this I shall be married to Mr. Ladley. Don't worry. Will write again from N.Y.   Lovingly,
> Alice.

From that time until a week before she had not heard from her daughter. Then she had a card, mailed from Times Square Station, New York City. The card merely said:

> Am well and working.   Alice.

The defense was visibly shaken. They had not expected this; and I thought even Mr. Ladley, whose calm had continued unbroken, paled.

So far all had gone well for the prosecution. They had proved a crime, as nearly as circumstantial evidence could prove a crime, and they had established a motive. But in the identification of the body, so far they had failed. The prosecution "rested," as they say, although they didn't rest much, on the afternoon of the third day.

The defense called first of all Eliza Shaeffer. She told of a woman answering the general description of Jennie Brice having spent two days at the Shaeffer farm at Horner. Being shown photographs of Jennie Brice, she said she thought it was the same woman, but was not certain. She told further of the woman leaving unexpectedly on Wednesday of that week from Thornville. On cross-examination, being shown the small photograph which Mr. Graves had shown me, she identified the woman in the group as being the woman in question. As the face was in shadow, she knew it more by the dress and hat: she described the black and white dress and the hat with red trimming.

The defense then called me. I had to admit that the dress and hat as described were almost certainly the ones I had seen on the bed in Jennie Brice's room the day before she disappeared. I could not say definitely whether the woman in the photograph was Jennie Brice or not; but under a magnifying glass I thought it might be.

After that the defense called Jonathan Alexander, the druggist. He testified that on the night in question he had been roused at half past three by the prisoner, who had said his wife was ill, and had purchased a bottle of a proprietary remedy from him. He made an excellent witness, I must say, and his identification was absolute.

After that the defense called Jennie Brice's sister, and endeavored to prove that Jennie Brice had had no such scar. It was shown that she was on intimate terms with her family and would hardly have concealed an operation of any gravity from them.

All in all the defense scored that day. They had shown that the prisoner had told the truth when he said he had gone to a pharmacy for medicine that night for his wife; and they had shown that a woman, answering the description of Jennie Brice, had spent two days in a town called Horner, and had gone from there on the Wednesday after the crime. They had shown too that this woman was dressed exactly as Jennie Brice had been.

And that was the way things stood on the afternoon of the fourth day, when court adjourned.

Mr. Reynolds was at home when I got there. He had been very much subdued since the developments of that first day of the trial, had sat mostly in his own room, and had brought me a bunch of jonquils as a peace offering. He even had the kettle boiling for tea when I got home.

"You have had a number of visitors," he said. "Our young friend Howell has been here, and Mr. Holcombe is back. He has a man in his room. I don't know who it is."

Mr. Holcombe came down a moment after, with his face beaming. He refused tea, and stood looking at me and rubbing his hands together.

"I think we've got him, Mrs. Pitman," he said, almost gaily. "The jury won't even go out of the box."

But further than that he would not explain. He said he had a witness locked in his room, and he'd be glad of supper for him, as they'd both come a long way. After that he went out and bought some oysters and so on and a bottle or two of beer. But as far as I know, he kept his unknown locked up all that night in the second-story front room. I don't think the man realized he was a prisoner. I went in to turn down the bed, and he was sitting by the window, reading the evening paper's account of the trial; an elderly gentleman, rather professional looking.

Mr. Holcombe slept on the upper landing of the hall that night, rolled in a blanket. Not that I think his witness even thought of escaping, but the little man was taking no chances. He was still in a state of excitement, and I doubt if he slept very much.

At eight o'clock that night the doorbell rang. It was Mr. Howell. I admitted him myself, and he followed me back to the dining room. I had not seen him for several weeks, and the change in him startled me. He was dressed carefully, but his eyes were sunk in his head, and he looked as if he had not slept for days.

Mr. Reynolds had gone upstairs, not finding me socially inclined, and I was alone.

"You haven't been sick, Mr. Howell, have you?" I asked.

He did not answer at once. He lit a cigarette and took a turn or two around the room. When he spoke it was as though he had only just realized my question.

"Oh, no," he said. "I'm well enough. I've been traveling about, that's all, and those infernal sleeping cars . . ."

His voice trailed off and I saw him looking at my mother's picture, with the jonquils beneath.

"That's curious!" he said, going closer. "It looks almost like Lida Harvey."

"My mother," I said simply.

"Have you seen her lately?"

"My mother?" I asked, startled.

"No, Lida."

"I saw her a few days ago."

"Here?"

"Yes. She came here, Mr. Howell, two weeks ago. She looks badly, as if she is worrying."

"You mean about me?" he asked eagerly.

"Yes, about you. What on earth possessed you to run away like that? It was idiotic. When my bro—when her uncle accused you of something you simply beat it, instead of facing things like a man."

"I was trying to find the one person who could clear me, Mrs. Pitman." He sat back, with his eyes closed. He looked ill enough to be in bed.

"What happened? Did you succeed?"

"No," he said, his voice bleak.

I thought perhaps he had not been eating and I offered to get him some food, as I had once before. But he refused, with the ghost of his boyish smile.

"I'm hungry, all right, but it's not food I want. I want to see Lida," he said. "I've got to see her, somehow."

I sat down across from him and tried to darn a tablecloth, but I could not sew. I kept seeing those two young things, each sick for a sight of the other, and from wishing they could have a minute together; finally I got to planning it for them.

"Perhaps," I said, "if you want it very much—"

"What do you think?"

"And if you will sit quiet, and stop lighting one cigarette after another until you drive me crazy, I might manage it for you. For five minutes," I said. "Not a second longer."

He came right over and put his arms around me.

"Who are you, anyhow?" he said. "You turn to the world the frozen mask of a Union Street boardinghouse landlady, but you are a gentlewoman by every instinct and training, and a girl at heart. Who are you?"

"I'll tell you what I am," I said. "I'm a romantic old fool, and you'd better let me do this quickly, before I change my mind."

He freed me at that, but he followed to the telephone, and stood by while I got Lida. He was in a perfect frenzy of excitement, flushing with anxiety, and in the middle of the conversation taking the receiver bodily from me and holding it to his own ear.

She said she thought she could get away. She spoke guardedly, as if Alma were near, but I gathered that she would come as soon as she could; and, from the way her voice broke, I knew she was as excited as the boy beside me.

She came, slipping in very quietly, at a quarter after ten that night, and I took her back to the dining room, where he was waiting. He did not make a move toward her, but stood there with his very heart in his eyes, looking at her. And at first she did not make a move either. She stood and stared at him, thin and white as he was, a wreck of himself. Then she made the first gesture.

"Ell darling!" she cried, and ran around the table to him as he held out his arms.

The schoolteacher was out, so I went into the parlor bedroom and sat in her silly cozy corner in the dark. I had done a wrong thing, and I was glad of it. And sitting there in the darkness, I went over my own life again. After all, it had been my own life. I had lived it. No one else had shaped it for me. And if it was cheerless and colorless now it had had its big moments. Life is measured by big moments.

If I let the two children in the dining room have fifteen big moments, instead of five, who can blame me? But I could not let them stay long. There were too many chances of interruption. And I did not yet know his story.

14

THE NEXT DAY was the sensational one of the trial. We went through every phase of contradiction: Jennie Brice was living. Jennie Brice was dead. The body found at Sewickley could not be Jennie Brice's. The body found at Sewickley was Jennie Brice's. And so it went on.

Then the defense did an unexpected thing in putting Mr. Ladley on the stand. That day for the first time he showed the wear and tear of the ordeal. He had no flower in his buttonhole, and the rims of his eyes were red from strain. But he was quite cool. His stage training had taught him not only to endure the eyes of the crowd, but to find in its gaze a sort of stimulant. He made a good witness, I must admit.

He replied to the usual questions easily. After five minutes or so Mr. Llewellyn got down to work.

"Mr. Ladley, you have said that your wife was ill the night of March fourth?"

"Yes."

"What was the nature of her illness?"

"She had a functional heart trouble, not serious."

"Will you tell us fully the events of that night?"

"I had been asleep when my wife wakened me. She asked for a medicine she used in these attacks. I got up and found the bottle, but it was empty. As she was nervous and frightened, I agreed to try to get some at a drugstore. I went downstairs, took Mrs. Pitman's boat, and went to several stores before I could awaken a pharmacist."

"You cut the boat loose?"

"Yes. It was tied in a woman's knot, or series of knots. I could not untie it, and I was in a hurry."

"How did you cut it?"

"With my pocketknife."

"You did not use Mrs. Pitman's bread knife?"

"I did not."

"And in cutting it you cut your wrist, did you?"

"Yes. The knife slipped. I have the scar still."

"What did you do then?"

"I went back to the room, and wiped off the blood with a towel."

"From whom did you get the medicine?"

"From Alexander's Pharmacy."

"At what time?"

"I am not certain. About three o'clock, probably."

"You went directly back home?"

Mr. Ladley hesitated. "No," he said finally. "My wife had had these attacks, but they were not serious. I was curious to see how the river front looked and rowed out too far. I was caught in the backwash of the flood and carried upstream for some distance."

"You came home after that?"

"Yes, at once. Mrs. Ladley was better and had dropped asleep. She wakened as I came in. She was disagreeable about the length of time I had been gone, and wouldn't let me explain. We quarreled, and she said she was going to leave me. I said that as she had threatened this before and had never done it, I would see that she really started. At daylight I rowed her to Federal Street."

"What did she take with her?"

"A small brown valise."

"How was she dressed?"

"In a black and white dress and hat, with a long black coat."

"What was the last you saw of her?"

"She was going across the Sixth Street bridge."

"Alone?"

"No. She went with a young man we knew."

There was a stir in the courtroom at this.

"Who was this young man?"

"A Mr. Howell, a reporter on a newspaper here."

"Have you seen Mr. Howell since your arrest?"

"No, sir. He has been out of the city."

I was so excited by this time that I could hardly hear. I missed some of the cross-examination. However, I do remember how, when the offense took over, the district attorney pulled Mr. Ladley's testimony to pieces, bit by bit.

"You say you cut the boat's painter with your pocketknife?"

"I did."

"Then how do you account for Mrs. Pitman's broken knife, with the blade found in your room?"

"I have no theory about it. She may have broken it herself. She had used it the day before to lift tacks out of a carpet."

That was true, of course, I had.

"That early Monday morning was cold, was it not?"

"Yes. Very."

"Then why did your wife leave without her fur coat?"

"I didn't know she had until we had left the house. Then I didn't ask her. She wouldn't speak to me."

"I see. But isn't it true that, upon a wet fur coat being shown you as your wife's, you said it could not be hers, as she had taken hers with her?"

"I do not recall such a statement."

"You recall a coat being shown you?"

"Yes. Mrs. Pitman brought a coat to my door, but I was working on a play I am writing, and I do not remember what I said. The coat was ruined. I did not want it. I probably said the first thing I thought of to get rid of the woman."

I got up at that. I'd held my peace about the bread knife, but this was too much. However, the moment I started to speak, somebody pushed me back into my chair and told me to be quiet.

"Now, you say you were in such a hurry to get this medicine for your wife that you cut the rope, thus cutting your wrist."

"Yes. I have the scar still."

"You could not wait to untie the boat, and yet you went along the river front to see how high the water was?"

"Her alarm had excited me. But when I got out, and remembered that the doctors had told us she would never die in an attack, I stopped worrying."

"You got the medicine first, you say?"

"Yes."

"Mr. Alexander has testified that you got the medicine at three-thirty. It has been shown that you left the house at two, and got back about four. Doesn't this show that with all your alarm you went to the river front first?"

"I was gone from two to four," he replied calmly. "Mr. Alexander must be wrong about the time I wakened him. I got the medicine first."

"When your wife left you at the bridge, did she say where she was going?"

"No, sir. She still wouldn't speak to me."

"You claim that this woman at Horner was your wife?"

"I think it likely. It's the sort of thing she would do."

"Was there an onyx clock in the second-story room when you moved into it?"

"I don't recall any clock."

"Your wife didn't take an onyx clock away with her?"

The courtroom tittered, and Mr. Ladley smiled. "No," he said. "Why should she?"

The defense called Mr. Howell next. He looked rested and somewhat happier for having seen Lida, but he was still pale, and he showed the strain of some hidden anxiety. What that anxiety was the next two days were to tell us all.

"Mr. Howell," Mr. Llewellyn asked, "you know the prisoner?"

"Slightly."

"State when you met him."

"On Sunday morning, March the fourth. I went to see him."

"Will you tell us the nature of that visit?"

"My paper had heard he was writing a play, intending to star in it himself. I was to get an interview, with photographs if possible."

"You saw his wife at that time?"

"Yes."

"When did you see her again?"

"The following morning, at six o'clock, or a little later. I walked across the Sixth Street bridge with her and put her on a train for Horner, Pennsylvania."

"You are positive it was Mrs. Brice?"

"Yes. I watched her get out of the boat, while her husband steadied it."

"If you knew all this, why didn't you come forward sooner?"

"I've been out of the city."

"But you knew the prisoner had been arrested and that this testimony of yours would be invaluable to him."

"Yes, sir. But I thought it necessary to produce Jennie Brice herself. My unsupported word—"

"You have been searching for Jennie Brice?"

"I have. Since March the eighth."

There was a stir in the courtroom at this, especially when he added that he had not been able to locate her. But the noise subsided as the attorney for the defense went on.

"How was she dressed when you saw her last?"

"She wore a red and black hat and a black coat. She carried a small brown valise."

"Thank you."

The cross-examination that followed did not shake his testimony. But it brought out some curious things. Mr. Howell refused to say how he happened to be at the end of the Sixth Street bridge at that hour, or why he had thought it necessary, on meeting a woman he claimed to have known only twenty-four hours, to go with her to the railway station and put her on a train.

Nevertheless, I could see that the jury was visibly impressed and much shaken. For Mr. Howell carried conviction in every word he said. He looked the district attorney in the eye, and once when our glances crossed he even smiled at me faintly. But I saw why he had tried to find Jennie Brice, and had dreaded testifying. Not a woman in that courtroom, and hardly a man, but believed when he left the stand that he was or had been Jennie Brice's lover. And as such was assisting her to leave her husband.

"Then you believe," the district attorney said at the end, "you believe, Mr. Howell, that Jennie Brice is living?"

"Jennie Brice was living on Monday morning, March the fifth," he said stubbornly.

"Miss Shaeffer has testified that on Wednesday this woman, the one you claim was Jennie Brice, sent a letter to you from Horner. Is that the case?"

"Yes."

"The letter was signed 'Jennie Brice'?"

"It was signed J.B."

"Will you show the court that letter?"

"I destroyed it. There was no reason for keeping it."

"It was a personal letter?"

"It merely said she had arrived safely, and not to let anyone know where she was."

"And yet you destroyed it?"

He hesitated.

"A postscript said to do so," he admitted finally.

"Why?"

"I don't know. An extra precaution probably. She didn't want to be found."

"You were under the impression that she was going to stay there?"

"She was to have remained for a week. So she said anyhow."

"And you have been searching for this woman for two months?"

He looked uncomfortable, but his voice was steady. "Yes," he said. "I wanted no miscarriage of justice."

He was telling the truth, even if it was not all the truth, and I believe had it gone to the jury then Mr. Ladley would have been acquitted. But late that afternoon things took a new turn. Counsel for the prosecution stated to the court that he had a new and important witness, and got permission to introduce this further evidence. The witness was a Doctor Littlefield, and proved to be my one-night tenant of the second-floor front.

Holcombe's prisoner of the night before took the stand. The doctor was less impressive in full daylight; he was a trifle shiny, a bit bulbous as to nose and indifferent as to fingernails. But his testimony was given with due professional weight.

"You are a doctor of medicine, Doctor Littlefield?" asked the district attorney.

"Yes, sir."

"In active practice?"

"I have a Cure for Inebriates in Des Moines, Iowa. I was formerly in general practice in New York City."

"You knew Jennie Ladley?"

"I had seen her at different theaters. And she consulted me professionally at one time in New York."

"You operated on her, I believe?"

"Yes. She came to me to have a name removed. It had been tattooed over her heart."

"You removed it?"

"Not at once. I tried fading the marks with goat's milk, but she was impatient. On the third visit to my office she demanded that the name be cut out."

"You did it?"

"Yes. She refused a general anesthetic and I used cocaine. The name was John, I believe of a former husband. She intended to marry again."

A titter ran over the courtroom. People strained to the utmost are always glad of an excuse to smile. The laughter of a wrought-up crowd always seems to me half hysterical.

"Have you seen photographs of the scar on the body found at Sewickley? Or the body itself?"

"No, sir, I have not."

"Will you describe the operation?"

"I made a transverse incision for the body of the name, and two vertical ones—one longer for the 'J,' the other shorter for the stem of the 'h.' There was a dot after the name. I made a half-inch incision for it."

"Will you sketch the cicatrix as you recall it?"

The doctor made a careful drawing on a pad that was passed to him. The drawing was much like this.

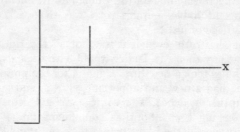

Line for line, dot for dot, it was the scar on the body found at Sewickley.

"You are sure the woman was Jennie Brice?"

"She sent me tickets for the theater shortly after. And I had an announcement of her marriage to the prisoner some weeks later."

"Were there any witnesses to the operation?"

"My assistant. I can produce him at any time."

That was not all of the trial, but it was the decisive moment. Shortly after that the jury withdrew, and for twenty-four hours not a word was heard from them.

15

AFTER TWENTY-FOUR HOURS' deliberation, the jury brought in a verdict of guilty. It was a first-degree verdict. Mr. Howell's unsupported word had lost out against a scar.

Contrary to my expectation Mr. Holcombe was not jubilant over the verdict. He came into the dining room that night and stood by the window, looking out into the yard.

"It isn't logical," he said. "In view of Howell's testimony, it's ridiculous! Heaven help us under this jury system, anyhow! Look at the facts! Howell knows the woman; he sees her on Monday morning, and puts her on a train to go out of town. The boy is telling the truth. He has nothing to gain by coming forward, and everything to lose. Very well. She was alive on Monday. We know where she was on Tuesday and Wednesday. Anyhow, during those days her gem of a husband was in jail. He was freed Thursday night, and from that time until his rearrest on the following Tuesday, I had him under observation every moment. He left the jail Thursday night, and on Saturday the body floated in at Sewickley. If it was done by Ladley it must have been done on Friday, and on Friday he was in view through the periscope all day!"

Mr. Reynolds came in and joined us. "There's only one way out that I see," he said mildly. "Two women have been fool enough to have a name tattooed over their hearts. No woman ever thought enough of me to have *my* name put on her."

"I hope not," I retorted. Mr. Reynolds's first name is Zachariah.

But, as Mr. Holcombe said, all that had been proved was that Jennie Brice was dead, probably murdered. He could not understand the defense letting the case go to the jury without their putting more stress on Mr. Howell's story. But we were to understand that soon, and many other things. Mr. Holcombe told me that evening of learning from John Bellows of the tattooed name on Jennie Brice and of how, after an almost endless search, he had found the man who had cut the name away.

At eight o'clock the doorbell rang. Mr. Reynolds had gone to lodge, he being an Elk and several other things, and much given to regalia put away in boxes, and having his picture in the newspapers in different outlandish costumes. Mr. Pitman used to say that man, being denied his natural love for barbaric adornment in his everyday clothing, took to the different fraternities as an excuse for decking himself out. But this has nothing to do with the doorbell.

It was old Isaac. He had a basket in his hand, and he stepped into the hall and placed it on the floor.

"Evening, Miss Bess," he said. "Can you see a bit of company tonight?"

"I can always see you," I replied. But he had not meant himself. He stepped to the door, and opening it beckoned to someone across the street. It was Lida.

She came in, her color a little heightened, and old Isaac stood back beaming at us both. I believe it was one of the crowning moments of the old man's life, thus to see his Miss Bess and Alma's child together.

"Is—is he here yet?" she asked me nervously.

"I didn't know he was coming." There was no need to ask which "he." There was only one for Lida.

"He telephoned me, and asked me to come here. Oh, Mrs. Pitman, I'm so afraid for him!" She had quite forgotten Isaac. I turned to the schoolteacher's room and opened the door. "The woman who belongs here is out at a lecture," I said. "Come in here, Ikkie, and I'll find the evening paper for you."

"'Ikkie'!" said Lida, and stood staring at me. I think I went white.

"The lady heah and I is old friends," Isaac said, with his splendid manner. "Her mothah, Miss Lida, her mothah—"

But even old Isaac choked up at that, and I closed the door on him.

"How queer!" Lida said, looking at me. "So Isaac knew your mother? Have you lived always in Allegheny, Mrs. Pitman?"

"I was born in Pittsburgh," I evaded. "I went away for a long time, but I always longed for the hurry and activity of the old home town. So here I am again."

Fortunately, like all the young, her own affairs engrossed her. She was flushed with the prospect of meeting her lover, tremulous over what the evening might bring. The middle-aged woman who had come back to the hurry of the old town, and who, pushed back into an eddy of the flood district, could only watch the activity and the life from behind a "Rooms to Let" sign, did not concern her much. Nor should she have.

Mr. Howell came soon after. He asked for her, and going back to the dining room kissed her quietly. He had an air of resolve, a sort of grim determination, which was a relief from the half-frantic look he had worn before. He asked to have Mr. Holcombe brought down, and so there were the four of us sitting around the table: Mr. Holcombe with his notebook, I with my mending, and the boy with one of Lida's hands frankly under his on the red tablecloth.

"I want to tell all of you the whole story," young Howell began. "Tomorrow I shall go to the district attorney and confess, but I want you all to have it first. I can't sleep again until I get it off my chest. Mrs. Pitman has suffered through me, and Mr. Holcombe here has spent money and time—"

Lida did not speak, but she drew her chair closer, and put her other hand over his.

"I want to get it straight, if I can. Let me see. It was on Sunday, the fourth, that the river came up, wasn't it? Yes. Well, on the Thursday before that I met you, Mr. Holcombe, in a restaurant in Pittsburgh. Do you remember?"

Mr. Holcombe nodded.

"We were talking of crime, and I said no man should be hanged on purely circumstantial evidence. You affirmed that a well-linked chain of circumstantial evidence could properly hang a man. We had a long argument, in which I was worsted. There was a third man at the table, Bronson, the business manager of the Liberty Theater."

"Who sided with you," put in Mr. Holcombe, "and whose views I refused to entertain because, as publicity man for a theater, he dealt in fiction rather than in fact."

"Precisely. You may recall, Mr. Holcombe, that you offered to hang any man we would name, given a proper chain of circumstantial evidence against him?"

"Yes."

"After you left Bronson spoke to me. He said business at the theater was bad, and complained of the way the papers used, or would not use, his stuff. He said the Liberty Theater had not had a proper deal, and that he was tempted to go over and bang one of the company on the head, and so get a little free advertising.

"I said he ought to be able to fake a good story, but he maintained that a newspaper could smell a faked story a mile away; and that anyhow all the good stunts had been pulled off. I agreed with him. I remember saying that nothing but a railroad wreck or a murder hit the public very hard these days, and that I didn't feel like wrecking the Pennsylvania Limited.

"He leaned over the table and looked at me. 'Well, how about a murder, then?' he said. 'You get the story for your paper, and I get some advertising for the theater. We need it, that's sure.'

"I laughed it off, and we separated. But at two o'clock Bronson called me up again. I met him in his office at the theater, and he told me that Jennie Brice, who was out of the cast that week, had asked for a week's vacation. She had heard of a farm at a town called Horner, and she wanted to go there to rest.

" 'Now the idea is this,' he said. 'She's living with her husband, and he has threatened her life more than once. It would be easy enough to frame up something to look as if he'd made away with her. We'd get a week of excitement, more advertising than we'd ordinarily get in a year; you get a corking news story, and find Jennie Brice at the end, getting the credit for that. Jennie gets a hundred dollars and a rest, and Ladley, her husband, gets, say, two hundred.'

"Mr. Bronson offered to put up the money, and I agreed. The flood came just then, and was considerable help. It made a good setting. I went to my city editor, and got an assignment to interview Ladley about this play of his. Then Bronson and I went together to see the Ladleys on Sunday morning, and as they needed money they agreed. But Ladley insisted on fifty dollars a week extra if he had to go to jail. We promised it, but we did not intend to let things go so far as that.

"In the Ladleys' room that Sunday morning, we worked it all out. The hardest thing was to get Jennie Brice's consent; but she agreed, finally. We arranged a list of clues to be left around, and Ladley was to go out in the night and to be heard coming back. I told him to quarrel with his wife that afternoon—although I don't believe they needed to be asked to do it—and I suggested also the shoe or slipper to be found floating around."

"Just a moment," said Mr. Holcombe, busy with his notebook. "Did you suggest the onyx clock?"

"No. No clock was mentioned. The clock has puzzled me right along. It didn't belong."

"Then what about the towel?"

"Yes. I said no murder was complete without blood, but he kicked on that—said he didn't mind the rest, but he'd be hanged if he was going to slash himself. But as it happened he cut his wrist while cutting the boat loose, so we had the towel after all."

"The pillow slip?" asked Mr. Holcombe. "Was it included?"

"Well, no. There was nothing said about a pillow slip. Didn't he say he burned it accidentally?"

"So he claimed." Mr. Holcombe made another entry in his book.

"Then I said every murder had a weapon. He was to have a pistol at first, but none of us owned one. Mrs. Ladley undertook to get a knife from Mrs. Pitman's kitchen and to leave it around, not in full view, but where it could be found."

"A broken knife?" Holcombe asked.

"No. Just a knife."

"He was to throw the knife into the water?"

"That wasn't arranged. I only gave him a general outline. He was to add any interesting details that might occur to him. The idea of course was to give the police plenty to work on, and just when they thought they had it all, and when the theater had had a lot of booming, and I had got a good story, to produce Jennie Brice, safe and well. We were not to appear in it at all. It would have worked perfectly, but we forgot to count on one thing. Jennie Brice hated her husband."

"Not really hated him!" Lida exclaimed.

"She did. She's letting him hang, isn't she? She could save him by coming forward now, and she won't do it. She's hiding so he will go to the gallows."

There was a pause at that. It seemed too incredible, too inhuman.

"Then, early that Monday morning, you smuggled Jennie Brice out of the city?"

"Yes. That was the only thing we bungled. We fixed the hour a little too late, and I was seen by Lida's uncle, walking across the bridge with a woman."

"Why did you meet her openly, and take her to the train?" Mr. Holcombe demanded irritably.

Howell bent forward and smiled across at the little man. "One of your own axioms, sir," he said. "Do the natural thing. Upset the customary order of events as little as possible. Jennie Brice went to the train, because that was where she wanted to go. But as Ladley was to protest that his wife had left town, and as the police would be searching for a solitary woman, I went with her. We went in a leisurely manner. I bought her a magazine and a morning paper, asked the porter to look after her, and in general acted the devoted husband seeing his wife off on a trip. I even"—he smiled—"I even promised to feed the canary."

Lida took her hands away. "Did you kiss her good-bye?" she demanded.

"Not even a chaste salute," he said. His spirits were rising. It was, as often happens, as if the mere confession removed the guilt. I have seen little boys who have broken a window show the same relief after telling about it.

"For a day or two Bronson and I sat back, enjoying the stir-up. Things turned out as we had expected. Business boomed at the theater. I got a good story, and some few kind words from my city editor. Then—the explosion came. I got a letter from Jennie Brice saying she was going away, and that it was no use trying to find her. I went to Horner, but I lost track of her completely. Even then we didn't believe things as bad as they turned out to be. We thought she was giving us a poor time, but that she would show up.

"Ladley was in a blue funk for a time. Bronson and I went to him. We told him how the thing had slipped up. We didn't want to go to the police and confess if we could help it. Finally, he agreed to stick it out until she was found, at a hundred dollars a week. It took all we could beg, borrow and steal. But now we have to come out with the story anyhow."

Mr. Holcombe sat up and closed his notebook with a snap. "I'm not so sure of that," he said impressively. "I wonder if you realize, young man, that having provided a perfect defense for this man Ladley, you provided him with every possible inducement to make away with his wife? Secure in your coming forward at the last minute and confessing the hoax to save him, was there anything he might not have dared with impunity?"

"But I tell you I took Jennie Brice out of town on Monday morning."

"Did you?" asked Mr. Holcombe sternly.

But at that, the schoolteacher, having come home and found old Isaac sound asleep in her cozy corner, set up such a screaming for the police that our meeting broke up. Nor would Mr. Holcombe explain any further.

16

MR. HOLCOMBE was up very early the next morning. I heard him moving around at five o'clock, and at six he banged at my door and demanded to know at what time the neighborhood rose. He had been up for an hour and there were no signs of life. He was more cheerful after he had had a cup of coffee, however, and commented on Lida's beauty, saying that Howell was a lucky fellow.

"That's what worries me, Mr. Holcombe," I said. "I am helping the affair along and what if it turns out badly?"

He looked at me over his glasses. "It isn't likely to turn out badly," he said. "I have never married, Mrs. Pitman, and I have missed a great deal out of life."

"Perhaps you're better off: if you had married and lost your wife—" I was thinking of Mr. Pitman.

"Not at all," he said with emphasis. "It's better to have married and lost than never to have married at all. Every man needs a good woman, and it doesn't matter how old he is. The older he is, the more he needs her. I am nearly sixty."

I was rather startled, and I almost dropped the fried potatoes. But the next morning he had got out his notebook and was going over the items again. "Pillow slip," he said, "knife broken, onyx clock—wouldn't think so much of the clock if he hadn't been so damnably anxious to hide the key—the discrepancy in time as revealed by the trial, yes, it's all clear as a bell. Mrs. Pitman, does that Maguire woman next door sleep all day?"

"She's up now," I said, looking out the window.

He was in the hall in a moment, only to come to the door later, hat in hand. "Is she the only other woman on the street who keeps boarders?"

"She's the only woman who doesn't," I snapped. "She'll keep anything that doesn't belong to her, except boarders."

"Ah! That's the case, is it?"

He lighted his corncob pipe and stood puffing at it and watching me. He made me uneasy. I thought he was going to continue the subject of every man needing a wife, and I'm afraid I had already decided to take him if he offered, and to put the schoolteacher out and have a real parlor again, but to keep Mr. Reynolds, he being tidy and no bother.

But when he spoke he was back to the crime again. "Did you ever work a typewriter?" he asked.

What with the surprise I was a little sharp. "I don't play any instrument except an egg beater." I replied shortly, and went on clearing the table.

"I wonder—do you remember about the village idiot and the horse? But of course you do, Mrs. Pitman; you are a woman of imagination. Don't you think you could be Alice Murray for a few moments? Now think. You are a stenographer with theatrical ambitions. You meet an actor and you fall in love with him, and he with you."

"That's hard to imagine, that last."

"Not so hard," he said gently. "Now the actor is going to put you on the stage, perhaps in this new play, and someday he is going to marry you."

"Is that what he promised the girl?"

"According to some letters her mother found, yes. The actor is married, but he tells you he will divorce the wife; you are to wait for him, and in the meantime he wants you near him, away from the office where other men are apt to come in with letters to be typed, and pay attention to you. You are a pretty girl."

"It isn't necessary to overwork my imagination," I said, with a little bitterness. I had been a pretty girl, but what with work and worry—

"Now you are going to New York very soon, and in the meantime you have cut yourself off from all your people. You have no one but this man. What would you do? Where would you go?"

"How old was the girl?"

"Nineteen."

"I think," I said slowly, "that if I were nineteen and in love with a man, and hiding, I would stay as near him as possible. I'd be likely to get a window that could see his going out and coming in, a place so near that he could come often to see me."

"Bravo!" he exclaimed. "Of course, with your present wisdom and experience, you would do nothing so foolish. But this girl was in her teens. She was not very far away, for he probably saw her that Sunday afternoon, when he was out for two hours. And as the going was slow that day, and he had much to tell and explain, I figure she was not far off. Probably in this very neighborhood."

During the remainder of that morning I saw Mr. Holcombe at intervals, going from house to house along Union Street, making short excursions into side thoroughfares, coming back again and taking up his doorbell ringing with unflagging energy. I watched him off and on for two hours. At the end of that time he came back flushed and excited.

"I found the house," he said, wiping his glasses. "She was there, all right. Not so close as we had thought, but as close as she could get."

"And you can trace her?" I asked.

His face changed and saddened. "Poor child!" he said. "She is dead, Mrs. Pitman! She died in a New York hospital a day or two ago, giving premature birth to a child."

"Not the one at Sewickley!"

"No," he said patiently. "That was Jennie Brice."

"But Mr. Howell—"

"Mr. Howell is a young ass," he said with irritation. "He did not take Jennie Brice out of the city that morning. He took Alice Murray in Jennie Brice's clothing, and made up to look like her."

Well, that is five years ago. Five times since then the Allegheny River, from being a mild and inoffensive stream, carrying a few boats and a great deal of sewage, has become a raging destroyer and has filled our hearts with fear and our cellars with mud. Five times since then Molly Maguire has appropriated everything the flood carried from my premises to hers, and five times have I lifted my carpets and moved Mr. Holcombe, who occupies the parlor bedroom, to a second-floor room.

A few days ago, as I said at the beginning, we found poor Peter's body floating in the cellar, and as soon as the yard was dry enough I buried him there. He had grown fat and lazy, but I shall miss him.

Yesterday a riverman fell off a barge along the waterfront and was drowned. They dragged the river for his body, but they did not find him. But they found something, an onyx clock, with the tattered remnant of a muslin pillow slip wrapped around it. It only bore out the story as we had known it for five years.

The Murray girl had lived long enough to make a statement to the police, although Mr. Holcombe only learned this later. On the statement's being shown to Ladley in the jail, and his learning of the girl's death, he collapsed. He confessed before he was hanged, and his confession briefly was this:

He had met Alice Murray in connection with the typing of his play, and had fallen in love with her. He had disliked his wife intensely, and would have been glad to get rid of her in any way possible. He had not intended to kill her, however. He had planned to elope with the Murray girl, and awaiting an opportunity had persuaded her to leave home and to take a room near my house.

Here he had visited her daily, while his wife was at the theater.

They had planned to go to New York together on Monday, March the fifth. On Sunday, the fourth, however, Mr. Bronson and Mr. Howell had made their curious proposition. When he accepted, Philip Ladley maintained that he meant only to carry out the plan as suggested. But the temptation was too strong for him. That night, while his wife slept, he had strangled her.

I believe he was frantic with fear after he had done it. Then it occurred to him that if he made the body unrecognizable he would be safe enough. On that quiet Sunday night, when Mr. Reynolds reported all peaceful in the Ladley room, he had cut off the poor wretch's head and had tied it up in a pillow slip weighted with my onyx clock!

It is a curious fact about the case that the scar which his wife incurred to enable her to marry him was the means of his undoing. He insisted, and I believe he was telling the truth, that he did not know of the scar; that is, his wife had never told him of it, and had been able to conceal it. He thought she had probably used paraffin in some way.

In his final statement, written with great care and no little literary finish, he told the story in detail: of arranging the clues as Mr. Howell and Mr. Bronson had suggested, of going out in the boat with the body covered with a fur coat in the bottom of the skiff, of throwing it into the current above the Ninth Street bridge and of seeing the fur coat fall from the boat and be carried beyond his reach, of disposing of the head near the Seventh Street bridge, of going to a drugstore as per the Howell instructions, and of coming home at four o'clock, to find me at the head of the stairs.

Several points of confusion remained. One had been caused by Temple Hope's refusal to admit that the dress and hat which figured in the case were to be used by her the next week at the theater. Mr. Ladley insisted that this was the case, and that on that Sunday afternoon his wife had requested him to take them to Miss Hope; that they had quarreled as to whether they should be packed in a box or in the brown valise, and that he had visited Alice Murray instead. It was on the way there that the idea of finally getting rid of Jennie Brice came to him. And a method also, that of using the black and white striped dress of the dispute for the Murray girl to wear.

Another point of confusion had been the dismantling of his room that Monday night, sometime between the visit of Temple Hope and the return of Mr. Holcombe. This was to locate the scrap of paper containing the list of clues as suggested by young Howell, a list that might have brought about a premature discovery of the so-called hoax, and which had been mislaid.

To the girl he had told nothing of his plan. But he had told her she was to leave town on an early train the next morning. He gave her detailed instructions to wear his wife's clothes which he had taken with him, and to make herself up as nearly like Jennie Brice as she could. To carry out the deception, which he promised to explain later, she was to *be* Jennie Brice to young Howell. This he thought was safe, as Ellis Howell had only seen his wife once, and the girl was a fair actress herself.

His further instructions to her were simple: to go to the place at Horner where Jennie Brice had planned to go, but to use the name of "Bellows" there. And after she had been there for a day or two to go as quietly as possible to New York. He gave her the address of a boardinghouse where he could write her, and enough money to last until she could find work or he could join her.

He reasoned that as Alice Murray was to impersonate Jennie Brice, a Jennie Brice hiding from her husband, she would naturally change her name. And as the name Bellows has been hers by a previous marriage she might easily resume it. Thus, to establish his innocence, he had not only the evidence of Howell and Bronson that the whole thing was a gigantic hoax. He had also the evidence of Howell that he had started Jennie Brice to Horner that Monday morning, that she had reached Horner, had there assumed an incognito, as Mr. Pitman would say, and had later disappeared from there, maliciously concealing herself to work his undoing.

In all probability he would have gone free, the richer by a hundred dollars for each week of his imprisonment, but for two things. The flood which had brought opportunity to his door had brought Mr. Holcombe to feed Peter, the dog. And the same flood, which should have carried the headless body as far as Cairo, or even farther on down the Mississippi, had rejected it in an eddy below a clay bluff at Sewickley, with its pitiful covering washed from the scar.

Well, it is all over now. Mr. Ladley is dead, and poor Alice Murray, and even Peter lies in the yard. Mr. Reynolds made a small wooden cross over Peter's grave and carved "Till we meet again" on it. I suppose though that the next flood will find it in Molly Maguire's kitchen.

Ellis Howell and Lida are married. He inherited some money, I believe, and what with that and Lida's declaring she would either marry him in a church or elope, Alma had to consent. I went to the wedding and stood near the door, while Alma swept in, in gray velvet and a rose-colored hat. She has not improved with age, has Alma. But Lida, Lida under my mother's wedding veil, with her eyes like stars, seeing no one in the church in all that throng but the boy who waited at the end of the long church aisle—I wanted to run out and claim her, my own blood, my more than child.

I sat down and covered my face. And from the pew behind me someone leaned over and patted my shoulder.

"Miss Bess!" old Isaac said gently. "Don't take on, Miss Bess!"

He came the next day and brought me some lilies from the bride's bouquet, which she had sent me, and a bottle of champagne from the wedding supper. I had not tasted champagne for twenty years!

That is all of the story. On summer afternoons sometimes, when the house is hot, I go to the park and sit. I used to take Peter, but now he is dead. I like to see Lida's little boy. The nurse knows me by sight and lets me talk to the child. He can say my name quite plainly. But he does not call Alma "Grandmother." The nurse says she does not like it. He calls her "Nana."

Lida does not forget me. Especially at floodtimes she always comes to see if I am comfortable. The other day she brought me, with apologies, the velvet dress her mother had worn at her wedding. Alma had worn it but once, and now she was too stout for it. I took it. I am not proud, and I should like Molly Maguire to see it.

Mr. Holcombe asked me last night to marry him. He says he needs me, and that I need him.

I am a lonely woman, and getting old, and I'm tired of watching the gas meter. And besides, with Peter dead, I need a man in the house all the time. The flood district is none too orderly. Besides, when I have a wedding dress laid away and a bottle of good wine, it seems a pity not to use them.

At least I have kept my figure, and my mother's pearls are still in the bank. It seems queer, but Mr. Holcombe is quite well off. Besides, I have grown very fond of him.

I think I shall do it. It would be rather nice to ask Alma to the wedding, and see her face as I walk up the aisle.